A COOKIE
BEFORE DYING

Virginia Lowell

CHIVERS

British Library Cataloguing in Publication Data available

This Large Print edition published by AudioGO Ltd, Bath, 2013.
Published by arrangement with the Berkley Publishing Group, a division of Penguin Group (USA) Inc.

U.K. Hardcover   ISBN   978 1 4713 2780 3
U.K. Softcover   ISBN   978 1 4713 2781 0

Copyright © 2011 by Penguin Group (USA) Inc.

Printed and bound in Great Britain by
TJ International Limited

*For my sister, for years
of cookies and laughter*

ACKNOWLEDGMENTS

With each passing year, I grow more appreciative of the remarkable people who have touched my life. As always, I am endlessly grateful to my writer's group: K. J. Erickson, Ellen Hart, Mary Logue, and Pete Hautman. Many, many thanks to my editor, Michelle Vega, for her perceptive insights and her understanding during a difficult time. The staff at Berkley Prime Crime are the best of the best. A special thanks to the third Saturday potluck group for decades of friendship and fun. And, of course, my love and gratitude to my father and Marilyn, my sister, and my husband.

CHAPTER ONE

Olivia Greyson flicked a droplet of sweat off her forehead before it could dribble into her eyebrow. At six a.m. and already eighty-eight degrees, she hadn't expected to look out her bedroom window and find her front lawn covered in white. Browned dead grass maybe, but not crinkly white balls.

Perhaps she shouldn't have stayed up so late the previous night, Saturday or not. She and Maddie had brainstormed dozens of themed cookie cutter events for The Gingerbread House, enough for months to come. Maddie Briggs, best friend since childhood and now Olivia's business partner, had been in fine creative form, bubbling up ideas like a red-haired volcano. The effort had required a plate of decorated cookies and a generous amount of merlot. Very generous, judging from the empty bottles Olivia had rinsed and stowed in the recycling bin. In her own defense, one of the bottles had already been opened and used for cooking and salad dressing.

As Olivia stared at her lawn, a memory from high school popped into her mind. She and Maddie and a couple guy friends had TP'd a friend's house one night. The friend's parents hadn't found it funny, and Olivia and Maddie spent hours throwing out gobs of toilet paper after the guys left them to take the blame. If that was toilet paper on the lawn of The Gingerbread House, she would not give up until the culprits were caught and forced to clean it up. Olivia opened one window and unhooked the screen, letting fingers of hot, sticky air reach into her bedroom. The air conditioner in her bedroom might be approaching extinction, but at least it dried the air. She poked her head outside. Nope, there were no telltale lengths of tissue hanging from tree branches, and the shapes on the lawn looked crunched up, not round like rolls of toilet paper.

Olivia knew she'd have to go outside to investigate. She slipped into the last clean casual items in her summer wardrobe, red shorts and a pink tank top. A glance in the mirror confirmed that the colors were wrong for her auburn hair and medium complexion. An obsession with clothes wasn't one of Olivia's vices; however, this outfit was destined for the Chatterley Heights thrift shop. Right after she caught up on the laundry.

Olivia slapped the end of her unmade bed and two silky ears poked up from a fold in the blanket. "Come on, you lazy hunk of fur." Spunky, her little rescue Yorkshire terrier, yawned. "Yeah, I know it's early, but we need to look at something outside." At the word "outside," Spunky wriggled out from the covers, leaped to the floor, and followed his mistress down the hallway. His nails clicked on the tile floor of the kitchen as he trotted toward his empty food bowl.

"First things first." Olivia measured Italian roast into the Mr. Coffee, poured in some water, and hit the switch. She fed Spunky before heading down the hallway to the bathroom. By the time she returned, Mr. Coffee was spitting his last drops, and Spunky had licked his bowl shiny. With a whimper, he raised his big, brown eyes and cocked his head at Olivia.

"You are such a con artist. Do you really think I won't remember that I just filled your bowl?" Olivia slid his leash from a wall hook and shook it. "Come on, Spunky, adventure awaits."

Olivia lived above her store, The Gingerbread House, in the top floor of a small Queen Anne for which she proudly held a mortgage. At least her debt level had dipped a bit. She'd used part of an inheritance from her dear friend, Clarisse Chamberlain, to pay down the mortgage and refinance at a much lower interest rate. Before her death, Clarisse had encouraged Olivia in her dream of opening The Gingerbread House, the only store in town that specialized in cookie cutters. Olivia liked to think that Clarisse would approve of her decision to use some of her inheritance to secure the future of her business.

Now Olivia had the mystery of the white August lawn to solve, and she hoped it would turn out to be more comedy than tragedy.

When she and Spunky reached the foyer at the bottom of the staircase, Olivia tried the door leading to The Gingerbread House to make sure it was locked. It was. The front door lock and deadbolt were secure, as well. So a break-in hadn't accompanied whatever detritus awaited on her front lawn.

Olivia had barely opened the front door when Spunky squeezed through the crack. With all the strength in his five-pound body, he yanked sharply at his leash and managed to break from Olivia's grip.

"Spunky! You get your fuzzy little butt back here right now." True to his terrier nature, Spunky ignored her. Olivia was about to yell more forcefully when she stopped short, reminding herself that whoever had littered The Gingerbread House lawn might still be lurking about, perhaps with a camera and tape recorder. She didn't relish the idea of seeing herself on YouTube.

Olivia scanned her lawn in puzzlement. Apparently, someone had crunched up dozens of papers and tossed them around the entire front yard of The Gingerbread House. Olivia knew crunched-up paper when she saw it, and she was looking at lots of it. As far as she could tell, none of the other stores around the town square had suffered the same insult. It must have happened after two a.m., or Maddie would have noticed when she'd headed for home.

Spunky sniffed at a nearby paper snowball. When a gust of hot wind shifted it, he leaped backward and yapped furiously.

"Spunky, hush. It's Sunday morning. Sensible people are trying to sleep."

Spunky pounced on the ball. Clutching it in his teeth, he growled and shook his head back and forth. As she crossed the lawn to join him, Olivia leaned down and scooped up one of the papers. She snatched the end of Spunky's leash from the ground and looped it around her wrist so she could use both hands. The paper was so saturated with humidity, it made no crinkling sound as she smoothed it on her thigh.

"What fresh hell is this?" Olivia's words hung in the still, heavy air. Spunky whimpered and skittered around her feet as she stared at the huge capital letters across the top of the notice:

SUGAR KILLS!!!

Did you know:
- Sugar is the leading cause of obesity, heart disease, and diabetes?
- Eating sugar causes cancer?
- If you eat sugar while you're pregnant, it causes birth defects?
- You'll have to run five miles to work off one cookie? Ten miles if the cookie is iced?

STOP YOUR SUGAR HABIT NOW!!!

Join me at The Vegetable Plate every Tuesday evening from 7:00 to 8:00 to learn how to take your life back from the DEMON SUGAR. We'll talk about ways to escape its clutches and live sugar-free forever. We'll confront the agony and devastation of Sugar Addiction. And we'll share recipes.

Refreshments will be served: herbal teas and fresh organic vegetables.

Olivia reached into the pocket of her shorts, slid out her cell, and speed-dialed Maddie Briggs. Maddie answered on the second ring and, as usual, began chattering at once. "Hey, I was thinking, wouldn't it be fun to have an early morning store event and serve breakfast cookies?"

"Breakfast . . ."

"Cookies, right. Like egg-shaped cookies, wavy slices of bacon, toast and sweet rolls and sausage links and coffee cups and —"

"Got it," Olivia said. "Don't forget the slices of cold pizza." She had recently acknowledged her addiction to pizza for breakfast, lunch, dinner, and bedtime snacks. As of yet, she hadn't determined whether any intervention was called for. "And empty merlot bottles," she added. "They were all over my kitchen this morning."

"Ouch, don't remind me," Maddie said. "So shall we bake today? We have that nice new freezer to fill, and I long to wield a rolling pin once more."

"First, you need to get right over here and take a look at The Gingerbread House lawn," Olivia said. "It might make you want to wield that rolling pin for another purpose."

"Intriguing," Maddie said. "What's up?"

"Something odd and disturbing. You'll want to read it for yourself."

"Read? Did someone spray-paint naughty words on the grass? Read them to me. You can abbreviate if you're embarrassed." When Olivia hesitated, Maddie added, "Right now, Livie. As in this instant. I'm dying of curiosity here."

Olivia brushed dew-limp hair off her forehead with the back of her hand. "Not spray paint. Paper. The lawn is covered with balled-up paper notices. I'm holding one of them. The two-word heading is 'Sugar Kills,' which ought to give you the general idea. And I bet I can guess who wrote it."

"Charlene Critch, rhymes with —" A fierce round of Yorkie yapping drowned out Maddie's voice.

"Spunky agrees with you," Olivia said. "He is barking in the direction of the store next door. The store that is not the Heights Hardware."

"Ah, The Vegetable Plate," Maddie said. "Spunky is such a discerning little creature.

16

Read me the rest of it."

"Hm?"

"Charlene's rant, Livie, what else does it say?"

"I think Spunky's on to something," Olivia said.

"Yes, we've established that. Now, I beg of you, read."

"I thought I saw a light go on and off upstairs in The Vegetable Plate," Olivia said. "Isn't Charlene using the top floor for storage?"

"It's six thirty in the morning. Charlene's probably up there sharpening her fangs for a breakfast of raw rutabaga. Or maybe that's where she keeps a secret stash of chocolate, or her printing press, or —"

"I don't think so. Charlene's car isn't in her spot, and she lives fifteen miles out of town. Hush, Spunky," Olivia commanded as she picked him up and tucked him into the circle of her arm. She unlocked the front door of The Gingerbread House and pushed the squirming dog into the foyer. Spunky spun around and leaped for the door, but Olivia managed to close it in time.

"Sorry, Kiddo, I'll be right back." As Olivia headed across the damp lawn toward the The Vegetable Plate, she realized her cell phone was squawking. "Maddie?"

"Who else would it be? What the heck is going on?"

"I'm sure you're right and it's nothing," Olivia said, "but I'm going to peek through the display window of The Vegetable Plate, just to make sure everything looks normal." Olivia glanced up at the top floor of the store and saw no lights. When she reached the front display window, she cupped her hands around her eyes and pressed her nose against the glass. The Vegetable Plate's sales area occupied the former parlor of a modest Victorian summer home. Unlike The Gingerbread House, Charlene Critch's store had no other windows scattered around the room, so Olivia could make out only the sales counter plus a few outlines of display tables.

"Maddie? Are you still there?"

"Waiting impatiently."

"I can't see much inside The Vegetable Plate. Maybe I imagined the light upstairs, or it could have been the sun reflecting off the glass. I'll make sure the front door is . . ." The doorknob turned in Olivia's hand. "Uh oh."

"What does 'uh oh' mean, Livie? Livie?"

With a light push, Olivia opened the door a few inches.

"Livie, speak to me. Now." Maddie's voice

seemed to leap out of the cell phone.

"Keep it down, Maddie. I'm betting Charlene forgot to lock her door. I'll poke my head inside and take a quick look around. I'll make sure everything is okay, don't fuss. I'll lock the front door on my way out."

"Livie, don't wander around in there alone. What if there's a burglar inside, or a maniacal killer? At least wait for me, I'll be right there."

"Stop fretting. I'll be fine."

"I'm out the door, Livie. Don't hang up."

"Uh huh." Olivia hung up. She eased open the front door and listened. Hearing nothing beyond the usual creaking associated with old houses, she entered and shut the door behind her. The store went pitch dark. Olivia remembered a light switch located to the left of the entrance. She felt for it along the wall and flipped on the overhead lights. Her hand closed around her cell phone as she took in the condition of The Vegetable Plate.

Charlene Critch was neat and precise, from her personal grooming to her store inventory. The Vegetable Plate exemplified a place for everything and nothing even slightly out of place. Not now, though. Right inside the front door, Olivia had nearly crunched several bottles of vitamin supplements tossed on the floor. On the wall behind the cash register, Charlene's favorite poster — YOUR MOTHER WAS RIGHT: EAT YOUR VEGETABLES! — hung like a limp tablecloth from one remaining tack. A wall bookshelf, normally stuffed with health food cookbooks, was empty, its contents strewn on the floor, spines broken and covers bent.

The door to Charlene's cooler stood wide open. Organic cheeses and ready-to-eat tofu sandwiches lay in a pile on the floor, as if someone had swept them out of the cooler in one movement. The cool air dissipated quickly in the hot room. Olivia reached out to close the door but changed her mind. The scene suggested a hurried, impatient search by an intruder who might have been careless enough to leave fingerprints.

Only one item appeared untouched — Charlene's cash register. Had the intruder assumed the cash would be locked in a safe overnight? Or maybe cash wasn't the motive for the break-in. Except there hadn't been an actual break-in, had there? Olivia examined the front door lock and saw no damage. Either the intruder possessed a key or Charlene had left the store unlocked Saturday evening. Olivia tried to imagine Charlene forgetting such an important detail — or any detail, for that matter —

and failed. Charlene loved The Vegetable Plate. Olivia thought about how she'd feel if she walked into The Gingerbread House one morning and found her beloved cookie cutters tossed on the floor and stepped on, her precious cookbooks and baking equipment ripped and smashed. Her heart would crumple. Impossible as Charlene could be, Olivia felt a surge of empathy for her.

Olivia flipped open her cell phone, intending to call Chatterley Heights' sheriff, Del Jenkins. Hesitating, she listened to the store. Had she heard a sound coming from the hallway that led to the kitchen? The Vegetable Plate was smaller than The Gingerbread House, having only a few rooms downstairs and a dormer upstairs. The kitchen at the back of the store led out to a tiny, overgrown back yard.

There it was again. Olivia heard a faint click, like magnets catching as a cabinet door opens or closes. She shut the cover on her cell phone. If the kitchen was in the same chaotic state as the sales area, Charlene might be back there straightening up. Maybe she'd already phoned the sheriff.

To be on the safe side, Olivia approached the kitchen as softly as she could, sidestepping a trail of broken mugs that used to read, DRINK YOUR VEGGIES! Luckily, she had worn her running shoes. Not that she ran much in August. In the sweltering heat, not even her fetching little Yorkie could convince her to go for a jog.

The kitchen door was the type that swung in and out to facilitate carrying heavy, hot casseroles into the dining room and stacks of dirty plates back to the kitchen sink. Olivia nudged the door a fraction, enough to allow a peek into the kitchen. She could see a narrow swath across the room to the back door, which hung open. At first, she heard nothing. Maybe an animal had wandered inside and caused all this damage while hunting for food. No, only an animal of human height and dexterity could have ripped a poster off a wall and opened the cheese cooler. Besides, a hungry animal wouldn't have left the cheese on the floor, neatly wrapped.

Olivia eased the kitchen door open wider to reveal a row of cabinets along the wall. No one was in sight, but now she could hear a faint shuffling sound. She inched the door farther, a millimeter at a time.

"Damn." The whispered curse dripped venom yet was so soft that Olivia couldn't tell whether the voice was male or female. If she could only get a glimpse of a foot or a shoulder . . .

"I'll *kill* her." This time the voice sounded male, but Olivia didn't recognize it.

A crash, followed by the tinkling of broken glass, startled Olivia into backing away from the kitchen door too quickly. The door swung toward her, then back into the kitchen. Now Olivia was the one cursing to herself. She'd announced her presence to the intruder. He would either run away or barge through the door toward her, and it would happen fast.

Olivia backed aside from the swinging door while she flipped open her cell phone. She had the police department on speed dial, so she didn't bother with 911. When the kitchen door didn't move, she assumed the intruder had escaped out the back. By the first ring, Olivia had crossed the empty kitchen, glass crunching beneath her feet. She ran out the open door in time to see a man's back disappear into a line of arborvitae.

"Chatterley Heights Police Department. Sheriff Jenkins speaking."

It was the voice Olivia had hoped to hear. "Del, it's me. There's been a break-in at The Vegetable Plate. I just saw a man run through the back yard, heading north."

"On my way," Del said. "Can you describe the guy?"

"I only saw his back from a distance, but he looked and moved like a fairly young man. He was tall, I'd say, and slender, athletic. Dark hair. Jeans and a blue T-shirt."

"How dark was his hair? How long was it? Was it shaggy? Neatly cut?"

Olivia closed her eyes and remembered the man's hair lifting as he ran. "Dark brown, I'd say, not black. Professionally trimmed. It wasn't really short, but not long and shaggy, either."

"Nothing else?"

"Sorry."

"Okay, I'll send out an APB and be there as soon as possible. You stay in The Gingerbread House and I'll come talk to you later."

"Del, I'm —"

"I mean it, Livie. Sit this one out, okay?" The sheriff's cell phone clicked off.

Too late for that. Olivia figured it would take Del no more than a few minutes to realize she couldn't have seen the intruder run off if she'd been in The Gingerbread House — she didn't have a view of Charlene's back yard. Del would be irritated, but so be it. The two of them had been tiptoeing around each other in an almost-relationship since the previous spring, when Olivia had become embroiled in the investigation of her dear friend Clarisse's death.

She knew his concern for her was real, but could she help it if crime popped up right next door?

On her way back through The Vegetable Plate kitchen, Olivia left cabinet doors hanging and tried to avoid the broken glass. She'd already tampered enough with the scene, though for a good cause. She didn't envy Charlene having to clean up the mess. Maybe she and Maddie could lend a hand; it might improve their relationship with her.

"OH. MY. GOD." Charlene's voice, petulant at the best of times, punched the air with such force that Olivia stepped backward. She crunched a pile of glass shards loud enough to be heard through the closed kitchen door. "What was that?" Charlene shrieked. "Oh my god, he's still here."

"Knock it off, Charlene, it's probably Livie." The swinging door opened, and Maddie appeared. "Wow." She took in the emptied cupboards and broken glass. "Who won?"

Charlene pushed past Maddie. "Oh my God, did *you* make this mess?"

"Of course not." Olivia glanced down at her feet, planted amid the remains of what might have been pricey water goblets. "I thought I saw an intruder in your store, and I came over to investigate. He was going through your cupboards, so I assume he's also the one who tossed your glassware on the floor." She heard the irritation in her own voice and banished all thought of helping Charlene with the cleanup.

"Well, you certainly didn't try to save anything, did you. And my 'glassware' was crystal. Do you have any idea how much those goblets were worth? No, of course you don't."

It was common knowledge that Olivia had recently inherited an enviable sum of money, at least for the average person, plus an even more enviable collection of vintage cookie cutters, so it struck her that Charlene's family must be quite well off. Perhaps the man who broke into The Vegetable Plate was aware of that.

"Hey," Maddie said. "You have no right to talk to Livie that way. She was trying to help, not that you care."

"Well, it looks to me like she made things worse by interfering."

"In fact," Olivia said, "I was able to call the sheriff and give him a partial description of the intruder, as well as his direction when he took off. He was tall and slender with dark brown hair. Does that sound like anyone you know?"

As always, Charlene had applied her

makeup with skill and attention to detail, but it couldn't hide a sudden shift in her emotions. She hugged her arms around her slender rib cage and dug her manicured fingernails into the bare flesh of her upper arms.

"Charlene? You know who did this, don't you?" Olivia pointed toward the piles of glass, sparkling as they caught the overhead light. "Was that man looking for something in particular? Because he didn't have to trash your belongings. That was done with anger. It was personal." She reached toward Charlene's shoulder.

Charlene pulled back. "I don't know anyone who would do this to me." She lifted her chin. "At least, not a man. A jealous woman, maybe, but not a man. Anyway, I don't believe you really saw anyone. You were probably hallucinating. A sugar high will do that."

With a derisive snort, Maddie said, "Hah! And what were you on when you threw those stupid flyers all over our lawn?"

"Are you deaf? I told you a hundred times on the way over, I did not throw those flyers on your silly lawn. Although whoever did it deserves a medal."

Maddie's freckled cheeks flushed. "What the heck is that supposed to mean?"

"You know perfectly well you are killing innocent people with all that sugar you're stuffing down their throats. You should be arrested."

"Well, at least *our* customers actually *enjoy* what we offer. All you do is manipulate people with fear and guilt."

"Murderer!"

"Zealot!"

"Go to your rooms, both of you!" Maddie and Charlene turned to stare at Olivia, who had stunned them and herself by shouting.

"Is that you, Livie?" Sheriff Del Jenkins called from inside the store. Moments later, he appeared at the kitchen door, showing no sign that he had heard a squabble. With a grim smile at Olivia, Del said, "Why am I not surprised to find you still here." When no one spoke, he added, "Charlene, Maddie, any chance I can get past you and into the kitchen, so I can do my job?"

"Sorry," Maddie said. "Of course you can. We were about to call a truce and break for coffee. Want some?"

"Tea," Charlene said. "Coffee is bad for the blood pressure. I only drink herbal tea. No sugar, of course."

Olivia shot a warning glance in Maddie's direction. Aside from a surreptitious rolling of her eyes, Maddie allowed Charlene's insistence on sugarless tea to go unchallenged.

As for Charlene, the fight had gone out of her. Her shoulders slumped as she glanced into her ruined kitchen. "I guess we'll have to use the little microwave I keep in the store to make tea. I'll get some water from the bathroom."

Once Charlene was out of sight, Maddie said, "I'll go to The Gingerbread House and grab some coffee for us. Won't take long. Maybe I'll bring some cookies."

Watching Maddie's retreating back, Olivia said to Del, "I'm afraid I had to run through the kitchen to see the intruder, but otherwise I don't think I touched anything. The door to the back yard was already open."

"What's with all that paper I saw on your lawn?" Del asked as he surveyed the damage in Charlene's kitchen. "I have to admit, I picked one up and read it. Looked like something Ms. Critch might write."

"Charlene didn't deny writing the notice, but she insists she didn't throw all those copies on our property," Olivia said. "And no, I did not race over here in a rage and destroy Charlene's store for revenge."

"I wasn't implying that you did," Del said with the faintest hint of a smile. "You seemed to be the only one *not* in a rage."

■ ■ ■ ■

Maddie rolled the trash can onto the lawn and began to toss paper basketballs.

"I suppose we should be recycling all this paper," Olivia said.

"Or we could borrow a super-sized fan from the hardware and blow the stuff onto Charlene's lawn. This humidity adds some real heft. It would be a shame to waste such an opportunity." Maddie sank an overhead ball into the can. "Nailed it," she said. "After I left, what did Del have to say about the break-in? Any suspects?"

"Not that he mentioned. At least he doesn't seem to suspect us. However, in future you might want to control your irritation with Charlene, in public anyway. You did sound as if you'd happily thrash her with a ten-pound bag of sugar."

"Oh that," Maddie said with a dismissive laugh. "Del knows I'm harmless."

Olivia found a tissue in the pocket of her shorts and used it to blot perspiration from her forehead. "This qualifies as aerobic activity," she said, "for which it is way too hot. We need a rake."

"I'll pick one up from the hardware when I meet Lucas for lunch." Maddie's still newish love, Lucas Ashford, was the quiet and, to use Maddie's description, yummy owner of the Heights Hardware. "Although it won't be much use until the next time Charlene decides to decorate our lawn in her own special way. Why would you worry that Del would suspect us of trashing The Vegetable Pile?"

"The Vegetable *Plate*. As if you didn't know."

"Slip of the tongue."

Olivia scooped up a paper. "The content of this flyer might look to some folks like a motive."

"Point taken. It's clear as day Charlene wrote these, and I could cheerfully stuff them down her throat." With fists planted on her curvy hips and curls spiraling wildly, Maddie did resemble an avenging goddess. "If I were that sort of person," she added. "Which I am not."

Olivia dumped a load into the can and dried her arms on her shorts. "What do we really know about Charlene?"

"Not much from my end," Maddie said. "I asked my aunt Sadie if she remembered anything about the Critch family. She thought they'd lived a few miles out of Chatterley Heights years ago and moved away when Charlene was little. She might have been thinking of another family, though. I don't remember Charlene at all, but she is a bit younger than we are. Hence her juvenile behavior."

"She's somewhere around twenty-five," Olivia said, "which would make her six or seven years younger than we are and a couple years younger than Jason."

"Your brother is more mature than Charlene, which isn't saying a lot," Maddie said. "No offense meant."

"None taken."

"Here's what I don't get," Maddie said. "Why would Charlene think it was such a good idea to dump a truckload of crinkled-up flyers on the dew-soaked lawn of The Gingerbread House? What does she get out of it?"

"I don't think Charlene did this. I suspect it might have something to do with the man I saw running from her store."

"The man who, according to Charlene, is a figment of your sugar-addled imagination?"

"Which made me very curious," Olivia said. A lock of damp auburn hair fell across her forehead, and she blew it away from her eyes. "Why would Charlene deny the existence of someone who had vandalized her beloved store? She tried to blame us, but that didn't go anywhere. I doubt she believed it herself."

Curiosity sparked in Maddie's green eyes. "Maybe she's being stalked. If she knows her stalker, why wouldn't she say so?"

"I don't know about the stalking part, but she certainly clammed up at my description of the man I saw running from her kitchen. I'll bet you a gingerbread cookie cutter family that she knows who it was but doesn't want his identity revealed. Maybe it's someone she cares about. Which is why we should learn more about Charlene Critch."

"You can't kid me, Livie Greyson. You are seriously addicted to mysteries. Don't think I haven't noticed the Agatha Christies you keep taking out of the library. Don't get me wrong, I grew up with Nancy Drew, but you'll have to unearth Charlene's secrets by yourself. The less I know about her, the happier I'll be."

"I'll grant she can be irritating, but why do you dislike her so much?"

Maddie scooped up some papers, balled them together, and smashed them into the full trash can. "Because Charlene is skinny and blonde and her hair always behaves no matter what the humidity."

With a puzzled frown, Olivia said, "But you are curvy and have red hair with personality. What's the problem?"

Maddie kicked at one of the few remaining wads of paper. "I guess it's what Heather Irwin said to me last week. I stopped in at the library to talk about the cookies for Gwen and Herbie's baby shower — did you know that Heather is organizing it? Anyway, Heather dragged me into her office to talk about some things Charlene had said while she was checking out a few books. She doesn't like Charlene any better than I do, maybe even less."

"Charlene reads library books?" Olivia's question came out sarcastic, and Maddie grinned. In fact, Olivia was wondering why Charlene, with her vast and expensive wardrobe, didn't buy her own books.

"Good question," Maddie said. "Heather said they were mostly romances and some bogus reference book about poisons in the foods we eat. Anyway, if I may continue, Heather told me that Charlene asked a bunch of personal questions about Lucas and me. Like, are we really, *really* a couple? Why hasn't Lucas ever married? He's so attractive, is he afraid of commitment? And aren't I running out of time to have kids? Not that I'm insecure."

"Not since the seventh grade," Olivia said.

"Charlene, on the other hand, screams insecurity."

Maddie brightened. "You always know the right thing to say. Anyway, it might be fun to watch her try to flirt with Lucas. He doesn't know what the word means. Lord knows I wasted years getting nowhere with him, until I gave up and started treating him like the guy next door. Which he is. That's when he finally noticed me."

"That plus the scent of your baking as it drifted over to his hardware store. Never underestimate the power of decorated cookies." Olivia didn't add that once Lucas became interested in her, Maddie reverted, for a time, to middle-school-crush mode. That period was best forgotten.

With a sideways leap, Maddie disposed of the final paper ball. "Enough about Charlene. There is cookie dough in the fridge, and it's calling out to me."

Between them, they hauled the trash can back to its space in the alley behind The Gingerbread House. "Let's go in the front," Olivia said. "I left poor Spunky locked in the foyer."

They rounded the corner and found Sheriff Del standing at the door, frowning as he listened to Spunky's frantic barking. He relaxed when he saw them. "I was getting worried," Del said. "I wondered if you'd gotten knocked on your heads when you returned from The Vegetable Plate."

Olivia grinned. "Do you suspect crime behind every door?"

"Occupational hazard. Especially when you're around."

"Ouch."

"I see you got the lawn back to normal," Del said. "By the way, Charlene steadfastly denies any responsibility for those flyers. She insists you two set the whole thing up, including the break-in, so you could scare her off."

Maddie snorted. "Frankly, she isn't worth the trouble."

Olivia unlocked the front door, triggering an explosion of vicious barking from inside.

"Hush, Spunky, it's me. Want some coffee, Del? We were about to reward our clean-up work with a flurry of cookie construction. Besides, I have a few questions to ask you."

"I knew there'd be a catch," Del said. "Thanks, but I need to get back to the station. I only stopped by to let you know we have a suspect for the break-in. We need to check his alibi, then we'll be in touch about your identification."

"But I only saw his —"

"You saw his back as he ran off, I know, but it's worth a try. I'm tracking down some information, so I should be able to fill you in tomorrow. You're still closed on Mondays, right? Great. Meanwhile, keep your doors locked." Del left before Olivia could ask who the suspect was.

CHAPTER TWO

The small kitchen at the back of The Gingerbread House had acquired two new items since Olivia received her inheritance: a window air conditioner and a new freezer, which hummed with state-of-the-art efficiency next to the bruised old refrigerator. Without good air conditioning, August in eastern Maryland was not conducive to long, happy hours of cookie baking and decorating. Olivia preferred feeling connected with the outdoors, but not when the heat and humidity made her feel like a boiled potato. Besides, she'd told herself, controlled humidity was better for consistent cookie quality.

Olivia loved Mondays, when the store remained closed. She and Maddie could catch up on business chores and get a jump on preparing the various cookies they would need for the coming week. Now that they could afford to hire some help in the store, they'd begun to supply special-order cookies for private parties, in addition to their themed store events.

"Ready to roll," Maddie said. "If I can find my trusty rolling pin."

Olivia looked up from her paperwork. "Cupboard next to the sink, second shelf from the top."

"How'd it get there? I swear, Livie, you hide things on purpose so you can torture me."

Olivia reached into a drawer and tossed Maddie a clean towel to wipe the dough off her hands. "Nonsense," she said. "You are the resident genius, and I am merely your short-term memory."

"Did you remember to get more flour? This dough is a tad sticky."

"Top shelf, next to the sugar. Are you starting on the cookies for the Tucker baby shower this week?"

"Um, sure, that's on the agenda."

Something in Maddie's tone made Olivia suspicious. "That event is special to me. If it weren't for Gwen and Herbie's contacts with animal rescue groups, I wouldn't have found Spunky." At the sound of his name, the little Yorkie lifted his head a few inches from his blanket, then dropped back to sleep. "The lazy bum."

Maddie studied a package of meringue powder as if she'd never seen one before. "I'm making an extra batch of dough to try out some ideas. Anyway, I mixed two batches yesterday, and they're rolled and chilling in the fridge, so there'll be plenty to work with. Don't fuss, Livie, all will be well. Don't you have errands to run or something?"

"I thought I'd —" A knock on the alley door interrupted her. "Are you expecting Lucas?"

"Not really," Maddie said as she opened the door. "Hi, Del, what's up?"

The sheriff dropped his uniform hat on the counter and mopped his forehead with his shirtsleeve. "You two have the best air conditioning in town."

"Well, don't let it escape into the alley," Maddie said.

"Do you only want us for our air conditioning?" Olivia asked.

"It's a start," Del said, with a lopsided grin.

Maddie rolled her eyes. "Honestly, you two, get a room. I have cookies to cut."

"Look who's criticizing." Olivia felt a little ping of pleasure whenever she and Del flirted, but it had been all too rare since late June. Her ex-husband, Ryan, had shown up uninvited with his grand scheme to open a clinic to provide affordable surgery for poor patients. It was a nice idea, but Olivia knew Ryan too well. Surgery was all he really enjoyed doing. He'd get bored and frustrated with the administrative demands of a clinic. She found it hard to believe that he had really turned over a new leaf.

Olivia poured a glass of iced tea from a pitcher in the refrigerator, added a few ice cubes and a wedge of lemon, and handed it to Del. "Any news about the break-in next door?"

"Thanks." Del swallowed a large gulp of tea. "We do have a suspect, but no real proof. When Charlene called the family attorney, we had to release him."

"Charlene called the family attorney? You mean the suspect is — ?"

"Charlie Critch, Charlene's younger brother," Del said. "It would be great if you could get a look at him, Livie. He works as a mechanic at the garage," Del said. "Does your brother still work there?"

"Wow, the plot thickens." Maddie eased an unbaked cut-out cookie onto a length of parchment paper. "Livie, did you know Charlene had a brother?"

"I did not," Olivia said. "Why didn't we

know that? My brother must work with him."

"He moved here a couple months ago and keeps pretty much to himself," Del said. "He rents a room from Gwen Tucker's aunt Agnes, over on the east side of town. So far we haven't been able to get a lot of background on him. Doesn't seem to have much of a history, but Cody is scouring the Internet." If there was anything to find, Del's eager deputy, Cody Furlow, would hunt it down.

Olivia raised an eyebrow. "I'll drop by the garage with some cookies and see if I can get a look at — what was his name? Charlie? Charlene and Charlie. . . . Are they twins?"

"Charlie is at least five years younger," Del said. "No record, adult anyway. Charlene might not want to press charges but vandalism is still a crime. I'm real interested in that kid. He and his sister had a public falling out two days ago at the Chatterley Heights Café. About money, according to witnesses. Charlene has lots and Charlie doesn't. We're looking into their family circumstances." Del drained his iced tea and retrieved his uniform hat. "Let me know your impressions after you get a look at the kid. Maybe chat with him, take his mea-sure." A cloud of hot, wet air osmosed into the cool kitchen as he opened the alley door.

"You're welcome," Olivia said to his back.

Del paused and twisted around. "Thanks." A corner of his mouth curved upward. "For doing your duty as a citizen."

Olivia threw a pen at him, but it bounced off the closed door.

Olivia was well armed when she arrived at Struts & Bolts, Chatterley Heights' one and only garage. She carried a Gingerbread House box filled with two dozen decorated cookies representing various modes of transportation, from animal to mechanical. In addition to the cookies, Olivia had stopped by the Chatterley Heights Café to pick up lattés for the mechanics and for herself. For Struts Marinksy, the owner, Olivia had splurged on a café mocha with a shot of mint and chocolate-mint sprinkles on top.

"You are a goddess in human form," Struts said as Olivia handed her the hot cup, "but I'm afraid not even chocolate-mint sprinkles will give me the power to bring your old Valiant back to its former glory. I'm an automotive genius, true, but even I am not that good. Jason won't give up, though. He keeps working on the poor old thing."

"I have grieved and let go," Olivia said as she plopped onto the old kitchen chair Struts offered to customers. "I come bearing cookies." She nestled the gift box among the notes, order forms, and oil-splotched tools that cluttered Struts's desk.

Struts eyed the box, decorated with a fanciful gingerbread house on top and colorfully sketched gingerbread men and women tumbling down the sides. "What's the catch? I don't have a first-born, not likely to produce one, so it can't be that. Are you trying to find out my real name?"

"Already know it," Olivia said with a smug grin. "It's Angelika. Mom told me."

"That snitch."

"It's a lovely name."

"I hate it. Do I look like an Angelika?"

Olivia studied Struts's grease-streaked T-shirt and frayed jeans, along with the combat boots planted on top of her desk, and was inclined to agree with her. However, the hair that escaped from Struts's ponytail and fell around her face was a rich, dark blond, with streaks of auburn and no emerging gray roots. Struts was somewhere in her mid-forties, taller than average, with the lean-legged figure of a long-distance runner.

"Actually," Olivia said, "you look like an Angelika dressed like a Struts, but I get your point. Still, the nickname fits. Mind telling me how you got it?"

"Ellie didn't spill that, too? What the heck." Struts shrugged a slender yet well-muscled shoulder. "I grew up on a farm. We had this ornery old tractor with which I had a special relationship. I was the only one who could fix it. This embarrassed my six brothers, who gave me the name Struts and tried to pass me off as a foundling."

Olivia imagined growing up with six Jasons and cringed. "Must have been rough."

"Nah, I loved knowing my brothers were jealous of what I could do. I've got this intuitive gift with machinery. Your brother calls me the Engine Whisperer." Struts slid her feet to the floor and lifted the lid off Olivia's offering of cookies. "Whoa, these look stunning." She selected an old-fashioned steam engine candy-striped in fuchsia and soft pink. "Do I have to share?"

"Up to you."

Struts sank back in her chair, closed her eyes, and moaned softly as she chewed off the smoke stack. Having polished off the entire choo-choo, she reached for a purple

45

Model T Ford. "Always wanted a Tin Lizzie." As the hood headed for her mouth, she said, "So Livie, what do I owe you in return?"

"You heard about the break-in last night in Charlene Critch's store? And that I saw the intruder run away?"

Struts nodded as she nibbled on the Model T's wheels.

"Between you and me, I need an unobtrusive look at Charlie Critch from the back." When Struts's dark hazel eyes opened wide, Olivia added, "I think Charlie is younger than the guy I saw, but Sheriff Del wants me to be sure."

Struts gulped her mocha and licked a few sprinkles off her upper lip. "Then we'll use some of these cookies as bait. I sure hope Charlie isn't the guy you saw. I like him. Nice kid, good feel for engines. Jason is working this shift, too, so we'll have to include him. Man, that boy can eat."

"No kidding," Olivia said. "You might want to rescue a couple cookies for later."

"Had that thought myself." Struts grabbed a violet-and-yellow baby carriage and an electric orange bicycle with red sprinkles. She wrapped them in what looked like a clean rag and stowed them in her desk drawer. "Better eat them soon," she said.

"We've got mice. I'll call the boys in here."

"Before you do that, what do you know about Charlie and his sister?"

Sweeping errant strands of hair behind one ear, Struts said, "Not a lot of personal chatter goes on here, at least not when I'm around. But I've picked up a thing or two. I know Charlie worships that sister of his, god knows why. If he's the one who messed up Charlene's store, I'll eat a seatbelt. Still, there's something going on with him. He and his sister come from money, you know. Lots of it. Charlie told me once that both their parents are dead. Not a word about what they were like or how they died, just 'They're dead.' Period. Jason might know more. He and Charlie are tight."

"My mom mentioned Charlie's father was a plastic surgeon."

"Yeah, I knew that," Struts said. "When they lived here in town, Charles Critch Sr. used to drive every day to his clinic in some DC suburb. Made quite a bundle, or so I heard. That's why I said Charlie has some sort of problem; his father set up a trust fund for both kids. I know because I dated one of the managers at the Chatterley Heights bank, and he told me in the strictest confidence."

Struts slid her hand under The Gingerbread House box lid and snagged another cookie. It turned out to be a modern car shape with electric green icing and a squished front end. The word "Valiant" was painted across the front in leaf green lettering. "Pure artistry," Struts said. "It deserves to be saved." She slipped it into her desk drawer.

Olivia asked, "You mentioned a trust fund and some problem with Charlie?"

"Oh yeah, sorry. Not like me to get distracted, but your cookies . . . Anyway, my guy who worked at the bank, he dumped me, so he deserves to have his confidence betrayed. He told me Charles Critch Sr. set up this trust fund for both Charlene and Charlie. They each get a monthly stipend, a generous one, and then each inherits a big chunk of the fund at the age of twenty-five. That's why Charlene opened that silly store; she just turned twenty-five. Charlie is twenty, so he's got a while to wait, but I pay well. Also, he gets that monthly stipend, which I could retire on. So you'd think he'd be living well, have a nice apartment, all that. But he lives in one room, and the last two pay periods he asked me for an advance."

"If Charlie was used to having lots of money," Olivia said, "maybe he has trouble staying within his allowance."

"Maybe." Struts shrugged. "Lord knows credit card debt is a pit a lot of folks have slid down into, yours truly included." She pushed aside an untidy collection of papers to reveal a hairbrush. While she repaired her ponytail, Struts said, "When Charlie started working here, about four months ago, he'd show up in nice clothes, then change into his work clothes in the gents. Now he wears the same clothes over and over. They keep getting dingier. I think he only washes them on his days off. Hey, I don't care, I consider grease a badge of honor. But you gotta wonder." Struts splayed her strong hands on the desk. They were immaculate. "This work does a number on my nails, though. I have them done once a week," she said, frowning down at her left hand. She whipped a diamond nail file out of her desk drawer and smoothed a tiny jagged spot on her thumbnail.

"Do you know anything about Charlene?" Olivia asked.

Struts shrugged. "She's got her admirers."

"I gather you're not one of them?"

Struts snorted. "Your mom insists Charlene was shy in high school, but she reminds me of those in-crowd girls. Not fond of that type myself."

"Me neither," Olivia said, "though Mom keeps reminding me that as an adult I should suspend judgment."

"Too tiring," Struts said.

"Any idea how Charles Sr. died?"

"Sure do." Struts's lips curved in a half smile of malicious glee. "Charles had his wife Patty served with divorce papers while he went on an early honeymoon with his twenty-five-year-old nurse and second-wife-to-be." Strut's smile broadened. "As I heard the story, poor Charles didn't last the night. Too much excitement. He had a heart attack and died in some fancy hotel in Vegas."

"Interesting," Olivia said. "So then how did Charlene's mom die?"

Struts sighed. "That's a sad story. I knew Patty from way back when she dated my oldest brother, before Charles swept her off her little size-five, triple-A feet. She should have married my brother, maybe she wouldn't have morphed into a skinny witch. Anyway, after Charlie Sr. left her and then up and died, Patty inherited everything except the trust for Charlene and Charlie. So Charles Sr. got his comeuppance and Patty got it all. But was she happy?"

"I'm guessing not?"

"And you'd be right," Struts said. "Patty went into a tailspin and let go of the steering wheel. She started drinking, decided she was too fat — at maybe ninety pounds — so she got herself hooked on diet pills and then sleeping pills. Plus she still drank her meals. She died less than a year after Charles Sr. Nobody talks about exactly how she died, but I think we can guess."

"Those poor kids," Olivia said.

"Yeah." Struts picked up her half-eaten purple Tin Lizzie cookie. "Pills, booze, and starvation. That's a sad way to go. Me, I'd rather sail a Maserati over a cliff." Struts made a dent in the Model T's back end and surveyed the damage while she chewed. "Did you know Model Ts mostly came in black?" she asked.

"I did not."

"I like it in purple," Struts said. "Very tasty." She reached across her desk and pressed the intercom button. "Break time, lads. Caffeine and sugar in my office." Whoops of joy penetrated the hum of the air conditioner.

Before the young men arrived, Struts took an old Baltimore & Ohio dining car plate off a hook on the wall. She spread a paper towel across it and placed a few cookies on top. "Gotta slow those boys down or they'll plow right through those cookies."

Olivia said, "Somehow I'll have to get a

good look at Charlie from the back."

"Don't fret, I'll make it happen." Struts swept her nail file and hairbrush into her desk drawer, perhaps to preserve her tough-woman-mechanic reputation.

Charlie Critch and Olivia's younger brother, Jason, crowded into the small office, filling it with movement and noise. The smell of gasoline trailed in behind them. They tore into the plate of cookies as if they hadn't seen food for days. A turquoise race car decorated with black flames and a royal blue baby carriage with tulip-red wheels disappeared into their mouths without even a murmur of admiration for their artistry.

"Hey, Sis, this latté is cold," Jason said.

"You're welcome."

Charlie Critch gave her a shy smile and toasted her with his latté. "Thanks for the coffee and cookies, Ms. Greyson."

"Call me Livie." Olivia tried to envision Charlie as an enraged store invader, but his quiet, respectful voice made it tough. At twenty, he still had the gangly look of a teenager who has just reached his full height, which Olivia estimated to be about six-foot-two. At six-foot-one, her brother was a shade shorter. Both young men had neatly trimmed brown hair and slender builds. In fact, now that she saw the two together, both of them looked similar to the man she'd seen running away from Charlene's store.

Jason snatched the last cookie on the plate, a burnt-orange airplane with cinnamon candies for windows. As it flew toward his mouth, he glanced at Charlie's thin face and hesitated. Without comment, Jason cracked the plane in half and handed a piece to the younger and clearly ravenous man.

"You're Charlene's brother, aren't you?" Olivia asked Charlie. "How have you been settling in here in Chatterley Heights?"

"Great." Charlie smiled, revealing a mouthful of well-tended, perfectly straight teeth with a clump of orange icing stuck between the front incisors. "I love working on cars," he added, with a sideways glance at Struts.

"It's too bad about Charlene's store," Olivia said.

Charlie's boyish face tightened, but he didn't comment.

"Any idea who might have done such a thing to your sister? I mean, you've both lived here only a short time, so it's hard to believe anyone in Chatterley Heights would have developed a grudge against her." Olivia held her breath, hoping she hadn't overdone it.

To her surprise, it wasn't Charlie who re-acted. Her brother, who had been slouching on the corner of Struts's desk, straightened and slid to his feet. He thrust out his chin in what Olivia called his bulldog look. "Grudge? Who said anything about a grudge? Charlene's a sweet kid. No reason anyone would want to hurt her." Jason slipped his hands in his pockets and re-treated to the windowsill.

Struts winked an eye at Olivia. "How about it, Charlie? I believe we can safely as-sume you've known your sister longer than any of us. Can you think of anyone who might have it in for her?"

Charlie crossed his arms as if he thought his chest might escape from his body. "No one," he said. "Maybe some people don't take to Charlene right off the bat, but she's always stuck by me. She doesn't deserve to get hurt."

While Olivia digested Charlie's informa-tion, spoken and tacit, Struts pushed the cookie box toward the two young men. "Sustenance," she said. "Boys need their daily sugar and butter." Jason was nearest, so he reached into the box and plucked out a burgundy spaceship with pale pink polka dots, which he kept for himself. He handed Charlie a Santa's sleigh in mint green with grape trim.

"Hey Charlie," Struts said, giving Olivia a glance filled with meaning. "Since you're here, does that Toyota parked out on the street look like it's got a flat?" She nodded her head toward the office window behind her desk. Charlie crossed the room, offering Olivia a clear view of his back.

"Which Toyota?" Charlie asked, as his head moved from left to right. "There's five of them. Two red Corollas, one of them this year's model; a blue Camry with a dent in the driver's door; a green Camry, maybe ten years old; and a red truck."

"I think it was one of the red Corollas," Struts said. "Or maybe the truck."

Jason joined Charlie at the window. Struts smirked at Olivia as both of the men's heads swiveled back and forth, hunting for a flat tire. "I think your eyesight's going, Boss," Jason said, turning to face her. "All the tires look fine to me."

"Me, too," Charlie said. "Want us to go out and take a closer look?"

"Nah, I guess I was dreaming about more walk-in business," Struts said. "Okay, guys, you've finished off the cookies, so back to work." Once the door had closed behind them, she turned to Olivia. "Well?"

"Honestly, I can't be sure. Charlie doesn't

55

seem the type to smash up a store, and it sounds like he's close to his sister, but . . ." Olivia shrugged and tossed her empty latté cup into the wastebasket as she rose to leave.

"Fine mechanic, too," Struts said. "I sure hope he isn't a crazed criminal, I'd hate to lose him. Besides, Jason would probably kill him if he hurt Charlene."

"What . . . ?" Olivia gaped at Struts.

Struts laughed. "And here I thought mothers were the last to know. Jason has quite a thing, as they say, for Charlene. No accounting for taste, but he is male, so there you are."

"Jason and Charlene," Olivia said. The thought of Charlene Critch as a sister-in-law made detached compassion a tougher sell. "Are they getting serious? Does Mom really know about this?"

"Yeah, Ellie is aware. As for getting serious, Jason clearly is. Charlene, who knows? She'd flirt with a fire hydrant if it wore pants."

"If that woman hurts my baby brother, I'll . . ." Olivia stopped herself in time. She was too familiar with murder to say it lightly. She thought it, though.

Struts opened her desk drawer and rummaged inside it. Slamming the drawer shut with her foot, she reached across to Olivia.

"Here." She held out the electric green Valiant with the smashed front end. "You need a cookie."

CHAPTER THREE

Olivia returned to The Gingerbread House to find the kitchen air conditioner at war with the overworked oven. Maddie had been busy. Cut-out cookies were cooling on three racks, while four lengths of parchment paper held more cut-out shapes ready for baking.

"Is that lime zest I smell?" Olivia asked.

Maddie pulled an iPod bud from her ear. "You found a crime nest?"

"Close. Lime zest. Did you put lime zest in the cookie dough?"

"It seemed appropriate," Maddie said. "What did you find out at the garage?"

"I'm about to call Del, you can listen in." Olivia called Del's cell phone, hoping to avoid having to leave a message.

Del answered in one ring; at least it sounded like Del's voice. "Harrow?"

"Del, is that you? You sound like you're drowning."

"Eating an egg salad sandwich in my squad car. So, did you get a look at Charlie Critch?"

"I met Charlie and got some background about him from Struts Marinsky over at the garage. Also, I got a good look at his back. But I still can't be sure he's the man I saw. He's got the right build and short brown hair, but . . . The intruder in Charlene's store seemed older to me. I'm not sure why. Maybe it was his voice."

"What about his voice?" Del said.

"The intruder's voice was angry, harsh. Charlie struck me as shy, with a quiet, boyish voice. I asked how his sister was holding up after the break-in, and I'd swear the kid almost crumpled. He tried to hold it in, but he was quite upset. He seems to care for her."

A soft murmur came from Maddie's direction: "It takes all kinds. . . ."

"One other thing," Olivia said. "I'd swear he was hiding something. He seemed evasive about whether he knew of anyone who might have a grudge against Charlene. He insisted no one would want to hurt her, but then he said she 'didn't deserve' to be hurt. Anyway, it seemed odd to me. Also, Struts thinks Charlie is having money problems."

"Okay, I'll do some more digging," Del

said. "You could keep your ears open, but otherwise, you're relieved of duty."

"What have you dug up so far?" Olivia asked. "Anything about Charlie's past? Does Charlene have a secret life?"

"Give me a break, Livie. You know I can't share the details of an ongoing investigation with you."

"Hey, you sent me off to look at a suspect for you — which cost me two dozen decorated cookies, by the way."

Del chuckled. "You're right, I should reimburse you for the cookies, so how about —"

"What, a dozen jelly doughnuts?"

"Dinner tonight. At that new restaurant, Bon Vivant. My treat."

"Oh." Olivia felt Maddie's sudden interest, despite her intense focus as she centered a new batch of cookies in the oven. "Can't," Olivia said, attempting a monotone. "Gotta meet my mom at her rumba lesson at seven."

"I'd pay good money to see that," Del said. "How about an early dinner? It'll be less crowded, anyway. That place is getting popular."

"Well . . ."

"Good, I'll pick you up at five. And Livie, I want you to stay in one piece, so thanks for your help, but don't start investigating on your own, okay?"

"I'll meet you there. I need my car," Livie said before flipping shut her cell phone. She had half a mind to stand him up. On the other hand, even an early dinner called for a glass or two of wine, which might relax Del's professional boundaries. Olivia's interest was more than curiosity. The break-in at The Vegetable Plate was too close for comfort.

Maddie opened the oven door to pull out a sheet of cookies, baked to perfection. A puff of hot air, buttery sweet and edged with citrus, escaped into the kitchen. "So what's this about you and the rumba?" she asked. "Who are you, and what have you done with my dignified friend?" She opened a cupboard door and began pulling down small bottles of gel food coloring for icing. "Unless . . ." She spun around, a bottle of electric purple clutched to her chest. "You're taking lessons so you and Del can go dancing, aren't you? The rumba is an excellent choice." With the bottle of purple gel coloring as her partner, Maddie began to dance around the kitchen worktable. Maddie's sensuous hip action made Olivia wish she had suggested that her mother meet her for breakfast the next morning instead.

Maddie swayed back to the cupboards, where she retrieved confectioners' sugar, meringue powder, and lemon extract for the royal icing. She added a set of measuring cups and deposited her armload on the table, next to the mixer. "So," she said as she opened the package of meringue. "You and Del. Tell me all."

Olivia lunged for one of the cooled, undecorated cookies. "I'll die if I don't try one of these right away." She nibbled off a protruding part that looked like a stem. "Mmm," she said, closing her eyes. She went for another bite, then stopped and frowned at the cookie in her hand. Her gaze traveled over the racks of cooling cookies and moved on to the rows of undecorated shapes. "I thought you were preparing for Gwen and Herbie's baby shower. These don't look like baby carriages or rattles or onesies to me."

Maddie poured confectioners' sugar into the mixing bowl, wielding her measuring cups with focused nonchalance.

"This is an apple, right?" Olivia held out her half-eaten cookie. She then pointed toward freshly baked cookies cooling on a sheet of parchment paper. "That one looks like a carrot, and I bet that's a sweet potato." She picked up a long, narrow, curved shape.

"Is this . . . a sweet pea? Maddie, you've baked a whole batch of fruits and vegetables. Why do I sense some cunning plot in that devious mind of yours? Please tell me you're not —"

The kitchen telephone startled Olivia, and she answered without checking Caller ID.

"Livie?" The deep voice belonged to Olivia's ex-husband, Ryan. He sounded tentative, which wasn't like him. "Livie, I know I promised not to call for six months, but I wanted you to know how much progress we've made on the new clinic. The response from other surgeons has been incredible."

"I'm glad for you, Ryan, but right now I —"

"Five minutes, okay? We've found a perfect building, a clinic that went under at the beginning of the recession. It went into foreclosure, and we got it for a song. It's even near a bus line for families that don't own cars."

Ryan sounded like the eager, hopeful man Olivia had fallen in love with, but she reminded herself how quickly he could change moods. "That sounds great," she said, "but —"

"Also, we've already convinced three surgeons to commit two days a month each. Well, one of them is me, and I'll be donating half of my surgery time, at least for now. Plus Joanie has been working day and night writing grants to drum up funding."

"Joanie?" Olivia glanced over at Maddie, who was mixing a new batch of cookie dough by hand, rather than drown out Livie's conversation with the whir of a mixer.

"You remember Joanie," Ryan said in the mellifluous voice he used when he wanted to gloss over a subject as if it were only of minor importance. "Joanie and I were in the same medical school class, but she decided she didn't want to practice, so now she writes applications for medical grants. Anyway, we've already been awarded a couple solid grants."

Olivia remembered Joanie well, though she'd spoken with her only once and for about three minutes, at a party given by one of Ryan's medical school professors. Joanie, with the girl-next-door name, had looked as if she'd come directly from a modeling runway. She'd worn a short, figure-hugging satiny dress that showed off her lovely shoulders and long legs. Excessively long, in Olivia's opinion. Then there was her hair, long and streaky blonde, which swayed as she walked. Joanie's gaze had scanned the party guests while she exchanged empty pleasantries with Olivia. Yes, she could imagine that Joanie was quite effective at scoring grant money.

Olivia's flash of remembered jealousy startled her. That's all it was, she told herself. Jealousy remembered. In the here and now, she felt relieved that Ryan might be involved with Joanie. Didn't she?

"Thanks for the update, Ryan," Olivia said. "I have to go now."

After she'd hung up, Olivia sat in silence, pulled into herself. Maddie seemed to understand her need for quiet. Moments passed before Olivia became aware of a shuffling sound outside the door that led to the alley behind The Gingerbread House. It could be a cat, or maybe Deputy Cody's black Lab, Buddy, had taken off again. No, it couldn't be Buddy, not unless he had learned to turn doorknobs. Olivia glanced at the dead bolt, then at the lock in the doorknob; neither was in its locked position. In hot, humid weather the door did tend to stick, so it might feel locked.

"What did his highness have to say this time?" Maddie was not a fan of Ryan, and her tone made that clear. "Livie?" she asked when Olivia didn't respond.

Olivia put her finger to her lips and nodded toward the door. When the knob jiggled again, she pointed to the rolling pin on the table. Maddie snatched it up and handed it to her. Holding the rolling pin poised to whack an intruder if necessary, Olivia twisted the knob and opened the door.

Maddie was the first to recognize a startled and familiar face under a broad-brimmed hat. "Snoopy?"

The rolling pin dropped to Olivia's side as she, too, recognized Sam Parnell standing in the doorway. He had flushed cheeks and a package under one arm. As always, he wore the full uniform — appropriate to the season, of course — of a United States Postal Service carrier. This wasn't the first time Sam had tried to get into their kitchen without knocking. He never seemed to learn.

No one called Sam by his nickname: Snoopy. At least not to his face. Red mottling began to creep up his neck.

Olivia opened the door wider. "Sam, what on earth were you thinking? You scared us to death. We thought you might be that intruder who broke into The Vegetable Plate."

Sam's flush deepened. His thin body seemed frozen in fight-or-flight stance. "I wasn't . . . I mean, some folks leave their alley doors unlocked on a workday, and this package arrived special delivery, so . . ." He held out the package. Olivia recognized the return address of a mail order firm that made lovely cookie cutters. She had ordered some in anticipation of holiday events in coming months.

"Thanks, I've been waiting for this," Olivia said, taking the package. "It's okay to come to the back door, Sam, but we'd appreciate it if you'd knock. We normally keep the door locked, anyway, even if we're working in the kitchen."

"Sure," Sam said. "I keep forgetting you picked up city habits living in Baltimore. Must have been tough, dealing with all that crime right outside your own front door."

Maddie snickered. "Yeah, Livie had to knock a few heads together to clean up her neighborhood."

Sam's small eyes darted from Olivia to Maddie and back. "Well, I can't stand around and yak all day." He spun around so fast his heavy mail bag slapped his back and threw him off balance. Olivia cringed when she heard Maddie giggle behind her.

"Let me get that door for you," Olivia said. "You've got quite a load there."

"Nothing I'm not used to," Sam said with dignity, nodding to Olivia as she held the door open. He paused before stepping into the alley. "By the way," he said, "you might want to check out Binnie's blog. She gave you two quite a spread." Chuckling, he added, "I guess any publicity is good, right?"

By the time Olivia locked and latched the door, Maddie had fired up the kitchen laptop and logged on to Binnie Sloan's blog, her newest adjunct to the *Weekly Chatter,* Chatterley Heights' only newspaper. For the most part, Binnie let her young niece, Nedra, handle the blog. Since Ned, as she preferred to be called, was a photographer and rarely spoke, the content was almost entirely photos, mostly of Chatterley Heights citizens looking startled, embarrassed, and angry. Often in that order.

Maddie flipped through the blog photos and said, "Ugh."

"How bad is it?"

Maddie answered with a low growl. "I advise you to call Mr. Willard."

"Seriously? You think we need an attorney?"

"If I'm going to kill Binnie and Ned, I'd better lawyer up." Maddie turned the laptop toward Olivia. "Take a look."

Olivia pulled a chair over to the small desk and squeezed next to Maddie, who scrolled back to the beginning of the photo display. Maddie muttered vengeful threats as she scanned through Ned's candid shots of the two of them cleaning scrunched-up paper off The Gingerbread House lawn.

"I hereby vow to do my laundry on a more regular basis," Olivia said when she saw herself in her red shorts and pink tank top.

"That's nothing," Maddie said. "Check out my hair. It looks like a bale of hay exploded on my head. I'm thinking I'll bash Ned with her own camera."

"I don't think this is worth a murder rap," Olivia said as the final photo appeared. "It's embarrassing and intrusive, but that's what Binnie and Ned are good at." She squinted and leaned toward the screen. "What's that?"

"What?"

"Right there, in the second-floor window of The Vegetable Plate." Olivia pointed to the blurred upper right edge of the photo.

Maddie peered over Olivia's shoulder. "I do see something, but . . ." Her fingers punched the keyboard. The photo became enlarged, and was blurrier, but a head-and-shoulders-shaped dark patch showed clearly in the top-floor window of The Vegetable Plate. "We'd better email this link to Del and Cody. Maybe they can get hold of the original. I'd love to see them confiscate Ned's camera. Can you tell if it's a man or a woman?"

"I can't see any hair," Olivia said. "The sun must be picking up the face because the room behind looks unlit. That makes sense if this is the store intruder, and he doesn't want to be caught searching for something. If it's Charlene, I think we might see the lightness of her hair; it's such a bright blond."

"Brighter than nature intended," Maddie said. "I wonder when Ned took this picture."

Olivia flipped back through all the photos. "You aren't in some of these, just me or the lawn, and the light is different in those pictures. I think Ned took these at two different times. I'm lucky she didn't post a shot of me going into The Vegetable Plate."

"Knowing Binnie," Maddie said, "she's holding it for ransom. She probably wants an interview with you."

"Wait a minute, I think I see something." Olivia picked up a pencil and lightly touched the grainy face on the screen. She traced the outline of a faint, dark curve separated by a lighter patch. "Those could be teeth," Olivia said. "I'll bet anything that's the man I saw running from the store. And he's laughing at us."

Chapter Four

Olivia arrived at the Bon Vivant a few minutes before five p.m. and found it already filling up. The restaurant had been open less than a month. Chatterley Heights residents had quickly discovered its charms, and a recent excellent review in the *Baltimore Sun* was now luring in more diners from the surrounding area. This was Olivia's first look inside.

Del hadn't yet arrived. The hostess — a tall, elegant redhead with a brilliant smile — skimmed around closely packed tables as she guided Olivia to a table for two next to a window. She pulled out a chair for Olivia and said, "The sheriff specifically requested one of our quieter tables with a view. May I bring you a glass of our house merlot while you wait?"

"I'll start with coffee, thanks. Cream and sugar."

The hostess flashed her snow-white incisors and disappeared. Within moments, a server appeared at the table with Olivia's coffee and two thick menus. Olivia sipped as she gazed out the window at a brick patio bordered with pink and red tea roses, all showcased against the lush hills in the distance. This was what kept her in Maryland despite the dripping heat of late summer. All this and cookies, too.

"What? No merlot?" Olivia jumped at the sound of Del's voice. Her chair started to tilt; Del steadied it. "Sorry," he said. "I'm too used to sneaking up on people."

"Do you plan to tell everyone in town that I like a glass of merlot now and then?"

Del grinned. "Everyone knows already. And just to warn you, everyone knows about your thing for pizza, too."

"I've watched you down quite a few slices," Olivia said. "Not to mention the ever-present ham-and-cheese sandwiches." Skimming her menu, she said, "Oh look, they serve pizza here. With roasted artichoke hearts and prosciutto, which make it both healthy and ham-like. Want to share one?"

"Sounds good to me." Del caught the waiter's eye. "And how about that glass of merlot?"

"Make it Chianti, in deference to the pseudo-Italian nature of the meal. And only if you will join me." Olivia had not forgotten that wine was a key part of her plan to find out what Del had learned about the break-in at The Vegetable Plate.

"Done." Del handed over the menus and leaned on his elbows on the table. "You look nice. I like the thing you did with your hair."

"Thanks," Olivia said with both pleasure and relief. She knew she should have worn one of her three dresses, but she planned to go directly from dinner to her mother's rumba class. "The thing I did with my hair," Olivia said, "is a barrette. That's a technical term."

"Unless it has to do with weapons, I won't remember it," Del said. "As promised, this meal is on me, with thanks for donating your time and cookies to help identify the man you saw leaving Charlene's store." Their wine arrived, and they clinked glasses. "Nice," Del said after his first sip. He gave Olivia a smile that warmed her from the inside, the kind of smile she hadn't seen for some time. She almost hated to pester him for information. However.

"Sorry I couldn't positively identify the intruder as Charlie Critch," Olivia said. "Although I liked the kid, so I'm also glad. He and Jason have become buddies. Of course, Jason likes Charlene, too, so he might not be the best judge of character." Olivia sipped her wine and vowed to memorize the label. She wasn't normally a fan of Chianti, but this stuff was tasty. "So do you have any specific reason to suspect that Charlie might be the intruder?"

Del's smile faded, but at least he didn't start ordering her to stay out of the investigation. "We don't have much at all yet. I've heard a great deal of gossip about their parents, but Charlene and Charlie are both strangely hard to investigate."

"Strangely?" Olivia asked.

"These days we can usually learn a lot about folks simply by searching for them on the Internet. But not these kids. As far as we can tell, neither of them uses sites like Facebook or Twitter or has a blog or even posts messages on anyone else's sites."

"Is it too much to hope that either of them has a police record? Come on, Del, don't make that face at me. I'm not simply curious. I'm not a gossip, either. The Gingerbread House is right next door to The Vegetable Plate, plus I suspect that whoever trashed Charlene's store did the same to our front lawn. So yeah, I need to know."

Del took a slow sip of his wine, let his gaze roam around the restaurant, squinted at the view from the window, and sipped again.

Olivia felt like canceling the pizza, pouring the wine on his head, and stalking out. Instead she said, "Nice try. Not going to work."

Del shook his head and laughed. "Lord help me if I ever have to interrogate you."

"I guess you'll have to assign someone else to do it. Or a whole team."

"You'd make mincemeat out of them."

"Oh please. Mincemeat? Decorated cookies, maybe." Olivia reached across the table and touched Del's hand with her fingertips. "I know you're worried for my safety, and I do appreciate that, but I hope you trust me to be rational. I'm not a danger addict. If a crime doesn't affect me or those I care about, I'll gladly leave it entirely to you."

"Except you seem to wind up caring about everyone you meet," Del said. "I believe you even care about Charlene Critch. Or is it really curiosity?"

Olivia drew her hand away. "A bit of both, I guess. Charlene can be profoundly irritating, no doubt about it, but there's also something lost about her. Mom told me she'd heard that Charlene was married briefly but her father had the marriage annulled."

Del frowned. "We looked for an ex-husband, but Charlene insisted she'd never been married, and we've found no record of a marriage. Usually we can unearth an annulment, but apparently the paperwork, if there was any, has disappeared. The Critch family was wealthy and powerful. Charles Sr. made it a point to curry the favor of people with clout. However, if there's an ex-husband, we'll find him eventually through friends and relatives."

"I suppose you've dug into her brother Charlie's past? Through official channels, I mean."

Del had apparently decided to trust Olivia, at least up to a point, because he answered without hesitation. "I've been checking with my sources in the DC Police Department. Nothing solid, but one buddy of mine said he'd heard the kid had a juvie record, which would be sealed. We ought to be able to dig it up, but for some reason we've come up empty so far. Has Jason mentioned anything about Charlie?"

"No, but I can grill him," Olivia said. "And speaking of food preparation, I believe that's our pizza wending toward us."

As their pizza and house salads arrived, Del added, "By the way, thanks for forwarding Binnie Sloan's blog link. She gave us the original photo, and we sent it along to the crime lab in Baltimore. Their photo expert might be able to enhance the guy's face in Charlene's window."

"I'm impressed," Olivia said. "How did you snag the original from Binnie without a warrant and a lengthy court fight?" She selected a large slice of pizza, one with lots of roasted artichoke hearts, and wedged the narrow end into her mouth before it could collapse.

"Easy," Del said. "I simply pointed out the consequences if they continued to take photos of you without your knowledge and permission. I informed them that The Gingerbread House is private property, along with your home and land, and that you had a legal right to bar both her and her niece from setting foot on or in either of them. Of course, they can still photograph you from the sidewalk, but if you forbid them from entering your store or even standing at the windows, it will seriously cramp their style."

"Wow," Olivia said. "Thank you."

"All part of the service."

As they both reached for a second piece of pizza, Olivia asked, "So does all this mean we are friends again?"

Del paused in mid-reach and raised his eyebrows. "Had we stopped being friends?"

Spreading some dressing on her salad of

baby greens, Olivia thanked genetics for her blush-resistant skin. "It's just that . . . a few months ago, it seemed maybe we were becoming more than friends. Or was I imagining things?" She wrapped her mouth around an extra-large forkful of salad in a clear case of nervous eating.

Del gave her free hand a quick, hard squeeze. "You weren't imagining things, but . . ."

Olivia wanted to encourage him to keep talking, but her mouth was crammed with greens. She tried to say "But what?" with her mouth full. It came out as "Ga-uh?"

Del threw his head back and laughed. A couple at a nearby table glanced at him and gave each other a knowing smile. "Okay," Del said once he'd quieted down. "If you promise not to choke yourself with green stuff, I'll talk. It's about your ex-husband. No, hear me out. I know you assured me the marriage is over, dead, never to be revived. And I know you were being sincere." Del picked a bit of crust off his plate and ate it.

Olivia sipped her wine and waited for him to elaborate, though it cost her a jittery stomach.

With a sigh, Del leaned toward Olivia. "Ryan is an impressive guy," he said. "I'll grant you he has a controlling nature, though when he suddenly showed up in your store, he did seem to be making an effort to lighten up. I think he wants you back."

"Not a chance," Olivia said. Her ex-husband had driven from Baltimore and appeared at The Gingerbread House without warning in mid-summer. He had babbled nonstop about his plans for a low-cost surgery clinic for the working poor, all the while pacing the sales floor and talking over customers who had questions about store items. To Olivia, it was an example of the best and the worst of Ryan. His enthusiasm could be infectious and alluring, but he often forgot that his listeners were separate from him and might have their own plans for their lives. Worst of all, Ryan had been in full swing when Del dropped in to ask if Olivia might be interested in dinner and a movie that evening. He couldn't find a place to break into Ryan's monologue, so he finally left. Olivia only found out Del's intentions much later, after the warmth between them abruptly cooled.

"Some breaks can't be mended," Olivia said. "Ryan has a good side, and that's what you saw, although you have to admit he was self-absorbed, too. The real problem is he tends to lose interest in his ideas once they demand too much time and administrative work. He loves to do surgery, and surgery is where he shines. He seemed to be making an effort to be less controlling because he wants me to move back to Baltimore and take care of all the stuff he hates to do. If I'm going to oversee a business, I'd much rather it be mine."

"I can understand that," Del said as a waiter arrived to refill their coffee cups. They both shook their heads when he asked if they wanted dessert. When the waiter was out of earshot, Del said, "I do think there was more to it. I think he misses you, and who wouldn't? Maybe you need to think about his offer for a while."

"Are you trying to get rid of me?" Teasing, Olivia narrowed her eyes at him. "Or wait, I get it. You've been listening to Charlene Critch, and you've decided I've brought too much sugar into your life."

"Or maybe not enough," Del said with a lopsided grin.

Olivia glanced at her watch and said reluctantly, "I've got to run. My mom's rumba lesson begins in fifteen minutes." But she stayed put and tilted her head at Del. "You've pulled back," she said. "That's your right, of course, only . . ." She sipped her coffee, took a deep breath, and asked, "Is Ryan the whole reason, or is there more?"

Del stared down into his coffee cup, out the window, anywhere but in her direction.

"You are free not to answer, of course," Olivia said. "Only, could you give me a verbal hint whether you plan to answer in the next three minutes or not? It's just that Mom's rumba lesson waits for no one, not even her one precious daughter."

Del's smile was fleeting. "You have a right to know, though I'd appreciate your keeping this between us. In a sense, it's about Ryan, but more about you. I mean you in relation to Ryan," he added when he saw the stricken expression on Olivia's face. "My marriage . . . Livie, I know it isn't fair to make this comparison, but I can't help it. My marriage ended because my wife left me for her ex-husband."

"Oh, Del, you —"

"Don't really want to talk about it right now," Del said. In a softer tone, he added, "If I'm not mistaken, it's time to rumba."

An unusual number of well-to-do families had settled in and around Chatterley Heights, which made the town a destination for hungry artists of all types, especially those willing and able to teach. Olivia's mother, Ellie, took full advantage of the opportunities available. On Monday evenings, she would be at her Latin dancing lesson.

The Chatterley Heights Dance Studio occupied a small building located southeast of the town square. A sister team of seamstresses had occupied the building until the early 1960s. The sisters died long before Olivia was born, but her mother had often described the elegant ball gowns and bridal trousseaus she'd admired in the large display window. Ellie had been a little girl in the fifties, but she remembered in vivid detail the delicate embroidery and tiny beads handstitched to satin gowns. Ellie had called it sweet karma that, after standing empty for years, the building was renovated for a dance studio. Grateful for the opportunity, underemployed dance teachers came regularly from Baltimore and DC to offer lessons in everything from hip-hop to square dancing.

Through the studio's front window, Olivia could see the dance floor, which covered what used to be the store's entire sales area. The dimmed lights left the edges of the room in near darkness. Her mother appeared to be alone on the dance floor, practicing some steps. Behind her, a light shone through a doorway, which Olivia guessed was the instructor's office. If she hurried, maybe she could catch a word with her mother alone.

Olivia stepped inside the building and felt a rush of cool, dry air. Ellie was across the room perfecting a spin that sent her long, gray hair flying out from her back. In contrast with her usual preference for loose, flowing outfits, Ellie wore a red knit dress that hugged her petite figure. A double row of short ruffles flounced around her knees as she executed a quick twisting movement.

Ellie caught sight of Olivia and waved. She held up one finger to say she'd be back in a minute and disappeared into the office. A moment later, music erupted from speakers around the dance floor, and Ellie emerged in the arms of one of the most gorgeous men Olivia had ever seen. He could have been anywhere from thirty to sixty. His tall, lean, perfectly controlled body swayed like silk in the wind, and he possessed a luxurious shock of white-streaked black hair that set off a chiseled face. He looked down at Ellie, who barely reached his shoulders, and smiled in a way that made Olivia feel squeamish.

"Quite a dancer, isn't he?"

Olivia spun around to find her stepfather, Allan Meyers, standing behind her in the shadows. Allan's broad, friendly face tightened as he watched his wife twirl away from her instructor, then back into the crook of his arm.

"Name's Raoul, of course," Allan said. "Doesn't seem to need a last name."

"Something tells me you're not here for a rumba lesson," Olivia said.

Allan laughed. "Your mother sang this fellow's praises so much, I thought I'd have a look-see for myself. Not that I'm worried, mind you."

"No reason you should be."

With his eyes glued to Ellie's movements, Allan asked, "You thinking about rumba lessons, too? You might want to step on it. This guy will be gone in two weeks." With a sheepish grin, he added, "Not that I'm counting the days."

The rumba came to an end, and Ellie danced over to them, swaying her hips in a way no daughter should have to witness. Allan handed Ellie a bottle of water from which she took a long swig. "I have a five-minute break while Raoul selects more music. And I'm afraid Allan and I have to leave right after the lesson. We have reservations for a romantic dinner at that new restaurant, Bon Vivant. Allan planned the whole thing." Ellie flashed a radiant smile at her husband.

Olivia decided not to mention that she'd just had dinner with Del at Bon Vivant. Her mother already dropped enough hints about the two of them. Living in the city had given Olivia a sense of personal privacy that had evaporated about two minutes after she'd moved back to Chatterley Heights.

Ellie took another swallow of water and handed the bottle back to Allan. "Now Livie, on the phone you said you wanted to know about the Critches? I'm afraid I rather lost track of them after they left Chatterley Heights for DC, but one hears things."

"I think Charlene Critch is hiding some-thing," Olivia said. "She knows who that prowler was, the one I found in her store. I'm sure of it. Del suspects her brother, Charlie." Olivia shook her head. "I visited Struts & Bolts and took a good look at him, but I'm not convinced Charlie is the man I saw. He does seem secretive, though. I'd like to know more about him, and about Charlene, too."

Allan laughed. "You sure came to the right person. When it comes to people, your mother knows all."

"I'm not so sure about that. Let me think." Ellie fingered her hair off one shoul-der to disentangle it from a dangly earring.

85

"The Critch family moved away from Chatterley Heights about ten years ago, right in the middle of the school year. I remember because it was Jason's senior year in high school, and he had such a crush on Charlene. After she left, he was down in the dumps for some time and had trouble concentrating. Although it was spring, after all, which undoubtedly had something to do with his distraction. You know what those last months of high school are like. There's so much on one's mind, all of it earth-shattering."

"The minutes march on, Mother."

"As they so often do when one is constantly reminded of them." Though Ellie's tone sounded innocent enough, Allan edged away out of range.

"Point taken," Olivia said.

"It's hard for teenagers to adjust to change," Ellie said. "Charlene is a couple years younger than Jason, so she was about fifteen when she had to leave all her friends. She was a pretty little thing, not so painfully thin as she is now. It gives her a hard look, don't you think? I suspect the poor girl has an eating disorder, which shouldn't be surprising with those parents of hers. So critical, especially Patty. She insisted her children be perfect, which of course children never are. Present company excluded, of course."

"Liar," Olivia said. "But back to the intruder?"

"I'm getting there, Livie. You're so impatient."

"I thought I was perfect."

"Now who's wasting time?" Ellie glanced back over her shoulder as Raoul crooked a come-hither index finger at her. "Hang on a moment, I have an idea." She glided across the dance floor to Raoul, who leaned down to her as she spoke. He nodded once.

Ellie waved toward Olivia and called, "Come along, both of you."

"But —"

"No buts, Livie. I refuse to miss a moment of my wonderful lesson."

Olivia had a bad feeling about what might be coming next. She glanced at her stepfather. With his husky build and hunched shoulders, he reminded her of a bull in the headlights.

As Raoul changed the compact disc, Ellie said, "This will be fun. And so fortuitous! I've always wanted both of you to take up dancing. It will keep you young, and wait until you see how exhilarating it is."

Olivia's bad feeling worsened.

"We will keep the dance slow and simple."

Raoul looked as if he had arrived yesterday from Latin America, but his accent was slight. "Ellie and I will demonstrate the basic steps of the rumba. We will then separate the ladies from the gentlemen. Or the gentleman, in this case." Raoul bowed his head in Allan's direction. "Normally, I would have a dance partner to instruct the ladies. Alas, here I teach alone. Therefore, I will first instruct the gentleman in his movements, and then the ladies in theirs. Ellie has learned the dance quickly and well, so she will dance with her husband. But first, Ellie and I will again demonstrate the rumba, as I noted that the two of you were in conversation while we danced earlier. Please pay careful attention."

"I really don't think this is —" As the music interrupted, Olivia shot an alarmed glance at her mother.

Raoul held out his hand to Ellie, who took it and allowed herself to be escorted again to the dance floor. She rested her right hand on Raoul's upper arm as he reached his left hand to her shoulder blade. Olivia sneaked a peek at Allan's scowling face. She sympathized. Over Ellie's head, Raoul called across the floor, "Watch our feet, the steps are quite simple. Think of a square."

To Olivia, the square image lasted about

twenty seconds. After that, the steps made no sense at all. If there was a pattern to them, she couldn't see it. Ellie and Raoul's dancing feet seemed to be going everywhere at once, and the hip movements became, to say the least, distracting.

When the dance ended, Raoul turned to Olivia and Allan. "There, you see? One makes a square, with small departures. Slow, quick-quick, slow. It is simple." With a tight, closed-lip smile, he held out his hand to Allan, who shrank back against the wall. With an elegant shrug, Raoul turned to Olivia and captured her hand. She felt her heart sink to about knee level.

Ellie took one look at her daughter's face and said, "I'm sorry, sweetie, I forgot that you need to repeat the steps slowly several times before they make sense to you. I'm afraid you inherited that from your dear father."

"Ah," said Raoul. "I shall teach you slowly."

Ellie slid between them. "That is so perceptive of you, Raoul, but first, perhaps I could try? It would be such good practice for me." Ellie grabbed Olivia's hand and dragged her toward the far end of the dance floor. As Raoul started to follow, she said, "No, no, you gentlemen take a break. We won't be a minute." Ellie slipped into the office and reappeared as the rumba music began again. She led Olivia to a dimly lit corner and said, "I know you hate this, Livie, and so does Allan, so I regretfully release my dream of having a twinkle-toed family. I shall orchestrate your escape. But first I thought we could talk more easily over here, away from the pressure. Raoul is so forceful."

Olivia glanced back across the room, where her stepfather and Raoul stood several feet apart, arms crossed over chests, watching them. "But poor Allan is alone with Raoul." Turning back to her mother, she asked, "Don't you find Raoul rather intimidating?"

"Not at all, dear. Besides, Allan is more than capable of taking care of himself. By the time we finish, he will probably know all there is to know about the financial aspects of Raoul's dancing career. Now, let's get to it, shall we?" She took Olivia's left hand and placed it against her upper arm. "Now Livie, you may ask your questions, but pay attention, as well. If I'm to give up the remainder of my dance lesson, at least I can have the satisfaction of teaching you a few steps. Now, start with your right foot and step backward. No, sweetie, your other right. That's it, but slower. Make it sultry. Next, two quick steps. . . . Now what else did you want to know about the Critches?"

Distracted and struggling to avoid a collision, Olivia stared down at her feet and watched as they completed a square — more or less, if she didn't count her false steps. So that's what Raoul meant by thinking about a square. Olivia relaxed a bit and remembered one of the questions she'd wanted to ask about the intruder in The Vegetable Plate. "Um . . . about the man who broke into Charlene's store," she said. "Could he be someone from Charlene's past? Her ex-husband, maybe?"

When her mother didn't launch into a convoluted story, Olivia glanced up at her face. Ellie's knitted eyebrows indicated thought. Olivia lost track of her feet and zigzagged right into her mother's undulating hip. Ellie didn't miss a step. With gentle pressure, she guided Olivia into position and hesitated a moment as her daughter stumbled back into rhythm.

"I might be thinking of someone else altogether," Ellie said, unruffled by the mishap. "But I do think that Charlene's brief, unfortunate marriage was a while back, at least seven or eight years, because I remember thinking how lucky your father and I were that we'd managed to stay happy despite how young we were when we married. I was only nineteen, and your father was twenty. Of course, we'd already lived together for a year at the commune."

"Too much information, Mom."

"Oops, I feel a spin coming on," Ellie said. Olivia jumped out of the way in time to avoid being whacked as her mother flung her arm out.

"I do love those spins," Ellie said. "Now where was I? Charles Sr. was the key, I think. You will have noticed that both children were named after their father? Arrogance, pure arrogance. Charles Sr. was a plastic surgeon, wildly successful, made piles of money. That's why they moved to DC. They bought a mansion, I heard, joined all the right clubs, put their children in private schools. Those poor young dears."

As the intensity of the music built, Olivia knew she was running out of time, but she decided not to interrupt. Her mother's stories nearly always yielded helpful information and insights. Eventually.

"They became reflections of their parents' worth, you see," Ellie said. "They had to look perfect and excel at everything. I remember hearing that Charles suggested Charlene have plastic surgery when she was still a teenager. And little Charlie, he became quite a problem. I believe he was thrown out of more than one private school."

Olivia decided to keep Charlie on her suspect list for the time being.

Ellie executed a final twirl out and back as the music ended. "Wasn't that fun?" Her cheeks had pinked up, but her breathing seemed normal.

"Mom, I really am sorry I used up your lesson. Allan said Raoul will be leaving soon."

"Don't worry, dear. I haven't broken it to Allan yet — he's feeling a bit overshadowed, you know — but Raoul told me during our dance that he likes Chatterley Heights so much, he has decided to stay indefinitely. Isn't that lovely? Now, about Charlene's marriage," she said. "I don't know the details, but I remember hearing that she married what they call a 'bad boy,' which isn't surprising when you think about it. I believe she was still in high school in DC when they eloped. Charles hired someone to track them down, or so I heard. I don't know exactly what happened then, but I assume the marriage was unhappy, since I remember hearing about an annulment. Poor Jason has never forgiven himself." Ellie flipped her hair over her head and fluffed it with her fingers.

"*Jason?* What does Jason have to do with it?"

"Oh, didn't I say? Jason is the one who introduced Charlene to the boy. After your father died, Jason felt so lost. Oh, I know you missed him, too, but you went off to college, and Jason sort of floated for a couple of years, keeping so much inside. Then I met Allan, and it all got worse. Jason was a senior by then. His grades began to slide, he didn't want to go to college, and he started skipping school to hang around with a group of dropouts. At the moment, I'm afraid I don't remember anything about them, including their names. Jason was secretive during that time. I'm sorry, Livie, I wish I knew more details. Only I suspect that the man Charlene married turned out to have a nasty side."

CHAPTER FIVE

A sudden piercing noise awakened Olivia from a deep sleep. When the sound repeated twice and went to voice mail, she finally recognized the opening bars of "Satisfaction" by the Rolling Stones. Not Olivia's favorite. It crossed her foggy mind that her mother, who danced to that song, might have reprogrammed the cell phone ring tone. But no, messing with ring tones was Maddie's specialty. Olivia decided it wasn't worth opening her eyes.

Before she could drift off again, Olivia heard voices murmuring nearby and felt a weight land on her stomach. The voices turned out to be the television turned on low. The weight on her stomach began to wiggle. She finally opened her eyes when Spunky licked her face.

It had been a long day. Trying to learn the rumba and talk at the same time had taken a surprising amount of energy. Olivia had fallen asleep on her living room sofa, lulled by the cooking channel. While she debated checking her voice mail or going straight to bed, Mick Jagger complained again about the absence of satisfaction in his life. Olivia answered just to make it stop.

"Livie, you have *got* to see this."

Olivia made a guttural sound in her throat.

"I'm serious, Livie, you need to wake up and look out your living room window. I know you're there; the light is on. So drag yourself over to that window and check out what's going on in the town square."

"Why?"

Maddie ignored the irritation in Olivia's voice. "Come *on.* I'm afraid it will disappear any minute. It's . . . it's amazing. Enchanting. Fantastical. Please, go to the window *now.* Oh, and turn the lights off. And bring your cell."

Spunky jumped off Olivia's chest and trotted to the front window, as if Maddie had communicated with him telepathically. By then, Olivia was awake enough for curiosity to overtake crankiness. She slid off the sofa, switched off the light, and joined Spunky at the window.

"Come on, Spunks," Olivia whispered. "Let's see what Aunt Maddie has cooked up for us this time. It had better be worth losing sleep over."

"I heard that." Maddie's voice crackled from the forgotten cell phone in Olivia's hand. "Talk to me."

Olivia pulled aside the edge of the damask curtain covering her front window, while Spunky jumped on top of the small Queen Anne–style desk centered under the windowsill. "Okay, we're looking out on the park," Olivia said into her cell. "What's so amazing? All I see are sleeping stores, moonlight on the rump of Fred P. Chatterley's horse, about half of the band shell in lamplight, and — Oh. . . . What on earth . . . ?" Olivia pressed her nose against the glass. She'd caught a glimpse of shimmery movement near the band shell, but now the park looked deserted.

"Wait for it," Maddie said, her voice hushed with excitement. "There, see it? Right in front of the band shell."

Whimpering softly, Spunky stood on his hind legs. His nails made a clicking sound as he steadied his front paws against the windowpane. Olivia placed her head next to his and looked in the same direction. She saw what looked like a curl of fog, almost ghostlike, an apparition. Which, of course, Olivia didn't believe in. Except maybe in the middle of the night.

"Isn't she amazing?" Maddie said. "It has to be a 'she,' don't you think? It doesn't look like the way a man would dance."

"Dance?" Olivia readjusted her mental context and sure enough, she saw a slender, sylph-like creature twirling in the moonlight. She seemed to be wearing a diaphanous white midlength gown with a flowing white cape that swirled around her shoulders as she pirouetted. A curved arm swooped over the dancer's head as she leaped into the air with a smooth grace Olivia could only dream of possessing. "Are those ballet steps?"

"Livie, my friend, you need to get out more. Of course those are ballet steps, and I'd be willing to bet my new silicone baking mats she has trained professionally. Who on earth could she be? I don't recall Chatterley Heights producing anyone so skilled. She could be a beginning ballerina practicing for her first appearance. Wouldn't that be exciting? I wish I could get a closer look at her. She seems tiny, but I can't tell from this distance. I suppose she could be very young."

Olivia said, "I remember my friend Stacey saying her daughter has been studying ballet at some school in DC. Maybe she sneaked out of the house to practice." Her excitement waning, Olivia yawned. "We need to get back to bed."

Maddie's laugh was loud enough to distract Spunky for a moment. "That isn't Rachel Harald," she said.

"How do you know?"

"Trust me. Rachel is bigger, and besides, I've seen her efforts. I went to her first-year recital last spring, just to relive the dancing days of my youth." Maddie made a clicking sound that Olivia recognized as frustrated curiosity. "I'm going to sneak around behind stores and see if I can get a peek at her. Otherwise, I'll never be able to concentrate again."

"Maddie, it's the middle of the night. Please go home and get some sleep."

"Already slept," Maddie said. "I'll keep the phone on, and you tell me if she moves to another location."

"Maddie, I'm tired. I —"

"Okay, I'm behind the hardware. Bless Lucas for leaving a back light on. Now I'm in back of Fred's." Like most town residents, Maddie shortened the full name of the men's clothing store Frederick's of Chatterley. "Once I get to the other side of the bookstore, I think I'll be close enough to the band shell to see her. Is she still there?"

"Yes, but —"

"I'm past Book Chat. I can see her," Maddie whispered into her cell. "But I can't see her face. It's too dark, and she seems to be avoiding the lamplight. She looks small and very slender, almost like a pre-teen girl. It's funny, though. . . ."

Now Olivia was hooked. "What?"

"Her hair," Maddie said. "It's long, nearly to her waist. And it looks pure white."

"Maybe that's why I thought she was wearing a cape," Olivia said. "So she must be quite a bit older than we thought."

"If only if I could see her face," Maddie said. "She's wearing something over her head, sort of a sack thing. She must be able to see through it, so it might be the same filmy fabric as her dress. Maybe it's a costume." Maddie sighed into her cell. "I'm losing her; she's dancing into the shadows, away from the band shell. I guess I'll have to try again another night. Anyway, I'm heading back to the store now, so you can run along to bed. And take that furry creature with you."

Olivia gathered Spunky under one arm. "Okay, see you tomorrow. You can open, as penance for waking me up." In the middle of a yawn, her brain registered Maddie's words. "Wait, why are you coming back here? I refuse to stay up the rest of the night speculating with you about the identity of the mysterious ballerina in white."

"Not to worry," Maddie said, sounding far too alert. "I've got some baking to do, but I will be silence itself. And I can open the store, no problem."

"What baking?"

"Oh, you know, a bit of this and that to fill out the display."

"What display?"

"I thought you were exhausted."

"What display, Maddie?"

"For our spontaneous morning event, the one we talked about."

"We never talked about a spontaneous morning event. I'd remember. I'm not *that* sleepy."

"Didn't we? I guess I thought about it so much, I was sure I'd mentioned it. No problem, I've got the whole thing under control. You don't have to do a thing, just sleep in a bit and show up whenever."

Olivia was about to press the point, but she asked herself, did she really want to know? Spunky had gone limp against her chest, and she'd had enough excitement for one night. Maddie's ideas could be on the wild side, but she was, for the most part, a sensible businesswoman. Maddie had learned a lot in the year or so they'd operated The Gingerbread House together, and she'd been wanting to plan an event entirely on her own. Besides, if you couldn't trust your best friend and business partner, who could you trust?

CHAPTER SIX

Olivia placed a tray of iced vegetables — the decorated sugar cookie kind — on a display table in the cookbook nook. The nook was once a formal dining room for the succession of families who had owned the Queen Anne home before it became The Gingerbread House. In the dignified room, with its crystal chandelier and built-in walnut hutch with leaded glass doors, Maddie's whimsical creations made quite a statement . . . like flashing neon lights in a medieval cathedral.

Olivia felt anxiety creep up her spine. The same worry had awakened her early that morning and sent her downstairs to the store well before opening. When she had seen Maddie cutting and baking cookies in vegetable shapes the previous day, Olivia was puzzled but not concerned. Even when Maddie returned to The Gingerbread House in the wee hours because she "had some baking to do," and then insisted to Olivia that the two of them had agreed to host a "spontaneous morning event" — which Olivia was certain they'd never discussed — even then, she'd taken Maddie at her word. However, Olivia bolted awake before her alarm, one phrase of Maddie's ringing in her head: "I've got the whole thing under control." What "whole thing," and why might it go out of control in the first place?

Olivia pondered the plate of cookies in front of her, with their wildly colored designs, and she knew the answers to her questions. Maddie was angry with Charlene Critch and convinced she had littered their store's lawn with anti-sugar propaganda. All the cookies Maddie had prepared for their morning event represented fruits and vegetables. Charlene worshipped fruits and vegetables, and she despised sugar. However, decorated cookies are made with sugar. Lots of it. Charlene was sure to hear about the event and unlikely to be amused by the irony.

An electric blue cookie shaped like an eggplant and decorated with a hot pink smiley face grinned at Olivia from the top of a pyramid. She plucked it off. After glancing around to be sure Maddie wasn't watching, Olivia exchanged it for a cookie from the middle of the stack, a sedate apple shape, mint green with a baby yellow stem. The eggplant's bright skin peeked out, but at least she'd hidden that gruesome face.

Olivia started at a clumping sound behind her and turned to see Maddie in full costume. Her laced-up leather boots explained her noisy entrance into the room. Maddie had decided on a farmer theme for her event persona. It was Tuesday, not a day the store's customers normally expected themed cookie events, but Maddie had given her imagination full rein. She wore red denim cutoffs that skimmed her curvy hips. The bottoms frayed up a good two inches to reveal flashes of thigh. Maddie had wrestled her curly red hair into puffy pigtails and plunked a straw hat on top. A tight white T-shirt and red suspenders completed the ensemble.

"Wow, those look great in here," Maddie said, nodding with satisfaction at the plate of vegetable-shaped cookies.

"Nice shorts," Olivia said, hoping to distract Maddie from the disappearance of the evil smirking eggplant. "Sure you'll be cool enough?"

Maddie arched an eyebrow at her. "I see you are wearing one of your several pairs of gray slacks. Sure you'll be warm enough?"

"You sound crabby."

"*You* moved my cookie, didn't you?" Maddie slid the eggplant from its hiding place and switched it with the apple cookie. Using both hands, she nestled the grinning vegetable back on top of the cookie pyramid. "I love this cookie. I think it's one of my best efforts." She pulled her cell phone from her back pocket and took three pictures of the display. "This goes on our website," she said.

"Over my dead —"

"Yoo-hoo, girls. I'm here." It was the breathy voice of their part-time clerk, Bertha Binkman.

Maddie said, "Sorry, Livie, I forgot to tell you I called Bertha in for an extra day. I think we'll need the help. We're in the nook, Bertha."

Bertha appeared, out of breath. Olivia was glad Bertha wasn't wheezing nearly so much these days, since she had lost at least twenty pounds. She was still well-rounded, but her health had improved considerably. Bertha had been at loose ends when her longtime employer and dear friend, Clarisse Chamberlain, had died the previous spring. Too bereft to remain in the Chamberlain home, where she'd been given a home for life in Clarisse's will, Bertha had used part of her inheritance to buy a small house in Chatterley Heights.

"Did you girls know there's a small crowd gathering outside? Oh my, Maddie, don't you look cute." Bertha caught sight of the cookie arrangement. "Are those especially for the event? When Maddie called, she mentioned we'd be celebrating foods. My, my, aren't they . . ." She caught sight of the blue confection on top. "Interesting."

"It's eight forty," Maddie said, checking her cell. "Come on, Bertha. We still have work to do." She headed for the main sales area, with Bertha following, her white eyebrows puckered in confusion.

Olivia stayed behind in the cookbook nook. As soon as she was alone, she snatched the cursed eggplant cookie, opened her mouth to its widest circumference, and aimed. With her first bite, she took out a third of the blue flesh plus most of the gruesome grinning mouth.

Olivia's mother poked her head into the nook. "Hello, dear," Ellie said. "Just thought I'd drop by." She wore loose, silky blue pants and a long matching blouse tied at her waist with a midnight blue sash. With her long hair swinging in rhythm, she flowed into the cookbook nook like a gentle ocean wave. "You have a bit of blue icing on your lip," she said.

"Mother, what on earth are you doing here?" Olivia asked as she wiped the telltale icing away from her mouth. "Don't you have a class in mountain climbing or hang gliding or something?"

"Don't be silly," Ellie said. "I gave up such dangerous activities when I turned sixty. I am, however, considering a class in hip-hop dancing. It looks like such fun, and I think it would be excellent exercise."

"Are you really my mother?"

Ellie smiled benignly at her daughter, who towered over her by eight inches. "One wonders at times." She took a long look at the plate of cookies, now missing its eggplant. "I was afraid of this," she said.

"How did you — ?"

"Allan and I stopped for breakfast at the café this morning. We ran into Bertha and that sweet beau of hers, Mr. Willard. Though why everyone doesn't simply call him Willard, I can't grasp. He is quite approachable."

"Mom, I really have to —"

"No, you don't. Not yet," Ellie said. "Trust me. When Allan and I ran into Bertha, she mentioned that Maddie had called her to The Gingerbread House to help with an event. Bertha said Maddie had

108

described the event as 'unique and challenging.' Imagining those words coming from Maddie's mouth gave me a flicker of apprehension. I left half a serving of eggs Benedict on my plate to come rushing over here."

Olivia herself felt a shiver of foreboding. Her mother might seem vague at times, even to her family, but Ellie possessed an impressive ability to read people and situations. With trepidation, Olivia asked, "Do you suspect Maddie dreamed up this event with someone in mind? A certain someone who worships vegetables? Because I sure do, and I've been in the store since five o'clock this morning, trying desperately to think of a way to prevent a disaster. I've had one idea that might deflect some attention away from Charlene, but . . ." Olivia slid a candy-striped banana from the cookie pyramid and began to nibble. "I can't understand it. Maddie has been acting like a completely different person lately."

Olivia's peripheral vision caught Bertha walking past the nook entrance, followed by Sam Parnell, their postal carrier. Since the store wasn't yet open, Bertha must have offered him a cookie. *Good. The faster the cookies disappear, the earlier the event will be over,* Olivia thought.

"We'll examine Maddie's psyche later," Ellie said. "Right now we'd better concentrate on damage control. This is Chatterley Heights. Charlene is bound to hear that her beliefs are being mocked. It's no use hiding in here with your cookbooks, munching away at the evidence. Although . . ." She reached for an ear of fuchsia corn covered in yellow sugar sprinkles. "This looks diseased. I'd better do away with it."

"I saw Maddie making these cookies yesterday," Olivia said. "I should have known better. If she weren't my lifelong friend . . ."

"Yes, and lovable despite her sometimes misguided impulses."

"I know, I know," Olivia said. "I don't believe she really means any harm."

"Maddie gets an idea and runs with it," Ellie said. "Like the gingerbread man. And rather like that younger brother of yours." She held a thoughtful index finger to her chin. Olivia noticed the nail was painted the same deep blue as the sash around her waist. "Perhaps we should revisit the question of Maddie's psyche. You mentioned she hasn't been herself lately. Do you think something is bothering her? I only ask because Jason tends to wind up like a top when anything goes awry in his world."

"Now that you mention it, I have noticed it's been a while since I heard the words 'Lucas and I' burst giddily from Maddie's lips. When I've asked about their plans, she sounds distant. Maybe they've had a fight."

"I wouldn't be surprised if that's the problem." Ellie polished off her corn cookie and brushed the crumbs from her fingers. "I believe I will give up my yoga class for once. I like Maddie, and I like Charlene, despite her unsettling sensitivities. I think I might be able to help calm the atmosphere."

"Mother, you are the best."

"Yes, dear. Now, tell me your plan to deflect your customers' attention from Maddie's exuberant creations."

"Okay, first the simple part. I'll announce early and often that the fruits and vegetables represent a harvest theme. I mean, it is August, so that should sound perfectly reasonable. However, I'm not taking any chances. I've also devised one of our special contests. Come over here, I'll show you." Olivia led her mother into the main part of the store. The bright summer sun shone through numerous leaded-glass window-panes, imposing geometric shapes of shadow and light on the tables loaded with cookie cutter displays, baking gadgets, and plates piled with decorated cookies. Strings of cookie cutters festooned the circumference of the room, looping down from thin wire originally meant for hanging pictures. More cookie cutters, clustered into mobiles, tinkled in the light breeze from the new air conditioner.

The mobiles dipped low enough for customers to touch. Olivia stopped at one of them, a collection of bird shapes. Maddie and Bertha both scurried back and forth from the kitchen, preparing for the event, so Olivia lowered her voice. "We've had themed mobiles in the store since we opened," she said, "but these are different. I created some new themes, and I added one special cookie cutter to each mobile." She cupped her hand under a cutter in the middle of the mobile. "Like this one. What do you think makes this different from the others?"

"Aren't you always reminding me to pick up the pace?"

"Work with me, Mom. I need to know if this game will be intriguing and distracting or merely impossible and irritating."

Ellie touched the cookie cutter, which at her diminutive height required her to lift up on tiptoe. "It's unusual," she said. "An antique, isn't it?" When Olivia nodded, Ellie added, "It is made of tin, I believe, and in lovely condition." She stepped back and inspected the entire mobile. "Well, it must be the only vintage cutter in the grouping, right? Is that the point of the contest?"

"Give me some credit, Mom. Yes, it's the only vintage cutter, but there's one more step. Tell me what the shape is."

Ellie frowned up at the vintage cookie cutter. "It looks familiar, but I can't put a name to the shape. I can name all the others, though. Chicken, cardinal, dove, turkey, and so on, but this one looks like a generic bird."

"In the interests of time," Olivia said, "I'll give you a hint. Far back in the last millennium, when you were a youngster, there was an organization to which you belonged. I remember you telling me that you joined at the tender age of —"

"Six." Ellie clapped her hands and bounced on her toes, as if she had reverted back to that age. "I know the answer now. That sweet cookie cutter is a bluebird, the symbol for little girls who were in training to become Camp Fire Girls. We were called the Blue Birds. Although I don't believe that's the name anymore, especially now that boys are allowed to join, which is only fair, of course, but it does change —"

"Do you think this might work?"

113

"What, dear?"

Olivia suppressed a sigh. "Okay, nutshell plan. I announce a contest to customers. They must identify the only vintage cookie cutter in each mobile and correctly name its shape. The customer who gets the most right wins one of the cutters, whichever he or she chooses."

Ellie ran her finger along the hemmed edge of the bluebird cutter. "This is such a wonderful cookie cutter, so lovingly preserved. I assume it came from Clarisse's collection? Are you sure you'd want to give it away? Now Livie, before you interrupt, yes, I'm certain this contest will be intriguing enough to keep many customers from wondering about the reason for so many oddly decorated vegetable cookies."

"Thanks, Mom. And you're right, all the vintage cutters come from Clarisse's collection. I do hate to give up any of them, but I know Clarisse would understand. She loved this town. It would have broken her heart to see Maddie and me feuding with a fellow businesswoman."

Ellie squeezed Olivia's crossed arms. "You do realize that Charlene will still hear about this event." As Ellie shook her head, a long spiral of hair slid over her shoulder. "Poor Charlene. She was always sensitive. Perhaps even oversensitive, though I dislike that term. It's so judgmental, as if anyone could say how much sensitivity is too much."

Olivia stared out the window at the view of the town square. It looked so peaceful. She remembered summer days when she would hide from the sun in the band shell, with its stone benches and small dance floor. She'd lived in Baltimore, but she had to return home before she understood that life in a small town wasn't any simpler than it was in the city. Anger, jealousy, and resentment all flared as frequently in Chatterley Heights as they had in Baltimore. If anything, Olivia was finding it harder to escape here in her little hometown.

"Sweetie, don't hunch up your shoulders like that," Ellie said. "It isn't good for your posture. I honestly think this is a brilliant contest idea. It will surely put everyone in a good mood and moderate the upsetting effect of Charlene's reaction, which is likely to be dramatic." She straightened her jacket and tightened the sash. "I see that I have my work cut out for me." Her face lit with delight as she added, "I believe I made a pun — cookie cutters, my work cut out for . . ."

"I get it, Mom." Olivia's tone softened with hope. "Does this really mean you'll stay to help me, um, handle the Charlene/ Maddie situation?"

"Of course, Livie. It's what I do best."

Two hours into Maddie's surprise event, The Gingerbread House held more customers than Olivia had ever seen on a Tuesday morning. Charlene Critch had not shown up, and Olivia had heard no mention of her from any customers. However, Olivia reminded herself, there were still plenty of hours left before closing time. Charlene could walk through the front door at any moment.

Olivia felt a tug on the back of her hair and heard her brother's voice say, "Hey, Olive Oyl, great shindig." Jason hoisted his tall, thin self onto a display ledge that jutted out from the wall. He narrowly missed a porcelain bowl brimming with handmade copper cookie cutters. Olivia grabbed the bowl and moved it to a high shelf.

"You break it, you buy it," she said in her elder sister voice.

"Uh huh. Hey, Charlie, over here!" Jason yelled, waving his arm. "Charlie's here," he said.

"I gathered that."

"This is my day off from the garage," Jason said. "Charlie's been working since six thirty, so he gets an early lunch. We heard about Maddie's cool cookies, and we thought, hey, why not. Boy, are we hungry."

"So . . . you two are meeting here for a cookie before lunch?"

"Guess again," Jason said. "I mean, think about it, Sis. These aren't just cookies; they are *fruit* and *vegetable* cookies, something we hardworking guys need lots and lots of, right?"

Olivia glanced around at the dwindling supply of cookies and the many hands reaching for more. Maybe they really might run out of cookies early, before Charlene had a chance to show up.

"By the way, great contest idea," Jason said. "I already picked out the cookie cutter I want when I win."

Olivia arched her eyebrows at him. "You? A cookie cutter?"

Jason lowered his voice and leaned toward her ear. "Not just any cookie cutter, Liv. It's probably the closest I'll get to a Duesenberg. I don't expect you to know what —"

"Of course I know what a Dues—" More quietly, Olivia said, "I know what it is. Clarisse had it specially made for her husband, Martin, because he was restoring a 1930 Due— car he'd gotten cheaply. He loved that car."

"Cool," Jason said. "Which model? Never mind. See, I want that cutter thing to hang in the 1957 Ford Fairlane I've been working on. I found it rusting in a farmer's field and told Struts. She made an offer on it; got it for practically nothing. But the best part is, she said if I find the parts and restore it on my own time, she'll let me have it. Hey, here comes lunch." Jason pointed toward the kitchen door, through which Maddie emerged, chewing on a piece of hay and carrying a large plate stacked high with decorated fruit and vegetable cookies. Charlie Critch stood nearby. He smiled at Maddie and said something. Maddie handed him the tray and waved her hand as if to say, "Put it anywhere." When she disappeared back into the kitchen, Charlie flashed a broad grin across the room at Jason and lifted the cookie-laden plate above his head. Jason waved and slid off his perch. "Gotta get a picture of this," he said, holding his cell phone above customers' heads. "Later, Liv. Can't wait till you hand over my prize."

"What makes you think you'll win the contest?"

Jason winked at her. "Maddie gave me a few little hints."

Olivia decided that she and Maddie were

due for another talk. Not that it would do any good. Maddie was Maddie, impulsive in her generosity, impulsive in . . . just about everything. Olivia began to wonder if moving back to Baltimore to work with Ryan wasn't such a bad idea after all. However, her mood brightened as she watched her brother and Charlie Critch laugh together and stuff decorated cookies into their mouths. They both cared about Charlene. If it hadn't occurred to either of them that Maddie's cookies might be interpreted as a slap at Charlene, maybe no one would make the connection.

An eruption of laughter distracted Olivia from visions of Charlene on the warpath. A group of women had clustered near a large mobile, which hung in front of the picture window looking out on the Chatterley Heights town square. Maddie had designed the mobile using a baby theme, and Olivia had added a copper cookie cutter shaped like an infant's rattle. Clarisse had bought the cutter to celebrate the birth of her elder son. Heather Irwin, the young librarian at the Chatterley Heights Library, was touching the copper rattle as she spoke to her good friend, Gwen Tucker. Heather, normally shy, looked happy. Olivia had heard she had a new boyfriend, which might explain the color in her cheeks.

Gwen Tucker, along with her husband, Herbie, ran the Chatterley Paws no-kill animal shelter. At the moment, Gwen was pregnant, and she looked it. Fine-boned and about five feet tall, she was lugging eight months of healthy baby. Which reminded Olivia that she and Maddie had promised eight dozen decorated cookies for the baby shower Heather was organizing for Gwen on Wednesday evening. Maddie would have to pull off one of her frenzied baking miracles.

Olivia started at a light touch on the back of her shoulder, and a deep male voice said, "Livie? Could I talk to you for a minute?" She spun around and looked up several inches to Lucas Ashford's handsome and worried face. "I didn't mean to startle you," Lucas said. "I just . . . I know this is a really bad time, but . . ." He ran strong fingers through his dark hair and heaved a sigh that should have sounded manly, but the poor guy looked more like a tot who'd lost his puppy.

Over Lucas's shoulder, Olivia saw Maddie push backward through the kitchen door, holding a large tray of cookies. She turned around and handed the tray off to Bertha. Maddie glanced around the crowded store with a pleased expression until her gaze landed on the back of Lucas's head. Her smile melted into sadness, or so it seemed to Olivia. As Maddie spun around and vanished into the kitchen, Olivia said, "Yes, Lucas, let's talk. Now is fine. Let's see if we can find a spot in the cookbook nook."

The relief on Lucas's face was palpable. He followed Olivia closely through the sales floor, around groups of customers who seemed more interested in eating cookies and trading guesses about cookie cutter shapes than in purchasing anything. In forlorn silence, he stood at Olivia's elbow as customers stopped her and tried to wheedle hints about which cutter was the special one or whether they'd guessed the shape correctly.

Olivia had hung all her mobiles in the main sales area, so the cookbook nook was relatively quiet. The stack of cookies she had deposited in the nook before the store opened was now reduced to a few colorful crumbs. She led Lucas over to the two leather easy chairs arranged in a corner.

"It's . . . it's about Maddie," Lucas said. He sighed, then sighed again.

Olivia nodded her encouragement. Lucas wasn't much of a talker, and Maddie tended to interpret for him. Olivia wanted to give him the chance to say, in his own words, what was going on between the two of them. She might not be able to fix the situation, but at least she would know what it was.

Lucas bent his long torso forward and leaned on his forearms. Staring down at his intertwined fingers, he said, "Maddie is a real special woman. She's beautiful, she's smart and funny and . . ."

Uh-oh, he's breaking up with her. Olivia wished she had a cookie to cram into her mouth; she wanted so much to intervene.

"I don't know, maybe I'm not interesting enough. I don't talk a lot. Maybe she's tired of me being quiet, but I think I'm a pretty good listener, and . . . and I love her with all my heart."

And she adores you. What's the problem? "Lucas, could you fill me in a bit? Have you two had a fight or . . . ?"

Lucas's startled eyes lifted to Olivia's face. Despite his chiseled features, his confusion gave him a boyish look. "Oh, I . . . I guess I assumed Maddie had confided in you. Sunday evening I asked her to marry me. She said no, and she won't talk about it."

By eleven forty-five, Olivia allowed herself to be hopeful that the store event would finish without incident. She was less hopeful about her ability to rescue Maddie and Lucas's romance. Friendly, exuberant Maddie could close up like Chatterley Heights on a Sunday evening. When she did, it was serious. Olivia had lived in Baltimore for twelve years, through college and her marriage. She and Maddie had chatted often by phone, emailed, visited now and then. To be honest, though, living in separate locations had allowed each of them to limit how much to share with the other. Olivia had to admit she'd been tight-lipped about the problems she and Ryan were having, at least until she'd made the decision to leave her marriage. Had Maddie hidden a painful experience or two, as well?

Olivia had scheduled the announcement of the cookie cutter contest winner for twelve forty-five, so customers who couldn't get away from work until their lunch hours would have at least some chance to participate. With luck, the crowd would clear out by one o'clock or shortly thereafter. Charlene must have heard about Maddie's vegetable and fruit cookies by now and thought nothing of it.

Bertha waved to Olivia from behind the counter, where a line of customers waited to make purchases. Finally. Olivia had begun to wonder if her contest idea was so successful it had distracted folks from their new collection of hand-embroidered tea towels and their recently acquired vintage Wilton cookie cutter sets. Maddie had brought out the last of the cookies and was working the sales floor, so Olivia waved back to Bertha and headed toward the sales counter to help at the cash register. By the time she got there, the line had expanded to ten customers.

Fifteen minutes later, Olivia and Bertha had reduced the line to two customers. Olivia had a chance to survey the sales floor, which had grown denser with the arrival of the lunch crowd. The front door opened to admit a young couple she'd never seen before and, right behind them, Sam Parnell. She remembered he'd delivered their mail at about nine a.m., as usual. He was dressed in full uniform, complete with the hat that rarely left his head, but he wasn't carrying his mailbag. Olivia assumed he'd decided to stop by on his lunch hour. Since the very first day The Gingerbread House opened its doors, Olivia could not remember Sam ever giving up his precious lunch hour to drop by. This could mean only one thing: Sam thought there was juicy gossip to be had, or perhaps helped along. Sam's nickname — Snoopy — was well earned. Olivia's hope for a confrontation-free event began to fade.

Olivia's peace of mind took another hit when the front door again opened and in walked Binnie Sloan, the barrel-shaped editor of the *Weekly Chatter,* followed by her skinny young niece, Nedra. As Olivia knew from personal experience, the *Weekly Chatter* was not known for its adherence to journalistic standards.

Maybe, Olivia told herself, Binnie and Ned had come to cover the cookie cutter contest. Right. And Sam was there only to snag a cookie or three, despite his diabetes. Olivia noticed he did seem to be examining a half-full tray of decorated cookies with great interest. Finally, he selected one and took a bite. Binnie came up behind him, grabbed two cookies, and bit through both at the same time, as if they were a ham sandwich. Ned took a photo of the tray but did not indulge.

Another flurry of customers distracted Olivia for a time. When she was once again free to glance around, she saw Sam Parnell and Binnie Sloan in conversation, apparently about a sheet of paper that each of them held. Olivia told herself that they were simply comparing notes about the contest, but she didn't find herself convincing. Her apprehension spiked higher. Turning to

Bertha, she asked, "Will you be all right handling the register for a while? I'd like to check with Maddie to see how close we are to announcing a contest winner."

"The pace seems to be settling down," Bertha said. "You go right on ahead now."

Olivia spotted Maddie standing in the opening to the cookbook nook, where she could see and be seen. In the crook of her right arm, she held a mixing bowl into which folks were depositing half-sized sheets of peach-colored paper. Maddie's attention, however, was focused on the full-sized sheet of white paper in her left hand. As Olivia approached, she noticed red splotches on Maddie's pale, freckled cheeks.

"Something tells me," Olivia said when she reached Maddie, "that you aren't reading the contest results."

Without comment, Maddie handed the sheet of paper to Olivia, who recognized it at once as a copy of Charlene Critch's anti-sugar manifesto that she and Maddie had spent Sunday afternoon cleaning off The Gingerbread House lawn.

"So Charlene printed more of these things?"

"Take another look," Maddie said. "Then check out those folks who are just arriving."

Obeying the last order first, Olivia watched

as three women — customers who made regular trips from Clarksville in search of vintage cookie cutters — closed the store door behind them. Instead of plunging eagerly toward the ever-changing cookie cutter display as they usually did, the women paused to skim the papers they held. Their expressions appeared to range from bemused to concerned.

With chilled anticipation, Olivia turned her attention to the latest edition of Charlene's diatribe against the demon sugar. The opening warning that "Sugar Kills" hadn't changed, though Charlene had added an additional exclamation point. It was followed, as before, with a list of pseudo facts about how sugar accomplishes its dastardly effects. In this version, the claims were even more outrageous and, Olivia realized, more personal:

- WARNING: Don't be fooled by a little lime zest. Cookies shaped like fruits and vegetables are still just clumps of sugar, and sugar is a weapon of human destruction.
- Sugar causes obesity, heart disease, diabetes, cancer, and dementia. If you are eating an iced cookie while reading this, you have shortened your life by

several months.

- If you are pregnant and consuming sugar at this moment, you are condemning your baby to a life of illness and early death.
- No amount of exercise can undo the damage those cookies are doing to your bodies right this minute.
- Ask yourselves this question: What kind of person provides daily megadoses of sweet poison to an entire town?

If you are worried about your health and your loved ones, come to The Vegetable Plate this evening at seven o'clock. We will plan how to take back our lives from the destructive effects of sugar in our own town.

"Wow," Olivia said. "It seems we are a public menace. I'm wondering if we should call the police and have ourselves arrested."

Maddie glowered. "I don't find it amusing. Charlene is trying to destroy our business. I think we should sue her. I mean, this is illegal, right? You still have Mr. Willard on retainer, don't you? So call him and ask if this is legal or not."

"I don't really see the need to keep an attorney on retainer, though I could certainly talk to him if it would make you feel better. But Maddie, nobody could possibly take this stuff seriously. It's completely over-the-top. I'm more concerned about Charlene's state of mind. She seems . . ."

"Insane? Bonkers? Several cookies short of a mass poisoning?"

Olivia heard a gentle laugh as her mother joined them, also holding the offending paper. "Maddie, dear," Ellie said, "I must agree with Livie, and not only because she is my daughter. On numerous occasions, I have not agreed with her in the least, such as —"

"Mom, could we focus on the part where you think I'm right?"

"Certainly, Livie." With a motherly squeeze to Maddie's shoulders, Ellie said, "I do understand your feelings, Maddie. Those outlandish claims are more than lies; they are a profound insult, not only to your integrity but also to the intelligence of your customers. No, I don't believe Charlene is clinically insane. I do sense that something is deeply amiss in her life, though, and this is her way of . . . I don't know, assuming control?"

"Are you taking a class in Jungian analysis, Mom?"

Ellie patted her daughter's arm. "No, dear, it wouldn't provide nearly enough exercise for me. All I'm suggesting is that we turn our attention to Charlene's current situation. For instance, who tore apart her store, and why hasn't this person picked on other stores in Chatterley Heights? I have to wonder if Charlene is being tortured by a personal enemy, and maybe she feels alone. Perhaps we should talk to her, try to —"

"Uh oh," Olivia said.

"Now hear me out," Ellie said.

"No, I mean 'uh oh,' as in, look who is coming through the front door."

Olivia noticed that the decibel level of customer chatter dropped a notch and several hands pulled back from the cookie trays as Charlene Critch closed the front door behind her. She was dressed to perfection in a figureskimming, pink-and-white striped sundress. The stripes were vertical, of course, to emphasize Charlene's slight figure. Her blond hair was gathered into a ponytail, with tendrils framing her face. From a distance, she could pass for a teenager.

Olivia accepted the inevitable: if there was to be a confrontation, she should be the one to handle it. For the long, complex process of creating decorated cookies, Maddie had infinite patience. For people, not so much. Forming her lips into a smile, Olivia wove through her customers and around display tables toward the front of the store.

Charlene watched Olivia's approach with a cold stare. She didn't speak until they were face-to-face. "How *could* you?" she said, loud enough to be heard by everyone in the store.

"How could *I*? All I did was —"

"Do you think I'm so dense I wouldn't understand what you and Maddie are trying to do? I knew *she* was mean enough to try a stunt like this, but I can't believe you played along. I ought to sue both of you."

"Sue *us*? Look, all we did was host a celebration of the harvest. I really don't think that is grounds for a lawsuit. If anything, you're the one that —"

"This is just so . . ." Charlene's brown eyes began to glisten with tears. "So *mean*. You were only pretending to be kind to me after my store got broken into. And now you're trying to destroy my business." Her thin chest heaved as she tried to catch her breath.

"Charlene, let's talk somewhere else."

"Don't even bother to deny it. The evidence it right there." Charlene pointed toward a nearby table, where a tray held three uneaten cookies: a magenta apple with a grinning pink worm, a cornflower blue carrot, and something that looked like a turnip with the icing licked off. "You and Maddie are trying to trick everybody into believing that healthy eating doesn't matter, so they won't come to my Healthy Eating Club, or maybe even my store. You're trying to ruin me, and . . . and you're willing to poison everyone in Chatterley Heights to do it." Tears spilled down her cheeks, dragging her mascara and foundation with them.

In a flash, Olivia reached two understandings. First, Charlene probably believed everything she had written in her announcement. And second, her thickly applied makeup was an attempt to hide a black eye.

Charlene sniffled and swiped the tears off her cheeks. She seemed unaware that the bruised skin around her left eye had begun to show. "Anyway," she said, "I didn't come to talk to you. I need to talk to your brother."

"Charlie? I think I saw him over by the coffee table, near the window facing the square." Olivia waved her hand in the general direction of the window. "But Charlene, are you sure you're all right? I couldn't help but notice —"

"You're the one who's out of it," Charlene

said. "I think all that sugar has eaten holes in your brain. Charlie is my brother, not yours. I'm here to talk to Jason. *Your* brother."

That superior edge had slipped back into Charlene's voice. For a split second, Olivia wanted to slap her; then she remembered that someone already had. Olivia looked around for her mother. Wasn't this where she was supposed to take over and calm the atmosphere? "I wasn't aware you and Jason were friends," Olivia said and instantly wished she'd stuffed a cookie in her own mouth. Charlene and Jason had been friends in high school.

"This is a small town," Charlene said. "As you know, your *younger* brother is in my age group. Why wouldn't we be friends?"

"Jason was in the cookbook nook a little while ago." Olivia's tone was curt, but she was beyond caring. "He was eating cookies. Lots of cookies." *So much for "handling" the situation with patience.*

Charlene's perfect little chin lifted a notch. "Then I'd better find him fast. I've wasted too much time waiting for your sugar-soaked brain to focus. I need to save Jason from the same fate."

"It's time to announce the contest winner,"

Maddie said as she handed Olivia a Gingerbread House recipe card with one name on it.

Olivia glanced at the name and whispered, "Jason was convinced he would win. Looks like you didn't give him enough hints."

"Give me some credit, Livie. I'm not a complete pushover. I gave him a couple hints, like the Duesenberg, but it turns out he isn't the only old car fanatic in the crowd. Also, Jason isn't a baker, so he hasn't developed the knack of identifying shapes. He thought the baby rattle was a barbell. It seems he didn't process the whole baby context of the mobile."

"He really wanted that Duesenberg cutter," Olivia said. Maybe she would give it to him — if he didn't irritate her too much beforehand.

"Believe me, everyone knows how much Jason wants that cutter," Maddie said. "I'd feel bad for him except he's been whispering with Charlene in the nook. They seem pretty cozy. Just thought I'd warn you. Now let's get cracking, the troops are assembling."

Olivia and Maddie headed toward the picture window looking out on the town square. Customers watched in hushed silence, as if Olivia were about to announce the next governor of Maryland. *Gotta love those cookie cutter fans.*

"Thank you all for finding time on a Tuesday morning to join us for this impromptu celebration of the harvest and the eventual return of cool, crisp weather." Olivia searched faces for Charlene but didn't see her. She didn't see Jason, either, which seemed odd given his longing to win the Duesenberg cutter. "I know many of you need to get back to work, so I'll get right to the important part. Our cookie cutter contest winner today is . . . Gwen Tucker!"

As expected, Gwen selected the baby rattle for her free vintage cookie cutter. After congratulations, the majority of customers vacated the store, having feasted on a lunch of decorated cookies. For a fleeting moment, Olivia wondered if Charlene might have a point about The Gingerbread House being a den of wicked overindulgence. However, Charlene emerged alone from the cookbook nook and flung her a look of disdain, which erased Olivia's guilt. Instead of leaving the store, Charlene joined her brother Charlie at the beverage cart by the front door. She appeared to be fixing herself a cup of tea.

Ellie appeared beside Olivia. "Overall, that went quite well, don't you think?"

"Easy for you to say. You didn't have to deal with Charlene. Where were you, anyway?"

"Right behind you," Ellie said. "I could see you were doing fine, so I busied myself elsewhere."

"I wasn't doing fine at all. I got flustered and sounded like a nasty idiot."

"Yes, dear, and it was a very effective strategy. Charlene is so sadly insecure. You gave her the opportunity to feel superior, which soothed her righteous anger. I've used that approach myself on numerous occasions. You must have picked it up from me." Ellie glanced up at the Hansel and Gretel clock, so stunning and yet so difficult to read. Since it had been Ellie's gift, in celebration of The Gingerbread House's opening, no one minded its imperfections. Ellie said, "I have a voice lesson in either thirty or forty-five minutes, so we have just enough time."

"Time for what?" Olivia asked.

"For me to tell you what I have learned."

Spunky whimpered in ecstasy and ran circles around their ankles when Olivia and Ellie entered the upstairs apartment, leaving Maddie and Bertha to cover the store. On normal days he held court in the store, enjoying numerous ear scratches and the occasional treat from customers. On event days, however, he had to stay in the apartment. Crowds seemed to trigger memories of his puppy-mill days, which led to escape attempts.

Leaving her mother in the living room with the small Yorkie on her lap, Olivia brewed a pot of coffee and sliced some carrots and celery. Okay, maybe Charlene was getting to her. At the last minute, Olivia added some cheese crackers to the serving tray. And a couple dog treats, to make up for the ones Spunky missed because he'd been trapped upstairs all morning. Back in the living room, Spunky settled at Olivia's feet to crunch.

"Okay, talk," Olivia said. "What have you got on Charlene?"

"That sounds so harsh, dear. I've gleaned a bit of background, that's all. But first, I have a few things to share about Maddie and also about your brother."

"Old news, Mom. Maddie won't speak to Lucas because he asked her to marry him — don't ask me to explain it — and Jason is an idiot because he is besotted with Charlene."

Ellie nibbled on a carrot stick and smiled in that calm and knowing way that always made Olivia want to crush something. "Okay, Mom, out with it." Spunky's ears perked up at Olivia's tone.

"I am impressed," Ellie said as she selected a piece of celery. "Soon you won't need me to dig up information for you. However, that time has not come yet. As for Maddie's reaction to Lucas's proposal, I have a starting place for you. Maddie was about ten, as I remember, when her parents died in a car crash. I know that they were living in Clarksville at the time, and I occasionally saw her mother when my watercolor group wandered in her direction to find a picturesque scene to paint. Adele had been a part of our group before she married and moved away from Chatterley Heights. She always joined us when we gathered close to Clarksville, which we did at least once a month. Adele used to paint in the loveliest shades of pink and red to create a vibrant aura."

Olivia grabbed a handful of carrot sticks and bit off several tips at once.

"Livie, I promise I'm going somewhere with this. You see, Adele was a lot like Maddie — enthusiastic, full of energy and ideas. But a few months before the accident, she began to change. She grew quieter and much thinner and — this is significant, I think — she started painting with blues and purples."

Olivia dropped the carrots on her plate. "You think she was depressed? Or drinking, maybe?"

"I saw no evidence of drinking, but who knows? Mostly, she seemed terribly sad. I tried to question her about it the last time I ever saw her. She was vague, but she did say something about her husband having some problems. Apparently, she never shared her situation with anyone else from my circle, so I can only guess at what was going on. I did wonder if her husband was having an affair. Has Maddie ever talked about that time with you?"

Olivia shook her head. "All she's ever said is that her memory is a blur for the period surrounding the accident. Maddie doesn't like to dwell on anything that makes her feel sad. She's fine with anger, as you know. But even when her high school sweetheart Bobby suddenly broke off their engagement, she reacted more with panic. We agreed that Bobby had acted like a jerk, and Maddie recovered in record time." Olivia divided the remaining coffee between their cups and added milk and sugar to hers. She picked up a half-eaten carrot from her plate and wrinkled her nose. "I could use a cookie."

"Me, too," Ellie said. "I suppose there

aren't any left downstairs?"

"Cleaned out. However, not to worry, I always keep a small stash in the fridge. Because you never know. . . ."

"Absolutely. Besides, I have more information to share."

"I'll put another pot of coffee on," Olivia said. She gathered up the tired-looking vegetables and headed toward the kitchen. By the time the coffee was ready, she had chosen four decorated cookies in shapes as unlike fruits and vegetables as possible. She returned to the living room with the refilled tray, only to find Ellie balanced on one leg in a yoga position. Spunky was stretched over her foot as if he were worried she might fall over.

Her eyes closed, Ellie said, "Just a few more seconds, dear, and I will tell you what I've learned about Charlene, poor child."

"No problem, Mom. I'll eat one of your cookies while I'm waiting."

Ellie's only response was a serene smile. After another twenty or so seconds, she relaxed and opened her eyes. "Now I feel more centered," she said, settling cross-legged on the sofa.

"Your balance is impressive," Olivia said, "given your advanced age."

"Thank you, dear." Ellie's small, slender

hand hovered over the cookies and finally landed on a yellow heart shape decorated with dark pink curlicues. "Now, about Charlene Critch. I had a revealing chat with your brother after he and Charlene finished their little talk. Jason tried to be evasive, but as his mother I was able to read between the lines."

"Jason couldn't be evasive if you swiped his favorite wrench and held it for ransom."

"Which did make my task easier." Ellie savored a small bite of her cookie before saying, "Jason does like Charlene very much, as you said."

"I said he's besotted."

"Be that as it may, Jason sees another side of Charlene that you and Maddie do not. To him, she is vulnerable and sweet. I suspect Charlene is more comfortable with men than women, which is hardly surprising given how critical her mother, Patty, could be." Looking pensive, Ellie nibbled on her heart cookie.

Olivia worked on an orange-and-purple butterfly cookie, determined to be patient with her mother's unique delivery.

Ellie polished off her cookie and said, "I gathered from Jason that the abusive man in Charlene's past has followed her to Chatterley Heights. Jason let slip the name

141

Geoffrey. I suspect he is her ex-husband, the boy Jason introduced her to all those years ago. I assume you noticed Charlene's bruised eye?" When Olivia nodded, Ellie said, "I asked Jason point-blank about the eye, but he said she was shelving some new items and hit her cheek on the corner of a shelf. He was lying, of course. I always know when Jason is lying; his left eyelid twitches."

"You are scary, Mom."

"Thank you, dear."

"What about Charlene's brother, Charlie?" Olivia asked. "Could he be the one abusing her? He seems devoted to her, but that could be a sign of possessiveness."

Ellie pulled her knees up to her chest and leaned back against the sofa. Olivia felt a twinge of envy about her mother's flexibility. Maybe yoga wasn't such a revolting idea.

"I've seen Charlene and Charlie together, and I've never noticed possessiveness on the part of either of them," Ellie said. "In fact, I saw them yesterday morning. I was having an early breakfast at the Chatterley Café, and the two of them were there. They seemed deep in serious conversation, as if they were trying to solve a pressing problem. By the way, I noticed that Charlene paid the bill."

Having dispatched her second cookie,

Olivia settled back to sip her coffee. "That fits with what Struts Marinksy told me. Charlie doesn't seem to have any money, despite his inheritance."

"Interesting," Ellie said, checking her watch. "However, I've missed my voice lesson, and my classics reading group starts in half an hour. I need to pick up my copy of *Sense and Sensibility* on the way." She unrolled her petite body from the sofa and shook out the wrinkles in her loosely draped outfit. "We can both keep an eye on Charlene's safety, but there isn't much else we can do. Jason said she refuses to talk to the sheriff."

"I can at least mention to Del that someone might have blackened her eye," Olivia said. "Even if she denies it, he should know."

"You realize that Charlene will blame Jason for telling."

"I'll be discreet. After all, I'm not the only one who noticed the bruise."

Since Spunky had been stuck in the apartment all day, Olivia took him out for a short, brisk walk before returning to The Gingerbread House. It was near closing time, and Maddie was the only one left in the store. Olivia could hear her singing snatches of tunes along with her iPod.

Spunky had learned to open the kitchen door by running at it full speed and flinging his little body against it. Olivia heard Maddie's squeak of surprise when Spunky tumbled inside.

Maddie poked her upper body through the door, held out a squirming dog, and said, "Does this belong to you?"

"Never saw it before in my life," Olivia said.

"One day he's going to break his tiny neck." The instant Maddie plunked Spunky on the ground, he took off like a furry rocket and raced around the store. Watching the blur, Maddie said, "If he destroys any of our displays, I'll break it for him, the little darling."

Olivia laughed. "You would act just like Spunky if you'd been kept prisoner all day. How were sales?"

"Great! I will leave the counting to you, as always. You do the boring stuff, and I do the fun stuff. It works. And as resident gifted baker, I am about to tackle the cookies for Gwen and Herbie's baby shower tomorrow evening. Yes, I know, I should have them all cut out, baked, and in the freezer ready for icing, but things got a bit hectic." Maddie stuck her iPod buds in her ears and turned her back on Olivia. While

Maddie gathered ingredients and equipment for the cookies, Olivia collected the day's receipts and settled at her little kitchen desk. She'd hoped to talk with Maddie about Lucas's proposal and Charlene's response to their "harvest" cookie event, but she could tell the moment wasn't right. Maddie hadn't even brought up Charlene's bruised eye. When Maddie closed the door, it couldn't be blasted open with dynamite.

After a couple hours of dealing with numbers, Olivia was ready to call it quits for the day. Their sales had been good for a Tuesday, but not as impressive as most previous events, especially when she factored in the cost of all those cookies the customers had consumed.

"I'm beat," Olivia said. "I'm going to bed early tonight."

Spunky trotted over to her, but Maddie gave her a puzzled look and pulled her iPod buds from her ears. "You spoke?"

"I said I'm heading for bed. Are you planning to work all night?"

Maddie shook her head. "I'm actually tired, for once. I'll clean up in here and turn out the lights."

Olivia nestled her sleepy dog in one arm and closed the kitchen door behind her. With the store lights dimmed and the air conditioner on low, the light clink and dull shine of the cookie cutter mobiles reminded her of outdoor chimes. The store still smelled faintly of lime zest. At that moment, Olivia could not imagine leaving Chatterley Heights and moving back to Baltimore. The Gingerbread House had sneaked into her heart the way Spunky had as a puppy, the first time she'd held him.

Feeling expansive, Olivia decided to give her brother the Duesenberg cookie cutter he so coveted. Without turning up the lights, she wound through densely packed displays to the transportation mobile from which she'd hung the cutter. It wasn't there. Unable to comprehend what she was seeing, Olivia reached toward the spot where it had hung, on the right side of the mobile. It *had* to be there. Gwen had chosen the tin baby rattle cutter as her prize. And Jason wouldn't have taken the cutter on his own. Would he?

Maybe Maddie had given the Duesenberg to Jason. It would be like her to take pity on him because he hadn't won the contest, even with her hints. Olivia poked her head into the kitchen and waved to get Maddie's attention.

"Maddie, did you by any chance take that Duesenberg cookie cutter out of the transportation mobile?"

"Nope," Maddie said. "Not my job."

"It's gone."

"It can't be."

"Well, it is. Gone, absent, disappeared."

"Livie, you don't think Jason would . . . ?"

With a slow shake of her head, Olivia said, "I can't believe that he would. It's a valuable cutter, but Jason knows I'd let him have it free, or at least for next to nothing. Anyway, he seemed awfully focused on Charlene and her problems. It's hard to imagine he'd even have thought about it. Well, I won't worry about it tonight, and don't you, either. It'll turn up. Maybe it fell off and someone put it somewhere in the store. I'm sure we'll find it in the light of day. You look baked to a crisp. How many days has it been since you slept?"

Maddie yawned and stretched. "I'm fine. I went to bed early Sunday night."

"This is Tuesday evening. I'll clean up. You go home and get some rest."

For once, Maddie didn't argue.

CHAPTER SEVEN

Olivia lay awake and listed her midsummer resolutions. First, buy a new bedroom air conditioner. Second, never read the Cookie Cutter Collectors Club's latest *Cookie Crumbs* newsletter right before bed. Way too stimulating. She could read a thriller and still drift off, but looking at photos of vintage cutters made her want to run out and find an all-night flea market.

It didn't help Olivia's sleep problem that the temperature in her second-floor bedroom was in the mid-eighties with a dew point she could take a bath in. The Weather Channel had mentioned a storm nearby, possibly heading in their direction. It couldn't arrive soon enough.

Olivia lay spread-eagle on her bed wearing only panties and a loose cotton T-shirt that reached to her mid-thighs. When she'd first moved into her apartment, she had talked herself out of replacing the old window air conditioner in her bedroom. After all, it might be noisy and slow but it still worked. Frugality was her lifetime habit, inheritance or no inheritance. But with the distractions of Maddie's impromptu cookie event and Charlene's dramatic appearance, she hadn't remembered to turn the useless thing on until bedtime. The day's heat had snaked through the myriad, inevitable cracks in the old house and slithered up the staircase, gaining strength as it curled into her bedroom.

"I've been lying here for hours," Olivia muttered. She switched on the bedside lamp and checked her cell phone for the time. It was one a.m. "Okay, thirty-five minutes."

Spunky's tiny body stretched out flat at the foot of the bed, as far as possible from Olivia. When she spoke, he lifted his eyelids and dropped them shut in one smooth movement.

Olivia considered going to her kitchen and pouring herself a glass of wine. No, she had to open the store in the morning; she couldn't afford to feel groggy. She'd finished her last library book. Music never helped her to sleep, and the only television was in her living room, where the air conditioner was even older and louder.

Olivia shifted sideways to a cooler place

on the sheet. Forcing her eyes shut, she tried deep breathing, which her yoga-addicted mother insisted would relax her. It made her crabby. As if mirroring her mood, Spunky raised his head and growled. But he was looking toward the bedroom windows, not at Olivia. She sat up, listened, but heard only the racket made by the air conditioner.

"What is it, Spunks?"

Spunky fixed his limpid brown eyes on Olivia and whimpered. His head snapped back toward the window, ears perked. The air conditioner consumed one of two bedroom windows. Spunky leaped off the bed and trotted to the second, moonlight-filled pane, where he fidgeted and whined. When he gave Olivia his most heartrending look, the one with the pleading eyes and tilted head, Olivia turned off the bedside lamp and joined him at the window.

"I don't see anything," she said. Spunky stood on his hind legs and leaned his front paws on her shin. Olivia picked him up so he could look outside. "See? Dark of night, not a creature is stirring." Spunky's ears fell, then shot up again. This time Olivia heard it, too, even with the air conditioner whining in her right ear. She turned it off. The sound came through clearly, a howl that would have sent a chill down her spine if the room temperature hadn't already risen by at least a degree.

"Hang on a sec, kiddo," Olivia said, depositing Spunky at her feet. At once he began to hop on his back feet and paw at the wall. Olivia unlocked the window and lifted the crank, but the humidity-swollen frame stuck. She hit the wood with her fist and felt it shift. She hit it again, and the window cracked open, allowing heavy, wet air to penetrate the only slightly drier room. She cranked the pane wide.

Spunky yapped until Olivia picked him up. Together they peered out through the screen at what looked like black nothing until Olivia's eyes adjusted and the clouds parted to reveal streaks of moonlight. She began to distinguish large shapes: other buildings on either side of The Gingerbread House, trees in the town square, the lamp-light near the late-nineteenth-century band shell. Spunky wriggled his front paws free of Olivia's grasp and reached out to touch the screen. He yapped three times and went silent. A faint howl answered his call.

"Oh no, don't tell me." Olivia pressed her forehead against the screen. "Is Buddy out there, Spunks? Is that Buddy howling?" Spunky yapped and wagged his tail. "I'll take that as a yes." Deputy Sheriff Cody

Furlow's dog, Buddy, was huge, even for a black Labrador. However, the part about having black fur would explain why Olivia couldn't see him. Buddy and Spunky had forged a special bond and sometimes led one another into trouble, or out of it.

"Buddy sounds unhappy. Serves him right for running away." Spunky leaped out of Olivia's arms and ran to the bedroom door, which was closed to keep in the cooler air. Olivia sat on her bed and speed-dialed Cody's cell. The call went to voice mail. "Cody? This is Olivia Greyson. It's —" She checked her cell. "It's one twenty a.m., and I think Buddy ran off again. Unless he's home with you, he's probably the dog I can hear howling from the town square. Anyway, Spunky thinks it's him. Good luck."

Hoping her job was done, Olivia flopped back on her bed. Spunky had other ideas. He scratched the closed door, whimpering piteously. Olivia groaned. "All right, I'll make another call, but I'm not opening that door." Still on her back, she punched in her speed-dial code for the police department. She got a recording telling her to dial 911 for an emergency. At the end of the message, she was instructed to press "one" to leave a message for the Chatterley Heights Police Department. She questioned whether

Buddy on the loose would qualify as 911-worthy. However, it couldn't hurt to leave a message for Cody.

While Spunky paced between the door and the window, Olivia closed her eyes. She had done her duty, which ought to help her relax and fall asleep. She envisioned wading into a chocolate lake dotted with pink and yellow sugar sprinkles. She swam to the opposite shore and entered a real gingerbread house, minus the child-eating witch. The air smelled like ginger and cloves and cinnamon, and the shelves were stocked with iced gingerbread. She reached for a piece and felt how moist and light it was as she bit into it. A tiny sound made her glance down at her feet, where a marzipan puppy with licorice eyes gazed up at her. As she broke off a bit of gingerbread to give him, she became aware of an almond smell and realized the puppy was melting from the heat in the kitchen. The oven door was open and heat was pouring out, which meant the wicked witch was —

A breath-stopping howl reached her through the open bedroom window. Spunky answered with his own version, which sounded more like an extended yap.

"Thank goodness I didn't adopt a beagle," Olivia said. She rolled over on her stomach.

"You're really worried, aren't you, Spunks?" With tiny, galloping steps, Spunky ran to the bed, leaped onto it, jumped back down, and ran back to the window.

"What's more to the point," Olivia said, "you aren't going to let me sleep until we rescue Buddy. Though Lord knows what we'll do with the brute if we do manage to capture him." She slipped into jeans and a T-shirt and slid her cell phone into her pocket. She tried to pick up Spunky before opening her bedroom door, but he wiggled free and raced for the front door of the apartment. He held still long enough for Olivia to hook a leash on his collar, then stood on his hind feet and strained toward the door. "I'm worried, too," she told him as they headed out into the night. "I hope it isn't Cody he's howling over."

Dense, wet fog rolled in as they made their way across the town square, with Spunky barking and Buddy howling back. A vivid streak of lightning sliced the sky south of the park, followed by a loud boom and, a few seconds later, a long rumble. As all the lights in and around the town square blinked out, Olivia realized a major storm was moving in . . . and the booming sound hadn't been thunder. She hadn't thought to grab a raincoat, and she didn't even own a flashlight. She needed to start taking the Weather Channel more seriously. It would be too time-consuming to go back for rain gear. Better to find Buddy as quickly as possible and race back to the now darkened Gingerbread House. If the storm hit too fast and hard, they could all take shelter in the band shell.

The combination of dark and fog made it tough to determine direction, though a flash of lightning nearby illuminated the outline of the band shell. Olivia didn't catch sight of Buddy, though. She loosely held Spunky's leash and allowed him to lead her, which he did with fierce terrier determination. She was glad he weighed only five pounds and had minuscule legs, or he would have yanked her off her feet and dragged her through the damp grass.

Without hesitating to sniff the air, Spunky pulled Olivia around the band shell and toward the statue of Frederick P. Chatterley. As they passed the horse's rump, Olivia was able to make out Buddy's large form sitting on his haunches, his head lowered. He lifted his head as they neared. When he recognized Spunky, Buddy barked once and lowered his head again. He edged his front legs forward until his belly reached the wet grass, raised his head to the dark sky, and howled with a mournfulness that made even Spunky pause. Lightning slashed the darkness, illuminating the south end of the town square. A split second later came the rumbling of thunder. Olivia shivered as foreboding sliced through her. In that moment of light, she had seen a human form sprawled motionless on the grass, inches from Buddy's front paws.

With Spunky beside her, Olivia ran toward Buddy and knelt on the damp grass. "Cody?" Even as she whispered the question, Olivia realized that the prone form was not Deputy Cody. Cody was a skinny six-foot-three. She touched the man's jacket, then drew her hand away, remembering her rudimentary forensics. The material had felt like leather. Under his jacket, this man had the broad shoulders and muscled build of a weight lifter. He lay on his stomach, his face hidden from view. His head was bare, and his dew-soaked hair looked black.

Instinctively, Olivia reached toward his neck to feel for a pulse, then pulled back as she touched cold skin. A wave of revulsion turned her stomach. Spunky was braver, or at least more compelled by curiosity. He trotted around the dead man and sniffed his hand before Olivia yanked him back. Buddy's mournful brown eyes watched her as if expecting the human to take charge.

"Stop being such a wimp," Olivia muttered. "I meant me, not you," she said to Buddy. As the first raindrops landed on her back, she opened her cell and punched in 911.

Soaked to the skin, Olivia huddled between Spunky and Buddy, peering into the darkness to avoid looking at the dead man nearby. "I guess this is a two-dog night, huh, guys?" Neither dog laughed. Olivia heard a shout from somewhere close by, but the rain was falling so furiously she couldn't see more than a couple feet in any direction. The second shout was even closer, from somewhere to her left. "Hello?" she called.

"Where are you? Can't see a thing in this mess." It was Del's voice, worried and irritated and very welcome.

"Del, it's me, Livie. I'm — We are south of the band shell, right before you get to the statue."

Del sounded quite close and even more cross when he shouted, "Why on earth aren't you *inside* the band shell?" He arrived right behind her, panting but dry under a large umbrella. "Here, hold this," Del said, handing the umbrella to Olivia. He took off his raincoat and wrapped it around Olivia's trembling shoulders. Pulling on crime-scene gloves, he leaned over the prone body and felt for a pulse. "He's dead."

"I know."

Del pulled a flashlight from his uniform jacket pocket and squatted down, playing the light slowly over the body and along the soaked ground. Olivia tried not to watch, but she couldn't help herself. Del seemed interested in the area around the man's left shoulder. Olivia saw nothing but dark, wet grass. Del carefully lifted the man's shoulder off the ground enough to see beneath it. The grass, protected from rain by the man's chest, glistened with a dark liquid. Blood.

"Try to keep the umbrella over him, Liv. The scene is enough of a mess as it is." Del dialed his cell with his thumb. "I'm going to start with the assumption that you did not kill this man," he said as he waited for an answer to his call.

"Thanks ever s-so." Olivia shivered, but not from the sudden cooling of the air. Shock had begun to set in. Buddy edged closer to her, while Spunky, dripping wet and unusually subdued, snuggled up against her ankle.

"Cody, it's me," Del said into his cell. "Come to the park right away, south of the band shell, near the statue. Yeah, I'm aware there's a storm; I'm in it. So is your dog, by the way, as well as a deceased male, Caucasian. Apparent stabbing victim. Don't quote me on that, I haven't found a weapon. It might be underneath him. Get here as fast as you can and bring a couple extra umbrellas."

Del snugged his cell into an inside pocket of his jacket. Without touching the body, he leaned in close with his flashlight. "Expensive leather jacket," he said. "What's this?" An object protruded from the man's right hand. As the light caught a metallic sheen, Olivia inhaled sharply. It looked to her like the shaped edge of a tin cookie cutter. She thought back to the Duesenberg cookie cutter that had gone missing after the store event. That was made of tin. She told herself that lots of cookie cutters were made of tin, and there were lots of tin cookie cutters floating around Chatterley Heights. Besides, the small object could be anything.

"I don't recognize the guy," Del said. "Any chance you do?"

"What? Oh. No, he doesn't look familiar." Olivia wrapped her arms tighter around herself. "Wait a sec," she said as the light reached the man's face. "Hand over the flashlight, will you? Thanks." Del held the umbrella while Olivia knelt down, her knees sinking into the squishy ground. Her stomach lurched, but she forced herself to lean closer to the body. She trained the light on the man's hair, which hung in short strings down the sides of his head. The layered ends were even and precise, indicating a professional trim. Earlier, the hair color had looked black, but now she could see it was dark brown. And the dampness had brought out natural curls. She sat back on her knees and slid the light up and down the man's torso.

A siren pealed in the distance. Spunky and Buddy lifted their heads and peered toward the sound. "That'll be Cody," Del said. "Did you notice something I should know about?"

"I can't be positive." Olivia struggled to her feet and traded the flashlight for the umbrella, "but I think this might be the man I saw running from Charlene's store."

"Okay, we'll get Charlene and her brother to see if they can identify him. They might stonewall, given they've tried so hard to keep his existence a secret."

"I might have a first name for you. Geoffrey," Olivia said. "He might be Charlene's ex-husband."

Del's mouth tightened. "Where did you

get this name? And why didn't you tell me earlier?"

"Hey, I just found out a few hours ago, and Mom wasn't even sure about the name. Or the marriage. She did say that this Geoffrey and Jason were friends, though, so Jason would know . . . unless he's keeping quiet for Charlene's sake." Spunky smacked his wet front paws on Olivia's leg and whimpered until she lifted him up and held him to her chest. The smell of wet dog comforted her.

"Anything else you haven't had a chance to tell me?" There was an edge of impatience to Del's tone.

Olivia counted to three before giving up on the power of meditation. "Look, Del, I am tired and wet and close to losing what's left of my dinner. If I wake up before dawn and think of some tidbit that might be important, I will call you instantly."

Del's shoulders dropped as if the wind had gone out of him. "Livie, I'm really —"

A shout told them Cody was in the town square and trying to locate them. Buddy leaped to his feet and barked joyfully. When his master's form became visible, Buddy shot toward him, nearly knocking him backward. "The crime scene guys will be here in about five minutes," Cody said once

161

he'd subdued Buddy.

"Good," Del said. "You take Livie and those wet piles of fur home, then come right back. I'll stay here." He turned back to his examination of the dead man without revealing to Olivia whether he'd been about to say he was really sorry or really angry with her. She wanted not to care, but she did.

CHAPTER EIGHT

As soon as she unlocked the door of The Gingerbread House and stepped inside the following morning, Olivia heard the whirring of the mixer. She thought she caught a whiff of lemon, too, or perhaps it was her nose expecting lemon to go along with icing. Spunky wriggled in the crook of her arm. Every morning, he explored the whole store inch by inch, making sure nothing dangerous lurked in the shadows. When she put him on the floor, he took off like a windup toy. She left him to his task and headed toward the kitchen.

The mixer had quieted, and Maddie's head poked through the kitchen door. "I thought I heard the clatter of little doggie claws," she said. She looked better rested than she had the night before, but her voice lacked its normal exuberance. Olivia missed it.

"Tell me you haven't been here for hours,"

Olivia said, hoping a touch of lightness would bring the old Maddie back.

"I haven't been here for hours," Maddie said. "Only one. If I don't get these cookies iced pronto, they won't be dry for Gwen and Herbie's baby shower this evening."

"Give me a few minutes to set up the cash register, then I'll help you." Olivia located Spunky in the doorway of the cookbook nook. "Hey, Spunks, mind the store until we open, okay?" When she turned back toward the kitchen, Maddie had already disappeared without even a thank-you. This was serious. With mild trepidation, Olivia entered the kitchen to find Maddie hovering over a baked cookie, the omnipresent iPod plugged in her ears. So intense was her concentration that her light eyebrows nearly touched each other as she guided a plastic pastry bag filled with dark pink icing around the edges of the cookie, piping the outline of a baby carriage.

Olivia opened the small wall safe hidden behind the kitchen desk and began to count out bills and coins for the cash register. She scooped up the money and dropped it into a zippered bag. Maddie had moved on to another cookie, so Olivia decided not to interrupt until she'd set up the register and was ready to help. However, as she approached the door to the main sales area, Maddie looked up.

Maddie capped the tip of her pastry bag. "I called Bertha to come in for opening. We'll probably be swamped again, and I need to concentrate," she said. "You, sit."

"What's up?" Olivia asked as she pulled over a chair.

Maddie hauled herself up on the kitchen counter. "Since when don't you tell me instantly the moment something important happens, like, you find a dead body in the town square?"

"Maddie, of course I was planning to tell you every detail, but this is the first chance I've had, and you were working so intently. . . ."

"When I say 'tell,' I mean call or throw pebbles at my window to wake me up, whatever works. Do you know how I found out about your little nighttime tripping-over-a-murder-victim escapade? Sitting at the breakfast table with Aunt Sadie, that's how. She got a call from a friend in the gossip chain. She almost choked on her oatmeal. She's nearly seventy, you know. She can't handle that kind of shock."

"Your aunt Sadie was chewing oatmeal while talking on the phone?"

"Don't change the subject." Maddie had

been narrowing her eyes at her best friend since the age of ten. "If you must know, I overslept, so Aunt Sadie got it into her head that I was dying of consumption or something. She insisted on making me oatmeal, which in my opinion is only good for cookies. Now stop stalling and tell me everything, every minute detail, even if Sheriff Del swore you to secrecy. *Especially* if Del swore you to secrecy." She slid off the counter and retrieved her pastry bag. "I'll decorate," she said. "You talk."

Olivia spilled the whole story and felt better for it. When she'd finished, she poured herself the last cup of coffee, added generous amounts of cream and sugar, and started another pot.

As Maddie piped a cookie with baby pink icing, she asked, "So do you figure this Geoffrey is the jerk who gave Charlene a black eye?" Her head was bent over her cookie. "Because, between you and me, much as I dislike Charlene, I wouldn't blame her if she iced him. It was probably self-defense, anyway."

"There's one detail I haven't told you yet," Olivia said. "It might point to a suspect. I just hope it isn't one of us."

Maddie paused to glance up at Olivia. "Tell me at once. It might be interesting to be a suspect . . . for about five minutes," she said, smoothly picking up her icing where she'd left off.

"I think Geoffrey — if that's who he turns out to be — was holding a cookie cutter when he died. Anyway, I saw something in his hand that looked like the edge of a cutter."

Maddie frowned but did not interrupt her flooding. "What was it made of?"

"The light was bad," Olivia said, "but it looked like tin."

"Like our missing Duesenberg."

"Yup. I plan to have a quiet chat with Jason as soon as —" The kitchen phone rang. Olivia was within reach, so she answered. "Mom, am I glad to hear from —"

"Yes, dear, but you won't be glad to hear my news." Ellie's normally calm voice sounded tight, as if she were holding herself together. "I've just had a call from the sheriff. Your brother has been arrested on suspicion of murdering Charlene's ex-husband, Geoffrey King."

"What? No, not Jason, not in a million years. Del is out of his mind."

"Normally, I would agree," Ellie said, "but Jason turned himself in. Livie, he has confessed to murder. And according to the sheriff, my own son refuses to speak to me.

You've got to get down there and talk some sense into that boy. Please, Livie, right away. I'm on my way to The Gingerbread House; I'll take care of the store, you talk to your brother. Only please hurry."

"I'm out the door. I'll call Mr. Willard from my cell. We need an attorney pronto."

Aloysius Willard Smythe, attorney at law, was waiting outside the police station when Olivia arrived. Mr. Willard, as he was generally called, did not look his usual calm self. His long, thin fingers fidgeted with the buttons on his suit coat, and his quick, dark eyes roamed restlessly until he recognized Olivia striding toward him.

"This is a terrible turn of events," Mr. Willard said as he patted Olivia's shoulder like a concerned uncle. "Your poor mother must be frantic with worry."

"As am I," Olivia said. "I could throttle Jason, the bonehead."

Mr. Willard's gaunt face blanched. "Do you believe that your brother might actually have committed — ?"

"No, of course not," Olivia said. "Jason isn't a murderer, just an idiot. I do believe that he is afraid Charlene Critch might have killed her ex-husband. I'm fairly certain this Geoffrey King gave her a black eye, probably not for the first time, and I wouldn't be surprised if he'd been threatening her with worse."

"Ah, I see," said Mr. Willard. "In which case, the law would go much easier on Ms. Critch than it will on Jason."

"Which makes my brother an idiot. Right. Anyway, now we have to figure out how to help him. I doubt he'll help himself, not unless the real killer is arrested and turns out not to be his precious Charlene."

"Do you happen to know if Jason might be able to produce an alibi?" Mr. Willard asked in a fatalistic tone, as if he suspected it wouldn't be that easy.

"I haven't a clue," said Olivia. "Even if he could, he won't."

Mr. Willard waved his hand toward a bench behind them. "I suggest we sit for a few moments to develop our strategy. As you know, I do not practice criminal law, but I know several excellent defense attorneys, should the need arise. I can handle the preliminaries, but meanwhile we — meaning you, since you know your brother better than I — must think of a way to convince him to say no more without benefit of counsel."

Olivia wanted more than anything to storm into the jail and stuff a rag in Jason's mouth, but she agreed to sit down and work out a strategy. "A plan is a good idea," she said. "I always feel better when I have a plan."

For several minutes, they sat side-by-side on the wooden bench, Mr. Willard with his fingers laced together on his lap, Olivia in barely contained panic. The only plan she could think of involved bribing the police department with dozens of decorated cookies in law enforcement shapes. Bright blue service revolvers came to mind. Maybe some tulip red squad cars trimmed with gold luster dust paint, and of course a jail cell with bars formed from silver dragées. Olivia envisioned Jason's stubborn, frightened face behind the bars. She slowed and deepened her breathing to clear her mind of lovely iced distractions. Jason needed her, whether he'd admit it or not.

"I have something of a plan," Olivia said, "but you might not like it. I know Sheriff Del will hate it, so I don't intend to tell him. He'll figure it out, of course." She shrugged her shoulders. "But there isn't much he can do about it."

"Ah," said Mr. Willard. "You intend to find out who actually killed that unfortunate young man. And how might that intention convince young Jason to cease confessing at once?"

"Because Jason knows I can do it. Last spring he actually said how impressed he was when I helped solve a murder. I think that's the first and only time he has ever acknowledged that I might have a functioning brain. And he knows I love him, even when I can't stand him, so he knows I'll never give up. The hardest part will be convincing him that I'm not convinced Charlene killed her ex-husband."

Mr. Willard arched his bony fingers and began to tap his fingertips against each other. Olivia knew the gesture and hoped it meant he was taking her plan seriously. He was probably making an organized mental list of all the dangers. Mr. Willard's fingers stopped tapping, and he said, "I, too, know what you are capable of accomplishing once you are determined to do so. As your attorney, I cannot officially sanction your plan; however, time is of the essence." His long body unfurled as he stood and offered her his hand. "And time is, as they say, a-wasting."

Sheriff Del Jenkins plowed his fingers through his already well-furrowed hair. "Livie, I swear to you, Jason barged in here and confessed to murdering Geoffrey King. I wasn't even considering him as a suspect, at least not yet."

"What do you mean, 'not yet'? If you have any evidence, I have a right to know." Olivia had refused to take a seat in Del's office, which allowed her to glare down at him from across his desk. Mr. Willard, silent and even taller, stood beside her.

Del looked more helpless than angry. "I agree," he said, "you have a right to know. Once Jason confessed, I had to start investigating. It's my job. I checked his alibi for yesterday evening, up to the time you found King."

"And?"

Del rolled his office chair sideways toward Deputy Cody, who sat across the room at his computer, trying to look as if he were working. "Cody," Del said, "bring Olivia and Mr. Willard some coffee, will you? Cream and sugar for Livie." He directed a questioning glance at Mr. Willard.

"Black, thank you. I drink milk only in cappuccinos."

Del's mouth twitched for a moment. "Our budget doesn't stretch beyond a ten-year-old Mr. Coffee, I'm afraid."

By the time Cody brought their coffee, Olivia had decided to take pity on Del. He loved Chatterley Heights, and he wasn't likely to take pleasure in arresting someone he'd known for years. He was, however, more than likely to put up his guard if he realized how determined Olivia was to identify the real killer. She accepted her cup and slid into a chair facing Del's desk. Mr. Willard followed her example. She could almost hear Del's sigh of relief as he dropped into his own squeaky desk chair.

"I'm glad you're here, too," Del said to Mr. Willard. "That boy needs to understand the trouble he's gotten himself into by confessing. I was following a lead that suggested the killer might be from out of town, but now I have to investigate Jason. And I have to tell you, his alibi isn't solid."

Olivia sat forward in her chair. "What lead were you following? Could it clear Jason?"

Del hesitated, then asked Mr. Willard, "Are you here in your official capacity?"

Mr. Willard nodded. "Olivia has placed me on retainer to assist in her attempts to protect Jason. As I have reminded her, I am not a criminal attorney, but for now I am representing Jason's interests."

Del sipped his coffee and appeared to come to a decision. "Okay, I'll tell you what we have so far. You might want to hire your own investigator." His brown eyes darkened as he leaned toward Olivia. "Livie, I don't want to hear that you have taken on any investigating by yourself, okay?"

With a slow nod, Olivia said, "I understand."

Del held her eyes a moment longer before reaching toward a file on his desk. "Okay, Jason's story goes like this: Charlene Critch confided in him that her ex-husband, Geoffrey King, showed up at her store a few weeks ago." Del glanced up from his notes. "We've interviewed both Charlene and her brother, Charlie, and they agreed with Jason's summary of his movements yesterday up until about eleven p.m."

"Wait," Olivia said. "They were all together yesterday evening?"

"Right, at least that's what they claim. They all agree that King — who, by the way, Charlene insists was not really her husband because her father got the marriage annulled. Anyway, King had recently been released from prison after serving a sentence for robbing a jewelry store. He tracked down Charlene because he knew she had come into her trust money. He figured she'd pay him to go away. Charlene says she gave him some money, but he kept hanging around."

"Big surprise," Olivia said under her breath.

"Charlene admitted that King hit her on several occasions. She claims he did so when she refused to give him more money."

"But you don't believe her?" Mr. Willard asked.

With a shrug, Del said, "I don't have a strong reason not to believe her. It certainly fits King's MO."

Olivia said, "I'm not convinced Charlene's story explains what I saw and heard while King ransacked the kitchen in The Vegetable Plate."

Del riffled through his file and extracted one page. "According to my report, you heard him say, 'I'll kill her,' by which we assume he meant Charlene. Is that accurate?"

"First he said 'Damn,' and he sounded furious," Olivia said. "At the time, I thought he might be looking for something important to him, maybe something he thought Charlene had taken from him. And don't forget that the cash register was untouched. If all he wanted was money, it doesn't make a lot of sense for him to break a lot of valuable objects and ignore the cash register."

"Maybe the break-in was meant as a threat," Mr. Willard said. "Or, given the swearing and the vow to kill her, it might

175

have been an expression of extreme frustration at Ms. Critch's unwillingness to meet his financial demands."

"Maybe. . . ." Olivia thought back to that morning and pictured the scene in the kitchen. Rage, frustration . . . certainly King's violence expressed those emotions. But it sounded more like desperation. She had no proof, so she kept her idea to herself. She couldn't help but wonder if Charlene possessed something, maybe a document or an object, that could endanger Geoffrey King.

Mr. Willard cleared his throat. "Sheriff, may I ask how Mr. King was killed? I can promise you, by the way, that any information you are willing to share with us will be both appreciated and kept to ourselves."

Del hesitated a moment, then asked Olivia, "Will your silence extend to Maddie and your mother? Never mind, don't bother to answer. Of course it won't, and it wouldn't matter, anyway. The entire town will have heard some version of the story by this evening. I don't know how they do it."

Olivia almost choked on her coffee. "I think it's something in the water. How about this, Del: Mr. Willard, I'm certain, will maintain his professional silence." She glanced toward Mr. Willard, who nodded.

"And I'll use my very best judgment. I'll bite my tongue if someone passes on a rumor that Jason is an axe murderer. And I do understand that there may be details you want to keep secret even from me. As you say, I'll probably find them out, one way or another."

"I don't doubt it for a minute." Del retrieved the coffeepot. As he topped off their cups, he said, "King was stabbed. Time of death hasn't been established yet. We found a knife seemingly flung away from the scene. The crime scene unit is working on it. The storm messed up the scene pretty badly, but if there's anything to find, they will find it. All we can do is wait."

"What kind of knife was it?" Olivia asked.

"Next question?"

"Ah," said Mr. Willard. "One of those details to be kept secret. I have a question concerning my client, if I may, Sheriff. I assume you have more than young Jason's fondness for Ms. Critch, as well as his unfortunate confession, to indicate that he might be a viable suspect for Mr. King's murder?"

Del selected another page from his case file. "As I mentioned, Jason was with Charlene and Charlie until about eleven yesterday evening. According to Charlene, King had physically assaulted her earlier in the day — she claimed not to know why — and then he threatened to return to The Vegetable Plate that evening to 'torch the dump.' Charlene decided to guard the store all night. As if we didn't have police and a fire department." Del rolled his eyes toward the ceiling, apparently seeking divine assistance to understand human behavior. "Jason and Charlie offered to help guard both the store and Charlene. Just before eleven p.m., Charlie reminded Jason that he had an early shift at Struts & Bolts Garage the next morning. Charlene insisted Jason go home and get some sleep."

"Wait," Olivia said, "Charlie works at the garage, too."

"Charlie said his shift didn't start until noon, and Struts Marinsky confirmed. So Jason left at eleven and walked to his apartment by way of the town square. Jason claims he found Geoffrey King with a gas can and lighter, on his way to torch The Vegetable Plate. He struggled with King and killed him." Turning the page, Del said, "Back at her store, shortly after Jason left, Charlene claims she became impatient and told Charlie that it was 'just like Geoff to make a threat and then be too lazy to carry it out.' She said King had most likely started drinking and passed out. So she ordered Charlie to go home and get some sleep. Which he says he did."

Clearing his throat, Mr. Willard said, "Are we to believe that Ms. Critch remained alone in her store the remainder of the night? That sounds remarkably foolhardy and somewhat out of character, if I may say so."

Olivia let out a shaky laugh. "I'll bet she wanted a bath and some beauty sleep, plus an hour to do her makeup. That I could believe."

Her comment drew a brief smile from Del. "In fact, Charlene claims she left soon after her brother, at approximately 11:45 p.m., and went straight —"

"But doesn't that clear Jason?" Olivia asked. "If Charlie and Charlene left later, wouldn't they have seen the body on their way home?"

"Charlie Critch's rented room is in the northeast part of town, so he wouldn't have gone through the park."

"Unless he had a reason to, like seeing someone in the park," Olivia said.

"Duly noted," Del said. "Anyway, Charlene says she was afraid to cut through the park alone after dark, so she took the sidewalk straight south to her house. It made her nervous even to look toward the park, or so she said."

"If I may interject," said Mr. Willard, "are we to believe that a concerned brother such as Charlie would leave his sister to walk home alone in the middle of the night?"

"Good question." Del slapped his file shut and leaned his forearms on his desk. "I wondered that myself, but when I confronted Charlie about it, he shrugged and muttered something about obeying his big sister. He didn't sound resentful, simply embarrassed and a bit childlike. That detail does still bother me, though."

Olivia thought back to her conversation with Struts Marinsky about the relationship between Charlene and her much younger brother. "I have a mixed reaction," she said. "On the one hand, Charlene and Charlie must have formed a close bond because of their parents' self-obsession. Charlene must have been both mother and father to Charlie, and he seems to adore her almost as a dependent child would. So I can see him obeying Charlene against his better judgment. But there's another angle: Why would Charlene decide to send Charlie home first, despite her admitted fear of walking through the park? You know what I think? I think Jason is an innocent, besotted dupe, and his confession is hogwash. He's afraid Charlene killed King because she was the last to leave. Maybe she did. Or maybe Charlie killed him to protect his sister, and she's keeping quiet to protect him. Or they both did it."

Del sat in silence for some time, frowning at the closed file in front of him. When he raised his eyes to Olivia's face, he didn't look happy. "Here's what I think," he said. "We have too many possible suspects and too many lies. This will take time to sort out. Meanwhile, I have a confession from your brother, Livie, whether I want it or not. If he can't or won't recant and offer some believable explanation for his behavior, along with an alibi, I'm afraid he'll have to stay in jail."

"I told you I didn't want to talk to anyone," Jason said when Del brought Olivia and Mr. Willard to the town's one jail cell. A middle-aged man lay snoring on one of the two cots in the cell, apparently sleeping off a night of overimbibing. Jason's lanky frame huddled on the second cot, his arms linked around his knees. He looked to Olivia the way he had as a child, the day their father went to the hospital for the last time. She wanted to put her arms around him, as she had then. However, that was then, and this was now.

The defiance on Jason's face did not invite sisterly comfort.

"You said you wouldn't talk to your mother," Del said. "You didn't specify anyone else." He unlocked the cell and allowed Olivia and Mr. Willard to enter before locking it again. Pointing to a bell attached to the wall outside the cell, and within reach from inside, Del said, "Give me a ring when you've finished."

Once Del was out of earshot, Olivia sat on the end of the cot. Jason slid farther away and tightened his grip on his knees. "You're acting like an idiot, you know. And a selfish one, too. If it were up to me, I'd leave you here, but Mom is beside herself with worry." She felt her eyes tear up and turned her back on Jason. "I've hired Mr. Willard to protect your rights, and I don't like wasting money, so if you refuse to talk to him, I'll . . . I'll . . ." She rose and walked to the bars before turning to face him.

Jason's expression had softened, making him look younger still. He unfolded from the cot and said, "You'll never give me another cookie as long as you live?"

Olivia spit out a laugh. She gave him a hug, then socked him in the arm with her fist.

"Ow! Geez, Livie, you hit like a guy."

"When I'm mad enough. Now, listen to your big sister. If you think you're being self-sacrificing for Charlene's sake, give it up. You barely know her."

"You've got her all wrong, Livie. Charlene is sensitive. She's been through a lot; she told me all about Geoff King and what he did to her."

"So she killed him and is letting you take the rap for it? How sensitive is that?"

"*No*. It's just . . ." Jason circled the jail cell like a newly captured tiger. When he bumped the occupied cot, the snoozing drunk stirred and muttered, "Drinks on the house."

"If I may . . . ?" Mr. Willard tapped one bony finger on his lips. "Jason, your sister has engaged my services because she is fully aware of the dangerous situation in which you have landed yourself. I feel I need to warn you at once that if you persist in your murder confession, the police will interview you and ask for a statement. The police are overworked. They will stop looking for other suspects once you have given them a signed confession. At each step, it becomes more difficult for you to extricate yourself."

Jason said nothing, but he seemed to be listening.

"I am not myself a defense attorney, but I

will find one for you, if necessary. First, though, I need to ask you a question. Since I am currently acting as your attorney, I will not reveal your answer to the police. Do you have a strong reason to believe that Charlene Critch killed her ex-husband?"

"I . . . well . . ." Jason flung out his hands in a gesture of helplessness. Olivia wanted to protect him and slap him.

Olivia realized that Mr. Willard was trying to find out, indirectly, if Jason really had stabbed Geoffrey King. When Jason sent a pleading look in her direction, Olivia asked, "Do you want me to leave so you can talk to Mr. Willard in private?"

Jason's hands dropped back to his sides. "No, you can stay, Liv. The answer to your question, Mr. Willard, is no. I don't really know if Charlene killed Geoff. I just assumed because . . . well, Charlie wouldn't walk through the park to go home, so it couldn't have been him."

And it wasn't you, either, you complete and utter nincompoop. Olivia kept this observation to herself.

Dropping down on his cot, Jason looked up at Olivia and said, "I really care about her, Liv. I know she can come across as . . . But underneath she's still the same girl I knew in high school. You know, kind of shy and easy to talk to."

Olivia didn't know how much more of her tongue was left to bite. On the other hand, maybe Charlene had become herself again with Jason. And maybe she killed her abusive ex-husband and was allowing Jason to take the blame. "Jason," she said, "tell me something. Did you take the Duesenberg cookie cutter from the store when you didn't win it?"

"What? Of course not," Jason said. "Why would I do that?"

Olivia said nothing.

"Look," Jason said, "I know I've made a mess for everyone, and I'm really sorry you and Mom are so upset, but here's the thing . . . I don't have any *evidence* that Charlene didn't . . . you know, but I'm positive she didn't. I can't let her . . . ." Jason paused, frowning. "I couldn't let Charlene get hurt anymore. So that's why I killed Geoffrey King. I saw him in the park, and I knew what he was there for. I'm sorry, Livie, but that's all there is to it."

Olivia fixed him with a sisterly glare. "How did you kill him?"

His chin lifted in defiance, Jason turned his back on Olivia and said, "Thanks for your concern, Mr. Willard, but my mind is made up. I'd like you both to leave now."

185

He withdrew again to his cot, back pressed against the wall, arms around his knees.

Mr. Willard rang the bell, and Del came to unlock the door. Before leaving the cell, Olivia turned to face her brother. "Jason, you really are being an idiot. You know that, right?"

Jason gave her a sad smile. "I love you, too, Olive Oyl."

CHAPTER NINE

Olivia cringed as she approached The Gingerbread House and saw the gathering crowd. Several small groups milled around on the lawn, while a steady stream of customers passed in and out of the front door. Through the large front window, she could see the store was packed. She stopped to check her watch under the Parisian-striped awning that shaded Lady Chatterley's Clothing Boutique for Elegant Ladies. Twelve thirty, halfway through the lunch hour. Her mother would be frantic for news about Jason, so Olivia gave her a quick call to let her know that he was okay and she'd be back at the store soon with more details.

Also, Olivia was starving. The Chatterley Café was nearby, but the line went out the door and trailed all the way across the sidewalk to the curb. Pete's Diner, on the other hand, looked like it could use a customer. The diner was across the town square from Lady Chatterley's, near the statue of Frederick P. Chatterley. In the park, a cluster of curious townspeople were kicking the grass around the area where Olivia had found Geoffrey King's body. She decided to take the long way to Pete's Diner, around the square, rather than brave a bunch of avid clue seekers.

Having reached Joe's Diner unaccosted, Olivia relaxed at a secluded table and glanced through the short, grease-stained sheet of paper referred to as the "old" menu. Meatloaf sandwich with a side of mashed potatoes jumped off the page and begged to be ordered. The "new" laminated menu offered such items as scallops in garlic sauce, which she loved, but it was more of a meatloaf-and-potatoes kind of day. Olivia felt the need for substantive fuel with the calming qualities of tomato sauce.

"Olivia Greyson. Thought you'd deserted us for that fancy place on the edge of town." Ida, who had waitressed at Pete's off and on for much of her adult life, greeted everyone with tired sarcasm. Olivia found it oddly comforting. "So what'll it be?" Ida eyed the menu in Olivia's hand. "Must be tired of all that radicchio and pomegranate juice or whatever it is they concoct over there at Bone Vittles, huh?"

Olivia giggled and relaxed a bit more. She realized she was one of only three customers in the diner. By the front window, two retired men lingered over coffee while they watched the clue-hunting action in the park. "Well, Ida, Bon Vivant is a nice place, but they don't offer meatloaf sandwiches with mashed potatoes, and that's what I'm in the mood for. And coffee."

"Lots of cream, sugar's on the table, and extra tomato sauce." It wasn't a question; Ida knew her too well.

As soon as Ida left her table, Olivia speed-dialed Del. He answered on the second ring. "Don't tell me you've found another body."

"I haven't. Hope I never do. But I have an idea that didn't occur to me until I left the station. It's a long shot, but there might be a witness."

"You think someone saw the murder? Hang on, let me grab a pen. We buy them by the box, but there's never one . . . Okay, I found one. Now, who's this long-shot witness?"

"That's the problem, I don't know who she is, but . . . Wait a sec, my meal is arriving."

"Where are you?"

"Pete's."

"I'm on my way. But keep talking."

"Thanks, Ida," Olivia said as the waitress placed a bowl of extra tomato topping next to her sandwich plate. "Okay, Del, I can talk again. All I can tell you is that late Monday night — or maybe early Tuesday morning, Maddie would remember better — there was a woman dancing in the town square."

"Are you sure you weren't dreaming?"

"I told you, Maddie saw her, too. She came back to the store late to do some baking, and I'd fallen asleep on the couch. Well, never mind all that. Maddie called my cell, I looked out the window and saw the woman, and then Maddie —"

"Hang on, I'm at Pete's." Del came through the diner door, still holding his cell to his ear. When Ida saw him, he made a cup-sipping gesture to request coffee. Ida scowled at him but began to fill a cup. She delivered it a moment after he sat down across from Olivia.

"You ordering anything except your free coffee?" Ida asked.

"Ida, I've told you to charge me for coffee," Del said.

"If it was up to me, I'd charge you double, but Pete won't let me. He likes cops and firefighters. Don't ask me why." Shaking her head, she turned away.

"Wow, that sandwich looks great," Del said.

"Get your own, this baby is mine." Olivia curved a protective arm around her plate.

"Okay, about this woman you and Maddie saw. What did she look like?"

"Well . . ." Olivia was beginning to regret volunteering her information, such as it was. "I was in my living room, so I couldn't see anything except this diaphanous white blur sort of leaping and twirling near the band shell. She was dancing beautifully. Maddie said she might be a ballerina, but what do I know? She danced away from the light, and I never saw her again. But Maddie sneaked around in back of the stores east of the square to get a closer look, and she described what she saw to me. She said the woman was slender and had white hair."

"So she was older?" Del asked. Ida clattered a plate down in front of him. "A meatloaf sandwich? But I didn't order —"

"Pete said to bring you one. On the house. Of course. When Pete goes broke, I'll lose my job. You just think about that." Ida shuffled off, muttering to herself.

Del grinned. "That was code for 'leave a big tip.' I always leave a tip worth the cost of the meal plus twenty percent, and Ida knows it. She loves to bully me. Now, did

191

Maddie assess this dancer's age?"

"No, she said the woman was wearing some sort of veil over her head, but her hair still looked white. I have a hard time imagining an older woman executing those leaps." Olivia took a bite of her meatloaf sandwich and sighed in appreciation.

"A dance teacher, maybe?" Del bit into his sandwich, squirting tomato sauce on his cheek. He swiped at it with his napkin.

Olivia shrugged. "As far as I know, Raoul is the only professional dance teacher in town."

"Raoul . . . Is he the Latin dancer all the women in town are swooning over?" There was a snide edge to Del's voice.

"Now, now," Olivia said. "Just because he is tall, lean, and exotically handsome is no reason to take a disliking to him. My mom likes him, and she's a good judge of character. Although Allan despises him."

"Well, there you are then." Dell dipped a corner of his sandwich in extra sauce and stuffed it into his mouth while he jotted in a small notebook. Olivia noticed a bit of tomato sauce dotting his chin. She used her napkin to wipe it away. Del gave her a lopsided grin, and she felt her stomach flip. "So, this Raoul guy, has he got a last name?"

Olivia wrote off her stomach flip to an

excess of spicy meatloaf topping. "Probably, but no one seems to know it. You're the cop, you find out."

"Have you spoken to anyone else about this woman? Do you have reason to believe she was in the park at the time of the murder? Does she dance every night, or at least on a regular basis?"

"No . . . not really . . . and I haven't a clue. You might ask Maddie. She seems to be out wandering the streets at night more than the average human being. Or for that matter, ask Charlene and Charlie. Or Jason. All I know is she was there the night before the murder at about the right time and in about the right place. If she was there at the same time Tuesday morning, she might have seen something. And if she saw something, she might be in danger."

Del pushed aside his empty plate and took out his wallet. "If this dancer witnessed a murder and the killer saw her, she might already be dead."

"Hey, wait up." The insistent voice came from behind Olivia as she passed in front of Frederick's, the men's clothing store. She spun around to find Ida, the waitress from Joe's Diner, hustling toward her. "You left so fast, I didn't get a chance to tell you something," Ida said. Years of toting heavy trays had kept her in good shape; her breathing was normal. "Joe said I could take my break early. There's something I want to tell you, and I don't want anyone listening in. Most people would think I'm crazy — maybe you will, too — but I know your mom, and she'd take me seriously."

At the mention of her mother as an understanding listener, Olivia mentally prepared for a story involving chakras and sit-ins. Ida, however, was well into her seventies, so Olivia told herself not to jump to conclusions. "Let's get out of the sun," she said.

Ida cast a nervous glance toward the town square, where the clue collectors had multiplied, divided into several groups, and spread across the length of the park. "Too crowded around here," she said. "Let's go to the playground. I like it there."

Not the suggestion Olivia expected, but it was close by and had a bench under an ancient oak tree. With Ida about three steps ahead, they walked to the old playground that had entertained schoolchildren up until a few years earlier, when the new Chatterley Heights Elementary School was built at the edge of town. Chatterley Heights lacked the resources to renovate the old brick school building, so it stood empty, its front door padlocked and windows boarded over.

Ida settled on an old wooden bench dotted with bird droppings. A few remaining strips of paint revealed the bench had once been red. With a repressed cringe, Olivia sat next to her. What the heck, she could wash up and change clothes before returning to the store. Ida's obvious anxiety had piqued her curiosity.

"Just so we're clear," Ida said, "I'm seventy-eight years old, but I've still got all the brains I was born with. I raised two kids, nursed a sick husband for ten years, and I traveled around the world after he passed on. I've seen a lot. But this . . ." Ida slid her hand into the deep pocket of her diner uniform. At first, Olivia wondered if she was searching for cigarettes, but Ida produced two pieces of hard candy. "Want one?" When Olivia shook her head, Ida said, "When I get nervous, I need butterscotch."

"I know what you mean."

Ida unwrapped a candy and popped it into her mouth. Her facial muscles relaxed.

"Ida, do you know something about the murder that happened in the park last night? Because if you do, it's really Sheriff Del you should be talking to. I can pass information on to him, of course, but he'll still want to hear it from you."

Shaking her head, Ida said, "It's not that simple." She unwrapped the second butterscotch candy and sucked on it like a drowning person desperate for air. Her hand dove into her pocket and resurfaced with two more wrapped candies.

Olivia began to wonder if she'd get back to The Gingerbread House before closing.

"Ghosts are real, you know." Ida had spoken with two candies in her mouth, so Olivia wondered if she'd heard right.

"Ida? Did you say . . . ?"

"Ghosts. I said ghosts. You're kind of young to be hard of hearing." Ida's tone had returned to feisty normal. "I know exactly how that sheriff would react if I told him what I'm about to tell you. Oh, he'd pretend to listen and maybe write something in that little notebook of his, only it'd probably be 'Call the loony bin, Ida's nuts.' But I know what I saw, and from the little bit I heard back at the diner, maybe you saw it, too."

Olivia's heart picked up speed. "Are you trying to tell me you've seen a woman dancing in the park? Because the sheriff would be most interested in hearing about that, believe me."

Ida inhaled another butterscotch. "I slaw . . ." She paused to swallow. "I saw a

196

ghost dancing in the park, is what I'm trying to say."

"Listen, Ida, if you saw someone in the park last night, you must tell Del. That woman could be a witness to murder."

"Ghosts can't witness to anything." Ida slapped her hands on her thighs, in a gesture of angry frustration. "Don't know why I bother. Young people today, no imagination. Your mother would listen to me."

Ida started to stand up, but Olivia grabbed her elbow and pulled her back down onto the bench. "Wait. Ida, I do believe in ghosts."

"You don't."

"Okay, I don't, but that doesn't matter. I do want to know what you saw. Because Maddie and I both saw a white figure dancing in the park the night before last, and I'll agree that she looked ghostlike."

"She was a ghost."

"Understood. Have a butterscotch and tell me what you saw. Please?"

"Let go of my arm."

"Well, okay." Olivia was half convinced Ida would run for it, but she complied.

Ida did move, but only to put some distance between herself and Olivia. "I wish your mom were here."

"Me, too," Olivia said with conviction.

Ida retrieved another candy. "My last one," she said, slitting her eyes at Olivia. "Don't interrupt." When Olivia nodded in assent, Ida nestled the wrapped butterscotch between her palms as if she were warming it, or perhaps drawing comfort from it. "After my husband died," she said, "I sold the house, cashed out the insurance money, and had me one heck of a trip around the world. Always wanted to do that. I didn't come back till I ran out of money. Anyway, it was fine while it lasted. Like I said, I've seen a lot in my seventy-eight years, and a lot of it was while I was on that trip." Ida studied Olivia's face. "You getting bored? Young people these days don't have much patience for long stories."

Olivia raised both hands in denial. "Nope. No boredom, none whatsoever."

"Well, anyway, it was traveling the world that made me understand about ghosts being real. Most other countries are lots older than we are, you know. I saw castles that were maybe a thousand years old and still standing. Mostly, anyway. When a place has been around that long, it collects whole families of ghosts. I met a lot of people who'd seen ghosts, talked to them even."

Olivia was having trouble following Ida's logic, but she said nothing.

"I know a ghost when I see one," Ida said. "And that's what I saw. More than once, too."

Olivia nodded and remained mute.

"You see, when I got back from my trip, I had no money and no house, so I figured I'd better get a job. Pete hired me back right away. Pete's a cranky old cuss, but he's got a heart. He advanced me enough money to rent a room. I'd planned to save until I had enough to maybe rent a little house, but I got so used to living in one room, I decided to save my money for another trip. I figure I'll have enough in another year or so." Ida opened her hands, smiled at her wrapped candy, and closed her hands around it again.

Olivia clenched her teeth to keep herself from checking her watch.

"Pete, bless him, he lets me eat free at the diner during the day and use the kitchen at night. I don't need much sleep, never did. Some nights I stay in the diner kitchen till maybe three or so in the morning, cooking up some dishes to eat when I'm not working. Then I take them home and heat them up in a microwave. That way I don't need my own kitchen. And that's how I came to see that ghost." Finally, Ida closed her mouth around her last piece of candy and closed her eyes.

Olivia sneaked a peek at her watch. One forty-five. She'd promised to be back in the store by one p.m. She hoped Maddie had asked Bertha to stay. Ellie would be beside herself waiting for Olivia to report to her about Jason.

Ida said, "Pete's kitchen has a small window looking out on the park. After I put a dish in the oven, I like to turn out the light, sip some coffee, and look out the window at the park in the moonlight."

Olivia began to relax, realizing that, finally, she was about to hear Ida's story.

"A few weeks or so ago, I saw something move on the south side of the band shell where the light reaches from the lamp. So I went to the window and kept a close watch. At first, I thought maybe I'd imagined the whole thing, or maybe it was just a stray dog running after a squirrel. Then I saw it again. It looked like swirling smoke — you know, like when a bonfire goes out? Only it didn't keep going up toward the sky; it swirled up and back down again like . . ."

"Like a dancer?"

"Exactly. A ghost dancer. Because I could see right through it, I knew it couldn't be a real live dancer."

Having broken her silence without mishap, Olivia ventured out again. "Could you describe the . . . the ghost to me? Was it wearing anything?"

Deep ridges formed down from the sides of her nose as Ida frowned in concentration. "Something white," she said. "It was kind of a see-through white, though, like there wasn't anything inside. Maybe the ghost put on a long veil so it could feel human again. Now I think of it, though, it did seem to have a head."

"Ida, would you say it was male or female? The ghost, I mean."

"Oh, it had to have been a girl in life," Ida said. "She was so graceful, like a real dancer. A boy would be more athletic. Anyway, it makes sense, given where she keeps appearing. I mean, she dances around the band shell like she's playing peekaboo with a boy, and we both know who that boy would have been." Ida's thin gray eyebrows lifted high, sending a wave of wrinkles rippling across her forehead.

"Um. . . ."

"Oh, you young people, with your computers and your pie-phones."

"I think you might mean iPhones?"

"That's what I said. You have no sense of history. Didn't you ever hear the stories about Frederick P. Chatterley? He had an eye for the ladies, you know, especially the pretty young ones. You should hear the stories my grandmother used to tell me, though I had to swear not to tell my mother, of course."

With a sigh of pleasure, Ida drifted off into her memories. As much as Olivia wanted to hear those stories about the seamier side of the town's founding father, she wanted more information about the dancer in the park. "Ida, you said the girl ghost keeps appearing. How often did you see her?"

"Oh goodness, I lost count. I stay in the diner to cook maybe two or three times a week. Except some nights I don't stay late enough. She doesn't show up before midnight. I think she must be haunting the park because of something that happened to her in the wee hours of the morning. And I'll bet you anything it has something to do with Frederick P. —"

"How long does she stay?" Olivia could no longer contain her impatience, but it didn't seem to matter.

"You see, that's why I'm sure something happened to her in the park, because she starts dancing right after midnight and disappears into the ether by about one thirty in the morning. She simply lifts up and evaporates." Ida checked her watch and began to gather up her small pile of shiny yellow candy wrappers. "Well, except for that one time, of course," she said as she walked to the trash bin.

"Wait. What time? What happened?"

Ida dumped her wrappers in the bin and said, "Gotta get back to work."

"I'll walk with you."

"Step on it, then," Ida said. "I can't afford to lose this job." As they walked past the rusty jungle gym, she said, "They ought to take that thing down. A kid could get hurt on it. Not that I've seen a kid in this playground since the new school got built."

"So you were saying . . . about the time the dancer was off schedule?"

"Don't get a bee in your bonnet, I'm trying to remember. I think it was a week ago, maybe two. I do remember the ghost hadn't been dancing for very long, so it probably wasn't even one a.m. yet. She did one of those steps where she kind of leaped and spun in a circle and then balanced on one leg with one arm stretched out. You know what I mean?"

"Sort of." Olivia vowed to learn more about ballet. Maddie would know. "Then what happened?"

"Something grabbed her. I couldn't see what it was, but it was dark and strong, probably a demon. The ghost tried to get away. I could see her struggling, but the thing was really strong. It got hold of both her wrists and started dragging her." Ida chuckled, which so surprised Olivia that she tripped on a section of broken sidewalk. She recovered her balance to find Ida eyeing her with amusement. "You must take after your father," Ida said.

"I guess I was startled when you laughed just now," Olivia said, trying to sound curious rather than defensive. In many ways, she did take after her father, whose clumsiness was the stuff of family legend. However, Olivia told herself, she rarely walked into walls. So there.

"Oh that," Ida said. "I laughed because I was remembering how that little spirit got away. You'd hardly think she could do it without any substance to her, but when the evil thing lifted her off the ground by her shoulders — or what would have been her shoulders, if ghosts had shoulders. . . . Anyway, she was off the ground when she sort of arched her back and then kicked him so hard he dropped her. She was gone in a flash."

Olivia grew quiet as they approached Pete's Diner. She felt uneasy with the thought that Ida had witnessed an attempted assault and hadn't thought to call the police.

As she opened the diner door, Ida said, "You can tell that sheriff what I've told you, but I won't talk to him about it. He wouldn't believe me, anyway, and I've got enough problems with my kids thinking I'm senile and wanting to put me in a home."

"Del wouldn't —"

"Like I said, ghosts can't be witnesses. Besides, if a powerful demon couldn't pin down that dancing sprite, no human policeman has a chance."

"That may be," Olivia said, "but if you remember anything you haven't told me about the dancer in the park or the . . . whatever it was that grabbed her, it's your duty to call the police. A man was killed last night. We need to let the authorities decide what is evidence and what isn't."

"Well, they can do it without me." The door to Pete's Diner closed with a slam.

Chapter Ten

"So you're saying that Ida witnessed an attempted assault and failed to report it?" Del's irritation came through clearly on Olivia's cell. She paused on the sidewalk as two men carrying suit bags exited Frederick's of Chatterley. This was a conversation she wanted to finish before arriving back at her own place of business.

"Del, don't be too hard on Ida; she's a total believer in ghosts and goblins. There was no reasoning with her. Besides, I think she has given us some important information, even if we can't prove it yet. Now we know that the unidentified dancer goes to the park at more or less the same time on a more or less regular basis. Maddie and I saw her after the encounter that Ida described, so we know she wasn't scared off by it."

"Which might say more about her sanity than her courage," Del said.

"Point taken." Olivia had almost reached The Gingerbread House, so she stopped under a tree to finish her call. "Either way, we know the dancer encountered a man who tried to assault her, and it's likely that man was Geoffrey King. We know he'd been hanging around The Vegetable Plate at night, and we know he was violent. Who knows, maybe he made a habit of accosting any woman he met."

"Did you say you thought the dancer's hair was white?" Del asked.

"That's what Maddie said, and Ida mentioned a white head, too. They might have been fooled by a veil of some sort, though." When Maddie appeared in the front window of The Gingerbread House, hands on her hips, Olivia said, "Del, I need to get back to work. Why did you ask about the dancer's hair color?"

"Because Geoffrey King, from what we're learning about him, didn't strike me as the kind of guy who'd pay any attention to a woman older than late twenties. He seems to have left behind a string of angry sweet-young-things."

"Lots of suspects," Olivia said. "Anyway, he might not have been interested in her. Maybe he was threatening her." Maddie started waving her arms toward Olivia.

"Gotta go, Del. Maddie is having a breakdown."

"I thought you'd never get back." Maddie tried and failed to rake her fingers through her wildly disarranged hair. "You wouldn't believe . . ."

Olivia took it seriously when Maddie was not her usual what-me-worry? self. "What's wrong?"

"You would not believe . . ."

"Yes, we've covered that. Now tell me what's wrong." Olivia pulled Maddie by the wrist through the store and into the kitchen, where she pushed her frazzled friend onto a chair. Handing her a cup of coffee, Olivia said, "Okay, deep breath, that's it. Now speak."

Maddie took a swallow of coffee and said, "I'm all right. All morning I've been panting to hear everything about Jason and the murder, but now we've got a situation on our hands. And yes, I take responsibility. I should have started the cookies earlier, and I should never have planned that stupid vegetable event just to poke fun at Charlene. So it's all my fault, I'm a terrible businesswoman, mea culpa. See? I can speak some French, too."

"That was Latin," Olivia said and wished

at once that she hadn't. Maddie looked like she might be on the verge of tears. Olivia pulled over a chair and sat facing her. "Maddie, Maddie, friend of my youth and forever, you can tell me. What's going on? Has something happened to Lucas? Or your aunt Sadie?"

"No, nothing like that." With an impatient shake of her head, Maddie increased the volume of her hair by a third. "It's about the baby shower at Gwen and Herbie's this evening. Gwen called. You know that Heather was supposed to host the shower, right? I mean, they are neighbors and best friends, too. Well, Heather called Gwen and said she'd come down with a bad sore throat. Gwen said she sounded really bad. With Gwen being so pregnant, there's no way she could risk getting a bad virus. What if something happened to the baby? So Gwen asked if I could take over and run the show from their house, Herbie and Gwen's. I said 'sure,' because I figured I'd have time to decorate the cookies and get them dry enough to transport, and Bertha could take care of the store."

"Okay, so what's the hitch?"

"Well, first we've been busier than usual because of the murder last night and you finding the body. Bertha was here, and your mom showed up to help while you were talking to Jason, but I swear some customers were only here to pump your mom about you and the body and Jason. So I was out on the floor all morning and through lunch. Your mom wants to hear every detail of your visit with Jason in jail, by the way."

So much was happening so fast, Olivia felt as if her visit to her jailed brother must have taken place yesterday. And her mother was still waiting to hear about it. "And . . . ?" she asked.

After a huge sigh, Maddie said, "And I promised Gwen I'd deliver the cookies by about four and stay to help her set up. She wasn't expecting to host the shower at their house, and what with her being so very, very pregnant . . ."

Olivia glanced up at the clock over the sink. "So we have about an hour and a half to finish decorating the cookies? They won't all be dry, but we can lay them out in cake pans for transport. They will probably be fine for a seven p.m. event. I know you finished some cookies this morning. How many are left to be decorated?"

"Um. . . ." Maddie's eyes swiveled around the kitchen worktable, which was covered with cooling racks of undecorated cookies. The kitchen counter, behind them, was lined with more plain, baked cookies on sheets of parchment paper. Then Maddie cast a bereft glance at the refrigerator. Olivia guessed it held many, many more cut-out shapes yet to be iced. "I finished six," Maddie said. "So, well, seven and a half dozen."

"But I thought you'd decorated several dozen on Sunday. Or was it Monday?"

"Both," Maddie said. "But most of them were, um, fruit and vegetable shapes. I thought I'd have plenty of time to make baby shower shapes, and I did get them all baked. Well, mostly. I defrosted a couple dozen round shapes to fill out the order for eight dozen. I figured I could pipe some smiling baby faces on those. Or something. I'm really, really sorry, Livie."

Olivia missed her mentor and friend, Clarisse Chamberlain. Clarisse would have told her not to waste time on recriminations, face problems head-on, and when all else fails, chalk it up to experience. "Maddie, my friend," Olivia said, "when the going gets tough, the tough start decorating cookies. Here's the plan." She emptied the grounds from their Mr. Coffee and inserted a clean filter. "You rev up that mixer and churn out some royal icing while I check in with Mom about Jason. I'll keep it brief; there isn't much hopeful news. We will decorate like crazy for an hour, which is all we'll have by then. I can rig something up in my PT Cruiser to transport the cookies, and I'll deliver whatever we've finished by four. I'll stay and help Gwen prep her house for the shower while you finish up the cookies."

Maddie was already yanking royal icing ingredients off shelves. "I can drive the rest of the cookies to Gwen and Herbie's farm after I close, but I can't be in the store helping customers. Can you entice Bertha to stay the afternoon?"

"I'll see what I can do."

While Maddie snapped the beaters into the mixer, Olivia poked her head into the store. Bertha was behind the sales counter ringing up a sale. Olivia joined her and bagged a set of cookie cutters for a customer who was checking her watch. Before another customer could move within earshot, Olivia said, "Bertha, remember when you mentioned you could handle the store on your own for a while if Maddie and I got tied up with events? Well, now's your chance. We're in a crunch with this baby shower, so how about time-and-a-half for this afternoon, plus managerial experience, plus our undying gratitude?"

Doubt flickered in Bertha's eyes as she

asked, "I'd love to try, but would I be completely alone?"

Business had lightened up since that morning. The customers who remained were skimming cookbooks and examining cookie cutters with genuine interest. One woman was taking a close look at the red mixer with so many attachments even Maddie didn't know what they all did. "Maddie will be working in the kitchen until closing," Olivia said, "in case you have an emergency question. And I thought I'd talk to my mom about . . ." As if Ellie had heard, she emerged from the cookbook nook, spotted Olivia, and aimed right for her. From Ellie's expression, it was clearly time to break the news about Jason's insistence that he had murdered Geoffrey King. "Hang on, Bertha, I'll be back in a few minutes."

Olivia met her mother halfway and said, "Let's talk in private." Olivia led the way out the front door and into the foyer, where she unlocked the door leading to her apartment. At the top of the stairs, she unlocked her apartment. A ball of fur catapulted through the door the instant it opened. Olivia grabbed Spunky's middle as he flew past. "I banished him to the apartment this morning before racing off to visit Jason." Holding the whimpering, squirming dog, she led her mother to the living room.

"Let me," Ellie said, taking Spunky from Olivia's grasp. The Yorkie calmed down at once. Olivia was impressed. Even in her agitated state, her mother could calm a beast driven to escape.

"I'm sorry it's been so frantic," Olivia said, "and it's about to get more so. Mom, I'm really sorry, but I have to get right back down to help Maddie in the kitchen. We've got a crisis with Gwen and Herbie's shower. Could you possibly help Bertha mind the store this afternoon? Maddie will be in the kitchen working like a madwoman until —"

"Yes, of course I will, but what about Jason?"

"Jason . . ." Olivia threw up her hands and flopped down on the sofa. "Jason is an idiot."

"At the moment, I'd have to agree with you," Ellie said as she sat next to Olivia. Spunky settled in her lap and curled into a ball. "So I assume he won't recant his ridiculous confession?"

"Nope. And he still won't talk to you or Allan."

"Oh Livie, what are we going to do? How can we get Jason out of this horrible mess?" Tears filled Ellie's eyes and spilled down her cheeks. Spunky sat up in her lap and whimpered.

Fighting her own tears, Olivia put an arm around her mother's shoulders. "I don't know. I'll find a way." It was a rash promise, but failure was unthinkable.

"How are we going to spring your brother from jail?" Maddie asked as she piped a pink yawn onto a round baby-face cookie.

"Cute," Olivia said, glancing at the cookie. She was relieved that Maddie, after her bout of panic and guilt, had thrown herself into the task of decorating nearly eight dozen cookies in less than three hours. Together, they'd been able to finish almost two dozen already, and it was only two forty-five. "I'm afraid Jason will have to experience incarceration for some time, since he refuses to help himself. It'll take time to dig up anything that might be useful."

"But you have a plan, right?" Maddie looked up from the sparse blue hair she was piping onto another round baby-face cookie.

"Nope."

"You have no plan? That's worrisome," Maddie said. "What did Del have to say?"

"That his hands are tied." Olivia hated to keep secrets, especially since Maddie could be very helpful with problem solving. However, a promise was a promise. Del would stop trusting her if she revealed anything that might affect his investigation. On the other hand, there was no law against being sneaky. "Until I think of something, maybe we should work on our own mystery — what happened to Clarisse's Duesenberg cookie cutter?"

"I looked everywhere I could think of," Maddie said. "Unfortunately, I've run out of places to search. I mentioned it to Bertha — casually, so she wouldn't get upset. She hadn't seen it, didn't even know it had disappeared." Maddie picked up a cookie she had just finished. "You'll love this one."

"Hm?" Olivia was piping red and navy dots on a baby carriage.

"Who does this remind you of?" Maddie held the cookie under Olivia's gaze. It looked like a baby face with blue dots for eyes, messy clumps of yellow hair, and a jagged red mouth.

"Now that's just mean," Olivia said.

"Yet cathartic. I'd eat it, but we need every cookie." Maddie placed baby Charlene next to a pink-and-red teddy bear.

Olivia added her baby carriage to the row. "How sure are you that Charlene won't be at the baby shower this evening?"

"Positive. Gwen gave me the invitation list, in case I was inspired to match any cookies to guests or their kids."

"Can I see that list?"

"Sure, as long as you read and decorate simultaneously and with equal efficiency." Maddie opened a kitchen drawer and drew out a folded sheet of paper, which she unfolded and placed next to Olivia. "We are on this list, in case you were worried."

Olivia selected a baby bootie for her next project and gathered pastry bags of baby blue and navy icing. Since Gwen and Herbie had declined to learn their baby's sex, Olivia and Maddie had decided to use a variety of icing colors. Before removing the covers from the metal tips, she put aside her pastry bags to look through the names on Gwen's list. Charlene Critch wasn't there, as Maddie had promised, and neither were Charlie Critch and Olivia's brother, Jason. Her mother and stepfather were listed with "regrets" next to their names. They would be too upset to feel like socializing. Otherwise, at least half the people on the list had been in The Gingerbread House during the infamous "harvest" event on Tuesday.

"Excellent," Olivia said, picking up her bag of baby blue icing. "I feel the onset of a plan."

"Oh goodie," said Maddie. "Do I get to help?"

"Check in with me when you bring the rest of the cookies to Gwen and Herbie's house. By then I should know if it's a dud."

Olivia parked her silver PT Cruiser in the alley outside the kitchen of The Gingerbread House. She had bought it used, in excellent condition, and she loved its roominess. She'd splurged and had The Gingerbread House logo painted on both sides. Whenever she opened the car door, she smelled a faint spiciness left over from the dozens of decorated cookies she and Maddie had delivered to private events.

By three thirty, Olivia and Maddie had managed to finish decorating four dozen of the eight dozen cookies for the Tuckers' baby shower. Olivia had packed them in single layers inside sheet cake pans to allow the icing to continue to harden. She wedged the pans in the back seat so they wouldn't shift around during transport.

Before starting the car, she took a small flashlight from her pocket and wedged it into the glove compartment. Having learned her lesson the night before, she'd called Lucas at the hardware and asked him to drop off half a dozen flashlights of various sizes.

Gwen and Herbie Tucker owned a small farm west of town, about a fifteen-minute drive from The Gingerbread House. Olivia checked her watch. It was already ten minutes to four, but she couldn't afford to speed, in case she hit a bump and sent the cookies flying. Before starting the PT's engine, she called the Tuckers' number from her cell and left a message that she was on her way.

Olivia barely noticed the scenery. The part of her brain not engaged in avoiding bumps in the road was busy trying out questions to ask the baby shower guests. She wished she could have gotten some information from Jason. Drat that boy. Didn't he care how much trouble he was in? Or what he was doing to his mother and stepfather? How could he have gotten so hung up on Charlene that he'd even consider sacrificing his life on the off chance she'd killed her ex-husband?

Or did Jason know for certain that Charlene killed Geoffrey King?

As Olivia turned onto the long driveway to the Tucker farm, she asked herself one last question: Might Jason have killed Geoffrey King in an attempt to protect the woman he loved? Could he have been so stupid and misguided? As much as she loved

her brother, her answer to her own question
was a firm *yes*.

CHAPTER ELEVEN

Gwen Tucker opened the front door of her nineteenth-century farmhouse, took a pan of cookies from Olivia's hands, and said, "If it's a girl, I'll name her Olivia."

Following Gwen through a foyer crammed with muddy boots, Olivia said, "My brother calls me Olive Oyl. Just information you might want to consider."

Gwen's laugh had a frantic edge. "Maybe it will be a boy. I could name him Oliver." She slid the pan onto an already crowded kitchen counter. "Although one of our dogs is named Oliver, so that might be confusing. Anyway, I want you to know how incredibly grateful we are to you and Maddie for pinch-hitting today. Poor Heather, she sounded awful on the phone. Here it is, hotter than jalapeno, and she manages to get the flu."

Olivia flashed back to their store event on Tuesday and Heather's rosy cheeks. Maybe she hadn't been wearing makeup after all. "I fervently hope no one caught Heather's virus yesterday," she said. "That was quite a crowd we had."

"I'm drinking orange juice and hoping my flu shot still works." Gwen began to arrange cookies on large plates. "These look irresistible, as always. However, I shall resist, at least for now. I don't think my skin will stretch any farther." She was about five feet tall, and her current width looked a close second to her height.

"How can I help?" Olivia asked.

"I'm afraid the house needs some straightening. We've been so busy lately, what with preparing for the baby and moving Paws to our big barn." Both Gwen and Herbie were vet techs with a dream. They had opened the Chatterley Paws no-kill animal shelter about three years earlier and quickly found they needed more space. "That's the thing about a no-kill policy," Gwen said. "We spay and neuter our animals, but that only slows down the inevitable. Lately we've been getting pets from families who can't afford them anymore. It's so sad. I don't suppose you'd like a kitten? Or two?"

"Um . . . Bertha Binkman is allergic to cats, so no, but I'll spread the word."

"Maybe Maddie — ?"

"Did you mention something about a bathroom that needs cleaning? Point me to the noxious chemicals and I'll get to it. Can't have you breathing that stuff."

By five thirty p.m., Olivia had cleaned two bathrooms, decorated the living room, and made a bowl of punch. While arranging chairs, she realized there were only enough for ten guests. She found Gwen in the kitchen, cutting sandwiches into animal shapes.

"Oh gosh," Gwen said, "Heather was going to bring a bunch along with her. She keeps a huge supply of folding chairs for family picnics, and she carts them around in her truck. What can we do? Guests are arriving in less than two hours."

"I hate to bother Heather when she's not well," Olivia said, "but maybe I could drive to her place and pick up the chairs myself?"

"Oh, would you? That would be perfect. And you wouldn't have to bother her because I know where she stores the chairs — in the small barn way at the back of her property. Not the big barn behind her house; that's where she keeps her horse. She adores horses, you know. And cats, thank goodness. Just follow the gravel drive past the big barn to the beginning of a grove of trees, and you'll see the small barn. Heather never locks that barn because there's nothing of value in it. I mean, I guess the chairs are valuable, but they aren't books or horses. That's all Heather cares about, books and horses."

"You're sure I shouldn't call and warn her?"

"Totally sure. Even if she hears your car, she'll see the painting of The Gingerbread House on the side, and she'll know you're helping me. You're an angel to do this, Olivia. I will never, ever buy a cookie cutter from anyone but you and Maddie. I'd hug you, but . . ." She pointed to her rotund middle and laughed.

Heather Irwin's farm was several miles down the road from Gwen and Herbie's, in an isolated area of the countryside. Whereas the Tuckers had neighbors across the street, Heather was able to look out any window in her old farmhouse and see nothing but fields and trees. It was an ideal setting for a shy woman who loved books and horses.

Olivia turned onto the gravel drive that wound past Heather's place. She braked for a moment and rolled down her window, still wondering if she should let Heather know what she was doing. The quiet, dark house convinced her to drive on. If Heather had managed to fall asleep, it was better to leave her alone.

The drive curved in back of Heather's house to skirt around a large maroon barn. Like the farmhouse, the barn looked recently painted and in good repair. Olivia heard a horse whinny as she drove past. The gravel thinned and mixed with hard dirt as Olivia traveled through the middle of a fallow field toward the copse of trees where the small barn nestled. She wondered if the trees might once have marked a boundary between properties. The building's orientation seemed odd, facing into the trees rather than back toward Heather's house. The fields behind the barn had all gone fallow in a wild way, as if no one cared.

The little barn had seen better days, though maybe not much better. It looked like it was hand built by an amateur. Only a few remnants of brown paint dotted a door barely large enough to allow more than one animal at a time to enter. The door was unlatched. Olivia carefully wedged it open — she didn't trust the rusty hinges to hold it upright.

Little daylight penetrated the small, dirty windows, and the air smelled of rotting hay. Olivia heard the unmistakable rustling of little rodent feet scurrying to escape the human intruder. She decided it was best not to dawdle. The folding chairs were easy to locate. They leaned against the wall in neat stacks of four, close to the door. Ten stacks added up to forty chairs. The baby shower invitation list had contained about fifty guests, and most had accepted. The PT Cruiser could hold a lot, but it didn't have the capacity of a truck. Olivia decided to pack in as many as possible, and that would have to do.

Carrying four chairs at a time proved painful. On her first try, one chair slid from the middle of the stack and directly onto Olivia's big toe. She held on to the other three and limped to her car. Transporting two chairs at a time, she filled her trunk, then packed the back seat so high she wouldn't be able to see out her rear window. She thought she'd wedge a few more on the floor of the passenger's side of the front seat and then call it quits.

Olivia reentered the barn and picked up three chairs at a time, hoping to make this her last trip. Burning pain seared through the shoulder she had injured some months earlier in a car accident. She lowered her burden to the floor and closed her eyes, willing the pain to subside. As it eased, she became aware of an odor in the stale air, besides the natural ones she'd already learned to ignore. She smelled coffee.

Opening her eyes, Olivia slowly swiveled her head, trying to locate the direction of the odor. *This is silly, I don't have time for this.* But coffee? In a virtually empty, unused barn? Heather must have visited recently and dumped the remains of a cup of coffee on the dirt floor. Not today, though, if she was as ill as Gwen said she was. How long would the smell of coffee linger in the air, given the competition from ranker odors? An hour or two? Surely not an entire day. It wouldn't hurt to go fetch that new flashlight she'd put in her glove compartment and check out the source. She was probably making a big deal out of nothing, but given the unsolved murder hanging over the town, she'd feel better if she had a quick look around that barn.

The bright, hot daylight steadied her. Feeling silly, she dug out her little red flashlight and wedged it into the back pocket of her khaki pants. Back inside the barn, Olivia switched on the flashlight and began to explore. The rodents, she hoped, would be in hiding.

At first Olivia saw nothing in the barn that aroused her curiosity, only an abandoned pile of hay in one corner and a couple of tractor attachments she couldn't put names to; she wouldn't know a combine if it ran over her. Otherwise, the barn looked empty, with the exception of two stalls along the opposite wall. The door to one stall hung open, and the other was latched shut.

Olivia checked her watch, which she should have done earlier. She'd already spent nearly forty minutes on her errand. Gwen would be getting anxious for her to return. Okay, a quick check of the stalls, and if she found nothing, she would leave the coffee puzzle unsolved. Olivia crossed the barn and ran her flashlight around the insides of the open stall. The coffee smell was stronger, but she saw no evidence of any in the stall.

Olivia moved to the closed door of the second stall. She lifted the latch, then dropped it and jumped sideways as two rats ran past her feet to escape into the barn. Through the thudding in her head, Olivia listened for more scuttling sounds. After some moments of silence, she clutched the latch and rattled it. Three more rats ran out under the door. Olivia figured that any rodents left in the stall were either dead or armed. She knew she had to look inside, if only to convince herself there was nothing of importance to see.

The hinges creaked as Olivia swung the stall door open. *Geez, could this get more melodramatic?* She poked her head inside far enough to see one back corner, which she illuminated with her flashlight. What she saw explained the stale coffee smell — a landslide of paper coffee cups, some scrunched, others tossed with coffee still in them. Next to the pile stood one lone ceramic cup with its own brewing attachment. A pile of coffee grounds had been dumped next to it. Since the barn had no obvious source of electricity, the cup must have been brought from somewhere nearby. Heather's house, perhaps? Or there might be another farmhouse through the trees, if the barn had once belonged with another property.

Olivia stepped inside the stall and aimed her flashlight at the other back corner of the stall, where a blanket was spread over a lumpy pile. Olivia felt more curious than leery; she'd read enough police procedurals to know that her nose would probably have told her by now if the blanket hid a body. She'd already left her fingerprints all over the place, so she lifted a corner of the blanket and took a peek. Her flashlight revealed what looked like a collection of belongings. By now, she'd forgotten about the time. She gently peeled the blanket back.

"My, my, my," Olivia whispered. "What have we here?" She'd expected to see personal items, such as worn, used clothing, shoes, maybe a backpack. What she found was not what one would expect a homeless person to carry . . . unless that person was also a thief.

Olivia didn't touch anything, since it was unlikely the thief had bothered to clean off fingerprints. She settled on her knees and played her light around the pile. She saw a man's dress shirt with the tag still on it. The only store in town that carried such an expensive line of men's clothing was Fred's. A silky pink negligee with lace on the bodice might have come from Lady Chatterley's. A bottle of eighteen-year-old Glenlivet scotch, its seal broken, rested inside a silver wine bucket with Bon Vivant etched across the front. This was no ordinary thief. Stealing expensive scotch required skill, as did swiping a wine bucket from an upscale restaurant. There was more, but Olivia didn't dare move anything.

As she reached to replace the blanket, Olivia spotted a splotch of red through an opening deeper inside the pile, behind the silver bucket. Her light didn't reach it, but even in shadow the red looked too bright for blood. She inched closer for a better look. The object looked round with an indentation in the middle, from which a bit of brown protruded. For some reason, the shape reminded Olivia of a decorated cookie. It looked so familiar, as if she'd seen it before.

A stem. Of course. The brown bit was a stem protruding from the red flesh of an apple. No, not an apple. A tomato. Olivia knew where she had seen the object before. She didn't have to dig it out of the pile to know that the tomato decorated the handle of a knife sharp enough to peel an apple . . . or kill a man. The knife was part of a four-piece set owned by Charlene Critch.

Olivia dropped the blanket and ran from the barn, leaving behind the last three folding chairs.

"I'm telling you, Del, I didn't need to see the whole thing to know it was a knife from Charlene's set."

"You aren't driving, are you?" Del sounded worried.

"Oh, honestly, I have one little accident and suddenly I'm a menace to myself and others. All right, fine, I'll pull over. Don't hang up."

"Wouldn't dream of it."

Olivia found a gravel turnaround and shifted into park. "Okay, here's what I think," she said. "Geoffrey King must have stolen the knife, probably as a sort of veiled threat to Charlene. I mean, from what I've heard about him, he resented losing his rich wife, so it makes sense he'd steal whatever he could from her. Especially if he could make her fearful that he might use one of those knives to hurt her or her brother."

"Did you see anything that directly connected the items to Geoffrey King?"

"Who else would go around Chatterley Heights stealing expensive items? That had to be King's stash. Besides, I'm sure there's DNA and fingerprints all over the place." Olivia heard a car door slam in the background. "You don't intend to drive while we're talking, do you?"

"I'm allowed," Del said. "Or I could hang up, if that would make you more comfortable."

"Ah, but then you wouldn't hear the rest of my report." Olivia told him everything else she could remember, including the presence of a ceramic cup used to brew fresh coffee. "Maybe King stole the cup from Charlene, too. Or he must have found a way into Heather's house. Heather seems too cautious to hand a house key to someone she just met. Anyway, from the looks of that stall, King was seriously hooked on coffee."

Del said, "King might have offered to do some handyman work around the house so Heather would give him a key during the day."

"Geoffrey King? Handyman work? Wouldn't Heather get suspicious when nothing got done? She's quiet, but she isn't dense. And wouldn't she have noticed him coming and going from her barn? From the pile of paper coffee cups, he could easily have spent a couple of weeks holed up in that barn. Del, was one of those knives used to kill King?"

Del didn't answer.

Olivia switched on her ignition. "I intend to drive again, so I'd better hang up or you'll have me arrested. Be considerate when you get to Heather's place. She has some awful bug, so don't scare her with sirens. The house was dark when I left. She probably knocked herself out with cold medication, and she is undoubtedly contagious. If you give me whatever bug she's got, I'll have to kill you."

"Understood. Just in case, I'll wear a surgical mask when we go out to dinner on

Friday."

"Friday . . . ?" Olivia began. But Del's cell had gone dead.

It was six p.m. by the time Olivia reached the turn-in for the short drive leading to Gwen and Herbie Tucker's house. Only one hour to go before baby shower time. Her anxiety eased when she saw a little yellow Volkswagen and a red truck parked side-by-side near the side entrance. Gwen and Herbie owned the truck, so Herbie must have found someone to watch over the animals still residing at the Chatterley Paws shelter in town. He and Gwen were in the process of moving their furry charges to the renovated barn on their property. Maddie owned the yellow VW, which meant she'd finished the decorated cookie order in record time.

Maddie emerged from the side entrance and sprinted over to Olivia's car. "I'm to help you carry folding chairs," she said. "Where have you been so long? Gwen is frantic. I'm afraid that baby will pop just to get some rest. Thank goodness Gwen invited her obstetrician." Maddie hauled three chairs from the PT Cruiser's trunk.

Olivia lifted out two more chairs. "Don't run off," she said. "I've got a lot to tell you about why I was late getting back."

Maddie's eyes widened. "About the murder? Speak at once."

"Probably about the victim, anyway. Also, I have a plan for us, so we'll be multitasking this evening."

"Goody," Maddie said. "I am the queen of multitasking."

While they carried folding chairs into the house, Olivia gave Maddie a quick, quiet summary of Ida's story of the dancing ghost, the stolen items she'd found in Heather's barn, her conversation with Del, and the information she hoped the two of them could gather while they helped host the Tucker baby shower.

"Our timing is exquisite," Maddie said. "There's nothing like decorated cookies to quell suspicions and loosen lips."

"Except maybe wine, of which I saw several cases chilling in the basement."

"I'll take these last two chairs," Maddie said. "Your shoulder has been through enough. Besides, I'm younger."

"By mere months, but thanks for your concern." As she held open the side door for Maddie, Olivia asked, "Are we good to go? Any questions?"

"Ready and eager. Let's meet afterward to share information."

"Good idea," Olivia said. "My place, pizza

and merlot. It'll have to be frozen pizza, I'm afraid."

"Not to worry, I'll stop at the grocery on the way and pick up a few little enhancements."

By seven p.m., guests began arriving at Gwen and Herbie's house, parking wherever they could find a spot. The lawn would need reseeding. By eight, at least forty people had packed themselves into the house for the gift opening, after which many wandered outdoors to breathe. The cookies were gone and the wine half drunk, but Olivia hadn't managed to pry any useful information from the guests. She missed having her mother there to make gentle suggestions, but she understood why Ellie and Allan had declined the invitation. Fielding the inevitable questions about Jason's predicament would have been agony.

At least Maddie seemed to be making some headway. She'd flashed a thumbs-up at Olivia twice already. Noting that the wine supply was dwindling, Olivia made her way downstairs to get a few more bottles. When she returned to the kitchen, she found a tall, middle-aged woman using the bright light over the sink to check her makeup in her compact mirror. The woman arched her eyebrows unusually high, as if she were practicing a surprised expression. When she caught sight of Olivia, she said, "Why, it's Livie Greyson, isn't it?"

"I'm afraid I —"

"Oh, of course you don't recognize me. You were a tiny slip of a girl when I left Chatterley Heights. Of course, I wasn't much more than that myself, but, well, the years do march on, don't they? And now, here you are all grown up and then some, and I'm home again." She heaved a dramatic sigh.

Olivia noticed that the woman's eyebrows had remained arched throughout her speech. They were fixed in place, almost certainly by a surfeit of cosmetic surgery.

"Oh but I must reintroduce myself. I am Lenora Dove." She made her pronouncement as if there were nothing more to be said. When Olivia gave her a blank look, the corners of her scarlet lips drooped. "Well, I can see you are not a movie fan," she said. "Young people these days seem to prefer squinting into a tiny computer screen to reveling in the big screen. Lenora Dove is my screen name, though Lenora is also my given name. In private life, I am Mrs. Bertie Bouchenbein, though you might remember me as Lenora Tucker."

"Of course," Olivia said, "you are Herbie's aunt Len! I heard you were moving back to town. I'm so sorry about your husband. I never met him, but I'm sure you miss him deeply."

"Oh, I do indeed." As Lenora tilted her head in sadness, her sculpted dark blond curls remained glued in place. "By the way," she said, "I go only by Lenora now."

"Of course." Olivia wondered how long that would last. Old nicknames die hard. "Have you been back in town long?"

"For only a week," Lenora said, "but such an eventful week it has been. Brutal strangers and murders and arrests. . . ."

"Only one of each, actually." Olivia sounded defensive; she vowed to be more careful.

"I'm so sorry, I forgot the young man arrested is your brother. He wasn't even born when I left to seek my fortune in Hollywood. Such years. . . . I had parts in several films, you know, and I have it on the best authority that they will be reissued on DVD at any moment. That's all I had time for, though, only a few films, and then I met the love of my life, Bertie Bouchenbein. He was twenty years older than I, but what is age? A mere number. He cast me in a film he was producing, and the rest is marital history." Lenora touched a tissue to her cheek to imply emotion. "However, I am delighted to be back home."

Olivia did not doubt that statement. According to Herbie, Uncle Bertie and Aunt Len spent every penny they earned as fast as they could. Bertie died penniless and without life insurance.

"Your dear brother — what was his name again? Jake? Jimmy?"

"Jason."

"Yes, of course. Dear Jason will be vindicated. I feel it in my very being. I am quite sensitive, you know. It helped me enormously in all my acting roles. I am certain that nasty young man was killed by someone from the underworld. A loan shark, perhaps. He struck me as a grasping, greedy sort, and that type always needs money."

"You *met* him?"

"Didn't I mention that? I will never rid myself of the memory of that experience. A detestable young man. I met him briefly in that store, the one with all the vegetables."

"The Vegetable Plate. Charlene Critch owns it."

"Exactly. I am a vegetarian, you know. That's how I keep my slender figure. I visited little Charlene's vegetable patch late one evening and found the front door open.

The store was dark, but since I was in need of some items, I ventured inside. I heard voices behind a door, loud voices. I surmised the door must lead to a kitchen. I opened it and peeked inside. My goodness, what a scene met my gaze! They weren't aware of me at first, so I heard more than perhaps I should have, but really, it was just like walking in on a filming. Although of course it is nearly impossible to interrupt the actual filming of a movie scene. I remember once I —"

"So you heard Charlene and someone arguing?"

"I did indeed. That sylphlike girl was protecting herself from a man. He was tall and strong . . . quite well built, actually. But so very angry. Charlene was holding him off with a long knife. There was some sort of decoration at the top of the knife, but I only got a glimpse of the color. It was red, blood-red. The man was telling her she had to give him money or some other man was going to kill him. I naturally assumed he was talking about a loan shark situation. Years ago I had a part in a movie called *Dark, Dark City.* It was never released, some nonsense about a stolen script, but anyway, there were several unsavory characters threatening the hero with a slow, gruesome death because he couldn't pay back a loan."

"The man who was threatening Charlene, do you remember exactly what he said to her?" Olivia poured two glasses of wine and handed one to Lenora.

"I might." Lenora downed her wine and handed the empty glass to Olivia, who refilled it. "I'm very good at memorizing dialogue, you know. Let's see. . . ." She took a gulp from her second glass of wine. "Let me visualize the scene . . ." She closed her eyes. "The man was trying to grab little Charlene, who was fending him off with the knife. Then he said, 'If you don't give it to me, someone will arrive here from DC. He will be large and armed, and he'll be coming to kill me. Only I won't go down alone, you put that in your stupid noggin.' And then Charlene said, 'I hope he does kill you. If you don't leave Charlie alone, I'll point the guy in your direction.' I could never forget such great lines." Lenora drained her glass and held it out to Olivia. "I wouldn't mind another," she said.

While she filled Lenora's glass a third time, Olivia said, "You need to tell all this to Del as soon as possible. It could be really important."

"Del?"

"Our sheriff, Del Jenkins."

241

"Ooh, that delicious young man with the warm eyes. I'd be delighted to tell him anything."

Olivia was surprised to feel an instant prick of jealousy. Of course, Lenora was not a serious rival, but Olivia had assumed she was the only one who had noticed those warm brown eyes. A foolish assumption, clearly.

"I'll give Del a call and tell him to drop by." Olivia saw Lenora's eyes stray toward the wine bottle. "Or maybe I'll just tell him to call you to set up a time to meet. I'll let you tell him your story in your own words. You do have a superb memory for dialogue."

"So kind of you," Lenora said, pouring herself a fourth glass of wine. This time she kept the nearly empty bottle within easy reach.

Olivia thought maybe she would suggest that Del wait until the next morning to interview Lenora. Late morning.

"That Lenora Tucker is a hoot," Maddie said. "I liked her. We share a flair for the dramatic, and I can remember dialogue, too."

"Can you polish off a bottle of merlot in twenty minutes and still speak coherently?"

"Would I need to be standing upright, as well?"

"And maintain good posture."

"Then no, not a chance." The kitchen timer dinged, and Maddie opened the oven door to remove an enhanced pepperoni pizza. "Perfect," she said. "It needs a minute to set, then I'll slice it."

Spunky trotted into the kitchen, his nose twitching. "Sorry, Spunks," Olivia said. "It's the canned stuff for you." She filled his tiny food bowl and gave him fresh water.

"Did you learn anything else at the baby shower?" Maddie asked.

"Lenora Tucker was more or less it, and I didn't have to work very hard for that information."

"Well, it was useful information," Maddie said. "There was your productive visit to Heather's barn, too, so overall you did good. See, I can be magnanimous."

"I never said you weren't. Is it time to cut the pizza? I'm dying here."

"Done." Maddie ran a pizza cutter through the pizza and centered the pan on the table between them. She had worked wonders with a frozen pepperoni pizza. It was two inches thicker with chopped green pepper, onions, olives, fresh basil leaves, and bite-sized pieces of roasted chicken.

"Wow," Olivia said. "It looks like a decorated cookie."

"That was a compliment, right?"

Olivia nodded, having already filled her mouth. Spunky leaped to her lap, hoping a chunk of chicken might slip off her slice.

Maddie slid a piece onto her plate and said, "I've discovered that I love prying information out of people, especially when they don't know I'm doing it. Maybe my talents are wasted baking and decorating cookies."

Olivia paused in mid-chew.

"Naw," Maddie said, laughing at Olivia's stricken expression. "As long as I stick around you, I can do both. Now let me eat and then I'll relate the wondrous results of my sleuthing." She bit into her pizza. After a second bite, she reached into the back pocket of her jeans and extracted a folded, wrinkled piece of paper. "Notes," she said, as another bite headed toward her mouth. She smoothed the paper on the table and glanced through it.

"How about I read that while you chew," Olivia suggested.

"Keep your mitts off." Maddie rested her half-eaten slice on the edge of the pizza pan. "My strength is sufficiently restored. I will now present a dramatic interpretation of my stunning discoveries." She wiped her hands on a paper towel.

Olivia plunked Spunky on the floor and got up to start her Mr. Coffee. Maddie's dramatic interpretations could reach epic lengths.

"Okay," Maddie said, "let's begin with Charlene. My favorite suspect, as you know. However, I can be big enough to admit that I didn't find any solid evidence pointing to her as Geoffrey King's killer. I talked to several women who remembered Charlene from high school. They all said more or less the same thing: Charlene has certainly changed since then. In high school, she was shy and eager to be liked. Some kids sucked up to her because her family was filthy rich, while others, including my informants — at least, according to themselves — ignored the rich part and thought Charlene was insecure and, frankly, boring. She didn't date much, purportedly because her parents forbade it." The corners of Maddie's generous mouth tightened. "I should warn you that your brother's feelings for Charlene were well known among her peers. Charlene and Jason hung out together quite a bit during and after school hours, at least to the extent they could without her parents finding out."

"That matches what Mom told me," Olivia said, "except she didn't mention anything about Charlene feeling more than friendship for Jason."

"It seems your mother was not fully informed," Maddie said, "which has got to be a first. Jason and Charlene were inseparable. When her folks weren't watching, that is. Anyway, this close yet unsatisfying arrangement continued until Charlene was almost fifteen, when she had an apparent breakdown. She spent a month in a private hospital before returning to school."

"Really?" Olivia poured two cups of coffee and found some cream in the back of the refrigerator. "Mom didn't mention anything about Charlene being hospitalized."

Maddie said, "Charlene told her friends about it when she returned to school, but kids that age . . . they can be really secretive with their parents. Anyway, it's not like your mom was cozy with the senior Critches or their rich buddies, so maybe it's one of the few Chatterley Heights happenings she never got wind of."

"I guess," Olivia said. "Mom did mention Jason was having problems about that time. She also said Jason introduced Charlene to Geoffrey King, although Mom wasn't sure of his name."

"Affirmative," Maddie said. "That was after Charlene returned from the hospital. And guess what she'd been hospitalized for? She'd been starving herself. She went for days without food, only water, and finally she passed out in study hall. Chemistry class, I could understand, but study hall? Jason carried her to the nurse's office. Made quite an impression on the other girls. At any rate, the Critches hightailed it to DC very soon after, dragging their progeny along. Which I realize doesn't get us very far, but it does confirm Charlene's instability."

"Sort of," Olivia said, "but it also digs Jason in deeper. He has been protective of Charlene since high school."

"Luckily, I have much more. As it happens, one of Gwen's favorite aunts became Charlie Critch's landlady when he moved back here to be with his sister. She had a lot to say about young Charlie, not all of it good. Some of it is downright suspicious."

"I thought Charlie was generally likable." Olivia lifted a box of decorated cookies off the top of the refrigerator and switched it with the empty pizza pan. Spunky jumped from her chair onto the table and tried to climb into the box. "Spunky! Bad boy!"

Spunky ignored her. Olivia grabbed him around his middle, deposited him in the hallway, and shut the kitchen door. "You and I will be repeating puppy school," Olivia said through the door. "Again."

"Poor guy. I feel his pain," Maddie said as she reached into the cookie box and brought out a peppermint-striped pig.

"About Charlie?"

"Okay, this is good," Maddie said. "Gwen's aunt Agnes said that she was about to kick Charlie Critch out of her house, where he'd been renting a room since he moved back to town. It seems he fell behind on his rent and then stopped paying about a month ago. A couple weeks ago, he paid her all his back rent. And last week, he couldn't pay again. Also, she'd been noticing her food disappearing from the kitchen. He was allowed to cook his own food there, but he was supposed to buy it himself. She rarely saw any food in the fridge that she hadn't bought, but she figured he was eating fast food. So about a week ago, before the murder, Aunt Agnes gave Charlie an ultimatum: pay on time and stop pinching food, or find another place to room."

"Any idea when Charlie got to his room the night of the murder?"

"Aunt Agnes is feisty, but she's also a

pushover for a young man down on his luck. She told Del that Charlie was there this morning when she got up at six. She said he paid up all his past-due rent plus a week in advance and even cooked her some eggs he'd bought himself. She said she'd heard him come home last night. She wasn't sure exactly, but she thought it was around ten or eleven."

Olivia finished off a blue lamb cookie, which, combined with Spunky's pathetic whimper from the hallway, made her feel guilty. Besides, she could almost see the scratch marks on the kitchen door. When she cracked the door open, the little Yorkie shot through and skidded into a cabinet. "Oh Spunks, what am I going to do with you?" He limped over to her, favoring the front paw that had been injured during his puppy farm days. "Give me a break," she said, but she lifted him to her lap and scratched his ears. "So Charlie has an alibi for last night?"

"Well, here's the kicker," Maddie said. "I pressed for more detail, and Aunt Agnes's story got shaky. She began to contradict herself. Finally she admitted, just between her and me, that she'd fabricated part of her story. What really happened is, a few days after the morning of her ultimatum to

Charlie, she found more food missing. He was still behind on his rent, too. She kicked him out that evening when he got home from work."

"My, my," Olivia said. "So we don't know where Charlie was after he left The Vegetable Plate on the night of the murder. But why would Agnes fib?"

"She felt guilty about kicking him out, and she didn't want to get him into trouble. Personally, I think she has a soft spot for Charlie. She told me she was absolutely certain that Charlie could never have killed someone in cold blood. I guess I should have called Del right away," Maddie said, "but I hate to be the one to get sweet, misguided Aunt Agnes into trouble with the law."

"I'll call him when we've finished," Olivia said. "I can point him toward Agnes and let him get the story himself. I'll mention she said a few things at the baby shower that made you start wondering if she'd gotten the days mixed up."

"You'd lie for me?"

"It isn't a lie, exactly. It's more like . . . well, like using a royal icing mix when you're in a hurry, rather than taking the time to mix the ingredients yourself." Olivia reached into the cookie box and withdrew a purple Yorkie with big pink eyes. She put it back.

"You mean like a shortcut?" Maddie asked.

"A shortcut, yes."

"That doesn't make a lot of sense."

"I know," Olivia said, "but just go with it. What else did you learn?" She peered into the cookie box and chose a yellow cow with purple sprinkles. Finding it unappetizing, she left it on the table.

"Nothing," Maddie said. "Where do you suppose Charlie Critch has been staying since Agnes kicked him out?"

"Probably with Charlene. She's so protective of him, I can't see her making him sleep under a bridge."

Maddie picked up Olivia's cow cookie and bit off the tail. "I'm wondering if Charlie told Charlene about his predicament. Wouldn't she have come up with the money for his rent? Or at least fed him so he wouldn't have to steal food? Hey, what if that stash you found in Heather's barn was Charlie's, not Geoffrey King's?"

"If Charlie had all those valuable items at his disposal, wouldn't he try to sell them to get rent money and food? Or heck, why not steal food from a grocery store, if he was so good at stealing?"

251

"I guess," Maddie said. "I think we need to find out where Charlie has been bunking for the past week. Del won't want to tell us, and Charlie will probably lie to him, anyway. I'll bet Jason knows."

"My brother is not speaking to me," Olivia said. "And even if he were, he wouldn't want to make Charlie look suspicious."

"Just try, okay, Livie? I know you're feeling tired and scared. I can tell because cookies seem to irritate you when things feel out of control." Maddie closed the cookie box and slid it onto the top of the refrigerator. "So here's a plan for you. Get a good night's sleep, then go shake that brother of yours until he spills some information."

"Sure thing, Mom," Olivia said. "Only I'm afraid he'll cough up a more convincing confession."

CHAPTER TWELVE

Some folks revel in heat and humidity, oblivious to the shiny layer of sweat that covers the body, but Olivia Greyson wasn't one of them. Now that Spunky was no longer an exuberant puppy with an unpredictable bladder, he didn't need a walk every few hours. However, after a frantic day in The Gingerbread House, followed by the Tuckers' baby shower, the little Yorkie had been cooped up in Olivia's apartment for too long. She knew if she didn't take him for a long walk, he'd want to play all night.

By the time she and Maddie finished their pizza-fueled brainstorming about murder suspects, it was ten p.m. As soon as Maddie left for home, Olivia clicked a leash on Spunky's collar and allowed him to lead her downstairs. Heavy, damp air coated her as she locked the front door behind them. The humidity had no effect on Spunky's energy level. Olivia let him determine their direction, which he did by perking up his ears, sniffing the air, and yanking her forward. Their walks usually began with a romp through the town square, but a small group of flashlight-wielding clue hunters still wandered the park, shouting each time they thought they'd found a piece of evidence. Spunky seemed to disapprove of the noise level. He veered east on Park Street, leading Olivia away from the town square. Lovely Victorian-era houses, most of them small and well maintained, lined both sides of east Park Street. The glow from old-fashioned streetlamps, matching the one near the band shell in the town square, created an atmosphere of comfort and safety.

"I'm not worried about murderers on the loose," Olivia said to Spunky. "Not when I have you to protect me." Spunky wagged his tail at the sound of her voice but kept up his pressure on the leash. At Willow Road, he stopped to sniff the air.

"This is new territory for you," Olivia said as Spunky turned onto Willow Road. He dragged her south, toward a fire hydrant that hadn't seen refurbishing in many years. "Found a juicy one, have you," she said as Spunky eagerly sniffed every square inch. While he used the facilities, Olivia gazed around. On Willow Road, some of the oldest homes in Chatterley Heights mingled with small businesses and run-down bungalows. Olivia felt safe in every area of town; however, it was getting dark and a couple streetlights were out farther down the street. She tugged at Spunky's leash. He ignored her and stood his ground.

"Come on, Spunks, how about we go home and have a treat."

When Spunky's terrier stubbornness took hold, even the word "treat" failed to budge him. He strained forward, his little nails scraping the sidewalk.

"Oh, all right," Olivia said, "we can go on a ways, but then home." She loosened the leash, and Spunky led her on a brisk walk down Willow Road. After two blocks, he stopped beside a streetlamp and tilted his head as if listening. Olivia listened, too, and heard faint strains of music from farther down the street. Then she realized where they were — about half a block away from the Chatterley Heights Dance Studio.

Olivia figured it was about ten thirty, which seemed late for a dance lesson. Curious, she followed Spunky until they reached a vacant wooded lot across the street from the studio. They stopped under a darkened streetlamp. For once, Spunky exercised self-restraint and sat quietly on the sidewalk. The studio's floor-to-ceiling plateglass window had no curtain, tempting passersby to stop and observe lessons in progress. Olivia's mother had mentioned that it took some getting used to, but once she lost herself in the dancing she didn't notice being watched.

The spotlights above the dance floor were turned off, but a light from farther back in the studio faintly illuminated the back room. It appeared to be empty. Yet Olivia could hear music coming from the building, so either Raoul was still there or he'd left a classical radio station turned on. Or she assumed it was a classical station. Unlike Maddie, Olivia wasn't mad about music. Her knowledge of music began and ended with the folk and light rock her parents had played while she was growing up. Her father had liked several classical pieces, but Olivia couldn't distinguish Beethoven from Rachmaninoff. She knew as much about music as she did about cooking — with the exception, that is, of decorated cookie baking.

The music stopped in mid-phrase. Assuming the free concert had ended, Olivia tugged on Spunky's leash. His little legs tightened, and his silky ears perked as high as they could go. "I need to get up in the morning, you know," she said. "Some of us have a store to run and can't loll around all day filing our nails." Spunky, of course, ignored her.

The music began again, louder than before. This time, Olivia heard a recognizable waltz tune, lilting and lyrical, though she couldn't name the title or the composer. She watched the studio window as if it were a ballroom scene in a movie, and it became one. A couple materialized on the dance floor and began waltzing with such grace that Olivia suspected she wasn't watching a ballroom dancing lesson. Though she couldn't see his features, she could tell that the male dancer was tall. As the couple rounded the dance floor, the light emanating from the back room revealed the man's full head of hair. He had to be Raoul. The female dancer was hidden by his body as the couple danced through the sliver of light.

Spunky had settled on his haunches to watch the show, but Olivia was beginning to feel voyeuristic. In a mesmerizing swirl, the couple circled the dance floor again and again. Each time they passed close to the front window, Olivia strained to see Raoul's partner. She gathered the impression of a petite woman wearing a silky gown that flowed with her movements. Could she be the ballerina seen dancing in the town square at night?

Olivia lifted Spunky, who whimpered but didn't yap. "Let's get a bit closer," she whispered. Across the street and next to the studio, another unlit streetlamp kept one side of the building in darkness. Olivia waited for the waltzing couple to reach the back of the dance floor before she carried Spunky across the street. They settled in the dark, near the edge of the window. From where she stood, Olivia could see about half of the dance floor. Spunky remained quiet. Maybe he was as curious as Olivia about this lovely and mysterious scene.

The music ended. Holding Spunky firmly in both arms, Olivia leaned her right shoulder against the rough stone wall and peered into the studio. Spunky's head jerked as strains of another waltz began. This time even Olivia recognized the piece — "The Blue Danube." She heard the tinkle of feminine laughter and wondered if the choice of music amused the woman.

Now that Olivia was closer she could hear the occasional murmur of voices, though no clear words. As the couple glided near her hiding place, she flattened against the wall.

The dancers had taken their fourth turn around the floor, and Olivia still hadn't gotten a look at the woman's face or hair. She decided to be bolder. Leaning her cheek against the window frame, she looked inside. If they danced close enough and looked directly toward her, Raoul and his partner might see the outline of her head. Spunky kept quiet, his head swiveling as he followed the movements.

Olivia held her breath as the two waltzed closer and closer to her. She couldn't believe they hadn't noticed her. She could make out Raoul's face as he smiled down at his partner with tenderness. The woman lifted her face toward his and a lock of her hair escaped from the bun at the nape of her neck. The long strand fell down her back. In the dim light, it looked white, though it might have been white-blond.

At that moment, Spunky reverted to his noisy self, barking and squirming as if a pack of starving coyotes were bearing down on them. The young woman yanked away from Raoul and spun around to stare out the window. Olivia clutched Spunky against her chest as she flattened herself against the outside wall. She edged away from the window into the safety of darkness. For a split second, though, she had glimpsed the woman's face. It was a pale oval of perfection, except for one flaw — a long scar down her left cheek.

CHAPTER THIRTEEN

"I thought we agreed to meet at six a.m. How long have you been up?" Maddie said as she let herself into The Gingerbread House on Thursday morning. In her bright yellow tank top and matching shorts, she reminded Olivia of a sun sprite. "Hey, Spunky." At the sound of his name, the sleepy Yorkie lifted his head and yawned a yap. Olivia looked up from a star-shaped tin cookie cutter she was examining. "Couldn't sleep after what I saw last night. I think I found our ballerina."

Maddie squealed, setting Spunky off on a round of yapping. "Oops, sorry, Spunks, I got carried away." She picked him up to calm him. "So shouldn't we go over to meet this woman? Like, right now?"

"And chase her out of town? No, we need to be careful. She might be hiding for a reason." She told Maddie about the woman's disfigurement. "Anyway, I figured I might as well get started on a cookie cutter inventory. I want to see if the Duesenberg was our only missing cutter." Olivia squinted at a tiny adhesive label inside the star. "These tiny numbers are a pain to read."

"Probably because you're reading in near darkness." Maddie turned the lights to high and said, "Et voyeur!"

"I think you meant 'Et voilà,' but it's an interesting substitution."

"Fine. I will never again attempt to speak French."

"Probably wise," Olivia said. "Okay, I'm about halfway through our inventory list, and here's what I've found so far." She handed over a list of numbers, some with notes beside them.

Maddie groaned. "I'll never understand how you remember what number belongs to which cookie cutter. I need at least a description. Or a sketch would be best."

"I've explained it to you."

"Yeah, I know, it's a series of codes describing the characteristics of each cutter, so there's virtually no possibility of misidentifying one. Unless you are me. I'm only comfortable with numbers that end with the word 'dozen.' " Maddie scanned the list and whistled. "However, I totally understand your notes. Either we've gotten sloppy or someone has been pilfering cookie cutters from our displays. We are missing four."

"Five, counting the Duesenberg," Olivia said. "And we still have half the inventory to check. We'll get through these faster if you read the numbers to me."

"I've been known to see a two and call it a three, but sure, why not." Maddie began to recite numbers, while Olivia worked the codes in her head. Twenty minutes later, they'd finished the task.

"Seven cutters missing," Olivia said. She ran her fingers through her tangled hair and made a mental note to brush it before heading for the police station to talk to Jason.

"That might be a normal level of pilfering, more or less," Maddie said. "Cookie cutters are easy to slip into a pocket. We don't magnetize them or anything."

Olivia shook her head. "I do this inventory regularly, most recently last Friday. Since we opened The Gingerbread House, only two cutters have gone missing. As you may recall, the culprits turned out to be two middle-school boys shoplifting on a dare."

"Ah, good times," Maddie said. "I do remember those boys returned to the scene of the crime with their irate and embarrassed mothers, one of whom suggested a day in lockup might teach her son a lesson. Personally, I think she just wanted a break from her kid."

"I know I would," Olivia said. "We've left the same displays up since Tuesday, so there's no way of knowing when the cutters were taken and if they were taken all at once."

"We probably shouldn't have left Clarisse's vintage cutters on display," Maddie said. "Though it looks like we lucked out. Only her Duesenberg cutter went missing. The others are still here. Isn't that a bit strange? The vintage cutters are the most valuable. Why not steal them first?"

"I don't know." Olivia reached out to tap the vintage bluebird cookie cutter, the lowest one on the bird mobile. It drifted gently at the touch of her hand. "Maybe monetary value wasn't the point. Or the thief figured I'd have noticed the losses earlier if they were Clarisse's vintage cutters."

Maddie tapped an index finger against her lips. "There's another possibility," she said. "The stolen cutters might have sentimental value for whoever took them. Or, of course, it might be random stealing for the sake of stealing." Maddie skimmed the list in her hand. "Here are the stolen shapes: a star, a teapot, a carrot, a sailboat, a party dress, an apple — and the Duesenberg, of course. What an odd combination. The thief could be a man or a woman." She shrugged her shoulders and handed the list back to Olivia. "I vote for Charlene Critch."

Olivia laughed for the first time in days. "Why does that not surprise me. At least the list doesn't scream out my brother's name. Except for the Duesenberg, of course."

"I'm betting someone besides Jason had a reason for taking the Duesenberg," Maddie said. "And we'll find out what it is. So what's next, and does it involve cookies?"

"Good idea," Olivia said. "I need to focus." Olivia dimmed the store lights and gave Spunky a quick pat on the head. His tail flapped once. "You guard the store, Spunks. Maddie and I have work to do." Spunky closed his eyes as Olivia massaged his ears. When she let go, he circled his bed and sank down to sleep.

"That's one pooped pup," Maddie said.

"He had an exciting evening." Olivia led the way into the kitchen and flipped on the lights. "Now, in answer to your question, next we discuss suspects other than Jason. And yes, we need to whip up a batch of cookies for later."

"Excellent," Maddie said, reaching for the

trusty Artisan stand mixer. "Do we have time to make a new batch of dough, or should I see what's left in the freezer?"

"Better check the freezer. I'll need the cookies for later today when I visit Heather Irwin. If she's back at work, I should bring extra cookies for her assistants and for library patrons. See if there are any bookish shapes in the freezer. I'll help in a sec, as soon as I wash up." Olivia shut herself inside the little bathroom at the back of the kitchen. Seeing herself in the mirror made her glad she kept a few emergency items in the medicine cabinet. She washed her face before tackling her hair. Sun exposure had lightened the auburn color, while a hard night of sleep had pushed up a clump in back and flattened one side. Olivia was not vain, but she had her pride. She would not be seen in public with smashed and clumped-up hair. Especially not by Del. She found a tiny bottle of hotel shampoo in the cabinet and washed her hair in the sink. Finally, she applied lightly tinted sunblock; the radio had promised another hot, sunny day. A swipe of mascara, advertised not to run, and she was ready.

When Olivia reappeared in the kitchen, Maddie had laid out two dozen cookies to defrost on racks. Maddie looked up from her mixer and said, "Good, you washed your hair. I didn't want to say anything, but you looked like a Dust Bowl survivor."

"Thanks ever so."

"No charge." Maddie swept her arm toward the defrosting cookies. "Those are the bookiest shapes I could find. I even found a few actual book shapes. Also a lion — there's always a lion or two outside big, old libraries — plus some gingerbread house shapes that look sort of like the Chatterley Heights Library. Then we have an A, a B, and a C; gingerbread boys and girls; a few cats —"

"Cats?"

"You know, cats and bookstores, cats and mystery stories. . . . Work with me, Livie."

"Okay, just asking. Looks fine. Are you going to be using the mixer right away?"

"I need about ten minutes of wild imagining," Maddie said, "before I settle on the icing colors. Why?"

"I want to make a couple phone calls." Olivia glanced at the kitchen clock. "Seven thirty. Good, there's time. By the way, I called Bertha last night. She'll be here at eight forty-five to help you open."

"And you will be . . . ?"

"With luck, I'll be in jail, wrenching information out of that brother of mine."

"You might want to start with bribery," Maddie said as she stood on tiptoe to retrieve a box from the top of the refrigerator. "We have about half a dozen leftover baby shower cookies. Well, not exactly leftover; I lost count and made extras. I'm not good with numbers, so sue me."

"Luckily, you always seem to err on the side of too many," Olivia said. "I'll take them all, thanks." She settled at the kitchen phone with a pen and pad. Her hand on the receiver, she gathered her thoughts before dialing the police station. Del answered on the first ring.

"Del, it's me. I have a favor to ask, only you can't say no. I need to talk to my brother. Alone. I won't hurt him, I promise."

Del cleared his throat and hesitated. Never a good sign.

"Did I mention I'm bringing cookies?" Olivia heard a faint chuckle. A better sign.

After another moment of silence, Del said, "I'm thinking. It sounds like you want to ask Jason some questions you don't want me to know answers to, right? Don't answer that. He probably won't talk, but if you could convince him to . . . Time is getting short, Livie. I've been trying to keep him here while the investigation proceeds, but the Office of the State's Attorney is making noises about transferring Jason to the Circuit Court for arraignment. I've held them off for about as long as I can. Like I told you earlier, the process moves much faster once we have a confession."

"I know." Olivia fought back tears of despair. "Del, please let me talk to him alone. I think I can get through to him."

"Okay, but bring Mr. Willard again. If Jason has his attorney present, I can stay out of the picture without having to explain myself to the State's Attorney. Remember, even if Jason recants his confession, there might still be a trial, and I'd be called upon to testify. Unless he is cleared first, that is."

"I understand. Thanks, Del."

"Don't thank me. Get Jason to talk."

Olivia hung up and immediately dialed Mr. Willard's office. He agreed to meet at the police station at eight thirty before visiting Jason again. When that was settled, she called her mother's cell.

"Mom, I'm glad I caught you. Do you have a few minutes, or are you off to something or other?"

"I'm skipping many of my something-or-others," Ellie said. "I'm too upset about Jason. I guess yoga might help, but honestly, I don't think I could focus. Do you have one of your lovely plans, Livie? Is there any way you could convince Jason to talk to me?"

Once again, Olivia had to swallow her fears, this time for her mother. "I'm going to give it my best shot, Mom, I promise. Right now, you can help most by dredging your mind for some information. I'm still finding my way around after living in Baltimore for so long, so I need to pick your brain."

"Of course, dear. Aything I can offer."

"Thanks, Mom. First, have you any idea where Raoul lives? In town somewhere, or does he commute?"

"Raoul? He lives above the studio. Remember I told you about the two sisters who owned the building when it was a dress shop? When they bought the building, they had the upstairs renovated as a two-bedroom apartment, where they lived for more than thirty years. Did you know that they died within a week of each other? It was so —"

"Mom . . ."

"I'm sorry, I guess sometimes I want to escape to happier days."

"I know, Mom. It's going to get better, I promise. Meanwhile, you are my best source of information about all things Chatterley Heights. Do you happen to know who owns the dance studio building now?"

"Yes, but why . . . ? Never mind, I'm wasting time. The dance studio is owned by the Chatterley Heights Management and Rental Company. It is called M & R Company for short. Continue."

If her mother was making such a determined effort to stay on topic, she must be frantic with worry. "Where is this company, and who owns it?"

"It's west of the town square," Ellie said, "on Apple Blossom Road. I'm not sure of the exact address."

"That's okay. I'm looking it up on my laptop."

"As for the owner, I believe she's a former high school classmate of yours. She's divorced now, and I think she went back to her own name, as you did. Her name is Con —"

"Constance Overton." Olivia had found the M & R Company website and was staring at the photo of a woman whose existence she had forgotten about. "Oh dear," she said.

"Is there a problem?"

"I remember Constance. She thought I stole her boyfriend junior year."

"Now Livie, I'm sure she has forgotten all about . . . Wait, *you* stole another girl's boyfriend in high school?"

"What, you think I couldn't attract someone else's boyfriend? Anyway, she only thought I stole him. He was too timid to tell her he wanted to break up, so he just started asking me out. To be fair, Constance was mighty scary." Olivia remembered Constance Overton as tall, model slender, a cheerleader, smart, and destined to be homecoming queen. She'd had a commanding personality, in that she commanded those around her to do her bidding. Constance had vowed eternal vengeance on Olivia for crossing her. She wasn't the type to forget.

"I suspect she has changed, Livie. Life is not always kind," Ellie said.

Olivia looked at the picture of Constance on the M & R Company website. She was sitting behind an imposing desk, smiling into the camera. She still had lush blond hair and perfect features, and now she owned her own company. It seemed to Olivia that life had continued to shower favors on Constance Overton. "Well, all I can do is try."

"Does this have anything to do with Jason?" Ellie sounded desperate.

"I'm not sure." Olivia told her mother about watching Raoul and a lovely woman with a scarred cheek waltz together at the dance studio. "I'm wondering if this woman might have been dancing in the park at the time of the murder. Do you have any idea who she might be? Is Raoul married or involved with someone?"

"Goodness, I have no idea. Such an attractive man, one would assume he is involved, but he never mentions his private life. I've never seen him with anyone. I'm fairly sure no one else has, either. At least, I've heard no gossip. I'll ask around."

"Good idea," Livie said. "Do you know his teaching schedule? Does he ever leave town . . . to teach elsewhere, maybe?"

"Let me think."

Olivia could almost see her mother searching her memory. Ellie, normally serene and fluid in her movements, had a habit of playing with her hair when she was upset. When Olivia's father was dying, Ellie had absently braided and unbraided the lower half of her long tresses. Now Olivia could almost see her trying to braid with one hand.

"The only information I know for sure," Ellie said, "is Raoul's teaching schedule. He teaches Monday through Wednesday, plus Saturday, from nine a.m. to eight p.m., including the noon hour because some students work full time. He says it is best not to eat until he has finished dancing. He also teaches on Fridays from nine a.m. to five p.m. He takes Thursdays and Sundays off. Does that help?"

"Why Thursdays?" Olivia asked.

"That's a mystery. I've heard that he leaves town on Thursdays and doesn't return until evening. I do know that Sunday is his day of worship. He is quite devout. I've heard from several friends that he goes to early Mass at St. Francis every morning. Sunday Mass, too. My friend Julia told me he goes to confession right after early Mass every Friday. She was impressed."

"Perfect," Olivia said. "Thanks, Mom, this really helps."

"I'm glad, Livie. Do you think Raoul's friend might be able to clear Jason?"

"I hope so." Olivia glanced at Maddie, who was trying to pipe green icing onto a cookie and listen to the phone conversation at the same time. Maddie paused, her eyebrow raised in a question. Olivia gave her a thumbs-up.

"Livie, you'll be careful, won't you? I couldn't bear it if both my children . . ."

Olivia knew her mother's fingers were torturing her hair. "I'm always careful," Olivia said. "Do me a favor, Mom. Go to your yoga class."

"I'll try."

As soon as Olivia hung up, Maddie asked, "So what was all that about Raoul's schedule? Are we going to break into the dance studio? Do you think the ballerina is a live-in girlfriend? Don't even think of going alone, Olivia Greyson, because much as I love The Gingerbread House, I will not mind the store while you have all the fun. I thrive on excitement. It is the blood of my life."

" 'Blood of my life' . . . ?"

With an impatient shrug, Maddie said, " 'Life's blood' is so hackneyed. Answer my questions."

"I will, later. Right now I'm due to meet Mr. Willard at the police station. We'll twist both of Jason's arms until he squeals. It's for his own good."

"Jason still refuses to see you." Sheriff Del stared into his coffee cup with puffy eyes. His shoulders drooped as if he were too exhausted to sit up straight.

Olivia and Mr. Willard exchanged glances. "Del, level with us," Olivia said. "Have you uncovered enough evidence to convict Jason without his confession?"

Del sighed and stared into his coffee. "Here's how it is," he said. "If he hadn't confessed, your brother would be a person of interest among several persons of interest. We wouldn't have enough to arrest him, let alone convict. He can't produce an alibi, but neither can Charlene or Charlie Critch, both of whom have motives. However, we don't have enough to arrest either of them yet, so Jason is sacrificing himself for no compelling reason."

"So you're confirming my brother is being stupid," Olivia said.

"Blunt," said Del, "yet accurate. You know how I feel about your penchant for getting involved in police business, but, frankly, I'm getting desperate."

"If I may," Mr. Willard said. "Have you any reason to believe that Jason is innocent?"

Del stared up at the ceiling and wiggled his fingers on the arm of his office chair. Finally, he said, "So far, I've been able to convince the State's Attorney to hold off arraigning him for a few more days. The reason is this — and I cannot stress enough that you must keep this to yourselves — Jason can't seem to identify the murder weapon. He knows the victim was stabbed, but he could have heard or guessed that. He's vague when it comes to details. Of course, he could be hedging to create doubt in my mind."

"My brother, and I say this with love, is not that clever," Olivia said.

Mr. Willard cleared his throat. "I am inclined to agree. Jason has always struck me as a young man without guile."

Del rocked his chair gently and frowned at his desk. After some moments, Olivia said, "I hear things, see things. Remember, I filled you in on the cache of stolen goods in Heather Irwin's barn, as well as everything Maddie and I heard at Gwen and Herbie's baby shower. You wouldn't have heard about the loan shark threatening Geoffrey King and King's use of that threat to put more pressure on Charlene if I hadn't told you to interview Lenora Tucker."

With a brief smile, Del said, "Quite a character. Though I keep wondering if she embellished her memory with scenes from a movie."

"It was helpful, though, right?"

"That remains to be seen."

"The knife . . . it was from The Vegetable Plate kitchen, wasn't it? Charlene had a set of four knives, each decorated at the top of the handle with a different vegetable. I saw one of them, the tomato knife, among the stolen items in Heather's barn."

Del's gaze met her eyes but he said nothing.

"One of the remaining three knives was used to kill King. I'm right, aren't I?"

With a sigh, Del nodded his head. "Keep that information to yourselves."

"Of course," Olivia said. "And we won't tell Jason, you can be sure of that. He'd use the knowledge to cement his confession. Del, if we could put our information together . . . I'm not trying to interfere, but I can't sit back and wait for Jason to get himself convicted of a crime I am absolutely certain he did not commit." Olivia did not mention seeing Raoul dance with the mysterious woman from the park. She was afraid Del might barge into the dance studio with a search warrant, causing Raoul to disappear, along with his partner.

"You first," Del said.

To catch him up, Olivia quickly told him about the cookie cutters missing from The Gingerbread House, adding, "When I found Geoffrey King's body I thought I saw something shiny and silvery in his hand. It looked like the edge of a cookie cutter. Was it?"

Del fetched the coffeepot and filled their cups before responding to Olivia's information. "Okay, yeah, we found a cookie cutter in King's hand. No clear indication as to how it got there, whether he grabbed it from his killer or it was placed in his hand. No fingerprints but his. We didn't know what it was meant to be, but it sounds like the Duesenberg shape you described." Del took a sip of coffee. "So thanks for that."

"So what about the knife that killed Geoffrey King?" Olivia asked.

Del stared into his coffee cup for several moments before he said, "We found the knife flung a few yards from the body. No usable fingerprints. The storm washed off most of the blood, but there was enough for analysis. It was King's."

"What did the knife look like?" Mr. Willard asked. "It is essential that we know this detail."

Del nodded. "All right. It was about eight inches long, including the decoration at the top, which looked like a very orange pumpkin."

"Thank you, Del," Olivia said. "Can we see Jason now? Even though he refuses to talk to us?"

"I'll lock both of you in with him, then it's up to you." Del took the jail key off a hook and led them down the hallway toward the cell. "When it comes right down to it," Del said, "a guy under arrest for murder can't demand a lot of privacy."

■ ■ ■ ■

"I know you didn't murder Geoffrey King, so you might as well drop the self-sacrificing hero act," Olivia said. Jason's bones looked ready to break through his skin. "You look awful. You haven't gone on a hunger strike, have you? Are you trying to kill your mother?"

"I'm not trying to do anything to anybody," Jason said.

"Here." Olivia handed him a Gingerbread House bag. "Maddie sent these. Sugar in various shapes and colors, all delicious. Personally, I'm for letting you starve to death for what you are doing to your loved ones, but Maddie has a softer heart."

Jason tossed the bag next to him on his bunk, but his eyes strayed in the bag's direction. He reached for it, pulled out a pink bunny cookie, and bit off the ear. "Thank Maddie for me," he mumbled through a mouthful of crumbs.

"Okay, Jason," Olivia said, "tell me how you killed Geoffrey King."

Jason's open face tightened with suspicion. "Why?"

"Because if you can convince me you

really killed him, I promise I'll stop bugging you."

Jason munched his way through a gingerbread teddy bear, deep in thought. When teddy was no more, Jason said, "I stabbed him."

"I see. With what did you stab him?"

"A knife."

"What kind of knife?"

"A knife kind of knife. Geez, what do you want from me?"

Olivia grabbed the cookie bag out of her brother's hand. Jason's bereft expression made him look young and vulnerable . . . and scared. Olivia pressed harder. "Describe the knife to me, in precise detail. And tell me where you got it."

Jason's dark wavy hair hung in greasy strings, and his frantic hazel eyes searched the tiny cell. Olivia wanted to throw her arms around his thin shoulders. She steeled herself and asked again, "Where did you get the knife?"

"From Charlene's kitchen," he said.

Olivia felt the blood rush to her head. Jason was probably spouting an obvious answer, since he'd spent so much time with Charlene. But still. . . .

Mr. Willard must have sensed her confusion. He dragged his visitor's stool close to

281

Jason's bed, looked him in the eyes, and said, "I am not convinced. The Vegetable Plate is replete with knives. Precisely what type of knife did you select? What did it look like?"

"I . . ." Jason's mouth hung open, as if he'd forgotten how to form words.

Mr. Willard shifted his stool closer. "Jason, this should not be a difficult question. What type of knife did you take from Charlene Critch's kitchen? We are waiting." His voice had lost its normal diffident quality.

"Big," Jason said, barely above a whisper. "It was big."

"How big? You are a mechanic, are you not? You ought to be able to estimate the size of a tool. How long was the blade?"

"A foot."

"Twelve inches? Are you sure?"

"Maybe bigger. Or smaller, I don't remember."

"Which is it, bigger or smaller?"

"I told you, I don't know. It was night, so it was dark."

With a stern frown, Mr. Willard asked, "Are you claiming it was dark in Ms. Critch's kitchen? Where was she at the time? If it was dark, how did you know where to find this knife? Did Ms. Critch find it for you?"

"No! Charlene . . . she wasn't there. Don't you try to blame her for anything." Jason shifted from confused little boy to angry protector.

"All right then, describe this foot-long knife. Make us see it." Mr. Willard had transformed from a gentle elderly man to . . . Perry Mason.

Jason hadn't once looked toward Olivia for support. He was in Mr. Willard's power. The fear and tension melted from Olivia's body as she turned her brother's cross-examination over to an expert.

"I told you, I don't remember what it looked like." Jason was wilting from exhaustion. "It was just a knife, a big knife. There wasn't anything about it worth remembering, I guess."

"You don't remember the knife you so carefully selected and with which you stabbed a man to death?"

"Um . . . No."

"Mr. King was a strong man," Mr. Willard said. "How did you manage to stab him without being harmed yourself?"

"I surprised him by . . . I stabbed him in the back." Jason glanced uncertainly from Mr. Willard's face to Olivia's.

Mr. Willard scraped back his stool and stood, towering over Jason. "Young man, you are lying. You did not steal a knife, and you did not, as you keep insisting, stab Geoffrey King. Let me give you some advice. Next time you want to take credit for someone else's murder, make sure you get the details straight before you confess."

To Olivia's surprise and relief, Jason crumpled. His sullen bravado gave way to a trail of tears down each cheek, which made him look even more like the little boy whose birth Olivia had once resented. She sat on his cot and put an arm around his shoulders. "You've really made a muddle of it this time, little brother."

Mr. Willard, once again mild-mannered and concerned, folded his long body onto his tiny stool. "You must tell us the truth, Jason. Begin with the night of the murder."

Jason sniffled with manly vigor. Olivia dug a tissue from a pocket in her khaki pants and handed it to him. She edged away, knowing that her brother's nose blowing could rattle furniture. When the air was calm again, Olivia said, "Start with the time you left The Vegetable Plate on the night Geoffrey King died. Were you the first to leave?"

Jason nodded. "I kept yawning and nodding off, so Charlene told me to go home and get some sleep. Charlie said he'd stay all night. He planned to keep guard downstairs so he'd hear if Geoffrey tried to break in. Charlene wanted to stay with him, but Charlie told her to go upstairs and try to sleep on this little air mattress she keeps up there. Charlie borrowed Charlene's cell phone and said he'd call 911 at the first sign of trouble. I wanted to help guard Charlene, but she insisted, and I really was pretty tired."

"What time did you leave the store?" Mr. Willard asked.

"Eleven. I know because I checked Charlene's cell to make sure it was charged. The battery was down about half, so I told Charlie to plug it in. He went to find the charger as I left. Can I have another tissue, Livie?"

Olivia dug out a tissue and said, "This is my last one. Don't blow it all at once."

Jason was too miserable to crack a smile. "I cut through the town square, like always," he said. "I hurried because it felt like it was going to rain. I didn't see anybody or anything. Honest. Cross my heart and hope to . . ." Jason's shoulders slumped.

Olivia rubbed her brother's back the way her mother used to when he was croupy as a little boy. "I'm confused about one thing," she said. "If Charlie stayed all night, why did you make a point of saying he wouldn't have seen anything because his route home didn't go through the park?"

"I got confused, too," Jason said. "The next morning, when everyone knew about Geoffrey, Charlene told me she sent Charlie home right after me. Charlene said he didn't want to go, but she insisted. Charlie usually does what Charlene tells him to do. She locked all the doors behind him and stuck chairs under the doorknobs and kept her cell with her while she slept upstairs. And that's all I know."

Olivia pondered the implications of Jason's story, which sounded reasonable to her . . . except for the part about Charlene Critch being so concerned about everyone else's sleep. The fact that she chose to stay alone in the store sounded suspicious. What if she had already planned to kill Geoffrey if he did show up? She wouldn't want Charlie involved. And what about Charlie? He didn't have a home to go to, so perhaps he decided to sleep in the park. He might have reasoned that he could keep an eye on The Vegetable House from the band shell. Maybe Charlie took a knife from the store's kitchen, in case he had a run-in with Geoffrey King.

Mr. Willard checked his watch and stood up. "As your attorney," he said to Jason, "I strongly advise you to stop confessing to a crime you did not commit. We will inform the sheriff that you are recanting your confession. Agreed?"

Jason nodded his assent. To Olivia, her little brother looked liked a boy who needed a nap. It saddened her to think of him curled up on a hard cot, isolated and scared. "One last question, Jason. When you stupidly . . ." *Deep breath, release slowly, like Mom does.* "When you confessed to Geoffrey King's murder, was it because you wanted to protect Charlene only or because you wanted to protect both Charlene and Charlie?"

Jason's eyebrows shot up in surprise. "You don't think Charlie —"

"I don't think anything yet. Answer the question."

"I wanted to protect Charlene, of course. I mean, Geoffrey was a jerk, and I was the one who first introduced them. I felt responsible, you know? I didn't know what he was like then, but still . . . He treated Charlene really badly. He slugged her in the face last weekend, you know. If she killed him, it was in self-defense, but I knew she'd get in trouble anyway because she didn't call the police right away."

Mr. Willard cleared his throat twice. "Ja-

287

son, I must ask you this, and I urge you to be open with me. Do you have reason to believe that Charlene did kill her ex-husband in self-defense? Because if so, I can help her. I'll find her an excellent attorney, and she may avoid prison altogether."

"All I know is what I already told you."

Olivia kissed her brother's forehead and ruffled his stringy hair. "We'll get you out of this somehow," she said. "So stop confessing, start proclaiming your innocence, and if you remember anything else, call your attorney. Or me." She exchanged a glance with Mr. Willard, who nodded and closed the notebook in which he'd been recording the conversation. Before ringing the bell to summon Del or Cody to let them out, Olivia turned to her brother. "I'm sending Mom to see you. You *will* talk to her. Won't you." It wasn't a question.

"Yeah," Jason said. "Send her soon, okay?"

CHAPTER FOURTEEN

As Olivia burst into The Gingerbread House kitchen, Maddie's head snapped up and cornflower blue icing squirted onto the worktable. "Crap," Maddie said.

"Sorry," Olivia said. "I'm behind schedule. How are the library cookies for Heather going?"

"Slowly. If you intend to keep finding bodies and tracking down killers, we'll need more help in the store." Maddie refocused her pastry bag on a cookie shaped like a book and wrote READ A COOKIE on the cover. "How's Jason doing?"

"Better, if you don't count the need for a shower and deep depression. He has agreed to see Mom. Also, he confessed to making a false confession and has promised to confess no more. Then again, he is hopelessly in love with Charlene Critch."

"So it's a good news/bad news thing." Maddie finished her book cover and stretched. "I hope you're including me in some of this sleuthing around town. Much as I adore decorating cookies, my back is forgetting how to straighten up."

Olivia poked her head in the fridge and found a bowl covered with plastic wrap. "What's this?"

"My tuna salad," Maddie said. "Something to cleanse the palate between cookies. Try it. If I do say so myself, I have perfected the art of tuna salad."

"I'm starving. I might have missed breakfast this morning. I don't remember." Olivia found some bread that wasn't too dried out and piled tuna salad on a slice. "This is great. Is there any dish you can't create?"

"Liver and onions. Unless I leave out the liver part. What's next on the agenda?"

"Could you spare me a few of these cookies?" Olivia asked. "I need to bribe my next informant."

Maddie winced as she stretched her arms behind her back. "Ah, much better. Who is your next informant?"

"Constance Overton."

"You'd better take half a dozen cookies. I suspect she's still gunning for you, despite everything she's been through." Maddie selected a pastry bag filled with inky blue and tackled another book-shaped cookie.

"Everything she's been through?" Olivia asked. "Never mind, I don't have time. You can fill me in later." She selected six cookies with dry icing and placed them in a Gingerbread House bag. "Anything urgent, before I hit the trail?"

"Only that Bertha thinks she knows who has been stealing cookie cutters."

"No kidding. Who?"

"Charlene Critch."

"Now Maddie, are you sure you didn't put that notion into her head?"

"Absolutely positive. All I did was show Bertha the list of missing cutters and ask her to keep her eyes open because they might simply have gotten misplaced. Bertha read down the list and said to me, 'I think it might be poor little Charlene.' I asked why she thought that and she said, 'Well, I could be wrong, but I know I saw her holding at least three of those cookie cutters during the harvest event.' They were all on mobiles," Maddie said, "so it was easy to see what Charlene was holding. Bertha said she had a wistful look on her face, like maybe they reminded her of something."

"Not enough to convict," Olivia said as she headed for the door leading to the back alley.

"Not yet."

■ ■ ■ ■

The Chatterley Heights Management and Rental Company turned out to be half of a renovated duplex. It had once been a Queen Anne summer house much like Olivia's, but smaller and split in half rather than into two levels. The exterior was in the process of being restored and repainted. The right half of the building housed a chiropractor, while the left front door sported a sign that read M & R COMPANY. The crisp block letters felt efficient and cold.

Olivia hadn't called ahead for an appointment. It had seemed like the best approach at the time. Now she wished she had at least some sense of how the adult Constance Overton might react to her. Olivia's watch read nine fifteen a.m. No time to worry about high school trauma. Jason was in jail and likely to stay there if she couldn't find the mysterious ballerina — a potential witness for the defense. Constance was her best shot.

A bell tinkled overhead as Olivia entered the front door of the M & R Company. She found herself in a narrow foyer containing an old-fashioned standing coat rack and a small table. The latter held a silver-footed tray. Olivia knew something about antiques, and this tray had once been used to deliver visiting cards to the lady of the house. Now it held business cards for *The Chatterley Heights Management and Rental Company, 19 Apple Blossom Road, Chatterley Heights, Maryland,* followed by *Constance Overton, M.B.A., Owner and Manager.*

As Olivia slipped one of the cards into her pants pocket, a commanding voice called from a room somewhere down the hallway. "Second door on the right. Come on in." The voice hadn't changed much, though it had grown deeper and more powerful. *Well, so have I.* Olivia straightened her spine, the way her mother was always telling her to, and strode toward the disembodied voice.

Constance Overton hadn't changed much, either, at least in looks. Her thick golden hair had darkened, and she now wore it short, layered, and blow-dried to create a sculpted wind-blown effect. Her face had filled out, but she still possessed a crystalline beauty. Olivia paused a moment and watched Constance's face shift from professional welcome to recognition. She did not stand up.

"Olivia Greyson. Well, well. I heard you were back in town. You are looking . . .

healthy. Sit down and tell me what I can do for you." She waved toward three antique chairs arranged in a semicircle in front of her imposing desk.

Olivia chose the center chair, which offered a soft needlework seat. "Hello, Constance. You seem to have done well for yourself." Her comment sounded banal. Wincing inwardly, Olivia said, "I think you might be able to help me with some information."

Constance relaxed against the back of her chair, which seemed higher than the one Olivia had chosen. "Now you've made me curious," Constance said. "I doubt you need rental property, since I heard you purchased the house with your little cookie store in it."

"Actually, Maddie and I — you remember Maddie Briggs, don't you? We co-manage The Gingerbread House, specializing in both modern and vintage cookie cutters." When Constance drew in a breath, presumably to interrupt, Olivia said quickly, "I came to you because I've been told you manage the property on Willow Road where the Chatterley Heights Dance Studio is located. I need information about the renter. This isn't idle curiosity on my part. You've probably heard about my brother, Jason?"

Constance cringed and said, "Sorry, my head is always thinking about business. I completely forgot that you were the one who found that man's body . . . and that your brother was arrested for the murder. As I remember, Jason was a good kid. No genius, maybe, but well meaning. How does all that relate to the renter of the dance studio?"

"I'm searching for a potential witness to the murder." Olivia felt relieved by the shift in Constance's demeanor — still curt but with a hint of empathy. They'd both grown up since high school; perhaps Constance had let go of the boyfriend-stealing episode from their youth. Maybe she didn't even remember it.

"And you think the dance instructor, Raoul, might be that witness?"

"In a sense."

"In what sense? And why should I reveal private information about one of my renters?"

"I didn't mean that you . . ." What was it her mother kept telling her about breathing? Oh yeah, keep doing it. "Do you know if Raoul lives in the property alone?" she asked.

Constance's penciled eyebrows shot up. "He assured me he would be living alone.

My rents include a portion of the cost of utilities. If someone else is living there with him, he should be paying higher rent, or the extra resident should be paying his or her own portion of the rent. I was specific about that. Do you have evidence someone is living with him full time?"

Olivia felt a strong need for a cookie. Then she remembered she had brought some. But where were they? "Hang on a sec, Constance. I left something on the table in the hallway." Olivia had the impression that Constance's eyelids had arched to her hairline, but she didn't pause to confirm. She hurried out to the table in the hallway and found the bag on top of the silver card holder. Constance's command to report to her office must have flustered her more than she'd realized. She resisted the urge to stuff a cookie in her mouth. With her luck, she'd wind up with crumbs on her chin.

When Olivia arrived back in the office, Constance was reading through some papers, her pen scratching notes on a pad. Olivia felt a compulsion to announce her presence. She resisted. Instead, she sat on her spindly chair, plunked the bag of cookies on Constance's desk, and opened the top. The mingled scents of lemon zest and ginger wafted into the air. The pen slowed, then stopped. Constance's eyes lifted from her work. She dropped her pen and reached for the bag. Olivia had to smile. A good cookie can tame the most aggressive of business school graduates.

Without comment, Constance reached into the bag and pulled out a frowning gingerbread boy dressed in purple and yellow stripes. The corner of Constance's mouth twitched. "Reminds me of a high school boyfriend of mine, the one who dumped me for another girl. What was his name? Shane?"

"Shawn," Olivia said.

"That's the one." Constance bit off the gingerbread boy's head.

"As you know very well," Olivia said, "the girl he began dating was me. You vowed eternal vengeance."

"Eternity is a long time," Constance mumbled, still chewing. She bit off a gingerbread arm and dragged the cookie bag out of Olivia's reach. When she had swallowed the last of the gingerbread cookie, Constance said, "Excellent quality. I assume Maddie is the chief baker?" She brushed crumbs off her desk and into her wastebasket. Then she smiled. "Bribe accepted and eternal vengeance canceled. Tell me how I can help Jason."

"Thank you." Olivia moved her chair closer and leaned her elbows on the desk. "First, can you tell me what Raoul's last name is? No one in town seems to have any idea, and I don't see how he could sign rental papers without one."

"Let me check," Constance said, opening a file drawer on the right side of her desk. She extracted what looked like a contract. "Yes, here it is. His legal name is Raoul Larssen."

"*Larssen?* Are you sure?"

"I remember now," Constance said. "I had the same reaction, so Raoul showed me his driver's license. He said he'd emigrated from Argentina as a young boy, accompanied by his widowed mother, who was a celebrated dancer. His mother managed to support them for a time by giving dance lessons, which is how he learned to dance. When Raoul was thirteen, his mother met and married a second-generation Swede named Sven Larssen, and mother and son took his name. Made sense to me."

"Did he mention having any family still alive?"

Constance said, "I always ask a few questions about family members, even for a month-to-month lease like this one. You never know when some kid will move back

298

in with the folks. Another resident means more use of utilities, maybe more damage, depending on whether the newcomer has come from, say, prison. Raoul said his mother and stepfather were deceased and his wife had died. I let it go at that. Are you going to tell me what this is all about?" Her hand slipped into the cookie bag and reappeared holding a pink rutabaga. "My kind of vegetable."

Olivia pondered how much to reveal to Constance. "It's important that Raoul not find out I've been asking about him," she said. "I don't have any reason to suspect him of anything, but I think he might know something or someone. . . . I don't know, I might be grasping at straws, but right now that's all I've got. Do you know what his wife's name was?"

Constance clutched the cookie bag to her chest as if she thought Olivia might claim it back. "The topic never came up," she said, "and I didn't ask. Not my business."

"I have a last request, and it's an odd one. You'll just have to trust me . . . despite my past alleged untrustworthiness."

"Explain."

"I have it on the best familial authority that Raoul leaves town every Thursday, and I need to get inside the dance studio. I know that borders on illegal, but —"

"You think someone else is living there, don't you? I'm very good at math, I can add two and two. Assuming that's your suspicion, I think we can do business. If Raoul has someone else living with him, I want to know. If I loan you the spare key, you are acting as my emissary, which isn't illegal. In return, you must tell me if you find evidence of another resident. Otherwise, I turn you in. Deal?" Constance's hand hovered near the file drawer.

"Deal. I might not be able to return it until tomorrow. My afternoon is jammed."

"I'll be looking over a new property tomorrow morning. Afternoon will be fine." Constance swung open her file drawer and brought out a zippered bag of keys. She handed over a key labeled with a combination of letters and numbers, reminiscent of Olivia's method for tracking cookie cutters. "A code, right?" Olivia asked.

"Of course. Wouldn't want my keys wandering around with actual addresses on them."

Olivia stood. "Thanks, Constance. I'm glad you haven't been planning my painful demise all these years. Drop by The Gingerbread House sometime."

As Olivia turned her back, Constance

said, "I'm afraid I'll have to order take-out cookies. I don't get out much." Olivia looked back to see Constance push back from her desk and wheel herself around it. "Unless The Gingerbread House is wheelchair accessible, that is." Constance laughed at Olivia's chagrined expression. "Car accident," she said. Her wheelchair was custom-made. The part that showed above her desk looked like a well-preserved mahogany rocking chair with carved roses above an embroidered back. The bottom was a state-of-the-art motorized wheelchair. When Olivia saw the soft paisley blanket covering Constance's lap, she realized that those lovely, long cheerleader legs were missing.

Olivia missed being with Maddie in The Gingerbread House. However, she had to work fast. Del might now believe that Jason was innocent of murder, but his confession — not to mention means, motive, and opportunity — could still send him to prison.

Olivia walked briskly, collecting a film of perspiration by the time she reached the dance studio. To divert attention, she passed the building, then doubled back through the alley to the rear entrance.

Constance had assured her the key opened

both the front and back doors, and it did. Olivia slipped inside the building and locked the door behind her. She found herself in darkness. As her eyes adjusted, she could make out windowless walls, a counter, and a table with two chairs. She hadn't thought to ask Constance for a floor plan. Some planner she turned out to be. It also never occurred to her to stop at home to pick up one of the new flashlights she had purchased after her dark and stormy night in the park. Olivia assumed she was in the small office that opened onto the dance floor. A ribbon of gray along the floor gave a clue to the location of the connecting door. Olivia headed toward the sliver of light, tripping over a chair leg on the way.

When she opened the door, Olivia saw daylight through the large front window and instinctively pulled back. She reminded herself that she would be invisible to someone looking into the dark studio. Probably. She wished Maddie were with her to lighten the mood. Breaking into homes, even with permission, wasn't as relaxing as, say, baking cookies. If Raoul returned early for some reason, her plan would backfire. He would pack up and leave town, and she might never locate the dancer in the park. *Jason, remember Jason.* That dancer might be her brother's only chance.

Olivia stepped out of the little office and scanned the dance floor. Aside from the front entrance, she didn't see any other doors. She reentered the office and closed the door behind her. She felt along the wall for the light switch and, defying caution, switched it on. So what if a pedestrian glanced inside the studio and saw light under the door? Besides her mother, how many people even knew Raoul's habit of leaving town on Thursdays?

The light revealed another closed door. It was unlocked, thank goodness. She opened it and found two light switches on a wall just inside. She flipped both. The office light turned off, and an overhead light came on, illuminating a narrow staircase. With a surge of hopeful energy, Olivia shut the door behind her and mounted the stairs.

The second floor reminded Olivia of her own apartment, with a central hallway and rooms on each side. She hurried past open doors leading into a living room, kitchen-dining room, bathroom, and a tiny room that looked like an office strewn with papers. At the end of the corridor, two bedrooms faced one another. At least, Olivia assumed they were both bedrooms. In the room to her left, she could see an unmade bed and two chairs strewn with various items of men's clothing, including dancing costumes.

The door to Olivia's right was closed. Attached to the doorjamb, she noticed a chain latch, the kind one might install on a front door to allow a resident to peek through without allowing access inside. Only this lock was on the outside of the door. Maybe it was left over from the era of the seamstress sisters? They'd grown old here; maybe one of them developed Alzheimer's and began to wander at night. She'd have to ask her mom. The metal didn't look worn, but the lock might have been used for only a short time.

Olivia tried the doorknob. It turned smoothly. Her heart quickened as she gently pushed the door inward and looked inside. The room was cluttered with discarded clothing, and there could be no doubt that it belonged to a woman. That woman was the ballerina in the park, the woman she'd seen waltzing in Raoul's arms. As she picked her way around piles of clothing, Olivia speed-dialed Maddie.

"Livie, don't worry, I've finished the cookies for Heather, and the store is quiet at the moment. So tell me everything." Maddie's voice was breathy with excitement. "Did you get into the dance studio? Did Constance Overton demand her vengeance after all these years?"

"I'll tell you about Constance later," Olivia said. "Long story. Anyway, she gave me a key and I am at this moment in the bedroom of our mysterious ballerina." She waited for Maddie's squeal to subside. "I'm at a small desk in the corner. No papers, just a laptop, maybe three or four years old." Olivia lifted the lid. "Turned off," she said. "Too bad."

"Now if you'd brought me along," Maddie said, "I'd fire that thing up in no time. I could probably even guess her password."

"I don't doubt it." Olivia took in the rest of the bedroom. "From the state of this room, I'd say our girl has issues. Apparently, she has never heard of a clothes hanger. Or else there are none left. The closet is stuffed. I envy her wardrobe, though. So thoroughly diaphanous. She has a sewing machine set up. It's an old Singer, must have been left by the previous owners. And there are piles of lovely fabrics."

"Ooh, she found the stash," Maddie said. "Aunt Sadie once told me the sisters kept a huge supply of gorgeous fabric in their attic. She always wondered what happened to it."

Olivia picked up a pill bottle from a

bedside table. "Listen to this, Maddie. Our ballerina takes pills. The label is for some generic drug with a multisyllabic name. I don't recognize it. Hang on a sec." She put down the phone and rummaged in her pocket for something to write on. She found an old receipt. Using a fabric marking pencil, she jotted down the drug name. She replaced the pill bottle as she'd found it and retrieved her cell.

"Maddie, you would love the closet. It's crammed full of costumes. Not just dancing dresses, but actual costumes with head-dresses and capes and . . . Wow, there must be twenty pairs of toe shoes and even more pairs of ballet slippers in here. Our dancer must have been a real ballerina. Maybe that scar on her face ended her career and made her unstable."

"We might be able to dig something up on the Internet," Maddie said. "That's my specialty."

"One more question for you, Maddie, and then I need to hang up. Did your aunt Sadie ever say anything about what happened to the sisters who owned this place? Did they sell it and retire to Florida or something?"

"It was sad," Maddie said. "The older sister went senile, and the younger one tried to take care of her and the store at the same time. It was too much stress for the younger sister. She had a massive heart attack. Aunt Sadie said it happened on a weekend, so it was Monday before anyone realized something was wrong. The police broke into the store and found older sis wandering around half-dressed and agitated. Younger sis was dead on the floor of the kitchen. Why?"

"I'll tell you later," Olivia said. "I'm behind schedule. See you soon." She closed her cell and took one last look around the bedroom. The costumes in the closet were tightly packed, but it wouldn't hurt to look through them. Olivia's watch read ten twenty, which left plenty of time to question Heather Irwin about the stolen items found in her barn.

Olivia set to work, moving through the costumes one by one, luxuriating in the fine silks and satins as they slid through her hands. She remembered wanting to be a ballerina when she grew up . . . until the first time she tried to dance en pointe in real toe shoes. Her poor little toes felt crushed as her entire weight balanced on those wooden tips. She lasted about a week before deciding to switch to horseback riding. That hurt, too, but not as much.

When Olivia was about three fourths of the way through the costume collection, she came to a dress composed of many translucent layers of white fabric. This might be the costume she and Maddie saw the ballerina dance in that night in the park. The next dress was white, also, as well as several more beyond it. Olivia examined each, not sure what she was looking for. After three more costumes, she found it — a large rip down the bodice and into the skirt. Olivia took the dress from the closet and held it under the bedside light. The rip could have happened during a struggle.

Reluctantly, Olivia slid the dress back on its hanger. Del would want to know everything she had found, but she wanted to put off her confession as long as possible. Del was beginning to trust her, or at least she hoped he was. He wouldn't be happy to learn she'd been riffling through belongings without their owner's permission.

Olivia was finishing her inspection of the dance costumes when her cell phone rang. It was her mother. She answered at once.

"Livie, it's . . . You've got to come right away. I don't know what to do."

"What is it, Mom? You sound upset."

"Of course I'm upset. You would be, too. They are taking Jason away."

"Away? Who are 'they'?"

"The police, of course. The ones from

Baltimore or Howard County, I don't know. I only know they are taking him away to be charged with murder. Del said they've found some evidence that Jason killed Geoffrey King."

CHAPTER FIFTEEN

Olivia entered the Chatterley Heights police station and felt as if she'd stumbled into an Agatha Christie novel, adapted for the stage, with her mother performing the role of Miss Jane Marple. Ellie Greyson-Meyers, all four-foot-eleven inches of her, single-handedly faced off two uniformed police officers. She stood between them and her son, apparently using reason to delay the inevitable. Olivia cringed when she saw Jason's hands and feet so tightly shackled he could barely shuffle. He looked young and frightened; she wanted to ruffle his hair and comfort him. She moved toward him, and at once an officer stepped in front of her. Del gave her a slight shake of his head.

"Livie, thank God you're here," Ellie said. "Allan left town at the worst possible moment. You talk to them."

"Mom, I'm not sure what I . . ."

"Tell them they can't take Jason away. His

confession was a lie, he's admitted that."

Sounding tired, Del said, "They have some evidence, Ellie."

"What evidence?" Ellie said. "And it had better be good." She planted her fists on her hips, straightened her spine, and gave the officers a hard stare. Miss Marple, Olivia thought, with a hint of Dirty Harry.

The two officers exchanged a quick glance before the taller of them said, "Blood evidence. I guess the crime lab found your son's blood on the deceased's shirt. Now we'd better get going, and you need to get out of the way, ma'am."

"Wait a minute," Olivia said, stepping closer to her mother. "It was storming the night Geoffrey King was murdered. I ought to know; I found his body, and it was soaked. How did the lab extract a clear blood sample?"

"Look, all I know is, the guy had a jacket on, and the crime lab found a dry patch with blood. You'll have to ask them how they got it." The officer snorted. "If you can get one of them to talk to you. All they do is run around complaining how understaffed they are and how they don't have time to breathe."

Olivia slipped her arm around her mother, whose shoulders felt as if they'd been carved from stone. "I'm no expert either, guys, I'm just confused. If they're so busy, how did they manage to produce a DNA match so fast? I mean, I do know it takes a lot longer to do a DNA analysis than television shows would have you believe."

The second officer, shorter and older, cracked a smile. "No kidding. Anyway, I guess the State's Attorney decided what the lab got was good enough for now. She wants to move on this."

Del had been standing off to the side, in neutral territory. Now he joined Olivia and Ellie. "When the State's Attorney called," he said, "she told me the lab had produced a 'match' with Jason. So which is it, a match or good enough?"

The older officer crossed his arms over his chest. "Both," he said. "The blood sample was a match to the prisoner's blood type, and when you add that to his confession, it's enough to move ahead with. Look, Sheriff, we're sympathetic. We know this is your town; you probably watched the kid grow up. Maybe he's a good kid, never been in trouble before. But we hear that all the time. Something made him snap, he killed a guy, it happens. We've got our job to do and no more time to sit around and argue."

"Blood type." Ellie's small hands bunched

into fists. "Jason is type O-positive. That's the most common blood type there is."

"She's right," Olivia said. "Did the State's Attorney even consider Charlene and Charlie Critch's blood types? They are both suspects, too. Or what about me? I found the body, and I'm type O-positive."

The tall officer shrugged. "We can arrest you, too, if that would make you feel better."

Del strolled toward the officers and said, "Look, guys, I'm not trying to hang you up, but you can understand why I'm not happy." Although his tone sounded even and reasonable, Olivia noticed tension in his neck muscles. "We've got a kid here who confessed to a murder because he was afraid his girlfriend stabbed her abusive ex-husband in self-defense and didn't call the police right away. It was noble and stupid, and we've all seen it before. Now the kid has recanted. We have an obligation to provide more proof than a blood type before we charge him." As the tall officer frowned and inhaled to respond, Del added, "So here's what I propose. I'm going to put in a call to the State's Attorney. Let me talk this over with her, see what she says. Okay? Meanwhile, you guys go have an early lunch at The Chatterley Café, on us." Del checked his watch. "Take your time."

The tall officer hesitated for only a moment. "Yeah, okay," he said. "We could use some lunch. But when we get back here, no more stalling, okay?"

"Sure," Del said. "Not a problem. You'll like the Chatterley. Order the Reuben with the works."

When the front door of the police station clanked shut behind the two officers, Olivia and Ellie both threw their arms around Del, who started to topple. Olivia grabbed his shoulders to steady him. "Del, you were great. Thank you!"

"Thanks, but don't get too hopeful. I know the State's Attorney. She's smart and ambitious. She doesn't like dawdling on cases. She thinks it makes the office look lazy, and that doesn't sit well with voters. But I'll see what I can do."

Ellie dragged an office chair behind Jason and pushed him into it. She placed her hands on his thin shoulders and kissed him on the top of the head. "We'll get you out of this if I have to stage a one-woman sit-in."

"She'd do it, too," Olivia said to Del. "She was a terror in the late sixties and early seventies."

"She's still a terror," Del said lightly.

"Now let me make that call." He motioned across the room to Cody to take Jason back to his cell, then retreated into his private office and closed the door.

Once Jason had been led away, Ellie wilted into the visitor's chair and curled into a ball. Olivia stepped outside the building and dialed Maddie's cell.

"Livie, what's going on? I've been hearing all sorts of rumors."

Olivia filled her in on Jason's situation and the rest of her visit to the dance studio. "I need more information about Raoul and this mysterious dancing companion of his. With all those costumes in her closet, she must have been a professional ballerina."

"She still dances beautifully," Maddie said. "Maybe whatever caused her scar didn't affect her ability or skill, but she was so traumatized she withdrew from the public eye. If that's what happened, maybe I could find something online about it. I wish we knew her name."

"About that," Olivia said. "I did find out Raoul's last name from Constance. Which reminds me, why didn't someone tell me Constance is in a wheelchair?"

"Thought you knew. Honestly, I think city life destroyed your knack for gossip. You've been back in town over a year now. How long does it take to catch up? Anyway, the store's getting busy again. Tell me Raoul's last name."

"Raoul Larssen." Olivia waited until Maddie's laughter subsided before she spelled it out. "See what you can find on the Internet and call as soon as you have something."

"What are you going to do?" Maddie asked.

"I'll stay here until we hear from the State's Attorney. Whatever she decides, we have to move fast if we're going to save Jason's neck. I'll stop by to pick up the cookies for Heather. I'm hoping she has some secrets to share. How's Spunky?"

"Lording it over the store. We'll have to order more Yorkshire terrier cookie cutters. Customers keep buying them as soon as they meet that little guy."

"Yeah, he's a born sales-pup." Olivia checked her watch. Past noon already. She'd meant to be back in The Gingerbread House for the whole afternoon. "Do you have plans for this evening?"

"No plans."

The subtle change in Maddie's voice told Olivia that all had not healed between her and Lucas. It was about time to be an interfering friend. "Good. We'll need the evening to bake and research and plan."

■ ■ ■ ■

"Your mom is with Jason, back in his cell," Del said when Olivia returned. "I talked the State's Attorney into backing off for a bit. She admitted Charlene and Charlie Critch both have O-positive blood, but she figured Jason's confession was the clincher. I sympathized with the budget cuts she's gotten socked with lately and pointed out that Jason would be one more prisoner in an overpopulated holding cell. I offered to do more legwork for her. However, if we don't have anything by Saturday morning, she's sending officers to transport Jason. He's already on the arraignment schedule for Monday morning."

"A day and a half. At least that's something," Olivia said.

"And, Livie, when I said 'us,' I meant Cody and me. You are not to get involved this time. Yes, I know you've been helpful, but this could get dangerous. So stay out of this. Do you hear me?"

"Not a word."

"*Livie,* listen —"

"If I want to put myself in danger to help my brother, I have that right."

"You're putting Maddie in danger, too.

317

Heck, last time you put *Spunky* in danger."

"Spunky will be staying home this time."

The front door of the police station opened and the two officers entered, looking cheerful and well fed. Del put his face close to Olivia's, lowered his voice, and said, "If you get yourself or anyone else injured, I'll . . . I'll . . ."

An angry retort flashed through Olivia's mind. She repressed it, spun around, and stalked out of the police station into sweltering heat.

CHAPTER SIXTEEN

Armed with a Gingerbread House cookie box in one hand and a cookie in the other, Olivia set out for the Chatterley Heights Library and a chat with Heather Irwin, Head Librarian. The library was located at the opposite corner of the town square, so the shortest route was through the park. Olivia was relieved to see that the clue-hunting murder-gawkers had finally given up.

Del's order to her not to try to help her own brother had left Olivia feeling both irritable and guilty. After all, Del had saved Jason from being dragged off in shackles. She was grateful for that. On the other hand, he had practically threatened her. She'd had no choice but to walk out on him.

Let it go, Livie. Jason needs you.

Enjoying the soft cushion of grass, Olivia zigzagged from one shade tree to the next. Her cranky mood began to improve. It didn't hurt that she was munching on a violet cookie shaped like a book, entitled *Purple Prose.*

The Chatterley Heights Public Library was housed in a small brick building next to the post office. A flower box decorated a square window near the front door. The first thing Olivia noticed was that the petunias were fried. Heather kept those flowers watered with the anxious concern of a new mother. She must be quite ill.

As Olivia entered the library, a bell dinged over the door. Two wide-eyed young faces turned to her, at first with hope, then with despair. High school girls, probably, working a summer job to earn money for college. The reason for their despair became evident at once. Everywhere she looked, Olivia saw unshelved books teetering in stacks up to ten high. Without provocation, one stack collapsed and several books slid off a table. One of the girls, a petite redhead, tried to stem the flow and managed to rescue one book.

"So," Olivia said, "I gather Heather is still home sick?"

The second assistant, a thin girl with bowed shoulders, gave her a half-nod. Olivia took this as an exhausted yes. "I'm sure she'll be back soon," Olivia said. When this didn't seem to cheer the girls, she opened her box of cookies. "You two look like you need a pick-me-up." She held the box out to them. "Have a cookie."

Olivia could feel the air lighten, such was the power of Maddie's cookies. Taking turns, the girls chose one cookie each. Olivia noticed that neither selected a book shape. "I'll go check on Heather at home," she said. On her way out, she left four more cookies.

Heather Irwin's farmhouse was as dark as it had been when Olivia found the stash of stolen items in one of the barns. She hesitated at the front door, worried that Heather might be bedridden. Maybe she shouldn't be disturbed. Or maybe she should be moved to a hospital soon.

Olivia rang the doorbell and heard it reverberate inside the house. She waited, listening for the sound of a voice or feet clumping down the stairs. She tried to turn the knob and found the door securely locked. She rang the doorbell again, longer this time. Olivia checked her watch, waited, checked again. A seed of concern took root and flowered into full-blown worry. Heather might be so ill she couldn't get out of bed. Or worse. Olivia considered calling Del; this might be an emergency.

Get a grip, Livie. Maybe Heather was out in her barn, feeding her horse and her collection of barn cats. She might even now be on her way in to work, although Olivia thought she would have recognized Heather's truck on the road. Heather's truck. Olivia deposited her box of cookies on the front seat of her own car before walking around to the back of the house. The garage door was open, revealing Heather's green pick-up inside. Olivia put her hand on the hood; the engine was cold.

The house looked as dark from the back as it had from the front. Olivia walked through the back yard, which needed mowing, and toward Heather's large barn. The door was latched from the outside. She lifted the latch and pulled open the barn door, which required her full weight to accomplish. She stepped inside, called out Heather's name. A horse neighed and several cats meowed, but not with the desperation of starvation. In fact, Olivia saw several bowls half full of dry cat food lined up along one wall. One small black cat ran up to her and wound around her ankles before heading for the food.

Olivia closed up the barn and circled the house. She saw no lights, either upstairs or downstairs. She pressed her nose against the kitchen window, the only one without a curtain. The kitchen had that lived-in look, with dirty dishes piled next to the sink and a coffee mug on the table. The mug looked like the same design as the one Olivia had found in the small barn.

If Geoffrey King had been hiding out in Heather's small, rarely used barn, he might also have picked the lock to her house and taken a mug. Perhaps more. Olivia's worry increased as she imagined Heather walking into her kitchen and finding King brewing himself a cup of coffee. King was a violent man. Heather had been calling in sick to the library every day, so she probably wasn't dead or dying, but she might be black and blue. Maybe she was simply staying out of sight until her bruises healed. Maybe she was hiding from King, not yet aware he couldn't hurt her any . . .

Wait a minute. None of this makes sense. . . . Heather Irwin might be quiet and solitary, but she was also strong and athletic. And smart. She had to know by now that Geoffrey King was dead. If she could open her heavy barn door and feed her animals, then she wasn't bedridden. What if Heather's mysterious boyfriend was Geoffrey King? Heather was shy and hadn't been in a relationship for some time. King could be charming, especially with women who were insecure about their attractiveness. Suddenly, it made sense that no one had seen this boyfriend, including Heather's good friend and neighbor, Gwen Tucker.

Geoffrey King stayed out of sight, operating in the darkness. Maybe he stashed stolen items in Heather's small barn because he knew she rarely went into it. But what if she'd found the loot? Olivia remembered Charlene Critch's black eye. If King had become violent with Heather, he wouldn't have been careful about it. Heather's face would undoubtedly tell the tale. And King had been murdered.

Olivia left the kitchen window and headed up the gravel driveway toward her car, dialing the police station number with her thumb. Del answered before the first ring ended. "Del? Listen, I think I might have something for —" Olivia heard the roar of a powerful engine and spun toward the sound. Heather's green truck exploded from the garage and sped straight toward her. Olivia leaped sideways off the gravel driveway, onto the lawn. Losing her balance, she collapsed into a ball and rolled, the way a ski instructor had once taught her. It had become second nature to Olivia. She had never become a confident skier, so she'd had plenty of time to practice falling.

Taking it slow, Olivia rolled to a sitting position. Heather's green truck was already out of sight. Olivia checked for broken bones. Her injured shoulder felt sore but, on the whole, not too bad. She heard a tinny voice yelling from the grass and realized her cell had flown from her hand when she fell. At least it still worked. She followed the voice, picked up her phone, and said, "Who is this?"

"Olivia? Are you okay? *You* called *me*, remember?"

"Del, of course. I'm fine, really, only a bit shook up. However, I am pleased to report that our murder suspect list has just increased by one."

CHAPTER SEVENTEEN

"How come you get to have all the excitement?" Maddie said. She opened the box of cookies Olivia had taken with her to Heather Irwin's farmhouse. "We might as well eat these. Good thing you stashed them in your car before Heather could run over them. What a waste that would have been."

"Thanks for your concern about my person," Olivia said, reaching into the box. She pulled out a pink book-shaped cookie dusted with darker pink sugar sprinkles. "They say reading is broadening," she said.

"Try not to think about it," Maddie said before biting the roof off a library-shaped cookie. While she chewed, she retrieved her laptop from the kitchen desk. "We weren't too busy today, which was bad for our bottom line but good for research." Depositing her cookie on a plate, Maddie opened the lid of her computer. "I bookmarked the good stuff." When her bookmark list appeared on the screen, Maddie hooked her ankle around a chair and dragged it next to Olivia's at the kitchen table. She set the computer between them. "I had to do a lot of digging to get to this point, for which I want adequate appreciation."

Olivia reached back to the kitchen counter, grabbed Maddie's half-eaten library, and handed it to her. "Have a cookie. Hey, your cookies are the best on earth. What appreciation could be more adequate?"

Maddie slid the box out of Olivia's reach. "Brat. No more cookies for you. Now concentrate." She clicked on a bookmark and up popped the website for the Royal Winnipeg Ballet, based in Manitoba.

"Manitoba, wow," Olivia said. "How do they stay warm in those skimpy costumes?"

"Oh, the ignorance. Ballet is hard work. Sit up front at a ballet sometime; you can watch the dancers sweat."

"Sounds like fun, but I'll pass. What have you found?"

"Wait'll you see, Livie, you will beam with pride. At first I thought it was a mistake on the Internet — and really, how could that be? But then I figured it out. Don't fidget, I'm getting there. Presentation is everything. Okay, first we have to go back some years.

For that I had to find an obsessive-compulsive ballet blogger, which wasn't hard. Ballet is easy to obsess about."

While Maddie squinted at her bookmark list, Olivia inched closer and closer until she could reach around and grab the cookie box. "Brain food," Olivia said in response to Maddie's glare.

"Here we are," Maddie said. "I found this blogger who has collected the names of principal dancers and soloists for every year going back more than fifty years, almost to the troupe's beginning. I skimmed through all of them. Just when I felt blindness begin to descend, I found this." Maddie scrolled back to 1980 and tapped her fingernail against one name on the screen, listed under the category "Principal Players."

Olivia leaned close to make out the tiny print. "Lara Larssen. You don't think . . . ? The last name is spelled the same as Raoul's, but couldn't that be a coincidence?"

"I found a short bio on another website that mentioned Lara was married to a Latin dancer. How many Latin dancers named Larssen can there be on the earth at one time? Lara would have been twenty or so at that time, and I'd guess Raoul to be in his mid-fifties right now, so it fits."

Thinking back to her conversation with

Constance Overton, Olivia said, "Raoul told Constance his wife was dead, but we have only his word for that. Maybe she's in hiding for reasons relating to the scar on her cheek." She did some quick math. "But would our ballerina in the park really be so old? Lara Larssen would be pushing fifty. Could she do all those leaps?"

"Maybe," Maddie said, "if she'd kept dancing and hadn't suffered a major injury. The question is, why? Who dances outdoors in the middle of the night?"

Olivia selected a rectangular cookie decorated as a library card. "Someone who still longs to express herself? Not that I know anything about this artistic expression stuff."

"However, you could be on to something, in your own fuzzy way."

"Or she could be mentally unbalanced," Olivia said.

"Also not unheard of in the artistic world. It would explain why she stays hidden during the day." Maddie scrolled up to 1982 and pointed to the screen. "I have a suspicion that the young Lara Larssen's ballet career was cut short. First, read this list."

Olivia scooted her chair next to Maddie's and scanned another list of dancers. "Okay, so Lara Larssen was still a principal player in 1982."

"This is two years after she was hired by the Royal Winnipeg Ballet." Maddie switched to another screen. "And here it lists Lara Larssen as the dancer chosen to play the role of Clara in *The Nutcracker.* That's pretty heady stuff for a young ballerina. I found a review of her performance that called her the next Margot Fonteyn."

"Margot Fonteyn . . . wasn't she a soap opera star?" Olivia asked.

Maddie was too excited by her Internet discoveries to react. "Now it gets even more interesting," she said, pointing to the screen. "This is the list for the following year, 1983."

"I don't see Lara's name," Olivia said.

"Exactly. She has disappeared, never to dance again, at least in public. I haven't been able to track down another mention of her. You'd think there'd be something on the Internet, given what a splash she made and how mysteriously she disappeared."

"I suppose you searched for death notices?"

"Of course," Maddie said. "No luck. However, I left a question for the blogger who put together this fantastic history-of-the-ballet website. Maybe she'll know something. In fact, let me check again and see if she's had time to respond."

Maddie's fingers bounced around the computer keys, reminding Olivia of little ballet feet. While she waited, Olivia got up to fill the dishwasher and wondered if Del had found Heather Irwin and her speeding green truck. She doubted Heather would disappear forever. She loved her horse too much to leave him without care. She even loved the barn cats and had given each one a name.

"Eureka!" Maddie paused a few moments to read the blogger's response to her question. "Okay, Livie, here's the scoop. Lara was a gifted dancer, but she was of a delicate constitution complicated by feelings of inadequacy, or that's what the blogger tells me. This is, after all, the Internet, so the information might be anything from total truth to romantic hogwash. Anyway, she says Lara developed a serious problem with anorexia. In those days, ballerinas had to be tiny. They got weighed all the time. Lots of ballerinas had problems with anorexia and bulimia. It's still a problem. Sad."

"Any information about Lara's ultimate fate?" Olivia asked.

"Let me finish. Nope, my blogger says she fell off the edge of the earth. I guess we struck out on this one."

"Not to worry, we'll keep searching." The

Gingerbread House cookie box held two more cookies. Olivia handed the gold lion with blue dragée eyes to Maddie. Olivia bit into the other cookie, a library building decorated with pale green ivy leaves.

"I need to do some cutting and baking this evening," Maddie said. "We've managed to run through most of the supply in the freezer. Want to help?"

"I do," said Olivia. "Should we grab a pizza?"

Staring at her computer screen, Maddie said, "I agreed to have dinner with Lucas tonight." She didn't sound happy. "I should be back in an hour."

"Maddie? Is there something you want to talk about?" Olivia sat down next to her.

Maddie shook her head at the computer screen.

"Maybe later?"

Maddie shrugged her shoulders and stood up. "Back in an hour. Then you can lay out your plan. Because I know you have one, and it better be good. We have about thirty-six hours to save your brother."

After Maddie left, Olivia finished cleaning the kitchen and got out ingredients in preparation for their baking session that evening. She wished she were half as well organized as everyone seemed to think she was. She had managed, without forethought, to add Heather as a suspect in Geoffrey King's death. She'd almost, but not really, found the mysterious dancer in the park, who may or may not have witnessed Geoffrey King's murder. And if she had witnessed the murder, she might be incapable of testifying due to mental disturbance. The suspects she hadn't tackled at all were the obvious ones: Charlene and Charlie Critch.

A subdued Maddie returned to The Gingerbread House kitchen in less than an hour. When she began to page through a decorated cookie cookbook that she knew by heart, Olivia couldn't stand the tension another minute. She needed Maddie at her best, not distracted and mopey. "How's Lucas these days?"

Maddie's eyes flitted up to Olivia's face and down again. "Fine."

" 'Fine' is not an acceptable answer," Olivia said. She heard the impatience in her own voice and didn't care. "Tell me what is going on between you and Lucas. One minute he is the love of your life and the next he's just . . . fine."

"Come on, Livie, it's no big deal. These things cool down, that's all."

"Not that fast and not without a reason."

Olivia filled Mr. Coffee with water, threw in some ground coffee, and snapped the switch. "Madeline Briggs, you and I need to talk."

"I thought you were worried about Jason. Your brother, remember? Suddenly my love life is more important than your own brother's *actual* life?"

"Don't change the subject. Sit." Olivia grabbed a chair and pressed it against the back of Maddie's legs until she had to sit down.

"Hey," Maddie said. "When did you get so bossy?"

"I'm an elder child, I was born bossy." Olivia poured two cups of coffee and put one in front of Maddie. After delivering the cream and sugar, she said, "Look, Maddie, I've been watching you pretend to be your usual super-perky, enthusiastic self, but you're unhappy. When you're unhappy, it isn't much fun around here."

Maddie's freckled face took on a sullen look as she sipped her coffee.

"Okay," Olivia said, "here's what I know. I know that Lucas asked you to marry him."

Maddie's cup rattled on its saucer. "How did you — ?"

"Because Lucas is beyond upset. He talked to me about it. He wants to understand. He's afraid of losing you. Maddie, you've been nuts about Lucas for years. What happened?"

Maddie poured herself another cup of coffee and stirred in silence.

Olivia said, more gently, "Lucas is a great guy, and he loves you. You know that. You will never convince me that you've suddenly lost interest in him. That isn't you. You're loyal. It took you a long time to get over Bobby after he broke your engagement that summer after high school, and Lucas is a much better person. Wait, is that it? Are you afraid the Bobby thing will happen again?"

Maddie dismissed the idea with a wave of her hand and a shake of her head. Progress.

"Then what?"

"Look, Livie, I really, truly don't want to talk about this."

"I get that." Olivia drained the last of the coffee in her cup. If her taste buds were accurate, she had tossed in about twice the correct amount of ground beans. Her heart had picked up about thirty beats per minute. She started a second pot, lower octane. "This has something to do with your parents, doesn't it?"

"What? How did you . . . ? Of course not."

"Nice try," Olivia said, "but I know you too well. You never want to talk about your parents. Maddie, I know how traumatic it is to lose a parent, and you lost both of them at a very young age. But there was something else going on, wasn't there?" When Maddie said nothing, Olivia added, "Mom mentioned that she saw your mother a few times in those months before the accident. She said your mom seemed unhappy, that she was distracted, losing weight."

Maddie stared toward the kitchen floor, sniffled once, and tears began to dribble down her cheeks. Olivia went to her and put a hand on her shoulder. Maddie said, "I hate this."

"Yeah, I know." Olivia said. "You probably hate me right now, too."

"Yep." Maddie ripped off a paper towel and blew her nose. "The least you could have done was wait until we'd started making cookies."

"You're right. I'll undoubtedly rot in hell for that."

"Works for me." Maddie blew her nose again on another paper towel. "Ouch. Put tissues on the grocery list."

"Will do. How about telling me what happened with your parents? You'll feel better, I'll feel better, we can get to those cookies, maybe save my brother's life. . . ."

Maddie half-laughed. "Okay, all right.

Quick version. Mom was depressed, and I guess she started drinking. Anyway, looking back on her behavior, that's what I suspect. On the day of the accident, she was driving. Why, I don't know. Dad usually did all the driving. No one told me the part about Mom being at the wheel until I'd finished college. Aunt Sadie let it slip one day. That's about it."

"So . . . I guess I need a longer version because I'm not connecting the dots. Did you start worrying that marrying Lucas would turn you into a drunk?"

Maddie heaved a huge sigh. "If you're going to force me to talk about this, I really, really need to be baking."

"Okay by me. As you can see, I've lined up the ingredients. The butter is at room temperature. You only have to fire up the mixer." Olivia waved toward the neat line of flour, sugar, and extracts.

Maddie was already mixing flour and salt in a bowl, which she set aside near the mixer. "Mom was depressed. I know that much because I remember hearing one of her friends use the word, and I asked Mom what it meant. She said she was just feeling a little sad and not to worry about it. Dad was traveling a lot for work. I don't know, maybe she was lonely. Mom and Dad had always been so close, at least until those last few months. Dad seemed to be gone all the time, and Mom must have stopped eating because she lost a lot of weight."

"Do you think she might have been seriously ill?" Olivia put the flour away and refilled their coffee cups.

"No, Aunt Sadie would have told me. I do have to wonder if my dad was having an affair. That's something I would never be able to dredge out of Aunt Sadie. She thinks I'm still ten and terribly vulnerable."

"She loves you."

"Yeah, I know." Maddie yanked another towel off the roll. Her nose had turned red from the roughness of the paper.

While Maddie washed her hands, Olivia took a roll of toilet paper from the kitchen storage cabinet. She tore off the paper cover and plunked the whole roll on the table next to Maddie.

"Here's the irony, though," Maddie said as she measured sugar into the mixer bowl. "Hand me the butter, will you?"

"Irony?"

Maddie opened the wrapper and scraped globs of soft butter into the bowl with the sugar. "Mom and Dad were going off for a weekend away together the day they died. They were driving to the mountains, planning to stay in the same place they went for their honeymoon."

"Maybe they were trying to work things out?"

"What I remember so vividly was that when Mom leaned over to kiss me good-bye, I smelled her perfume. It was the first time I'd seen her smile in a long time. That was the last time I saw her." Maddie switched on the mixer, indicating she was done talking about her parents, and lowered the spinning blades into the sugar and butter.

Olivia reached for a hunk of toilet paper.

While Maddie made noise in the kitchen, Olivia picked up her cell and headed for the kitchen door. When Maddie paused the mixer and glanced up at her, Olivia said, "I want to call Del and find out what happened with Heather." Maddie nodded and went back to work.

Spunky was curled in a ball on the padded seat of an antique chair near the large front window. His head lifted when he saw Olivia. "Hey, you lazy bum." Spunky wagged his fluffy tail and tried to lick Olivia's face as she picked him up. When she sat on the brocade-covered seat, Spunky circled in her lap and collapsed into a ball again. Olivia wove her fingers into the silky fur that tended to fall over his eyes. Time for a trim. Spunky sighed with contentment as Olivia massaged his ears and stared out the window at the park. The setting sun lent a warm glow to the collection of copper cookie cutters hanging from tiny suction cups on the window. Sometimes she felt as if she lived in a real gingerbread house . . . except, of course, the oven was used only to bake cookies. Olivia had a feeling this might be her last contemplative moment for some time.

With her free hand, Olivia opened her cell phone and called Del. He answered immediately. "Livie, are you okay?"

"Fine, Del, really. I don't think Heather was actually aiming her truck at me. Did you find her?"

"We did, although we can't take much credit for it. She'd pulled over only a few miles from her farm. We found her curled up on the front seat, balling her eyes out. Getting anything coherent out of her took some time. She cried all the way back to the station and through most of the interview."

"Was I right? Is she a suspect?"

"We consider her a suspect, yes."

In her excitement, Olivia shifted suddenly, causing Spunky to tumble off her lap.

"That's good news for Jason," Del said. "Heather has a motive but no alibi. A knife similar to the murder weapon was part of the loot you found in her barn, so she might have had access to another in the same set. That's not for general consumption."

"Understood." Spunky lifted his front paws to Olivia's knees, scouting out the possibility of regaining her lap. She patted her thigh, and he jumped up. "Did you find out if Heather knew about the stolen goods in her barn?"

"Denied all knowledge. Claims she didn't know someone was hanging out there, that she rarely entered that barn."

"I'm inclined to believe her," Olivia said. "No horses, no cats . . . Heather loves animals. She'd have no reason to trek way out to a run-down barn unless there were animals to care for. Except . . ."

"What?"

"Well, I suppose she might have seen the stuff if she decided to check out the condition of the folding chairs. Gwen said Heather had volunteered to bring them to the baby shower. That's why I was there, to get those chairs."

"Thanks. I'll follow up on that. For now, we had to let her go. We had no evidence linking her to King's murder. However, since she has no alibi for the night of the murder, she stays on the list. Do I dare hope you will let me take it from here?"

With a light laugh, Olivia said, "One can always hope. I do have a request, and it has nothing to do with the murder. I know how busy you are, but could you see if you can find any information about the car accident that killed Maddie's parents? They lived in Clarksville when they died, but maybe you know someone who could dig up some details? Maddie won't check for herself, she doesn't want to know."

"But you think she should?"

"Long story, Del. Let's just leave it that Maddie needs to work through a few things before she can move on to another stage in her own life. I'd like to help her do that."

"I'll see what I can do. Are we still on for tomorrow evening?"

"Tomorrow? Friday?"

"Tomorrow would be Friday, that is correct. Dinner?"

"Oh gosh, Del, I'm so sorry. I sort of . . ."

"Forgot. I get it," Del said, a touch of curtness edging into his voice. "Did you make other plans?"

"Well . . . The Gingerbread House might be staying open late tomorrow for sort of a special event."

"Sort of a special event? Is it, by any chance, the sort of event where a guest might suddenly get whacked with a blunt object?"

"Del, you are so suspicious. Although you're a cop, so it's understandable, and besides, you're probably on the right track. We have so little time. I can't help thinking there are folks who know more than they realize. I'm looking for a way to get that information as fast as possible. I might decide it won't work."

"Well, let me know if you want me to hang around. Meanwhile, I'll put Cody to work on the Briggs' car accident."

"Oh, and I have one more request."

"Which is?

"It's about Jason." Olivia hesitated, searching for the right phrasing. When it eluded her, she went for blunt. "Jason needs to be here tomorrow evening. Now hear me out, Del. You and Cody can watch him every minute, as long as you're subtle about it."

With an exaggerated sigh, Del asked, "Are you planning to tell me why you think this bad idea is actually a good one?"

"Of course," Olivia said. "I want everyone to think Jason has been cleared."

"Again, why?"

"So that I can clear him, of course.

Thanks, you're the best." Olivia closed her phone before Del could respond.

A moment after Olivia hung up her cell, Maddie burst through the kitchen door. "Livie, that ex-husband of yours is on the line. I told him you'd been sold into slavery, but he ignored me. He always ignores me. You have to talk to him." Maddie disappeared into the kitchen without waiting for a response.

"Sorry, Spunks, you're on your own again." Olivia scooped him out of her lap and nestled him back onto the seat alone. He curled into the warm spot she'd left behind.

When Olivia entered the kitchen, Maddie had the mixer going as close as possible to the phone receiver. With a rhythmic *splat-splat,* the paddle whacked the ingredients into a smooth dough. Maddie slid the mixer farther away but didn't turn it off as Olivia lifted the phone receiver.

"Ryan?"

"What is that racket? Can't Maddie do that someplace else? I'm on the phone."

"You're actually in The Gingerbread House kitchen, Ryan." However, Olivia shot Maddie a pleading look, and the mixer stopped.

"That's better. Livie, listen, I've got great

news. The clinic is moving along faster than we ever anticipated, and we might be able to open in a month. I need to talk to you about that as soon as possible. I'll stop by tomorrow evening. We can go out to dinner somewhere. I know there isn't much in that little town, so we'll head out and find something more interesting. I'll pick you up at seven. I've got a lot —"

"Ryan, stop, take a breath. I'm glad the clinic plan is going well, but tomorrow is impossible for me. I have other plans."

"Cancel them. This is important."

"My plans are important, too, and I resent your —"

"Look, Livie, I don't have time to argue. I'm meeting tonight with a backer, and I can't be late. You and I have something very important to talk about, and it can't wait any longer. So I'll see you —"

"Ryan, do not come here tomorrow, do you hear me? Ryan?" Olivia slammed the phone on its cradle. "He hung up on me. Can you believe that?"

"Oh yes," Maddie said, "I can believe it. If he does show up, can I punch him in the nose? Or perhaps a more sensitive spot?"

"I can't worry about Ryan right now." Olivia flopped down on a chair. "We have only one more day to come up with something, anything, that will keep Jason from being taken away and booked for Geoffrey King's murder. I need to think."

"How can I help? Or I can be very quiet, if that would be better." Maddie retrieved a box from the top of the refrigerator and twisted off the lid. It took a few moments for Olivia to realize that Maddie was laying cookie cutters on the kitchen table.

"Are those new?" Olivia moved her chair closer.

"I can't get that ballerina out of my head," Maddie said. "So I ordered all the ballet cookie cutters I could find. I guess that makes it official; I am a cookie cutter addict. They are so fun and calming and . . . Livie?"

"Hmm?" Olivia held a cookie cutter in the shape of a leaping ballerina. "Does this step have a name?"

"Jeté," Maddie said.

"That's French."

"Is it? I guess I knew that once." Maddie began to roll out a ball of cookie dough she'd been cooling in the refrigerator. After several moments of silent concentration, she glanced at Olivia, who was still staring at the leaping ballerina cutter. "Livie, you have that look on your face. What's up?"

Olivia slid the ballet cookie cutters toward

Maddie. "Let's use only these cutters for tomorrow evening's event."

"Fine by me," Maddie said.

"How early can you be up tomorrow morning?"

Maddie glanced up from her half-rolled dough.

"This is me, remember? I can stay up all night. Why?"

Olivia flexed her tight shoulders. Worrying about Jason was getting to her. However, a good night's rest would have to wait. "I haven't returned Constance's key to her," she said. "We can still get into the dance studio."

"I thought Raoul was only gone on Thursdays," Maddie said.

"Rumor has it he goes to early Mass every weekday morning, followed by confession after Friday Mass. Any idea how long confession takes?"

With the back of her hand, Maddie pushed an errant lock of curly hair off her forehead, leaving a streak of flour behind. "According to one of my Catholic friends, the goal is to get in and out with some Hail Marys and a few Our Fathers, but if she's feeling really guilty about something, confession can stretch to maybe fifteen minutes. But she usually makes an appointment for one of those. If Raoul goes after Mass, there's probably a waiting line."

"Well then, we'll have to be efficient," Olivia said. "I need to find the ballerina of the park, and I'm assuming she doesn't go to Mass with Raoul."

Maddie dipped a ballet shoe cookie cutter in flour and positioned it on her rolled dough. "If we actually find her at home, won't she tell Raoul?"

"I don't think so," Olivia said as she selected a cookie cutter in the shape of a ballerina performing an arabesque. She dipped it in flour and handed it to Maddie. "Anyway, I'm guessing the woman will be out cold while Raoul is gone. I researched those pills I found next to Valentina's bed. They were powerful sleeping pills. I suspect Raoul has been drugging her. I would love to know why."

Maddie looked up from her cookie cutting, emerald eyes sparkling. "Wow. Do you think keeping her drugged might have something to do with King's murder? Like maybe Raoul has some reason he doesn't want her to be seen and identified? Maybe King got mixed up with mobsters. Maybe Raoul and the ballerina saw him and now they're in the Witness Protection Program!"

"I doubt it," Olivia said. "The Witness

Protection Program would never have allowed Raoul to continue dancing. He'd be too recognizable, too easy to track down."

"He'd have to give up dancing?" Maddie held a pirouetting ballerina cookie cutter in the palm of her hand. "How sad. Remind me never to witness a mob hit."

"Duly noted." Olivia slid a pan of cookies into the oven. "I have a theory about Raoul," she said. "The trouble is, I don't have a bit of evidence."

"What? Tell me!"

"It doesn't really qualify as a theory," Olivia said. "I keep thinking about Ida's story of the dancing ghost."

The oven timer dinged. Maddie wedged open the oven door to take a look, releasing the sweet-spicy fragrance of orange and nutmeg. "Perfect," she said. "One more batch and we're done with the baking. Ida's brain is a little on the buttery side, you know."

"I got that impression," Olivia said, "but maybe we shouldn't ignore every detail of her story."

"Like what?"

"Like her account of a man threatening the dancer. Ida described that incident in some detail, and I did find a dress with a rip in the front. She said the ballerina kicked him and got away. Ida seemed so pleased by the dancer's feistiness that I dismissed the story as fantasy, especially when I found out she didn't report the incident to the police. But what if it was true? We've been thinking of the dancer as an older woman reliving her lost days as a prima ballerina . . . as someone damaged, in need of protection from any human contact."

While the batches of cookies were baking, Maddie had managed to whip up a batch of royal icing and divide it into covered containers for coloring. She added three drops of medium pink gel food coloring to one container and stirred the icing. "If Ida wasn't hallucinating," Maddie said, "then it seems to me our ballerina is one strong chick. A fighter."

"And young," Olivia said. "The way Ida described the incident, it didn't sound like a typical mugging. Think about it, the man grabbed the dancer and lifted her off her feet."

"So you think this woman might not be Raoul's wife? But Livie, all those costumes you described to me, they must have been Lara's from the roles she danced with the Royal Winnipeg Ballet."

"I'm sure they are," Olivia said, "but . . . like mother, like daughter?"

"Raoul and Lara's daughter. . . . I wonder. Pregnancy would certainly explain Lara's interrupted career." Maddie twisted a lid on the icing container she'd been working on and sat at her laptop. "There are a lot of ballet fanatics out there. It's hard to believe one of them wouldn't have uncovered the fact that Lara had a daughter. And said daughter must have trained as a ballerina. Let me check her bio again." She typed in Lara Larssen and selected Wikipedia. Skimming the brief biography, Maddie said, "Sketchy. I'm surprised her ardent fans haven't filled in more details, but it happens all the time."

"Exactly," Olivia said. "Internet information can be wrong and full of holes. Someone would have to hunt down official and private documents to locate birth certificates and medical records. If there was no public notice, like a newspaper obituary, even finding a death could take a lot of effort. Lara only danced professionally for two years. Maybe those ardent ballet fans didn't think she was all that interesting."

"Point taken," Maddie said. "The Internet is less than godlike. Maybe the dancer is Lara and Raoul's daughter, but where does that get us? If Raoul is drugging her whenever he leaves the studio, we won't be able to talk to her. It seems like an awful risk for not much gain."

Olivia felt suddenly lightheaded and realized she had been hyperventilating. She'd already gotten away with sneaking into Raoul's living quarters, but she'd had all day to do it, and no one had been home. Now there was a good chance someone would be there, and their time would be short. She'd be dragging Maddie into danger, too. They might be caught, even arrested. Del would never forgive her. Then Olivia thought of Jason, her baby brother, being carted off in shackles, standing trial for murder. She wished she hadn't mentioned anything to Maddie. Luckily, she hadn't yet revealed her real reason for wanting to get into the dance studio again — Raoul's little private office upstairs. She was willing to bet he had records in there somewhere.

"You're right," Olivia said. "We'd be taking a big risk for little or no gain. I'll give Constance her key back tomorrow. Meanwhile, let's finish these cookies and get a good night's sleep for once."

They finished by two thirty Friday morning. Olivia sent Maddie home, left the kitchen a mess, and checked the store locks. A sleepy Yorkie snuggled against her chest as she lumbered up the stairs to her apartment. She told herself that leaving Maddie out was the best decision. She wouldn't have much time to search through Raoul's papers, if indeed she could find any helpful documents, but she'd do what she could. If she got caught, so be it. Her baby brother was worth the risk.

CHAPTER EIGHTEEN

Promptly at five forty-five Friday morning, after less than three hours of fitful sleep, Olivia gave Spunky extra food and a hug. She locked her apartment door, leaving behind her whining pet. Halfway down the stairs, she realized something was amiss in the foyer. She could see light streaming from the entrance to The Gingerbread House. She was already keyed up. A break-in at the store was the last thing she needed. She eased down the steps, mentally preparing herself for whatever disaster awaited. A light *thump-rattle* sound came from inside the store, like someone bumping into a display table. Olivia froze five steps from the bottom of the stairs and reached into her jeans pocket for her cell.

"I thought those stealthy steps might be you." Maddie's face peeked around the doorjamb. "Cutting it a little close, aren't we?" She wore black jeans and a black

T-shirt. Her bright red hair hid underneath a large beret. Black, of course. "What, you thought you could sneak off on an adventure without me? Please. I've known you too long to fall for your feeble effort to pretend you'd changed your mind. I could tell the moment you decided to go it alone. So come on, we need to be hiding outside the dance studio in time to see Raoul leave for Mass. Otherwise, we can't be sure he's gone."

Olivia heaved a dramatic sigh. "Oh, Maddie, Maddie, Maddie. You're my best friend, and you are totally nuts."

"If that's your way of admitting you can't outsmart me, then apology accepted. Now, let's get a move on."

Maddie turned off the store light while Olivia poked her head out the front door. Except for one car, the town square looked deserted. That wouldn't last long. Business owners would begin arriving anytime after six a.m., especially for the two restaurants, which opened at seven. "Let's go out the back," Olivia said. "I wish I'd thought this out better, but I was dead tired last night."

"Not to worry," Maddie said. "I'm at my best when I'm winging it. You did remember the key, right?"

Olivia felt the shape of it in her pocket.

"Present and accounted for. That much I planned."

They slipped into the empty alley behind The Gingerbread House. "Good thing it isn't garbage day," Olivia whispered. "Let's go behind the stores instead of down Willow Road, then we can cut through that little park across the street from the dance studio."

"Good idea," Maddie said. "No one uses that park much, and it's got lots of trees. Try to look like we're out for an early morning walk, in case some obsessive store owner decided to arrive early to do inventory or something. You never know."

Olivia and Maddie walked with brisk casualness down the alley behind the stores on the east side of the town square. They'd encountered no one by the time they reached the park that stretched for a block from Hickory Road to Willow Road. The wooded area wasn't really a park, simply a large lot that had gone wild after two small houses burned down decades earlier.

Once they'd decided on a spot to hide and watch for Raoul to leave for Mass, Maddie asked, "What if he takes the back door?"

"No reason he would," Olivia said. "Constance said he goes to St. Francis, which is on south Park Street. The greater danger is he might cut through these woods."

"That's so comforting."

"That's why we're staying on the north edge." Across the dance floor, Olivia saw a light flick on in the office at the rear of the studio. Instinctively, she drew back behind a tree, yanking Maddie with her.

"Ow," Maddie whispered. "I think you dislocated my shoulder."

"Sorry. Look, there's Raoul in that little room at the back." Within seconds, the light went out. For several moments, the dance floor looked deserted. Olivia moved out of cover of the tree to see better. "I think he did go out the back," she said, cursing herself for overconfidence.

"No, I can see him," Maddie said. "The front door is opening." This time it was she who strong-armed Olivia out of sight.

Dressed in a light gray suit, Raoul looked exotically handsome. He glanced up and down the street before he crossed the lawn and walked to the north side of the studio. Maddie groaned. "Oh geez, what now? He's supposed to go south."

Olivia shifted several trees over to get a better view of the studio's north side. She saw Raoul pause and look up at the top floor. "I think he's checking at our ballerina's window. Maybe he wants to be sure she's asleep, not watching for him to leave."

"Do you think he left her room unlocked?" Maddie asked. "We might be able to talk to her."

"He's leaving. I wonder if he was worried she hadn't swallowed those pills I saw next to her bed. Okay, he's out of sight, time to rumba." Olivia glanced up and down Willow Road. "No cars," she said. "This is a quiet area, thank goodness. Let's double back to the end of the block and go up the alley in back of the studio."

"Okay, but we'd better step on it." Maddie's strong legs took her quickly through the trees. Olivia had to rush to keep her in sight. Once in the open, they tried to look casual, especially when several cars drove past. By the time they reached the rear door, Olivia felt so wound up she fumbled as she tried to fit the key in the lock.

"Livie? Are you okay? Your hand is shaking."

"Just excited," Olivia said. "I felt a lot calmer yesterday when I had more time. Okay, we're in." She took a deep breath, which slowed her heart-beat. She couldn't afford a case of nerves, not with Jason's life on the line. She locked the door behind them and put her finger to her lips as she pointed to the staircase. "Our dancer is

358

probably upstairs," she whispered, "asleep or awake."

Maddie nodded. "I'll go check on the bedroom, if you want to get going in the study."

"Thanks." Olivia led the way upstairs. At the top, she pointed Maddie toward the bedroom. "I'll be there," she whispered, nodding toward the study. "Be careful." Maddie grinned like a kid playing a game of international espionage, which triggered one of Olivia's bad feelings. She told herself Maddie was reliable . . . for the most part. When it was important. Too late now, anyway.

In the small, littered study, Olivia realized at once that Raoul, though precise and meticulous as a dancer, had no organizational impulse when it came to paper. She headed for a wooden desk with two drawers. It looked old, battered rather than antique. Papers covered the top of the desk, the chair seat, and the bookshelves. There were papers on the floor and she didn't see evidence of any attempt to sort them into piles. Olivia felt overwhelmed. She wondered if Raoul experienced the same emotion, having to deal with all this paper. She scanned the top of the desk and saw numerous invoices, apparently for medical treatments, many of them stamped PAST DUE. Would an itinerant dance teacher be able to afford health insurance, let alone such an array of medical bills?

Olivia checked dates and found a pattern. The oldest papers were on the floor, more recent ones on the bookshelves, and the newest papers covered the desk. She extricated a letter from the chaotic desktop. It was a brief description of a patient's treatment progress, signed by a psychiatrist at The Psychiatric Institute of Washington in DC. Olivia was skimming through it, feeling guilty, when she heard a creaking sound behind her. She spun around to face the door.

"Hey, it's just me," Maddie whispered. "Wait'll you hear what I found out. What's wrong? You look like you're about to faint."

"This is me being excited. Read this." Olivia handed the letter to Maddie.

"Wow," Maddie said. *"Patient has regressed . . . down from ninety to eighty-five pounds . . . appears to be hallucinating about being attacked again . . . reliving trauma. . . .* The letter is dated yesterday. This must be where Raoul goes every Thursday."

"I'd bet on it," Olivia said. "I suspect that attack was no hallucination."

"So Ida wasn't imagining things." Maddie

took stock of the room. "Kind of messy, isn't he?"

"Probably overwhelmed."

"This patient," Maddie said, peering at the papers on the desk, "is she named anywhere? She's right down the hall, by the way. Sound asleep."

"The bedroom door was open? She might hear us."

"Not a chance," Maddie said. "The door is bolted shut on the outside. But here's what I wanted to tell you. There's a covered peephole in the door, aimed right at the bed. I saw our ballerina. At first, she was facing away, all curled up like a little girl. Then she turned over, which just about stopped my heart. But I got a good look at her, and you were right. Being so thin makes her face look older at first glance, but she is young. I'm betting she's Raoul's daughter. If we could only find a name on one of these reports. . . . Do these guys ever say anything but 'the patient this' or the 'the patient that'?"

"What you're holding might be a copy of the doctor's notes," Olivia said. "There should be some identifying information on the bills, at least." She shifted a few papers on the desk. "Here's one. And there it is! Her name is Valentina. Valentina Larssen."

"Yay!" Maddie clapped a hand over her mouth. "Sorry," she whispered. "I am subject to glee attacks. What do we do now?"

Olivia glanced at her watch. "We're running out of time. I really want to know if Valentina talked to the psychiatrist about her dancing in town square, what she might have seen. Even if he thought she was hallucinating, maybe he recorded the details."

"Where would we even start?"

"On the desk. That's the most recent stuff." Olivia was already riffling through the papers. In the midst of such disorganization, she told herself, surely Raoul would never notice anything had been moved.

Maddie peered out the window, which faced Willow Road. "The world is waking up out there. We'd better make it snappy."

Precious minutes passed as they pawed through papers, looking for anything that mentioned Valentina's night dancing. Olivia had become a woman obsessed, desperate to find evidence that might clear her brother. It was Maddie's turn to exhibit frayed nerves. She briefly helped the search but soon gave up to check the window and the hallway. She disappeared once to make sure Valentina was still asleep in her room.

Olivia could feel her concentration flag, dragged down by despair. The psychiatrist seemed to dismiss whatever Valentina said as the imaginings of a damaged psyche. "I think I hate psychiatrists," she muttered. Maddie did not comment. She was gone again, probably checking the shower to make sure Raoul wasn't hiding in it. Olivia knew her time was nearly up, that she was tempting disaster by staying longer. Only a few papers left, she told herself. What if the evidence was right there, in those last unexamined reports?

Olivia heard Maddie arrive at the study door, but she didn't look up. Her hand shaking, Olivia picked up a sheet of paper and skimmed the first paragraph. "This is it."

"What was that?" Maddie asked.

"The evidence," Olivia said as her eyes skimmed the page. "I think I've found it."

"No, *listen,*" Maddie hissed. "What was that sound?"

Olivia's body tightened.

"It's a door opening downstairs," Maddie said, staring at her with huge eyes in an ashen face. "We're too late."

Olivia raced to the window in time to see Raoul walk away from the front door, pick a newspaper off the lawn, and head back toward the studio. Her mind took off at a gallop. She and Maddie needed to be out the back entrance before Raoul could get upstairs to check on his daughter. Not even Maddie's legs could move that fast without making a racket. It couldn't be done.

The faint sound of whistling drifted upstairs. Raoul was inside now. The whistling grew louder; he must have been coming up the stairs. Maddie unfroze herself from the study doorway and stumbled into the room. Olivia zipped through a series of escape ideas, all of which led to their discovery and ultimate disgrace. Yet staying put would be equally disastrous. Raoul was likely to glance into or enter any upstairs room. There was no predicting which one or when.

"What are we going to do?" Maddie breathed in Olivia's ear.

"We have to stay in this room," Olivia whispered back. "No choice." The door had been slightly ajar when they arrived. Maybe they could flatten themselves against the wall beside it, so they'd be hidden if Raoul entered the study. No, if he stayed to do some work, he'd eventually hear them. Olivia scoured the room for other ideas. She saw another door, also ajar, which she eased open. A storage closet, big enough to hold a small wardrobe . . . or two grown women.

They heard whistling nearby. Raoul was

in the upstairs hallway. Olivia grasped Maddie by the upper arm and pulled her into the closet, leaving the door ajar.

The whistling stopped. Olivia sensed Raoul standing in the study doorway. She imagined him taking in the condition of the room. He might be noticing that his papers were not as he had left them.

Raoul began to whistle another tune, which sounded vaguely familiar. Olivia had heard it at her mother's dance lesson. A rumba. He was in the room. Olivia realized she was still holding the psychiatrist's notes she'd been so thrilled to find. The whistling stopped. Olivia didn't dare move for fear the paper might crinkle. All she could do was hope that Raoul wasn't searching for that one page.

The continued silence should have been reassuring, but Olivia's imagination filled it with specters of an enraged Raoul about to swing the closet door wide while he called 911. Maddie shifted a bit. She was closest to the open crack and was trying to see into the room. Before Olivia could stop her, Maddie edged the door open a few more inches and peeked through. Nothing happened. Maddie pushed the door wider and poked her head into the room. Pulling back inside, she whispered, "I think I hear him releasing the chain lock on Valentina's bedroom door. We could try to make a run for it." She tiptoed toward the office door.

"Too dangerous," Olivia said. "If she's asleep, he'll come right back out. Even if we get out of sight in time, he'll hear us run down the stairs."

Maddie peeked into the hallway, then hurried to the safety of the closet. "You nailed it," she said. "I saw his foot step out of the bedroom. I can hear him coming this way."

Olivia felt sweat collecting under the light bangs that waved across her forehead. At this rate, she'd need another shower before greeting customers.

"Okay, I think he's on the stairs." Maddie cracked open the closet door and listened. Olivia took the opportunity to fold the paper she'd been holding and stuff it into her jeans pocket.

"I don't hear a thing," Maddie said. "Maybe Raoul is downstairs. He starts teaching at nine, doesn't he?" She checked her watch. "Yikes, it's eight forty. How did that happen? We have no chance of escaping until Raoul is in the studio with a student, and we are supposed to open the store in twenty minutes. We're doomed."

"Probably," Olivia whispered, "but not because we'll be late opening the store. I

366

called Bertha and Mom last night."

"Whew. I may need to reconsider this thinking-ahead idea," Maddie said. "Raoul must be downstairs getting ready to teach. I'm about to suffocate in here." She pushed the door open wide enough to slide through. "All clear," she said, checking the hallway.

Olivia left the closet and went straight to the window. "I don't see a car parked in front," she said, "though anyone who lives in Chatterley Heights would probably walk to a lesson."

"Shh," Maddie said. "I hear something."

"It's music," Olivia said, "coming from downstairs. Which means Raoul could be in the office or out on the dance floor." Her mind began to click off possible escape ideas, but they all involved going through the office. "How can we know for sure that Raoul is in the dance studio?"

"Only one way to find out," Maddie said. Before Olivia could stop her, Maddie stepped into the hallway, leaving the door wide open. She looked down the hallway toward the staircase, as if preparing to sneak downstairs. Instead, she spun around ninety degrees and turned to stone. Olivia rushed toward the open doorway, her heart pounding inside her brain.

Maddie's jaw slowly dropped. "Livie," she

said. "You'd better come out here."

Olivia stepped out and joined Maddie. Light spilled into the dim hallway through the open door of the ballerina's bedroom. An ethereal creature dressed in layers of pink chiffon watched them. Her body was so slight that for a moment Olivia thought she was a mirage. But her face was real, the scar on her cheek unmistakable. Her light brown eyes regarded Olivia and Maddie in a calm and incurious way.

Olivia breathed the name, "Valentina."

"Yes," Valentina said, "though Daddy calls me Tiny. I know who you are. You are the ones who make beautiful cookies. You saw me dancing in the park. Daddy told me." Despite her size and childlike way of speaking, Valentina appeared to be in her mid-twenties.

"We just finished making some ballerina cookies," Olivia said, "in your honor. You dance so wonderfully."

A ghost of a smile touched Valentina's lips. "I would love to see the cookies. Daddy tells me I have to eat more. He doesn't know you are here, does he? If he did, he would have locked me in my room to protect me."

"We wanted to meet you, Valentina," Olivia said. "We need to ask you something important."

"Daddy wouldn't like that. You should leave before he sees you." Valentina cocked her head, as if to listen. A thick lock of straight, white-gold hair fell across her face, nearly obscuring the scar on her cheek. Olivia realized how beautiful she must have been. "Daddy will be on the dance floor right now," Valentina said. "He is warming up before he starts teaching. You can go out the back door. If you are quiet, Daddy won't see or hear you. He is in another world when he dances."

Olivia reached out a hand in supplication. "Please, Valentina, one question only, I promise. It would mean so much to me and my family. I have a younger brother, Jason. He is in trouble. The sheriff thinks he killed a bad man, but I know he didn't. All I want to know is if you were dancing in the park a few nights ago . . . Tuesday, the night of the storm. If you were, did you see anything, anyone?"

Small as she was, Valentina shrank into herself. She turned her face toward her bedroom but did not escape into it, which Olivia found hopeful, yet puzzling. The psychiatric report Olivia had read described a frail creature so damaged that she couldn't think or act rationally. Certainly, Valentina appeared to exist in a world of her own.

However, the Valentina standing before her, though delicate and damaged, might make a credible witness.

Valentina turned to face Olivia. Tears bunched in her eyes. She blinked until they burst and trickled down her face, following the line of the scar on her left cheek. "I didn't want to dance in the storm," she said.

"But before the storm," Olivia said. She could hear desperation in her own voice and took a deep breath to calm herself. "Did you see anything at all that night? Or anyone?"

Valentina's frail body began to shiver. She reached up to her cheek and touched her scar.

"Please, Valentina. Jason is my baby brother. He doesn't deserve this. I know he didn't kill that man. You are my brother's only hope." It was too much pressure; she knew it as soon as she said it. Valentina's face contorted in agony as she fled into her room. Olivia heard the click of a lock.

"We've got to get out of here," Maddie said. "Now!" She grabbed Olivia's arm and dragged her toward the staircase. Olivia didn't fight her. Her chance had evaporated, but she'd find another. Somehow.

With Maddie in the lead, they tiptoe-ran down the stairs. Maddie peeked into the kitchen and signaled the all clear. The tough part came next. The door leading from the kitchen into the dance studio stood wide open. A familiar waltz played on the CD player.

Maddie yanked her along by the upper arm. "It's three minutes to nine, and that waltz is almost over," she hissed in Olivia's ear. "Raoul will be coming into the kitchen to set up music for his students."

Olivia nodded and reached for the doorknob. It wouldn't turn. She remembered she'd flipped the lock from the inside to keep Raoul from becoming suspicious. A good idea at the time.

Olivia whispered in Maddie's ear, "The music needs to be loud enough to cover the sound of this lock."

Maddie nodded. She grabbed the doorknob with one hand, the lock with the other. The music grew softer. Olivia held her breath. Maddie's muscles twitched a split second before the music crescendoed. She timed it perfectly. The lock snapped, the door opened, and Olivia slipped through. Maddie was right behind her. She eased the door shut. "Should we lock it?"

Olivia shook her head. "Let's get out of here."

As they headed north up the alley, Olivia

paused and looked back. She could see the second-floor window of Valentina's room. A small figure, dressed in pink, was observing their escape. For reasons she could not name, Olivia felt a flicker of hope.

CHAPTER NINETEEN

The phone began ringing the instant Olivia stepped out of her shower, and it stopped in mid-ring as she reached for the receiver. She still felt hot after her race home from the dance studio. Even her lightest outfit, taupe pants and a matching blouse in the thinnest possible fabric, weighed on her skin like wool. However, wearing a bikini to work was not an option.

She threw her sweaty jeans and T-shirt into her clothes hamper and headed toward the kitchen, Spunky at her heels. As she bit into a slice of cold pizza, the phone rang again.

"Livie? It's Mom. I can hear you chewing, so don't try to talk. Everything is fine in the store, but Heather Irwin is in the kitchen, sobbing her heart out. I gave her coffee and some tissues from my bag."

Olivia swallowed. "Good, she's on my list."

"List? Never mind, I don't want to know."

"I'll be right down."

Spunky circled her ankles, disturbed by the unusual morning schedule, which had not included an outing. "Come on, little guy. Bertha will take care of you for a while." Spunky did not seem happy with this information, but an extra treat helped.

As Olivia entered The Gingerbread House, she imagined she could feel a heaviness in the air that was more than heat. Her mother was showing a customer the elegant embroidery stitches on a handcrafted apron. Ellie's shoulders rolled forward as if she were carrying a backpack filled with rocks. Olivia knew how she felt. When Ellie glanced in her direction, Olivia blew her a kiss and pointed toward the kitchen.

Heather Irwin sat bent over the kitchen table, her head on her arms. At the sound of the door opening, she raised her head. Her eyes were red-rimmed and bloodshot, and her lips looked chewed. "Oh, Livie, you're really okay?"

Olivia poured herself a cup of coffee, refilled Heather's cup, and sat across from her. "I'm fine. How about telling me what's been going on with you lately?"

Heather gave a slow nod but didn't speak.

Olivia reached over to a tray of ballerina cookies, selected a classic toe shoe iced with shiny raspberry luster dust, and handed it to Heather. "A cookie for your thoughts."

The gesture coaxed a sad smile from Heather, followed by a deluge of tears. "How . . . how can you be nice to me, after what I . . . ? I almost *killed* you. Only I didn't mean to, honestly, it just . . . I sort of . . ." She bit the toe off her cookie.

"I know you weren't aiming your truck for me, or you'd have hit me." This wasn't quite true, but recriminations would only waste time.

"Still, it was unforgivable." Heather sniffled. "Sheriff Del is talking about pressing charges for reckless driving. I deserve that. But mostly, I don't want you to hate me forever."

"I try to avoid the 'hatred forever' thing," Olivia said as she slid the plate of cookies in front of Heather. "However, if you want to speed up the forgive-and-forget process, there is something you could do for me."

"Anything."

"Tell me everything you know about Geoffrey King. I know it's a painful subject, but I'm trying to save my brother from prison, and I don't have much time."

Heather picked up a cookie shaped like a ballerina performing an arabesque. With a grim smile, she laid the cookie on a napkin and said, "That's fair. Embarrassing, but fair. As it happens, I know a lot. It's a mistake to lie to a librarian, you know. Some people assume we're shy and gullible, but we know how to dig up the dirt." Blinking back tears, Heather nibbled on her ballerina's pale blue toe.

Olivia refilled their coffee cups. She could feel the time pressure in the tightness of her shoulders. Since Heather owed her, she could afford to be blunt. "King hit you, didn't he?" Olivia could see a hint of yellow under Heather's foundation.

"Yes," Heather said. "I've never felt so humiliated, so *angry.* No man has ever hit me before. I could have killed . . ." She bit off the ballerina's shin.

"You aren't alone," Olivia said. "Did he think he had a reason to hit you?"

With a shaky hand, Heather wiped a crumb off her upper lip. "I'd gotten suspicious because he didn't want to meet any of my friends or go out with me in public. I started noticing some of my kitchen things were missing, and I couldn't find my new iPhone. When a hundred dollars disappeared from my wallet, that's when I knew Geoff had to be stealing from me. Nobody else had access to all that stuff."

"So he hit you when you confronted

him?" Olivia asked.

With a lopsided smile, Heather said, "Not exactly. First I searched for him on the Internet. He told me his name was Geoffrey Lord, which didn't match anyone in my search. I did find a blog discussion about a Geoffrey Duke, though, so I tried every royalty-related name I could think of, and that's how I found out his real name was King. Geoff was charming and cunning, but he wasn't exactly a creative genius."

"Wow," Olivia said. "Never mess with librarians."

"You bet." Heather's round face relaxed to its normal friendly diffidence. "I found out Geoff had a history of stealing from girlfriends. He also gave stolen gifts *to* girlfriends. He seemed to pick shy women who were too embarrassed to report him to the police. They sure unloaded online, though. They all said he was charming at first, and then he became demanding and critical and usually violent."

"Did any of the women mention whether he used weapons?"

Heather nodded. "Several women mentioned he'd threatened them with a knife. One woman needed a couple stitches in her chin. He didn't use a knife with me because . . . well, when I confronted him in my kitchen about the stealing, I'd locked away all my sharp utensils. He knew right where they belonged because he opened the drawers to look for them. When he realized I'd hidden them, he really lost it. He hit me in the face, and I fell down. I thought he was going to kill me. But he just smiled and left. I changed all my locks, just in case."

One driving purpose consumed Olivia's mind — to clear her brother of murder charges — and she had less than twenty-four hours to do it. Calming and questioning Heather Irwin had taken more than an hour, but it had been worth the time. Olivia hoped Heather hadn't killed Geoffrey King. She had a strong motive, though, and no alibi. And she was one smart cookie.

Maddie, Bertha, and her mom could handle the store, in case curiosity brought in more than the usual number of Friday customers. Olivia gulped down the rest of her coffee, took a filled Gingerbread House bag from the refrigerator, and exited into the alley.

The Vegetable Plate, right next door, was Olivia's first planned stop. To avoid being seen entering sugar-phobic Charlene's store holding what looked like a bag of cookies, Olivia followed the alley to the rear door.

Charlene would probably be in her kitchen. She had help who worked the sales floor much of the time, so she could experiment with healthy recipes.

Olivia peeked through the small kitchen window. She was in luck. Both Charlene and her brother Charlie sat at the worktable, their heads tilted toward each other as they talked. If she knocked, Olivia was afraid they might disappear. She tried the door-knob. It turned easily in her hand. She slipped inside so swiftly that the Critch siblings had no time to scrape back their chairs.

"I'm so glad to find both of you here," Olivia said as she closed the alley door behind her. "We need to talk."

"What the . . ." Charlene twisted to her feet. "A *civilized* person would knock. You of all people should remember that someone broke into my store."

"Yes, but the man who broke in is dead, isn't he? Which is why you feel safe enough to leave your back door unlocked."

Charlie put an arm around his sister's tight shoulders. "It's okay, Sis. I'm here, no one can hurt you."

"Especially not me." Olivia held out her bag. "I come with a peace offering." Before Charlene could start shrieking about the demon sugar, Olivia added, "These are cut-out vegetable sandwiches. Sorry about the bag, it's all I could find." She plunked her gift on the table between Charlene and Charlie. Pulling up a chair, Olivia said, "Sit down, please. I know this is abrupt, but I don't have a lot of time."

Charlene exchanged a quick glance with her brother. "We heard a rumor that Jason was being released."

Olivia, who had started the rumor and encouraged her friends and relatives to spread it around, said, "He is . . . for now. He's still the prime suspect, though. I want to clear him."

"Jason is my buddy," Charlie said, "but Charlene and I are suspects, too, so why should we help you?"

"If you are guilty, then you probably shouldn't help me. Or you could lie. But if you didn't kill Geoffrey King, you should have no problem answering my questions. I'm not the police. I have no interest in learning any of your secrets unless they help me find the real killer and free Jason." Olivia opened her bag of sandwiches. "If I do say so myself, these are works of art."

Charlene's button nose twitched. "I smell cucumber."

"Yep, freshly cut."

"I eat only organic vegetables."

Olivia nudged the bag closer to Charlene. "These vegetables are all organic. So is the whole-grain bread."

"How can I be sure?"

"My mother bought all of it right here at The Vegetable Plate yesterday afternoon."

Charlene hooked an index finger on the edge of the opening and peered inside. Frowning, she said, "I see mustard. I eat no commercial sandwich spreads. They contain sugar."

Olivia quashed a strong impulse to sigh and roll her eyes. "My mom made the mustard from organic dried, ground mustard seed. And she used pure spring water." *Thank you, Mom.*

Charlie opened a cupboard next to the sink and took out a large glass serving plate, which he rinsed and dried before setting it on the table. "Look, Livie," he said, "we both care about Jason, but I don't see how we can help. We didn't kill Geoff, I swear it."

Charlene began to arrange the cut-out sandwiches one by one on the glass plate. "These are pretty," she said, resting a lettuce shape against the curve of a banana. "Did Maddie make them?"

"I made them."

"Oh." Charlene picked up a radish-shaped sandwich and nibbled on the top leaves. "This really has radish in it."

"I do my best," Olivia said. This isn't the time to scream, she told her frantic, impatient self.

Charlene finished her radish sandwich and met Olivia's eyes. "Well? What do you need from me?"

"Me, too," Charlie said as he tossed an entire tomato-shaped sandwich into his mouth.

"Thank you both, for Jason's sake. Now just so I know, am I right, Charlene, that it was Geoffrey King who threw all those flyers on The Gingerbread House's lawn last Sunday morning?"

Charlene's tight mouth loosened into a sneer. "Oh yeah, that would be Geoff's work. I bet he was real pleased with himself, making me look like a jerk. He knew I wouldn't give him away. That would mean admitting he'd ever been a part of my life."

"Why would he do such an odd thing?"

Charlene picked up a celery-shaped sandwich and picked at the bread. A small pile of bread pellets formed on the table. "Geoff was all about showing how much smarter he was than everyone else in the entire world. He threw my leaflets on your lawn to get me in trouble with my neighbors — and to show me he could get to me anytime he wanted." With a smug smile, Charlene added, "Except he was dumb enough to look out the window to watch you and Maddie clean up. The sheriff showed me that picture Binnie took."

"You still didn't identify him, though?"

"It would have made things worse for me." Charlene shot a quick glance at her brother. Olivia saw the worry in her eyes and wondered who she was really protecting by keeping silent.

"I can understand that," Olivia said. "Just a few more questions. I'm still confused about where you two and Jason were on Tuesday night. The police don't confide in me, but I think there are other suspects. It's in your best interests to be open about your whereabouts at the time of the murder."

Charlene examined her pale rose nails for flaws. "What suspects?"

"Well, I heard you had a run-in with Geoffrey King about a loan shark that was after him."

"Who said that?"

Olivia shrugged. "Is it true?"

Charlene relaxed against the back of her chair. "You already know the answer, so why ask? Yeah, I held Geoff at bay with one of my vegetable knives, but that doesn't mean I used one of them to stab him."

"I never suggested you did, but I don't believe you've been truthful about where you were that night."

"I am not a liar." Charlene's denial lost points for its whiny tone.

Olivia turned her attention to Charlie. "You stayed in the store all night to protect your sister, didn't you? You wouldn't have left her there alone, not when King had threatened to burn it down. Also, I happen to know you had nowhere else to go. You'd lost your room."

Charlie slumped back and stared at the ceiling. "Charlene told me to say I'd gone home." He patted his sister's arm. "It's okay, Sis. I'm so sick of lying and hiding all the time. See, Charlene figured if she got accused of killing Geoff she could claim self-defense. But I'd had a lot of run-ins with him. I even threatened to kill him for hurting my sister. The worst is, Geoff was . . . well, he was blackmailing me. He was taking my monthly trust money and most of my salary, and he wanted more. I wanted to kill him, I really did. But it wasn't me."

"What was he blackmailing you for?"

"That's none of your business." Charlene

bolted to her feet. "I want you to leave. Now."

"No, Sis, it's all right." Charlie reached for her wrist. "Let's get this over with." Once she'd sat down, he said, "I have a juvie record for stealing cars. It's supposed to be sealed, but somehow Geoff got hold of a copy and threatened to show it to Struts. I'd have lost my job, and I'd never be able to work in a garage again. I love working with cars more than anything. I don't know how he got those records, but he did."

Charlene snorted in a less-than-ladylike way. "He probably sweet-talked some idiot of a clerk, and she fell for it."

"That all makes sense." Olivia hoped she sounded reassuring. "So then . . . are you saying Charlene left the store that night before you did?"

"No!" Charlene nudged closer to her brother. "The truth is, neither of us left. We both stayed all night like we planned . . . to protect the store from Geoff. That man was evil. He was more than capable of burning down my lovely Vegetable Plate, even with me in it." Charlene's hands flew toward the serving plate and scooped up four sandwiches. She cradled two in each hand as if they gave her comfort.

"Did you stay together?" Olivia asked. "In

the store, I mean."

"Yes," Charlene said.

"No." Charlie wove his fingers through his loose brown curls. "I know it doesn't look good, Sis, but you've got to stop lying to protect me." He leaned toward Olivia, elbows on the table, eyes beseeching. "Charlene slept upstairs. She has a cot up there. That's where I've been sleeping since I lost my room. That night I stayed downstairs and kept watch, and Charlene didn't come downstairs all night. I could have sneaked out and killed Geoff, but I swear I didn't."

"Are you saying you didn't see or hear anything while King was being killed?"

The plate of sandwiches rattled as Charlene's small fist hit the table. "My brother has answered enough of your questions. We only wanted to protect my store. Charlie didn't need to hurt Geoff."

"Why?"

"For the same reason I didn't — I could have sent Geoff to jail anytime I wanted to. It would have been . . . well, messy, but I'd have done it. The last time Geoff hit me, I told him I'd had it. I said if he didn't go away and leave us alone, I'd tell the police what I knew about him." Charlene's lower lip trembled.

"Tell the police what?" Olivia's voice

betrayed the desperation she felt. "What did you have on King? That's what he was searching for when I caught him in your kitchen, wasn't it?"

Charlene bolted to her feet and sent her chair teetering backward. Charlie caught it before it fell. "I need to check on my salesclerks," Charlene said. "We're done here." She clutched Charlie's upper arm and dragged him out of his chair.

Olivia, however, wasn't finished. She followed the Critch siblings through the kitchen door and into the store. Charlene conferred with two young female clerks, ignoring Olivia as she roamed the sales floor. She knew what she was looking for — the missing cookie cutters Bertha reported seeing in Charlene's hands. With luck, they might be on display.

The cookbook section seemed a good place to start. Cookie cutters make lovely shelf decorations. Olivia struck out there, so she checked the lamps scattered about. No cutters hung from the pull cords. Next she searched the store for the sparkle and shine of slicing gadgets, a logical place to exhibit cookie cutters. She located the display in a sunny spot near the cash register, along with two clerks, a customer, and Charlene.

An eager clerk offered to help her find the

perfect slicing tool for any need, but Olivia waved her off with "Just looking." *For my own property.* . . . And there they were, the cutters missing from The Gingerbread House. She had to admit they lent a touch of artistic gaiety to the jumble of knives, vegetable peelers, garlic crushers, and other slicing paraphernalia. She almost hated to claim them back.

Olivia counted six cookie cutters: a carrot and an apple, hanging from two jars filled with various types of peelers; a sailboat next to a fish-boning knife; a party dress looped over several lemon zesters; a teapot next to the zesters; and a star above the entire display. Olivia stepped back and surveyed the entire section. There was no vintage tin cutter in the shape of a classic Duesenberg.

"Why do you look shocked?"

Olivia spun around toward Charlene's voice "Did I look shocked?"

"Cookie cutters don't have to be linked with sugar. I thought of that before you brought those little vegetable sandwiches."

"I can see that," Olivia said. "I wasn't shocked, I just didn't remember you buying any cookie cutters."

Charlene cocked a perfectly shaped eyebrow at her. "Oh, I didn't buy these cookie cutters. Charlie bought them for me."

Charlene's expression softened as she reached out to touch the sailboat cutter. "When we were kids, Charlie and I used to take the family sailboat out on the lake at our vacation home. We'd spend hours drifting around, pretending we were explorers. Each of these shapes means something special to me. Charlie knows that. He can be a sweet brother sometimes."

"Yeah" Olivia said. "I've got one of those, too."

Charlene briefly met Olivia's eyes and said, "Jason is a good guy. I hope he gets cleared."

"Me, too." Olivia did not say aloud that Charlie almost certainly stole the cookie cutters from The Gingerbread House. She suspected he'd taken the Duesenberg cutter, too. Had he given it to Jason? Did the cutter fall out of Charlie's or Jason's pocket during a struggle with Geoffrey King? If so, the Duesenberg might have been King's dying attempt to identify his killer . . . and one sister was about to lose a baby brother.

CHAPTER TWENTY

Olivia walked the short distance back from The Vegetable Plate with ideas tumbling around in her head like cookie cutter mobiles in a windstorm. Each one tantalized her, but she couldn't decide which to grab. Charlene Critch clearly hated her ex-husband enough to kill him, especially since he persistently threatened, blackmailed, and stole from both her and her beloved brother. Moreover, Olivia now knew that Charlie Critch had stolen at least six of the seven cookie cutters missing from The Gingerbread House. Olivia was willing to bet he'd also stolen the Duesenberg cutter found in Geoffrey King's dead hand. Had he meant to give the cutter to Jason, who had wanted it so much? Did he, in fact, give the Duesenberg to Olivia's brother before King's murder?

Heather Irwin seemed genuinely contrite about nearly running Olivia down with her truck. She claimed that King struck her because she'd confronted him about stealing from her, which sounded in character for him. On the surface, Heather appeared shy and quiet. Underneath, she was smart, determined, and gutsy. She did her homework and planned ahead, all useful characteristics for someone bent on revenge.

Heather had revealed one intriguing bit of information. It seemed that Geoffrey King was drawn to knives, and he made a habit of aiming for the faces of his victims. King himself died from a knife wound. Valentina Larssen's lovely face was disfigured as the result of a knife wound. Maybe King had threatened to slash her other cheek as well. If Ida's recollection was correct, Valentina had a violent, nighttime encounter with King in the park — and a very protective father. All of which might be no more than a string of coincidences . . . but something to keep in mind.

"Were you planning to come inside sometime today?" Maddie's question reached Olivia through an open side window in The Gingerbread House. "You've been standing out there forever, lost in thought."

"Have I? Sorry." When Olivia focused on Maddie's face, she realized something was wrong. Maddie's freckles looked darker than usual against the pallor of her skin.

"We sort of need you in here," Maddie said. "Desperately."

"What's happened? Is it Jason?"

"Only indirectly," Maddie said. "Come see for yourself. I'll meet you around back."

When Olivia arrived at the alley entrance, Maddie stood waiting in the open doorway. She locked the door behind them. Without a word, Maddie opened the kitchen laptop.

"I have a very, very bad feeling about this," Olivia said, recognizing Binnie Sloan's blog spot on the screen.

"You'll feel worse after you read it," Maddie said. "At least there aren't any pictures." The kitchen phone rang. "That'll be doom calling," Maddie said as she reached for the receiver. "I'll negotiate our execution date. You read."

Olivia took a couple deep breaths and read:

Our intrepid girl sleuths, Olivia Greyson and Maddie Briggs, are at it again. With her brother, Jason, in stir on a *murder* rap, Olivia has resorted to breaking the law herself to dig up (or conjure up?) evidence to clear him. Our paper, the *Weekly Chatter,* has received an exclusive eyewitness report that Olivia and Maddie broke into the Chatterley Heights Dance Studio early this morning, while our handsome and mysterious Latin dance teacher, Raoul, prayed at St. Francis Catholic Church. Were the inseparable girl detectives looking for evidence . . . or were they planting it? We suspect they read too many Bobbsey Twins books as gullible children. Since Olivia returned to Chatterley Heights after years of big-city living, she has found herself mired in crime more than the average shop owner. So we have to wonder . . . What next? Check out the *Weekly Chatter*'s daily blog entries to keep up with the antics of our very own Nancy Drew and her sidekick, George. We welcome information and pay for photos.

As Olivia read through the piece again, her anxiety began to fade. She had an idea, or at least a crumb of an idea. She closed her eyes to let her mind chew on it for a while.

"How can you nap at a time like this?" Maddie flopped into a chair, ignoring the ringing phone. "I've answered four calls already. I'm going to tear that phone out of the wall in a minute." Binnie's blog entry was still on the laptop screen. Maddie snapped the lid closed to hide it. "Livie Greyson, we're about to get sent up the river with your brother, and you . . . you are smiling. Explain yourself."

Olivia lifted the laptop lid and pointed to the screen. "This piece of journalistic tripe is probably libelous," she said, "but it couldn't be more perfect for us." The phone began ringing again. "This could save us a lot of time."

"Or waste it." Maddie jumped up, took the ringing phone off the hook, and hung it up. Before it could ring again, she dropped the receiver on the table. "I learned about this so quickly because one of Lucas's employees is hooked on that blog. She was checking it on her cell phone when that entry showed up. How does Binnie get away with this?"

Olivia got up and put the phone back on the hook. "I'll deal with the calls in here. You keep track of your cell phone messages," she said. "All part of the plan."

"What plan?" Maddie was approaching hysteria.

The phone rang, and Olivia answered at once.

A strong, firm voice said, "Livie, it's Constance Overton. Thought I'd give you a heads-up. I called the sheriff and told him there was no break-in, that I'd given you a key to the dance studio to check something out for me. He sounded quizzical until I played the wheelchair card — you know, poor me, can't climb stairs and so on. I'll let you know later how many dozen cookies you owe me."

"It's worth every pound of butter," Olivia said. "Besides, it'll be fun to watch you plump up."

"Won't happen," Constance said. "My metabolism still thinks I play basketball. Good luck with whatever it is you and Maddie have gotten yourselves into this time. By the way, when do I get my key back?"

"If you can wait till tomorrow, I'll deliver it with cookies," Olivia said.

"Agreed."

Olivia hung up and turned to Maddie, who was sucking on her lower lip and checking her messages. "Constance cleared us of breaking-and-entering charges," Olivia said. "We owe her big time. And speaking of cookies, how many ballet ones do we have?"

"At least six dozen, maybe more," Maddie said. "As you can see, I've been working off my jitters." She waved her hand around the kitchen. Olivia had been so involved with immediate crises that she hadn't noticed the piles of dirty baking pans and utensils. Maddie opened the refrigerator door to reveal stacks of covered cake pans. "I'm trying to get the icing to harden more quickly," she said.

"Excellent," Olivia said. "Put half of them around the sales floor as soon as you remind me how to post a response to Binnie's blog. Oh, and would you ask Mom to come talk to me as soon as she can free herself from customers?"

"How about you tell me what's going on here." The color was returning to Maddie's cheeks.

"Fair enough," Olivia said. "We're having a celebration right after closing tonight. A few select guests will be invited. I've asked Del to bring Jason here, but we'll do this even if he refuses. I'm pretty sure that whoever killed Geoffrey King will be among our guests."

"What's to stop them from simply leaving town and disappearing?"

"After Binnie's latest blog entry? That would be like painting 'I'm guilty' on their back. I think it's more likely the killer might try to throw suspicion onto someone else."

"Okay, I'm game. Let me get you started on that blog entry. Hit Binnie between the eyes for me." Maddie opened the laptop and showed Olivia how to post a response. "Whatever you say, it'll be around town in minutes. Everyone is glued to this blog. Look, two new posts just appeared." She skimmed the entries. "Great, some high school kid is accusing his former physics teacher of the 'town square massacre.' Sounds like *somebody* should have studied for his physics final." Maddie stood up. "All yours." She arranged a tray of ballet cookies and headed to the sales floor.

Olivia's post to Binnie's blog was simple. She announced that Jason had been released due to new evidence gathered by the police, who expected to make an arrest very soon. The Gingerbread House, she said, would offer decorated ballerina cookies to well-wishers until closing at six p.m.

"Are you interruptible, Livie?" Ellie's gentle face appeared around the edge of the kitchen door. "Maddie seems to think you have a plan that includes me. If it involves saving Jason, I will do anything."

"I know, Mom. You're probably the only one who could pull this off. I need you to convince Charlene and Charlie to come to The Gingerbread House after closing today. I'm hoping Del will agree to bring Jason here, since I've been spreading it around town that he is being released."

Ellie pulled a handful of hair over her shoulder and began to braid the bottom half. "I see what you are doing, Livie, and I think it is dangerous. I know it works well in Agatha Christie novels when the detective gathers the suspects in one room and starts flinging accusations about, but this is the real world. Someone might get hurt. Oh, I wish Allan weren't out of town."

"Tomorrow morning, Jason will be transported to Circuit Court for arraignment. I don't have time to wrench information out of the suspects one by one. I need to get everyone talking fast. This is the only way I can think of to make that happen."

Olivia practiced patience while her mother unbraided her hair, then began again. Finally, Ellie tossed her hair over her shoulder and said, "I've got it. I know exactly how to get Charlene and Charlie to come here."

"Just like that?" Olivia asked. "How?"

"Were you aware that not one single person showed up for Charlene's first Healthy Eating Club meeting?"

"I'd forgotten all about that," Olivia said. "And your point would be . . . ?"

"I'll offer to help her get the club going. I can produce quite a number of friends, you know. While Charlene is feeling grateful and unsuspecting, I'll ask her to bring Charlie and join us to welcome Jason home. Charlie will do anything Charlene tells him to do."

"Clever. I appreciate the sacrifice."

"Oh, it's no sacrifice, Livie. You and Maddie will be going with me to the Healthy Eating Club. It will be such fun to spend time with both of you." With a motherly kiss on Olivia's forehead, Ellie said, "I'll go talk to Charlene and Charlie right now. Be back in a jiffy."

Olivia took time to visualize a sea of swirling blue icing before calling Heather Irwin. It was easy to convince Heather to drop by the store after closing for Jason's homecoming. After nearly running Olivia down with her truck, Heather jumped at the chance to show goodwill.

Next Olivia called Constance Overton.

"Livie," Constance said, "I was just thinking about you. And those cookies you owe me. . . ."

"Good, because I'm calling to put myself further in your debt. I'll owe you cookies for the next decade."

"Sounds delectable. What do you need?"

"I want Raoul Larssen to come here to the store after closing this evening. And I want him to bring his daughter, Valentina."

"His *daughter?* You didn't tell —"

"No time, Constance." Olivia quickly summarized what she'd discovered at the dance studio. "At the very least, Valentina is a probable witness to King's murder."

"Well, I guess I could play the heavy," Constance said, "and tell Raoul that I was ready to throw him out for breaking the terms of the lease, but you talked me out of it. Maybe you offered to pay the extra for the girl. I'll strongly suggest they visit you this evening to shower you with thanks. Something along those lines."

"That's better than any idea I came up with. If they don't show up, I'll have to go to them. Thanks, Constance."

"Sure. Only now I want more than cookies in exchange. I hear you got a nice inheritance recently."

"You want my inheritance?"

"Don't be silly," Constance said. "I pull in a hundred thousand a year. No, I want you to make The Gingerbread House wheelchair accessible."

"Done."

"And I want you to convince the other stores in town to do the same."

"Done and done."

CHAPTER TWENTY-ONE

As soon as Olivia locked the front door of The Gingerbread House at six p.m., her heart began to creep up her throat. Now that it was about to unfold, her plan to prove her brother's innocence felt flimsy and foolish. If only she had more time to think it out. . . .

"You seem jumpy, dear," Ellie said from behind Olivia's back, which made her jump. Ellie laughed. "I know you're having second thoughts about this evening," she said, "but really, what other choice do we have?"

"You sure know how to boost my confidence," Olivia said.

"Too much confidence can be dangerous." A worry wrinkle between Ellie's eyebrows betrayed her own unease. "I believe I'll take five minutes to center myself," she said.

As her mother drifted toward the cookbook nook, Olivia straightened her spine and headed for the kitchen. She opened the door and heard Bertha's voice say, "You'll slice your own arm off." The prediction was delivered with parental force.

Sounding snappish, Maddie said, "Would you rather be shot down like a . . . like a squirrel?" She held a chef's knife in one hand and a cucumber in the other. Her hair resembled a brush fire.

Olivia looked from one tight face to the other and asked, "Am I missing something?"

"Okay, you settle this," Maddie said, waving her knife in the air. "We've invited a bunch of murder suspects to our closed store. That might be safe in mystery movies, but in real life things could get messy. And dangerous. I think we should be armed."

"And I think that would only make the situation more dangerous," Bertha said, planting her fists on her slimming yet still ample hips.

If we were doing this for anyone but Jason . . . "Frankly," Olivia said, "right now I'm scared of both of you. If we greet our guests with weapons, they will turn tail and run. I might join them."

"But where's our backup? Are we supposed to do this alone?" Maddie pointed her knife at Bertha and Olivia for emphasis.

"Maddie, please, put down that knife. You're knocking years off my life expectancy. I agree with Bertha, no good can come of arming ourselves. Del and Cody will be here soon, I know they will." *I hope they will.*

Maddie checked the kitchen clock. "It is six fifteen. Our *murder* suspects will begin arriving in fifteen minutes. What are we supposed to do, pelt them with ballerina cookies?"

"If they even show up," Bertha said.

Behind Olivia, the kitchen door opened, and Ellie's voice, serene with an edge, said, "I am newly re-centered, and I intend to stay that way. Need I say more?" Her audience of three shook their heads in chastened unison. "Good," Ellie said. "Now, I hear noises outside the alley door. I predict our reinforcements have arrived."

Olivia swung open the door on the first knock. Mr. Willard entered first. He smiled at Bertha, who rushed to him and threw herself into his arms. It was a testament to his wiry strength that he didn't fall over. "Now dearest," he said, "I couldn't stay home and let you face this evening alone. Besides, someone might need an attorney."

Sheriff Del and Deputy Sheriff Cody followed, each grasping one of Jason's upper arms. Ellie shed her serenity and ran to her son.

Lucas Ashford brought up the rear. He wore jeans and a crisp blue T-shirt that revealed well-developed muscles. When he saw Maddie, his worried look softened into a tentative, bashful smile.

"Hey," Maddie said.

"Hey, yourself." Lucas edged to her side through the crowded kitchen. "I got worried."

"Worried is good." Maddie leaned against him. "So," she said, looking toward Del and Cody, "can I assume you guys brought some firepower?"

With a loud sigh, Del said, "We decided to leave our assault rifles at home, but we do have our service revolvers. Jason isn't a free man just yet."

"Oh," Maddie said. "Sorry, Jason, but don't you worry. We're about to smoke out the real killer."

Jason looked thin and tired and not exactly bursting with hope. Olivia felt a tight squeeze in her heart as she watched him stare at the floor. At the same time, her resolve strengthened. "It's almost showtime," she said softly.

In ten minutes, the cookie trays were scattered around the sales floor, and tea and coffee bubbled away. By six forty-five, no one had shown up. Seven o'clock came and went with the same result.

"Don't give up hope, dear," Ellie said. "I have a strong feeling this experiment will work."

Olivia had gone over and over the questions she hoped to ask her suspects. She needed another angle. "Del, did you look into Lenora Tucker's story about Geoffrey King being afraid of a loan shark he owed money to?"

"Yeah, I talked to King's parole officer, who asked around. It seems King wasn't lying about that, except he seemed to be keeping up his payments. If he was stealing enough high-end stuff, that might explain it. He sure couldn't keep a job."

"Also, he was blackmailing Charlie Critch and who knows who else," Olivia said.

At that moment, the front doorbell rang. Bertha bounced up to welcome Heather Irwin, who was followed by Charlene and Charlie Critch. Charlene carried a loaf of fresh whole wheat bread, which she tossed at Olivia before throwing her arms around Jason's neck. "Oh Jason, I'm so glad you're okay."

Jason held her tightly and buried his face in her shoulder. Charlie stood nearby, fidgeting with the ribbon on a bottle of red wine.

Bertha again answered the doorbell and Raoul Larssen entered the store. He wore a white shirt and jeans, which emphasized his muscular legs and broad shoulders. However, Olivia doubted anyone could mistake him for a construction worker. His dark eyes explored the store before coming to rest on Ellie Greyson. "Ah, my favorite pupil," he said. When Olivia greeted him, he executed a quick bow and handed her a bottle of Chilean cabernet sauvignon. Inexpensive, yet excellent. "I offer this in celebration of your brother's freedom," he said. "And also for your kindness. Ms. Overton explained to me that you begged her to be lenient with me for my . . . for omitting to mention my daughter's visit."

"How thoughtful of you," Olivia said.

"Ms. Overton said you offered to pay her the extra rent I owe her. This is too generous of you and not necessary. It was merely a mistake on my part. I have already taken care of the problem."

Ellie took the bottle from Olivia's hands. "This looks delicious, Raoul. Will you join me in a glass? You don't have to teach tonight, do you? I've been hoping for a chance to chat with you. What class will you be starting next?" Ellie removed the cork with the ease of experience and poured three glasses.

Raoul accepted his wine and took a small sip. "I am so sorry to tell you this, my dear Ellie, but we will be leaving soon. I have made arrangements to teach elsewhere. They want me to begin immediately, and my classes here are coming to an end, so . . ."

"Oh no!" Ellie said. "I was so hoping to meet your daughter. From what I've heard, she's a stunning ballerina. Livie has seen her dance, you know."

"And I want to talk to her," Olivia said. "She might have seen something in the park that could clear Jason."

Raoul's eyes narrowed with suspicion. "But I understood that your brother has been cleared of the . . . the crime."

"I know it's confusing," Olivia said. "Jason has been released because the police realized they don't have any more evidence against him than certain other possible suspects." She directed a deliberate glance across the room at Charlene and Charlie Critch, who were chatting with Jason, Bertha, and Mr. Willard.

Raoul took two sips of his wine before saying, "I'm afraid there is no time to visit. My new job begins so quickly, you see." An elegant shrug of his shoulders conveyed

407

regret, apology.

"Perhaps I could visit her," Olivia said. "We have enough help with the store. I could come over tomorrow morning for a short visit, say, at nine o'clock? I'll help her pack."

Raoul placed his empty wineglass on a table. "I'm afraid that won't be possible," he said. "She will be gone, I have made the arrangements. She needs quiet, rest. Ever since her . . . her accident, she has been so fragile. It would be useless to speak to her, anyway, because her memory is often unclear. I must get back to her now."

Before Raoul could back away, Ellie captured his arm. "Raoul, if this is the last time I will see you, then I will not allow you to leave so soon. You will have another glass of that delicious wine and meet my son, Jason. Livie, dear, would you . . . ?" She nodded toward the wine bottle. Olivia filled Raoul's empty glass and trotted behind her mother, who smoothly trapped Raoul inside the small circle surrounding Jason.

Olivia sidled up next to Del. In a voice loud enough for everyone to hear, she said, "How about holding a plate for me while I pack some ballerina cookies for Raoul to take back to his daughter?"

Del followed her to a tray piled with cookies. Olivia handed him a heavy paper plate, on which she arranged cookies shaped like toe shoes, ballet slippers, and ballerinas performing a variety of moves. "Raoul is desperate to keep me or anyone from talking to his daughter. He's going to get her out of town as soon as he leaves here, I'll bet on it."

Del leaned toward her. "And you think this is significant because . . . ?"

"I think Valentina knows something about King's murder. Raoul doesn't want her involved, he says, because she is so fragile. Only I can't help but wonder . . . Del, I'm going to play a hunch tonight, and I might need your help."

Del sighed.

"Enough with the sighing, okay? I know you don't want me involved, but I am, so either deal with it or . . . well, that's your only choice." Olivia covered the plate with plastic wrap. "Follow my lead. I want to find out what Charlene had on King. She claims it was the reason she wasn't really afraid of him."

"Maybe she was bluffing," Del said.

"Maybe, but I don't think so." Olivia met his eyes and saw worry in them. "I'm not afraid," she said with a teasing smile. "You have a gun."

With Del's help, Olivia delivered a tray of cookies and another of cut-out vegetable sandwiches to the quiet group. "Especially for you, Charlene," Olivia said as she placed the cut-out sandwiches within reach. Charlene actually smiled at her. After several peaceful moments had passed, Olivia said, "You know, Charlene, I'm really curious about something. When I checked on The Vegetable Plate and found Geoffrey King creating havoc, I heard him say something like, 'I'll kill her.' I had the sense he was looking for a particular item, something really important to him."

Charlene dabbed at her chin, where a drop of red juice had dripped from her tomato sandwich. "I can't imagine what."

"Well, I wondered because he was so violent, yet later you told me you weren't afraid of him."

Charlene shrugged and selected a carrot-shaped sandwich.

"Maybe it's something you didn't know you had," Del said. "It would sure be helpful to us if you could figure out what it might be."

"I have no idea." Charlene shifted her chair closer to Jason, who reached for her free hand.

"Well, I sure don't miss Geoffrey King,"

Charlie said. "I didn't kill him, but I was glad to get him off my back."

"Oh Charlie, you knew I could protect you," Charlene said.

"How?" Olivia asked. "With the evidence you had against Geoffrey King?"

In her most gentle, mothering voice, Ellie said, "You are among friends, Charlene. It can be such a relief to let go of secrets. One often finds they are not nearly as shameful as one thought they were."

With a casual shrug, Charlene said, "Oh, I'm not ashamed. I made a promise that I wouldn't use the information unless absolutely necessary. And now it won't ever be necessary. It would have stood up in court, though. I had a signature and everything."

"Is this something King was never prosecuted for?" Del asked.

"My friend never told anyone but me. She didn't want to press charges, even though I told her I'd support her. She said no one would believe either of us. So we came up with this idea that she'd write it all down, and I'd keep it safe."

"Do you still have all this information? Geoff never got hold of it?" Olivia asked.

Charlene snickered and said, "Geoff wasn't as smart as he thought he was. He tore apart my store, thinking I'd be silly enough to hide it there. It's in my safe-deposit box. Someday I'll burn it."

"Who was this woman, Charlene?" Del leaned toward her, pressing hard. "What was her name?"

"I'll keep her secret forever," Charlene said, her delicate chin in the air. "She deserves her privacy."

"But Geoffrey King was murdered," Del said, "and his killer hasn't been —"

"More wine, anyone?" Ellie said, holding a bottle in each hand. "Come on, this is a celebration."

When the atmosphere had settled, Olivia turned to Del. "So when do I get my Duesenberg back?"

"Your what?"

"Duesenberg, it's a —"

"Classic car, I know."

"Actually, it's a tin cookie cutter, and I want to give it to Jason as a homecoming gift."

"I forgot all about that." Jason's smile made him look more like the eager kid he'd been only days earlier. "Why does Del have it?"

"I didn't know I did," Del said. "I guess I should have asked you or Maddie what that cookie cutter shape was meant to be, but I wanted to keep it to myself. So much for that idea. Thanks, Livie."

"Don't mention it. Any idea how it got into the dead man's hand?" Olivia took careful note of her listeners' reactions. Bertha, Mr. Willard, and Cody maintained their watchful silence. Heather Irwin looked as if a weight had been lifted from her mind. Ellie smiled serenely, as usual. Raoul's expression was thoughtful, attentive. Charlene looked bored, Charlie stared at the floor, and Jason frowned at Charlie.

"Charlie?" Jason asked. "You didn't . . . did you? We talked about this. You said you'd stopped."

"I know, I know." Charlie's young face scrunched up as if he were about to cry. "It was for you, Jason. I felt bad that you didn't win it, like you wanted. Only I didn't give it to you because I realized you'd figure out I . . . stole it. I was going to sneak it back over here, but I never got the chance."

"Charlie!" Charlene balled up her fist at her brother but slammed the arm of her chair instead. "Those cookie cutters you gave me, you stole them, too, didn't you? Now look what you've done. You've gotten yourself in trouble again. You'll wind up in jail, Charlie. I can't bear it."

Jason reached his arm around Charlene's tight shoulders. "It's okay, Charlene, I'll pay

413

for the cutters. Charlie isn't . . . He takes things sometimes when he's under pressure, like with Geoff blackmailing him, and he only does it to please the people he loves."

Olivia did a mental double take. Who was this thoughtful adult pretending to be her brother? "There's another problem, Jason," she said. "Remember, the Duesenberg cookie cutter wound up in Geoffrey King's hand. So we have to wonder, did it fall out of the killer's pocket? Or did the killer or another person place it in his hand to implicate someone else?"

"No one will believe me," Charlie said, hanging his head, "but I lost it. All I know is it disappeared. I looked all over for it so I could bring it back to The Gingerbread House."

"That sounds pretty convenient," Del said. He signaled to Cody, who stood in back of Charlie's chair ready to arrest him.

"No!" Charlene linked arms with her brother. "Charlie had nothing to do with it. I put that tin thing in Geoff's hand. It never occurred to me that you might have stolen it, Charlie, or I wouldn't have. . . . I was trying to help you. When I found that Dues-whatever, I figured anybody could have dropped it in my store after shopping at The Gingerbread House, so I thought. . . . Oh, I don't know what I thought. I wanted to confuse the police so they wouldn't assume Charlie killed Geoff to protect me."

"But wait a minute," Olivia said. Her head was spinning. "How did you even know King was dead?"

"Because I saw the murder — or part of it, anyway. I was upstairs. I woke up and looked out the window onto the park and saw a man leaning down. There was enough light from the band shell lamp that I could see what looked like a body on the grass. The man who was leaning over picked up something and threw it away. Then he ran off."

"Which way?" Del asked.

"I'm not sure, it was getting really dark. Anyway, I ran downstairs and couldn't find Charlie, so I got scared and . . . That stupid cookie cutter was on a shelf under the cash register, so I grabbed it and ran outside." Charlene shivered. "I could tell right away that the dead man was Geoff. I was so afraid Charlie had killed him. I looked around until I found a knife in the grass. It was one of my vegetable knives. I didn't know what to do. I could hear thunder, and I thought, well, rain will wash off the knife. So I left it. Maybe that was stupid." Charlene shot an insecure glance at Jason.

Olivia asked, "That knife was part of a set, wasn't it, Charlene?"

Charlene nodded. "Geoff stole them one by one because he knew I loved them. I'll probably never get them back. Maybe I don't want to."

Olivia asked, "Weren't those knives found in your barn, Heather?"

Heather's normally open expression grew guarded. "I think you claimed you saw at least one knife when you found the stuff Geoff stole and hid in my small barn. But I never saw any of that. I practically never go near that barn. Anyway, this is the first I've heard of the cookie cutter Charlene says she planted in Geoff's dead hand."

Never mess with a librarian.

"I didn't mean to . . ." Charlene had lapsed into nervous whining. "I already explained, I only put that cookie cutter in Geoff's hand to confuse everybody."

"You certainly accomplished that," Del said. "You also managed to implicate Charlie, Olivia, Jason, Maddie, and others I'll probably think of later."

"No," Charlene said, "not Charlie. I ran back to The Vegetable Plate. I wasn't gone more than five or six minutes, and there was Charlie, curled up behind a bookcase, sound asleep. I hadn't thought to look for

416

him there. And he hadn't been outside because his shoes and pant legs were perfectly dry. I checked."

"He didn't wake up while you were running around the store or checking his pants?" Del asked.

"It would take a bomb to wake Charlie up," Charlene said in her old, snide voice. "I left him asleep and went back upstairs."

Del looked unconvinced. Olivia noticed that even her besotted brother regarded the love of his young life with puzzled concern. With Charlene on the defensive, Olivia decided to press harder. "Maybe you were gone longer than you thought," she said. "Charlie could have sneaked in the back door, changed his clothes, and pretended to be asleep."

"No!" Charlene looked to Jason for support and saw doubt on his face. "I'm not lying. It happened just like I said. Anyway, I keep telling you, Charlie didn't have to be afraid. I could —"

"You could protect Charlie, so you keep saying." Olivia held out her hands toward Charlene, palms up. "But how do we know you aren't protecting him with this improbable story about the Duesenberg cookie cutter? He already admitted that he stole it. It's much easier to believe that Charlie killed King and the cutter fell out of his pocket. Or if Charlie didn't do it, then you did, and you were trying to cast suspicion on Jason. Everyone knew Jason loved that cutter."

"But —" Frantic now, Charlene shot up from her chair. Her paper plate with the remains of a carrot sandwich scattered on the floor. Del stood up, his hand near his service revolver. Cody and Lucas moved in closer. Charlene reached beseechingly toward Jason, who looked like he was on the verge of collapse.

Olivia felt awful, but it was the only plan she had. "Charlene," she said more gently, "you might be able to convince us of your innocence, and of Charlie's, if the evidence you have against Geoffrey is powerful enough. It'll need to be good because we already know that he hit you and destroyed your property."

"It *is* powerful. I can bring it to you as soon as the banks open on Monday."

"We will go with you," Del said. "But meanwhile, tell us what we'll find in your safe-deposit box."

"It's as simple as that, Charlene," Olivia said. "Jason is still in danger, and he is my highest priority. If you refuse to convince us that you and Charlie had no reason to kill

King, we'll have to assume that you are lying."

Charlene sank back into her chair. "Oh, all right. It's just that I never wanted anyone to know about that time in my life. It was so humiliating. That's why I let Geoff get away with hitting me, even though I could put him in jail. But I suppose it doesn't matter anymore."

Jason intertwined his fingers with Charlene's, and her shoulders relaxed. "I was in the hospital for a while after my annulment. It wasn't the first time." Charlene locked eyes with Jason, her best high school friend. "I met someone there who knew Geoff, someone he'd hurt badly. She was in the hospital recovering. He did that a lot — hurt women. Anyway, she and I got to be friends, at least until I left the hospital. She didn't want to press charges. I never saw her again after that, but she gave me a signed note stating what Geoff did to her. She said if I needed protection from him, I could use the note, even if it meant giving it to the police."

Out of the corner of her eye, Olivia saw Del get up and stretch, as if he were satisfied and ready to leave. Cody checked his cell phone, and Raoul refilled his wineglass. Olivia felt a wave of exhaustion, but she wasn't ready to let go. There was more, she felt sure of it.

"Who was the woman you got the statement from?" Olivia asked. "What was her name?"

Charlene heaved an exhausted sigh. "Oh Livie, does it really matter? Let us have our privacy."

"Why were you both in the hospital? What kind of hospital was it?"

"There's no reason for you to be ashamed, Charlene," Jason said. "Tell them."

Charlene's lower lip began a pout, but a look from Jason reversed it. "We were being treated for anorexia," she said.

Olivia tried to catch Del's eye, but he was writing a text message. "And your friend, was she by any chance a lovely young ballerina who had been slashed down the cheek — ?" Olivia hopped sideways as the chair beside her did a somersault backward. A second earlier, Del had been sitting in that chair. He ran at Raoul, who threw his glass of wine at Del's eyes. His aim was perfect. Del hesitated for only a split second, wiping his eyes with his sleeve to clear his vision.

Cody was too far away to help, so he aimed his revolver at Raoul.

"No weapons," Del yelled. He raced across the sales floor, knocking over display tables as he positioned himself between Raoul and the front door. Del adopted a fighter's stance, bent forward, ready to tackle.

As if he had rehearsed for months, Raoul took a few running steps and lifted into the air like a gazelle. Startled, Del ducked. Raoul's long, outstretched legs cleared Del's back by inches and delivered him nearly to the front door. As Raoul reached toward it, the door opened on its own.

Olivia's ex-husband Ryan stood in the doorway. "There you are, Livie," Ryan said, looking past Raoul and Del, both frozen in place. "Sorry I'm late. This town is so small, I almost missed it." Raoul tried to push past Ryan, who was not accustomed to jostling by strangers. "Hey, buddy, watch it." With Del gaining on him, Raoul hit Ryan in the chest with a powerful shoulder. Ryan's face turned beet red.

Del and Cody were within grabbing distance of Raoul. Olivia, who knew Ryan's stubbornness and his temper, called out to him, "Ryan, get out of the way. Let the police handle this."

Ryan ignored her. He swung his fist into Raoul's stomach, then yowled in pain. Raoul stumbled backward into Del and Cody, throwing them off balance. All three fell in a heap on the floor. Del was the first to recover. He rolled up on his knees and got a firm hold on Raoul's wrists, while Cody slapped on some handcuffs. Raoul stopped struggling. To Olivia's surprise, he began to cry.

"What is this, the Wild West?" Ryan held his injured right hand gently in his left palm. "I think my hand is broken. I'm holding all of you responsible," he said to the three winded men. "If this damages my surgery career, I'm suing you all."

Olivia suppressed a giggle, telling herself she was simply nervous. Ryan didn't deserve to have his hand broken. Well, maybe he did. . . . The Gingerbread House was a mess. Tables lay on their sides, their precious cookie cutter displays spread all over the floor. Several mobiles hung crookedly, as if they'd been used as swinging vines. At least the expensive baking equipment had been spared.

Ryan caught sight of Olivia across the sales floor. "Livie, come over here. I'm taking you away from this . . . this uncivilized backwater right now."

Olivia ignored him.

"Olivia Greyson, do you hear me?"

Del shot a glance in Olivia's direction, and Maddie moved up beside her. Olivia felt perfectly calm as she gazed across the cluttered floor at her ex-husband. "You'd better get that hand looked at, Ryan," she said. "We have a small hospital in this backwater, but I think they own an X-ray machine. I'm sure Del or Cody will be glad to run you over there as soon as they are done here." Without waiting for a response, Olivia picked her way through cookie cutters to the table where the wine and glasses miraculously stood undamaged. She poured two glasses and handed one to Maddie. "To The Gingerbread House," she said, clinking Maddie's glass.

"Long may she live," Maddie said, the hint of a tear in her voice.

CHAPTER TWENTY-TWO

Olivia should have been deep in peaceful slumber, but her mind churned nonstop. Spunky crawled on top of her stomach and watched her face. "Sorry I'm restless, Spunks. Loose ends." She reached over and turned on her bedside light. Her cell read eleven twenty-seven. Maybe she'd gone to bed too early, but she'd felt worn out. She and Maddie had supervised the cleanup of the sales floor, much of which their guests had completed. Even Charlene and Charlie stayed to help. Afterward, they'd finished off the wine — with tea for Charlene, of course — and trundled off to their various homes and beds.

A detail was trying to work its way loose from Olivia's jumbled thoughts. She reviewed Del's report to her on Raoul's tearful confession. He admitted that Geoffrey King had brutally attacked and scarred his daughter Valentina. She'd been a promising but shy, insecure ballerina, trained privately by her equally shy and insecure mother, Lara. Lara's health had suffered because of her anorexia, and she'd died right as Valentina was about to audition for the Royal Winnipeg Ballet. Raoul claimed that his daughter was, if anything, even more talented than his wife. Valentina lived to dance, he'd said. Raoul had hoped her confidence would grow with success.

Lara's death changed everything. Without her mother's advice and encouragement, Valentina slid into the quicksand of self-doubt and perfectionism, which soon became anorexia and depression. That's when Geoffrey King entered her life. He completed her downfall and, by slashing her face, ensured she would never appear in public again.

After hearing rumors about the dancer in the park, Raoul realized Valentina wasn't taking the sleeping pills he'd gotten for her. He confessed he lost control when he realized King was in town and had threatened Valentina again. Raoul sneaked out to the park, figuring Geoff would be there waiting for Valentina, and stabbed him. Raoul swore his daughter had already run off before he killed Geoff.

It made perfect sense. Olivia felt sympathetic toward Raoul and hoped a judge and jury would go easy on him, although murder is murder. But something was bugging her. If she could only . . . Raoul told Del that Valentina was safely back in the care of her psychiatrist at the hospital in DC. He had seen the end coming, he said, when Constance Overton asked him to attend the celebration of Jason's release at The Gingerbread House. To Raoul, that meant the police had more evidence.

Olivia sat up and wedged her pillow behind her back. Spunky jumped off the bed, trotted to the bedroom door, and sat on his little haunches. "That makes two of us," Olivia said. "Let's have a snack."

In the kitchen, Spunky munched on a doggie treat while Olivia sipped warm chocolate milk and allowed herself one decorated cookie: a pair of bright red toe shoes. They reminded her of Valentina. Using Spunky as a sounding board, Olivia sorted her thoughts out loud. "Unless I'm misremembering," she said, "Raoul wasn't entirely consistent about why I couldn't talk to or visit Valentina. I think when he first told us about his new teaching job, he said 'we' would be leaving soon, as if Valentina was going with him. When Mom and I insisted on talking to her about what she might have seen in the park, Raoul's story began to change. First I think he said there wasn't time, they were leaving so quickly. Then he talked about how fragile Valentina was, she needed rest, he'd made arrangements, she'd be gone by morning. . . . It wasn't until his confession to Del that Raoul said he had already sent his daughter to the psychiatric hospital in DC."

Spunky finished his treat and gazed hopefully at his mistress. "What do you think, Spunks? Could Del have misinterpreted?" Spunky yapped at her and trotted toward the treat cupboard. "You're right, of course," Olivia said. "Del doesn't make mistakes like that." She glanced up at the kitchen wall clock. Nearly twelve thirty a.m. She didn't want to awaken Del for something that might be nothing. "On the other hand, what if Raoul really did make arrangements for Valentina to be picked up in the morning? And what if Valentina is all alone in the dance studio, waiting for her father to return?"

"I need to take a short trip," Olivia said. Spunky yapped and wagged his tail. "Alone," Olivia added. "You stay safe and snug in your bed." She changed into jeans and a black T-shirt and headed for the door, where she realized she'd forgotten her keys.

427

After locating her keys, she unlocked her apartment door, then remembered to fetch her cell phone. Halfway down the stairs, she decided to pack some ballerina cookies, in case Valentina was alone and scared. "It'll be dawn by the time I make it there," she muttered as she filled a Gingerbread Box with cookies. She'd forgotten to close the store door on the way in, so she told herself to pay attention as she carefully locked the door on her way out.

Olivia drove to Willow Road, parked at the north end of the block, and walked to the front door of the dance studio. The ground floor was in complete darkness, but Olivia had seen a faint light showing through the curtain covering Valentina's bedroom window.

Olivia still had the studio key she'd borrowed from Constance Overton. She unlocked the front door and slipped inside. She eased the door shut behind her and stood in the dark, letting her eyes adjust. A light switched on in the office across the dance floor. A slender form appeared in the doorway with the light behind her. Valentina hesitated for a few seconds, then cried out, "Daddy, you are so late." Light as air, Valentina glided across the dance floor toward Olivia. She halted abruptly when she realized the form in the dark was not her father.

"Valentina, please don't be frightened. It's Olivia Greyson. You remember me, don't you? My friend and I are the ones who make cookies." She held out her box. "I brought you some ballet cookies — ballerinas, toe shoes, ballet slippers. . . ."

Valentina glanced at the box and backed away. "Where is my daddy?" She was dressed all in pale blue: leotard, tights, ballet slippers, and a gathered skirt made of blue silk. Her waist-length white-blond hair hung loosely over her shoulders. Olivia noted that her delicate beauty was marred less by the scar on her cheek than by her excessive thinness. Her shoulder sockets showed beneath her stretched skin.

"He's . . . he's been delayed," Olivia said. "He asked me to come over and reassure you. I understood from your father that you haven't been feeling well lately? Can I help?" When Valentina didn't respond, Olivia said, "Your father might be quite late, so he asked me to stay with you for a while."

Valentina shook her head slowly. "That isn't what he said. I'm supposed to go back to the hospital. He said to pack a suitcase and someone would pick me up."

"Okay." Olivia thought frantically, aware

that Valentina could outrun her. "Yes, the hospital in DC. I can take you there."

Valentina took several quick, light steps backward. "No, a taxi will take me. Daddy planned it." She turned and ran into the office.

Olivia followed and was relieved to find that Valentina was gazing out the window into the dark alley. Maybe she was hoping her father would appear.

"I can call a taxi, if you'd like," Olivia said, taking her cell phone from her jeans pocket. "I'll do it right now."

"No!" Valentina spun around. Her eyes widened as she saw the cell phone. "You're going to call someone to take me away from Daddy. He warned me. No phone!"

"All right, it's okay." Olivia placed the cell on the countertop. "See? I won't call anyone."

Olivia barely had time to register her movements before Valentina had snatched the cell and fled up the staircase. Runs with Spunky had strengthened Olivia's legs, but not enough to keep up with a ballerina. The hallway was empty when she reached the second floor. She headed toward the light streaming through the open door of Valentina's room and found her sitting cross-legged on her bed. Next to her lay a packed suitcase. "Daddy isn't coming back, is he?" she asked.

"I . . . I don't know," Olivia said.

"Daddy always tried to keep me safe," Valentina said. "He made a plan to protect me, but his plans don't always work. So sometimes I have to make my own."

As Valentina unfolded her legs to stand up, Olivia thought of a bluebell opening to the sun. And then she cursed herself for being distracted by the girl's gracefulness. In a blur, Valentina had slipped out of the room and slammed the door shut. Olivia heard the slide of the chain lock on the outside of the door. She was trapped inside, and Valentina had her cell phone. Olivia spun around, looking for a phone. There was none. She tried the window and found it painted shut. She began to pound on the door, for all the good that would do.

Out of the corner of her eye, Olivia saw Valentina's bedside table. The bottle of pills, nearly full when she had examined it the day before, now lay on its side, empty. A half-full glass of water stood next to it.

Olivia paced the room, trying to focus her mind. How long before Valentina succumbed to an overdose? Would it be fatal? Out of frustration and desperation, Olivia kicked the door. And then she stopped, remembering Valentina's words, her apparent frailness, how she fought back when King attacked her in the park. . . . *So sometimes I have to make my own.*

Valentina's suitcase lay on the bed, closed but, as Olivia discovered, not locked. She dumped its contents and pawed through them. Costumes. Valentina had packed a selection of her mother's ballerina costumes but nothing else. Olivia's hands shook as she examined the costumes one by one. She came to one that was rolled up, not lovingly folded. Olivia spread the costume on the bed. It was a white, knee-length skirt of fine, lightweight satin sewn to the waistband of a white leotard. The bodice and arms of the leotard and the front of the skirt were badly stained with browned dried blood. There had been no attempt to wash off the blood, almost as if Valentina wanted to preserve the memory of stabbing Geoffrey King. If Valentina truly felt no guilt, Olivia could think of only one reason she would have left the evidence for others to find. To clear her father.

Olivia heard pounding from outside the bedroom window. It sounded like someone trying to get in the front door. She grabbed one of Valentina's toe shoes from her closet and slammed the wooden toe against the window. The pane began to crack. Thank goodness for old window glass. At least she made enough noise to get Del's attention; he was standing on the sidewalk, shouting up at her. He waved an object in the air and pointed toward the front door. Olivia giggled when she realized he was wielding a baseball bat. She moved Valentina's blood-stained clothing to her sewing machine table and sat on the bed to wait.

In short order, Olivia heard the chain lock slide open, and the bedroom door opened.

"Valentina," Olivia said, as soon as she saw Del. "She took pills. Did you find her?"

"In the kitchen, groggy but still conscious. The ambulance is on its way. In fact, I hear it now."

"How on earth did you know I was here?"

"Logic, my dear Greyson," Del said. "Plus Maddie and Spunky."

"Spunky?"

"It'll wait till morning. Seven a.m. at The Chatterley Café with Maddie and Lucas. Cody and I will let them know you're okay. You need to get some sleep, you look exhausted."

Olivia's muscles did feel weak and wobbly, and somehow she fell into Del's arms.

"Always wanted to rescue a damsel in distress," Del whispered, his face buried in her hair.

"Was the baseball bat part of your fantasy?" Olivia asked, pulling back to look at his face.

Del laughed. "Well, no, I usually imagined using my bare hands, but after watching your ex-husband yesterday evening, I decided to go with something tougher."

Olivia, Maddie, Del, and Lucas were first in line when The Chatterley Café opened Saturday morning. Olivia felt surprisingly chipper after her harrowing experience and only four hours of sleep. Her sleep had been all the better for knowing that Jason was safe in his childhood bedroom, being watched over and, even more important, fed by Ellie. Olivia had to admit that Charlene was being attentive to Jason, bringing him vegie burgers and fresh fruit to help him regain his strength. Jason seemed to welcome both the food and the attention.

"Spunky should be here," Maddie said when they'd been seated. "If it wasn't for him, Livie might have spent the night locked in that poor girl's bedroom while she was dying in the kitchen."

"Hey, I am perfectly capable of kicking down a door when necessary," Olivia said. "However, I have a new appreciation for

Spunky's escape artistry. He did take unfair advantage of my distraction last night, though, hiding behind my apartment door when I went back for my cell and then following me into the store while I boxed cookies. He needs a stern lecture."

"And extra treats," Del said. "I sure appreciate the little guy."

"I helped, too, you know," Maddie said as their breakfasts arrived. "Ooh, fresh-squeezed orange juice. I couldn't settle down to sleep, so I decided to do some baking. I'm the one who called Del when I found Spunky running around the store and Livie nowhere in sight."

"How did you find me?" Olivia asked as she lifted a forkful of egg and sausage omelette.

"That was me," Del said. "I just had a feeling you weren't done investigating, so when Maddie said your car was gone, I sent out an alert and started checking in town. When I didn't find your car near any of your known haunts, I just drove up and down the streets. Chatterley Heights isn't that big. Once I saw you'd parked near the dance studio, I figured something was up."

"Poor Valentina," Maddie said.

"Poor Raoul." Olivia speared a roasted potato and paused to admire it. "I assume he has been released?"

Del nodded. "But he insists on staying with his daughter in her cell. He feels responsible. If he'd realized sooner that Valentina was sneaking out, maybe he could have prevented the whole incident. If King hadn't been able to threaten Valentina, she wouldn't have gotten the knife away from him and used it to stab him."

"What will happen to her?"

"I don't know, Livie, but I suspect the courts will be lenient with her, even though she hid her responsibility for King's death. Since the case became public, several women in the Baltimore-DC area have come forward with allegations that King abused and stole from them. If their stories can be corroborated, Valentina might be able to plead self-defense. My guess is she will end up back in the hospital."

"*She lives to dance . . .*" Olivia murmured. "Raoul said that last evening, about Valentina. Not being able to dance freely might feel like execution to her."

"There's always dance therapy," Maddie said. "So Lucas, are you going to eat that slice of bacon?"

As Maddie reached toward Lucas's plate, Olivia caught a glimpse of green sparkle. "Hey, what's that?" She grabbed Maddie's

436

hand. "Is that an emerald?"

With a light laugh, Maddie said, "Wow, you're good. What gave it away, the green part? It matches my eyes. At least that's what Lucas told me."

Olivia noted her friend's sudden flush and said, "It isn't fair to torture me, I've had a rough night. Is this or is this not an engagement ring?"

"Not," Maddie said. "But close. It's an I-promise-to-think-about-it ring. Lucas and I had a long talk last night. He's a good listener. I'm going to work on the . . . the thing we talked about, Livie."

"I know this is none of my business," Del said, "although Livie did involve me a bit. Maddie, about your parents' accident."

Maddie's eyes flitted from Del to Olivia and back to Del, but she didn't explode. Or run away. "What about it?"

"It really was just an accident," Del said gently. "Cody and I did some digging. There was no alcohol, no drugs of any kind in their systems. Your aunt didn't tell you anything about this because she thought that was best. Your mom was being treated for depression related to early menopause. The pills made her feel worse, so she stopped them and began feeling much better. When your dad realized how unhappy she was, he cut back on his work to be with her. The accident . . . There was one witness, who wasn't quoted in any of the published reports. I don't know why, maybe because she was elderly. She said that a cat crossed the road in front of your parents' car, and your mother swerved to avoid it. That's what caused the crash. It wasn't intentional."

"Oh that's . . ." Tears streamed down Maddie's face. Lucas took one hand, and Olivia took the other. "That's so like my mom." She sniffled. "I don't suppose anyone has a tissue?"

Maddie was quieter for the remainder of breakfast, but Olivia wasn't worried. She didn't take the ring off; that was a good sign. After Maddie and Lucas left together, holding hands, Olivia and Del were quiet through a last cup of coffee. Olivia felt comfortable and shy at the same time.

"You know, Del," she said finally, "you're an okay guy." *Smooth, Livie.*

"Even if I'm too wimpy to punch in a door with my fists?"

"They're nice fists. I'd hate to see them broken."

Del picked up her hand and laced his fingers through hers. "Livie Greyson, you and I are due for a long, long talk. The

438

sooner the better."

Olivia squeezed his fingers. "How about tonight?"

The employees of Thorndike Press hope you have enjoyed this Large Print book. All our Thorndike, Wheeler, and Kennebec Large Print titles are designed for easy reading, and all our books are made to last. Other Thorndike Press Large Print books are available at your library, through selected bookstores, or directly from us.

For information about titles, please call:
 (800) 223-1244

or visit our Web site at:
 http://gale.cengage.com/thorndike

To share your comments, please write:
 Publisher
 Thorndike Press
 10 Water St., Suite 310
 Waterville, ME 04901